I0641924

STAN LEE'S RIFTWORLD: ODYSSEY

STAN LEE'S RIFTWORLD: ODYSSEY

Stan Lee and Bill McCay

A BYRON PREISS VISUAL PUBLICATIONS, INC. BOOK

iBooks
Habent Sua Fata Libelli

iBooks
Manhanset House
Dering Harbor, New York 11965

bricktower@aol.com • www.ibooksinc.com

All rights reserved under the International and Pan-American
Copyright Conventions. Printed in the United States by J. Boylston &
Company, Publishers, New York. No part of this publication may be
reproduced, stored in a retrieval system, or transmitted in any form or by
any means, electronic, or otherwise, without the prior written permission
of the copyright holder. The iBooks colophon is a trademark of
J. Boylston & Company, Publishers.

Copyright © 1996 by J. Boylston & Company, Publishers
Cover painting, interior illustrations and cover,
copyright © 1996 by J. Boylston & Company, Publishers
Afterword copyright © 1996 by Stan Lee
STAN LEE'S RIFTWORLD is a trademark of Byron Preiss Visual Publications

Back matter art by Dave Gibbons
Cover and interior design by Claude Goodwin
Edited by Howard Zimmerman

Special thanks to Lou Aronica, Ginjer Buchanan, Keith R.A. DeCandido,
and Steve Roman.

A Byron Preiss Visual Publications book.

Library of Congress Cataloging-in-Publication Data
McCay, William. Stan Lee's Riftworld, Odyssey.
        (Stan Lee's Riftworld) "A Byron Preiss Visual Publications book."
p. cm.
    [1. Science Fiction—Adventure. 2. Fiction—Science Fiction—Alien
        Contact. 3.] I. Gibbons, Dave, ill. II. Title. III.
        Series: Stan Lee. Riftworld.

ISBN 978-1-59687-676-7

Table of Contents

Stan Lee and Bill McCay

Introduction

His name was John—John Cameron. At least there seemed a flicker of recognition from deep inside his consciousness. Recognition, yet doubt . . .

Ah. It was an invented name, an assumed identity. A wall of amnesia cut across his sense of self. Conscious recollection stretched back little more than two years. The question was, *what* of those two years could he remember? With sudden clarity, he understood it was vitally important to recall as much of his limited history as he could . . .

A flash—himself, standing naked by a rural roadside. That was his beginning. Other memories trickled into a consciousness that, in self-defense, had turned in upon itself almost to the point of catatonia.

John had been held prisoner—paralyzed in a high-technology hell that made sensory deprivation seem like a mental massage. His consciousness had been enclosed in a sphere of impalpable force, divorced from his body, unable to reach out. Now that his mind had finally been freed, its reconnection to the flesh had resulted in sensory overload. His psyche had retreated nearly into unconsciousness, trying to regroup.

His choices in captivity had been either insanity or shutdown. As John sorted through his memories, he

1

wondered if shutdown had come too late. Some of his recollections seemed like the daydreams of madness.

John remembered finding his way to New York City, where he got a job with a comic-book company, the Fantasy Factory—the largest in the business. Perhaps that added to his problems with recall. His memories appeared to be infiltrated by cartoonish fantasies.

John's Fantasy Factory job seemed normal—even menial. He'd been a general-purpose clerk—a gofer. Yet those workaday memories were interspersed with recollections of bizarre powers. John had been able to detect other people's thoughts. It wasn't mind-reading, exactly. The effect was more like hearing a blaring radio through cheap wallboard.

He'd felt the frustration and embattled emotions emanating from the company's head, Harry Sturdley. The memories of that younger John were tinged with a respect verging on hero-worship for the creator of such comics heroes as the Rodent and the Sensational Six. And then there was Peg Faber. John had averted his mental gaze around Sturdley's pretty red-haired assistant, attracted yet afraid of revealing his confused emotions and extra-human abilities.

For mind-reading, John discovered, had been the least of his uncanny talents. He'd developed a capacity for— not teleportation, exactly. It was an ability to visit unguessed locations by way of a dimensional anomaly John called the Rift. John's first transition into the Rift had been a terrifying accident. His mind had gone blank, he'd somehow *twisted* his perceptions, and suddenly found himself falling endlessly through an infinite gulf. Exerting all his will, he'd returned to the real world, sweaty and shaking. In learning to master the necessary mental knack, John discovered he could return from the Rift to other Earthly locations—even faraway places he'd never visited before. Then he'd discovered currents in the Rift's emptiness. By following these, he'd landed in strange new worlds—outlandish, unearthly realms.

There was the world that seemed trapped in perpetual winter, where the human inhabitants were locked in a class system based on size. Humans of normal stature were called Lessers, slaves to their equally human but twenty-foot-tall Masters. A more pleasant destination was a world of rolling parkland punctuated by cities of gleaming towers, airy spires that soared half a mile or more into the sky. Vastly complicated three-dimensional traffic flows filled the air around the cities—human figures in what seemed to be flying armor. John had visited this locale again and again, filling sketchbooks with futuristic cityscapes. When Harry Sturdley had seen these . . .

But he was getting ahead of himself. Carefully, John worked to sort his memories chronologically. The turning point had come at a vituperative Fantasy Factory staff meeting. John had delivered coffee to find Harry Sturdley bitterly wishing that there were real superheroes. Perhaps too eager to please, John had used his immaterial powers to find a pair of titanic fugitives on the world of the giants. He'd brought the pair, Robert and Maurice, to Earth via the Rift.

Sturdley didn't know that the giants had arrived at his wish. But they certainly were the answer to his prayers. He christened the pair "Heroes" and entered into a Faustian bargain with Robert. The Fantasy Factory could issue comics relating the Heroes' real-life adventures . . . if John Cameron would bring more giants to Earth. Yes, during the transit through the Rift, the pair of titans had been able to pinpoint John as the dimensional manipulator using their own, somewhat lesser, mental powers.

John had Rifted himself away after his unconsidered action, fearful of the consequences. An unforeseen result of his disappearance was that Peg and two Fantasy Factory artists, Elvio Vital and Marty Burke, had been ordered to track down the suddenly errant John Cameron. They hadn't succeeded, but the air of mystery around John— the way he'd vanished, his assumed identity—had sparked Peg's interest.

She had helped John negotiate a deal with Harry Sturdley. If John transported more giants to Earth, he'd be given a shot at writing and illustrating the first of the Heroes' comic books—*The Incredible Robert*.

John had Rifted over another forty-eight giants—followers of Robert—all refugees from their homeworld's bloodthirsty politics.

The fifty giants had settled in to become real-life vigilantes and four-color superheroes, despite internal sniping from Marty Burke—and external attacks from news woman Leslie Ann Nasotrudere. Sturdley had made the mistake of embarrassing the powerful television reporter. Her quest for payback had taken the form of a vendetta against the giants. But despite journalistic probes into what their real motives might be, the giants made a dent in New York crime, and their comics sold like crazy.

Sturdley and the Fantasy Factory were riding high. But John, too, worried about the giants' private agenda. Robert, the leader of the giants and the hero of John's first comics title, had a will to power, and his followers were culturally conditioned to think of normal-sized humans as cattle. Some of the more hot-headed were openly contemptuous of humans' rights. John feared that behind the veil of public service lay a master plan with ugly consequences for the world.

Harry Sturdley, however, wouldn't hear a word against his brave new profit center. He planned to enlarge the Heroes line, launching new books at the San Diego Comics Convention, the world's largest conclave of comics professionals and fans.

John brought Peg to the West Coast convention by way of the Rift, and had a wonderful time as an artistic rising star—until he was shot by a group of assassins hired by Robert. The giants had targeted John because he alone controlled the power that had brought them to Earth—which could just as easily send them back. Wounded, John rescued himself, Peg, and Sturdley by going into the Rift. But he was forced to drift with the Rift currents—and ended up on the giants' homeworld. He'd blacked out during the Rift transit, and the three of them had been scattered across the surface of a hostile planet.

Fortunately, John landed in the one place on the primitive world where healing was available. He found himself in an underground, computer-run installation in what the giants called the *Forbidden Zone*—forbidden because it contained the forgotten secret of the Masters' beginnings.

The self-aware computer running the hidden base healed John. But it hoped to use his genes to fulfill its programming and create a new race of caretakers for the planet. Fearing that John would use his mental powers to escape, it had sealed his mind in an inhibitory field—the featureless prison that had nearly cracked his brain . . .

. . . Unless his brain was already cracked, and the history he'd just pieced together was totally delusional. But no—he *had* been freed from the shining sphere that had imprisoned his mind, and in the howling onrush of sensory data, he became aware of the mental presence of his fellow castaways, Peg and Harry. Somehow, their passage through the Rift had stirred the pair's latent psionic abilities.

Mind-to-mind, John had picked up fragmentary glimpses of their separate journeys across an inimical landscape. Sturdley had cowed an entire tribe of savages. Peg had mentally bound a male Lesser who'd attacked her, making him her personal slave.

Following a psychic spoor, the terrestrial exiles had tracked him to the Forbidden Zone, been captured by the computer, and compelled to participate in its chilling program. Peg, it seemed, had been filled with hormones to induce a pseudo-pregnancy as preparation for the implanting of a gene-altered fetus.

Peg and Harry were attempting an escape before this technological rape. And they needed John to get them into the Rift.

But—he couldn't. After months of a silence more profound than that of the tomb, normal sensory stimulus struck at him in dizzying bombardment. His response had been to retreat to this near-catatonic state.

Of course, a cold, reasonable voice in the back of his head pointed out, *you could be safely in a mental ward somewhere, and all this rigmarole merely the dementia of a true catatonic.*

He flinched from the thought. And at that moment, the shields he'd thrown up to protect his consciousness were breached. Desperate, clumsy fingers of immaterial force probed his mind. It was Peg, twining into his consciousness more closely than any embrace. Very, very real.

John, if you want to Rift, what do you use? she asked frantically.

He steadied a little in the maelstrom of incoming data, showing her the knack of transition. Her mental probes seemed to sink into his brain, to the exact neurons that fired to initiate the Rifting.

John was too weak, his mind still too disassociated, to achieve the transit. Peg added her mental energy to the process, but it still wasn't enough. Then John felt the presence of Harry Sturdley's mind as well. There was a fourth presence identified only as Mike—the primitive would-be rapist whom Peg had enthralled.

Their combined mind-force managed the dimensional twist, and then came the all-too-familiar feeling of never-ending vertigo. The four of them were falling through unbounded nothingness.

They were in the Rift. And with John only semi-conscious, their destination was unknown.

Prologue

"So," Robert said, his hands on his hips, "you're back."

"That's right," John Cameron responded, staring up at his adversary. "I'm back."

Cameron had to crane his neck to look Robert in the eye. Although John topped six feet, he barely came to the level of Robert's knees.

Robert and his people had established giant-sized reputations as superheroes. They'd made giant fortunes through their licensed comics deal with the Fantasy Factory, and even gotten a movie contract.

But Robert had even larger plans. He'd used his popularity to gain access to the lawmakers of the Lesser Domain known as the United States. By twisting these leaders to his will, he expected to precipitate a catastrophe that would cull the Lessers' numbers and reduce their vaunted technology.

Unfortunately, obstacles existed between Robert's conception and his plan's execution. One of his followers, the giant called Gideon, had tried to go over to the humans' side, attempting to warn Sturdley. The traitor had been captured and neutralized. But Sturdley had begun to doubt that the Heroes were altogether altruistic.

The main antagonist, however, had been the Lesser known as John Cameron. His memory was maimed—though his body was twenty years old, he bare-ly recalled two years of his past. But this nondescript human had the strange ability to control the Rift—the pathway between worlds.

With that power, he could banish the Heroes—or open the gateway for Robert's enemies. Robert couldn't afford to allow such a Lesser to remain free. He'd schemed with some New York criminals to have Cameron elimi-nated, but the Lessers had botched the job. John Cameron had vanished into the Rift, taking with him Harry Sturdley and another Lesser—Sturdley's female assistant, Peg Faber.

Since that disappearance, Robert had feared Cameron's eventual return . . . and planned for a final solution. Now the upstart Lesser had come back. And Robert was in a position to deal with him.

The giant's hands snapped out, seizing Cameron and yanking him into the air. Cameron did not resist. There was little he could do. In relation to Robert, the human was the size of a one-year-old.

Cameron's ribcage just fit in Robert's palms. Smiling, Robert squeezed, exerting crushing force. Harder, harder . . . but there was no satisfying *crunch* of bone, no sudden implosion of heart and lungs. Cameron hung relaxed in Robert's grasp. But the Lesser's body shifted, seeming to expand in the giant's straining hands.

How could the Lesser's ribs now be larger than Robert's palms? Panicking, Robert dismissed reasons. He went for the soft tissues of Cameron's throat, trying to mash them with his thumbs. The muscles in his fore-arms quivered, but he couldn't pulp the vulnerable air passages. A cold thought crashed through Robert's mind. Had Cameron somehow managed to develop the shields of immaterial force Robert's people used to protect themselves?

Robert tried to seize the human by his feet, meaning to swing him like a club against a nearby tree trunk. Novice shielding sometimes buckled under serious stress. And the threat of having one's head smashed in certainly qualified.

Cameron still didn't resist . . . but Robert couldn't pick him up. The human was more than half his size now! How could he keep growing?

Then Robert finally noticed that the tree he'd aimed to dash the human's brains against was also growing. That was flatly impossible.

Unless . . . they weren't expanding. Robert was shrinking.

He tried to flee this madness. But Cameron, now the same size as the former giant, ran him down and tackled him. Robert tried to escape, but his opponent, now grown larger, blocked his every move. Cameron still wasn't fighting with him. He seemed merely to be playing with his dwarfed foe.

Finally the disparity in their sizes reached the point where Cameron could pick Robert up, the former giant dangling between the human's hands like an infant. Then Robert wound up perched on one hand, staring at the ground that seemed a terrifying distance below.

At last, he sat on a broad plain he knew to be Cameron's palm. Vast shadows congealed overhead—the human's fingers, bending inward to make a fist. The world vanished in blackness as the fist engulfed Robert, making him one with his enemy . . .

Robert rose bolt upright from the greensward where he'd bedded down, shuddering from the realism of the nightmare, his mouth distorted in the rictus of a silent scream. Beside him, his mate Barbara stirred uncomfort-ably, her minimal mental powers detecting his distress.

With desperate precision, Robert extended a scalpel-like tendril of mind-stuff, quelling her mind. Then he redoubled his own mental shields and lay back again. But sleep did not come as Robert lay sightlessly staring up at the fall foliage of the trees overhead.

His people had never been ones for prophecies and portents. But something in this nightmare struck Robert as a breath of prescience. Did it herald Cameron's return? Did it foretell the ultimate result of the battle between them?

Robert lay stark and slightly chilled. For once he didn't feel like the leader of this band of giants—their would-be Master of Masters. All he wanted to do was cling to the soft, perfumed form sleeping beside him, as a drowning man might cleave to the piece of driftwood holding him afloat.

Chapter One

Peg Faber clung desperately to the other bodies tumbling through the nothingness of the Rift. Even so, Harry Sturdley, John Cameron, and Mike felt far away. Her attention was devoted to the mental probe she had driven into John Cameron's near-comatose brain, powering the weird mental circuitry that operated this dimensional portal. They'd been forced into a cosmic getaway—an escape for which John was badly hurting and Peg unready.

It wasn't easy—her fledgling control of the Rift was constantly being buffeted by gusts of emotion and memory blasting through John's brain.

They spun wildly, torn by a crosscurrent in the Rift. Peg's attempts to keep them together were complicated by a flash-recall of John's first experience with such eddies—educational, but distracting to Peg's frantic efforts to steady their transit.

Besides battling her own fear, she had the ghost of John's panic threatening their mind-link. Why the hell couldn't he remember a successful journey? Then maybe she'd get some useful tips on making this passage work.

Perversely, her anger at him seemed to trigger fond memories of her. Images flickered on the link—Peg at her desk at the Fantasy Factory, laughing at a joke John had ventured. Peg with her eyes wide, hurling herself out of an elevator and flinging her arms around him.

She remembered the second episode. It had followed the appearance of a pair of giants on Earth—giants that John had Rifted over in response to a silly wish of Harry Sturdley's. Harry had given Peg the job of finding John, who had mysteriously disappeared. After devoting days to a fruitless search, she returned to admit her failure— only to have John stop the elevator and try to jump aboard. She'd vacillated between wanting to kiss him and wanting to kill him.

The cluster of humans floating through the Rift void threatened to fly apart—and Peg realized almost too late that her inattention to the transit could doom them all. Grimly, she refocused her mental energies, trying to ignore the barrage of images threatening to swamp her mastery of the cosmic flux. Even the roiling of her outraged gut was pushed to second place. Bringing them through the Rift alive needed all her concentration.

She almost missed Sturdley's telepathic message informing her that they'd reached their destination. Only when Harry linked into her mental probe did Peg realize the time had come to send a new flux through the telepathic circuit linking them with John.

It had required both of them to power up that strange knot of "Rifting" cells in John's brain. After being held prisoner in a field that inhibited his mental powers, John was as dissociated as if he'd spent weeks in a sensory-deprivation tank. He hadn't been able to give directions, forcing Harry and Peg to use their own newfound psionic powers and hurtle their little group blindly into the Rift. The question now was whether or not they'd managed to escape.

The transition back to normal space was even more torturous than their fall through the alien void of the Rift. Peg felt squeezed, squashed, and *twisted* simultaneously in several directions.

Then they were belched out into reality, landing in a tangle of arms and legs on a huge patch of overgrown lawn. Peg levered herself up on shaky limbs. Her first instinct was to help John, who lay naked and helpless beside her. They'd spirited him out of a Frankensteinian nightmare in the subterranean science center on the giants' world. Forgotten by the very race it had spawned, the center had been declared a Forbidden Zone. But the ancient computer that ran the complex had remained crazily true to its programming, conducting bizarre genetic engineering experiments—with Harry, Peg, John, and Mike as the lab rats. Their escape attempt had been spurred by the fact that the computer had actually created an in vitro embryo and was tampering with Peg's hormonal balance, initiating a pseudo-pregnancy in preparation for implantation.

They'd fled into the Rift before that experiment reached culmination. But there were still repercussions. Right now, the nausea swirling in Peg's tortured stomach felt as much like morning sickness as motion sickness.

"I'll be damned," Harry's voice penetrated Peg's grogginess. "We've reached John's *Planet of the Superheroes!*"

Peg knew about the existence of this other world. She'd seen John's sketches of the skyscraping towers and flying armored figures. At the moment, however, Peg could care less about their location. She was too busy redecorating the lawn with what appeared to be the entire contents of her stomach.

As the last miserable spasm passed, a pair of boots intruded on Peg's low-to-the-ground field of vision.

Perfect, she thought. Here come the cops. We've probably broken some local ordinance about stepping on the grass—she clutched her stomach—or barfing in the park.

Peg forced her eyes upward, and instantly regretted the action. The figure before her was dressed in a suit of high-tech armor that would make Darth Vader jealous, although it appeared to have been painted by a color-blind artist high on LSD. A complicated pattern in searingly fluorescent greens and purples crawled over the shiny armor. Just looking at it set off Peg's stomach again. "Oh, *please*," she muttered in a constricted voice. Summoning up what was left of her strength, she called, "Harry—help!"

Sturdley turned and did an astonished double take. Whatever the folks around here used for propulsion, it was incredibly quiet. He stepped over to the armored figure, noting that there were others behind it assembling various complicated-looking machines.

Harry opted for what he considered a typical stranger-in-a-strange-land response, extending open hands and saying, "Hello! I'm Harry Sturdley. This is Peg Faber—excuse her, she's sick. And this is John Cameron, and Mike."

The looming form in the psychedelic armor remained still. Harry considered that a good sign. The last time he'd tried this act on an alien planet, he'd nearly gotten a spear in his gizzard.

"We're—I guess you can call us dimensional travelers. And we're having some difficulty. Our friend John isn't well, and we needed to get away from where we were. This was the nearest destination . . ."

A slightly raspy voice suddenly boomed from speakers hidden within the armor. "You . . . are . . . travelers."

Sturdley jumped a little to be addressed in his own language. "That's right. Do you speak English?"

An armored limb pointed to one of the constructions now rising around them. "This . . . can . . . guess. Difficulty. Need you to speak."

"Need me to speak?" Harry echoed. Then he understood. "That machinery is some sort of translator. You need to hear more of my language for it to process."

"Need more English," the armored figure agreed.

Sturdley complied, giving a brief rundown of their adventures and explaining the mysterious Rift as best he could. It was a relief to have someone to talk to. Peg sat on the grass, looking lousy, while Mike, busy taking care of John, barely glanced at the armored figures.

Once a sufficient vocabulary had been acquired, an exchange of information proceeded. The armored figure introduced himself as Triadon, and seemed considerably more friendly than the computer that had held them captive on the giants' world.

"I am a . . . scientist," Triadon explained after fishing the word from his translator. "I have been studying this Rift, the changes of . . . energy."

"Energy fluctuations." The words came from John Cameron, who had roused slightly. As Harry turned in surprise, his mind was brushed by a mental probe from John.

Idiot! Sturdley accused himself. His mental powers would speed the process of communication considerably—if he'd thought to use them. Sending out some unobtrusive probes of his own, Sturdley found that Triadon's interest in the Rift was far from academic.

"Our world, Argon, is in danger whenever this Rift opens," the scientist explained. The—" the term proved untranslatable— "get out."

Harry tried to zoom in. "Something—or *someone*—coming through the Rift? Aliens? Invaders?"

Triadon made a complicated gesture. "They come—"

"Where the hell do they come *from*?"

"Hell?" the scientist asked.

"A place of punishment," Sturdley quickly explained.

"Ah," Triadon said. "Hell. A place of sending away."

"Exile?" Sturdley hazarded. "So these people coming in—they aren't aliens."

"No. *You* are aliens—I can see that," Triadon said. "These are . . . *villains.*" The scientist picked the word from Harry's comics-oriented vocabulary.

"Criminals?" Harry said. "You send them into exile somewhere through the Rift?"

John Cameron's hoarse voice abruptly interrupted the conversation.

"Yes—criminals," John echoed. "And coming here!"

His eyes were open, staring blindly into the sky. High above them, Sturdley could make out minute, flying dots. They grew larger. Then, as if to make sure they'd be noticed, flaming bolts lashed downward from the descending forms, aimed squarely at Triadon and his assistants.

Chapter Two

The hawk-face of Kenneth Drivelle gazed piercingly from the television screen. Leslie Ann Nasotrudere had never thought of him as much of a talent—the high point of his career had been playing a TV detective thirty years ago. But she grudgingly had to admit that in his trench-coat, Drivelle had the perfect look for the host of a show like *Unresolved Enigmas*.

"One can find enigmas anywhere," Drivelle intoned in a deep, slightly hoarse voice. "But this is one for the books—the comic books."

"Hey!" Marty Burke leaned forward from his place on the couch beside Leslie Ann. "Here's our segment."

"*Our* segment?" the newscaster said a little sourly. "I seem to remember Network yanking the story out of my hands and giving it to those hacks in the entertainment division . . ."

Burke hushed her as Drivelle set the scene outside the San Diego Convention Center, relating the mysterious disappearance of Harry Sturdley, Peg Faber, and John Cameron from the midst of comicdom's largest annual convention.

"Goddammit!" Leslie Ann burst out as the screen then filled with the videotape of a group of masked attackers disrupting the Fantasy Factory's huge outdoor promotional event, drawing real weapons previously concealed as prop rayguns. "That's *my* tape!" she complained, her voice drowning out Drivelle's narration of the terror and chaos. This should have been *her* story, done as real news. Instead . . .

Burke flapped his arms, admonishing her to silence as he stared raptly at the screen. There was always an eyewitness interview after the clip, and he expected to see himself there.

He was disappointed. There was another talking head on the screen—a middle-aged man running to fat, dressed in black and with an all-too-obvious fresh haircut that left a visible demarcation between the summer's tan and the shortened length of the hair. In fact, the whole impression from the interviewee was that of a person freshly scrubbed for his fifteen minutes of fame. Only when the guy opened his mouth and a familiar braying voice issued out did Burke finally place him.

"They went with *Loony Lonnie Lancaster?* When they could have had me?" Marty was infuriated.

"You could actually see me there in the film clip," Lonnie Lancaster said with relish. "I was the guy in the Jumboy outfit for the costume parade. At the time of the attack, I was actually *talking* with John Cameron."

He shook his head sadly. "The kid was a real talent, a top-rate artist. What a shame we'll only have three books to remember him by."

"Aaaaah, they're probably high-priced collector's items by now," Burke spoke to the screen in disparaging tones.

"I tried to stop 'em," Lancaster went on. "Got my head cracked instead." He pointed with some pride to a crease that angled from the side of his forehead off across his temple. "So I was down and out when that giant—the Terrific Thomas—threw the car to try and cut the gunmen off. I was at least as close as they were. Maybe if I'd been conscious and looking the right way, I'd have seen what happened to Cameron, Sturdley, and the girl."

"Right," Burke said mockingly.

"At least he tried to help," Leslie Ann found herself saying. "You were just as close when the shooting started. But you managed to become the Invisible Man while the Cholesterol King over there became a hero."

Burke turned, his face flashing shock, anger, and hurt.

What did I ever see in him? Leslie Ann asked herself, looking at her lover as if for the first time. He'd been much more impressive as the rebel firebrand of the Fantasy Factory than as the guy in charge. Of course, he'd been a useful tool against Harry Sturdley. Sturdley had made the mistake of embarrassing her publicly, earning himself a top position on Leslie Ann's shit list.

But now Sturdley was dead, or kidnapped and his body disposed of, according to the theories being reviewed on the television screen.

She turned to Burke, only to be abruptly silenced by renewed frantic hand-waving. "Ah," Marty said with much satisfaction, "*here* I am."

His televised image sat behind a large desk—Harry Sturdley's desk, she realized—looking like some sort of overstuffed toy. Television added pounds to people, Leslie Ann knew. This fact was never more cruelly evident than now, as Burke pontificated on what a great loss to the comics community Harry's disappearance was. Pudgy and pompous, she thought. A deadly combination.

Burke frowned as his sound bite came to an end, and Ken Drivelle returned to wrap up the segment. "Damn," Marty complained, "they hardly used *any* of the stuff they taped. I had a great spiel about what the new Fantasy Factory would be like—you know, life after Sturdley."

"Those are the breaks," Leslie Ann said coldly. "Most raw footage winds up on the cutting room floor." She gave him an exasperated look. "Besides, the angle was Sturdley's disappearance, not his company."

"But we did get coverage." Burke beamed as if he were personally responsible. "I mean, it's free publicity, right? What's that saying? 'Speak of me well, speak of me ill, but speak of me.'"

Staring at the fatuous look on his face, Leslie Ann had to clamp her lips to keep from speaking ill of him right then and there.

Burke finally noticed her expression. "Aw, you're not still mad at me for agreeing to the interview, are you? That was a business decision—publicity, like I just said." He moved closer toward her on the couch. "Hey, I'd have loved working on the investigation with you, but that was the network's call. It's lousy luck that you got beaned with a bottle covering those riots."

He gestured tentatively toward her face. The swelling had gone down around her right eye and cheek, and the cuts had healed where she'd been hit. But Leslie Ann still sported a gorgeous shiner and major bruises. Her less-than-perfect looks had prompted the network to put her on temporary leave. She'd lose more weeks before she got back on the airwaves. The Sturdley story would be a dead issue by then.

Burke moved closer still, worming an arm around Leslie Ann's waist. "You know I'd never do anything to hurt you," he said, his breath coming a little faster. "I just want to make you feel good."

Leslie Ann intercepted Burke's free hand before it slipped under her robe, twisted free of his embrace, and rose to her feet.

"Not tonight, Marty," she told him in a flat, decisive voice. Now it was her turn to gesture toward the bruises on her face. "I've got a headache."

Westchester County was famed as an enclave of gracious living and quiet respectability. When Harry Sturdley had installed his giant superheroes up there on the grounds of an unused estate, the atmosphere took on a carnival-like quality. But with the departure of the newspeople and the efficient supervision of the giants, the area around the mansion now called Heroes' Manor had grown quiet again.

Few people in the neighborhood even knew that the Heroes had expanded their domain, purchasing the estate next door to theirs. Dr. Cedric Thonneger knew, and he was scared to death. The doctor was a prisoner of the giants in the ramshackle pseudoTudor monstrosity. The resident titans had ignored the house, choosing instead to restore the old boathouse on the property. They'd turned it into a combination lab and hospital, where Thonneger tended a single, enormous patient.

The doctor couldn't believe how he'd gotten sucked into this nightmare. He lived and conducted his practice in the neighborhood, so he was aware of the giants. He hadn't learned of their mind-reading abilities, however, until the leader of the Heroes had come to pay a call. Robert was quite polite, but equally inexorable, picking the doctor's mind to point out a number of medical misdeeds that Thonneger had committed.

It was sheer blackmail, but Robert had forced the doctor to close down his practice and come to work for the giants. His first look at the enormous, comatose form hidden in the boathouse told Thonneger that his patient—Gideon, he later learned the name—had sustained a vicious beating. The medical man had set to work on the welts, bruises, and the crusted lacerations on Gideon's wrists—proof he'd been bound while being beaten.

Thonneger hadn't been able to bring Gideon back to consciousness, a situation that oddly enough hadn't disturbed Robert. It seemed the head giant had some tests he wanted Thonneger to conduct on the comatose patient. Some of them were straightforward enough— obtaining sperm samples and storing them for possible artificial insemination. Next came requests for other experiments, designed to explore the genetic differences between the giants and the human population. In other circumstances, Thonneger might have relished the opportunity—this was sure-fire Nobel prize material.

But then Robert began pressing for research into the effects of radiation on the giants.

Thonneger was leery, having little experience in nuclear medicine. He'd already encountered the strange force-field that protected each of the giants. How would *that* react to irradiation?

Robert had become insistent, but Thonneger, then still living in his own house, had resisted.

Soon after, his dog was found dead.

Zoltan was no ordinary animal. He was a German shepherd, a big, fierce watchdog—purchased by Thonneger after Robert's first visit. The dog had been trained to stay in or near the house. Yet Zoltan had been found on a nearby parkway, his body crushed.

The police, of course, attributed the animal's death to accident—an encounter of the closest kind with an eighteenwheeler, perhaps.

But the afternoon after this verdict was announced, one of Robert's lieutenants—a giant named Thomas— had stopped by Thonneger's backyard. He smilingly announced that *he* was responsible for Zoltan's murder. Then, calmly pressing huge, muscular hands together, he indicated that the good doctor had better get to work on the radiation experiments.

Frightened out of his wits, Thonneger had begun, first trying x-rays and tracing isotopes through Gideon's bloodstream. The force-field did indeed have some strange effects—for instance, x-rays didn't penetrate too deeply. On a conscious subject, a stunning near-twenty-foot-tall redhead named Ruth, the doctor found that the field could apparently be thinned at various points. Loss of consciousness, however, brought the field up to maximum—a wonderful survival trait.

Robert had accepted the doctor's initial findings, devouring medical texts to get a deeper understanding. But the leader of the giants wasn't satisfied. He wanted additional experiments, more intrusive—more life-threatening. Thonneger had been scared before, but now his mood verged on hysteria.

An evening fog was blowing in off the lake, and the air held a clammy chill. The back door of the rundown mansion was out of true, and tendrils of mist curled round the edges. Thonneger pulled the sweater he was wearing more tightly around his plump frame. When winter came, he realized, it would be damned cold in there.

If he were still there by winter. If his patient—and Thonneger himself—were still alive.

Thonneger stepped out of the house and down a well-defined trail that led to the boathouse. The original owners must have kept a yacht berthed there, because the structure was on the large side. A key from the doctor's pocket unlocked the landward entrance, and Thonneger stepped inside.

A faint odor of antiseptic struck him as he entered the half-lit, high-arched enclosure. Most of the old bay had been floored over. The walls were lined with medical monitors that gave off faint beeps as lights on their boards glittered. Thonneger paid little attention to them. He had a duplicate set of telltales up at the house, connected by wire.

No, the object of his attention was the enormous still form that sprawled across the center of the room. Gideon lay quiet, the worst of his superficial injuries now healed. No hospital bed in the world could have held him, so he rested on a gigantic air mattress—the sort of thing that was advertised at neighborhood fun fairs as a "Moon Walk."

Thonneger slipped off his shoes and donned a white lab coat, then stepped onto the mattress, making his usual tour of inspection. The monitor probes were all taped in place, and the oxygen connection was fine. He began to make notes. Breathing regular, skin tone acceptable . . . Thonneger poked the recumbent form with a finger. Yes . . .

A figure noiselessly rose from the water at the lakeward side of the boathouse. Thonneger started as Robert climbed up onto the floor of the sickroom. The giants always entered the secret infirmary underwater, keeping their visits unseen.

Robert sat at the end of the flooring, drying himself and gazing at the patient and his doctor with a faintly sneering air. "Still the same?" he asked Thonneger in a low rumble.

The doctor nodded. "No change."

"Then if the subject remains stable, I expect you to begin the new course of experiments." Eyes like fist-sized blue marbles bored steadily into Thonneger's face.

The doctor gulped, wilting under the glare. "I—I'll start tomorrow," he said in a constricted voice.

On the planet Argon, panic reigned. Triadon and his technicians scrambled desperately as bolts of destruction flashed down on them from armored figures diving from the clouds. The greensward was now torn with blackened scars from near-misses. Sturdley saw one of Triadon's armored men take a blast full in the breastplate and collapse in a shower of sparks.

Harry himself was trying to escape the center of combat when he glanced back toward Peg. The onset of danger had apparently overcome her illness, but she hadn't run for it. Instead, she crouched over John Cameron's recumbent form in the stance of a tigress defending its cub. Mike's eyes were glued to the sky as the fliers surged ever closer, seeming to aim for John. He tugged fearfully at Peg's arm, only to be shaken off.

Her gaze was also directed skyward, although her eyes seemed unfocused. "Damnation, Harry! Most of 'em seem to be robots!"

Sturdley directed his own mental probes up toward the raiding force, confirming Peg's discovery. Most of their attackers were machines, while a few airborne humans hung back, directing the foray.

"Triadon!" Sturdley got the attention of the leader of the friendly Argonians and passed along the information. He and Peg helped the defenders by pinpointing the enemy's leaders. The assault faltered as its commanders had to plunge into evasive maneuvers.

But the robots responded to an override program. The mechanical attackers, about a foot higher than the armored humans, hit the ground and headed for Peg.

She moved to block the nearest robot, lashing out with a potent psionic thrust. It didn't work. The robot back-handed her away.

Peg went tumbling and the robot headed for John.

The thought crashed in Sturdley's brain. Sure—John! The one who controls the Rift! Of course they'd want him.

If anything happened to John, it would also mean that he and Peg would be stranded. Sturdley stepped forward, irresolute. Something had to be done, but his mental powers would be as useless as Peg's.

Peg staggered upright, a nimbus of energy playing among her unruly red curls as she tried another psychic attack on the robot, with minimal effect.

But the robot must have become aware of her as some sort of hindrance. It turned, this time leveling a weapon at the girl.

John abruptly came to life with an inarticulate cry, his eyes blazing as he rose to confront the mechanical merce-nary. An incandescent swath of energy swept round his entire body, then leapt to envelop the robot, which pro-ceeded to explode in an impressive pyrotechnic display.

John wasn't done. Ignoring the other robots closing in, he glared up, seeking one of the humans directing the attack. Sturdley felt a tremendous rush of mental energy.

The robots shot skyward in unison, as if the ground be-neath their feet had become molten lava. Triadon and his people went on the offensive, using weaponry built into their armor to fire at the retreating raiders.

John staggered over to Peg, reaching out to her. She sagged under his weight as he suddenly collapsed again. Only Mike's assistance kept the two of them from falling to the lawn.

Peg glanced up at Sturdley. "Even half out of it, he was stronger than the two of us together," she whispered.

"But right now, he's weak as a kitten," Harry replied. "We've got to find some help—"

"I will give as much help as I can," Triadon announced, appearing soundlessly at Harry's elbow. "Your friend and the young lady—Peg—seem sick. Besides, you all need a place to stay. The evil ones"— he looked up after the dwindling forms of their attackers—"were after you."

The newcomers rode on a flying equipment platform provided by Triadon. Passenger accommodations were nonexistent, but Peg managed to find some sort of tarp to cover John. She, Harry, and Mike flew exposed to the high-altitude chill as the open-bodied cargo craft flew on.

The skyscraping towers disappeared behind them as Triadon led his people away from the city. Peg and Sturdley were shivering by the time the platform swooped downward. They found themselves skimming across a greenish-gray tundra, broken in the distance by a rocky butte.

Shivers of cold turned to shivers of fear as the platform seemed to throw itself at the sheer cliff face. Just as Harry was about to scream a warning to the pilot, the stone cracked to reveal a titanic doorway.

"Wow," Peg muttered, impressed. "It's just like the place in that Dynasty comic—the Fortress—"

Harry stopped her with a wave of his hand. "We've got enough problems without copyright infringements," he said. "I'll name it . . . the Citadel of Silence."

Mike, who'd been staring in dazed wonder since the fight began, finally spoke up. "This *is* the land of the gods, isn't it?"

"What?" Peg turned her attention from John to Mike.

"I just—I—I . . . I'm sorry." Mike wouldn't even meet her eyes.

"Mike, what are you trying to say?"

"When I tried to—to, ah . . . when I met you."

Peg had first encountered Mike on the giants' grim home-world, where he and two fellow thralls had tried to rape her. She'd survived by seizing control of his mind, using his muscle and her martial arts training to pound the other two into the ground. She'd also made use of her new-found psychic powers to do a little brainwashing, convincing Mike he was in love with her, that he'd do *anything* to please her.

Before they escaped from the planet of the giants, Peg had released her mental hold on Mike. But his Bronze Age mentality was not at all prepared for what he'd seen in the past hour. "I didn't know then that you were a goddess. I would never have—" Mike's words tapered off into humble mumbling.

"Mike," Peg began with a trace of asperity.

But Harry cut her off with a warning gesture. "Don't rain on his parade," he said softly. "We may need Mike's respect to get him through whatever comes next."

As the flying platform moored inside a huge underground hangar, two of Triadon's technicians picked up John and led the visitors through a labyrinth of passages into a laboratory full of incomprehensible devices.

There was a medical exam in a big cocoon-like machine, more high-tech and considerably less intrusive than the computerized physicals they'd endured on the giants' world. While waiting for their turns in the automed, as it was called, Peg and Harry worked to expand the translation device's vocabulary. Mike entered the cocoon in silence, but his darting eyes betrayed his nervousness. John remained semiconscious through the procedure.

Triadon joined them when the exam was over. Peg and Harry had learned from the technicians that their defender was also the planet's leading scientist. As Triadon approached, the Argonian removed his helmet, revealing a craggily handsome face with piercing blue eyes and reddish gold hair that descended to a widow's peak on his forehead.

"Interesting," Triadon said, perusing a printout on some sort of translucent plastic material. "Two of you show traces of inoculations against several diseases we consider extinct. One of you seems to have never been inoculated against anything. And one—" he frowned, glancing at John. "One shows no trace of any infections at all."

His eyes went to Peg, and his face reddened slightly. "According to the body chemistry report, the young lady appears to be one week pregnant, except there doesn't appear to be a fetus . . ."

Peg's face reddened considerably more. "It's a long story," she sighed, "involving genetic experiments and a mad computer."

Triadon went back to scanning the printout when he suddenly dropped the flimsy plastic and stared at them as if they were radioactive. "And all of you bear the *gene of evil!*"

Chapter Three

"What the hell is an *evil gene?*" Harry Sturdley demanded.

"And why do you act as if it's catching?" Peg wanted to know.

"Please forgive me." Triadon had the grace to repress his shock. "The condition is so unknown these days that it was among the last tests conducted." He glanced at the two terrestrial castaways. "Over a thousand years ago, our scientists isolated the genetic cause for discord, personal friction, greed, deviance—and succeeded in artificially removing it from the population. For more than a millennium, our society has suffered no war, crime, social agitation . . ."

"*Utopia,*" Peg mouthed the word in wide-eyed wonder.

"Yeah—if you're a sheep," Sturdley responded as he gave Triadon a sharp look. "This 'deviance' you talk about. That's another word for 'change.' How many new inventions have been created lately on this wonderful world of yours? Are there any new art forms?"

Triadon hung his head. "No," he admitted, "there are none. Besides conflict, it seems that the evil gene controlled the source of creative thought."

"A thousand years of peace—at the price of stagnation," Peg said quietly. She shivered.

"I'm afraid the last breakthrough our people achieved in our technology was the hemisemidimensional paraperpen-diculatronic warp."

"That's quite a mouthful," Sturdley said. "I don't think your translator handled it well."

Triadon shrugged. "More simply, it's the machine that exiles our criminals into the interdimensional flux you call the Rift."

"I guess that clears it up," Harry said.

"You exile your criminals into the Rift?" Peg shuddered at the thought of falling eternally through nothingness. "Talk about cruel and unusual punishment."

"Our ancestors created the Sphere of Exile and remanded there all those who wouldn't be changed—those who threatened the stability of our civilization." Triadon's voice was defensive. "It was a normally unreachable location in the flux. The problem is that, of late, our planet has had visitations through the Rift. Someone has traversed the interdimensional flux—as you did—and in the process, reopened the connection from the Sphere of Exile to our world. Some of the criminals have come back to Argon and . . . well, you've seen what disasters they're causing."

Sturdley nodded. "The wolves have returned to devour the poor sheep, and you have no defense."

"Poor defenses," Triadon admitted. "In calmer days, my followers and I were shunned because we were tainted with the evil gene. We were considered throwbacks because of our mildly aggressive or creative tendencies. When Argon was threatened, we volunteered to form a defense group. Otherwise, The Consensus—that's our government—is virtually helpless. We are the only ones capable of fighting the Deviants."

"Well, now you've got reinforcements," Sturdley said grandly. "We've had *lots* of experience in dealing with villains—even high-tech ones."

Seeing that Peg was about to make a comment, Harry rushed to cut her off. "It's the least we can do, Triadon. After all, it's our appearance here—ours and John's—that caused this problem."

Sturdley rubbed his hands together, his thoughts flying rapidly. "We've got ESP, you've got armor. When we put it all together, the S-Force should have these guys on the run."

"S-Force?" Triadon was puzzled.

"Sure," Harry said with a big smile. "S, as in Sturdley."

Outfitted in a suit of Argonian armor, Harry found that flight required considerably more technique than he'd ever imagined when he had so light-heartedly given that power to his superheroes. Attitude control, elevation, heading—even the slightest movement brought what he considered a gross overcompensation from the armor's exoskeletal controls. As for the other systems, weapons and so on, he had no idea at all how they operated.

This was supposed to be a test flight, to acclimate Sturdley to the demands of the armor. But Harry was determined to do more than that, to prove the usefulness of this new alliance. On the pretext of wanting to test himself out in heavy traffic, he'd gotten the technicians accompanying him to lead the way to the nearest city.

It turned out to be the place where they'd tumbled out of the Rift—the capital city of Argon, Kaldoa. Harry admired the skyline of mile-high towers, so familiar from John's sketches. The viewpoint was different from hundreds of feet in the air. Harry wondered if Manhattan would look the same. He'd often dreamed of flying over the highrises there, of being a caped superhero.

In fact, flying in New York would probably be easier. Here he had to dodge numerous bodies hurtling around him. Triadon's people had explained something about the suit's automatic collision-avoidance system. Sturdley was depending on that circuitry now as he blundered through the airborne traffic, paying little attention to his course as he flung out psychic probes.

The minds he touched were placid, quiet, well-adjusted . . . dull as hell. But somewhere down there had to be a mind with criminal intent, a mind that would stand out among these psychic sheep like a bloodied wolf.

Sturdley didn't find such a mind. Instead, he discovered a body without a mind at all.

Zeroing in on the contact, Sturdley's probes revealed electronic circuitry and mechanical contraptions beneath human-sized armor and human-seeming skin.

"There's a *robot* lurking on the top landing stage of that tower," Harry snapped to the closest technician, a guy named Melador who'd managed to match his crazy flight pattern.

Melador followed Sturdley's pointing finger. "That's the Consensus Computer Spire!"

The three technicians accompanying Sturdley peeled off and swooped toward the landing stage. Harry remained where he was, hanging in midair. He wouldn't be much help in any rough-and-tumble. But his abilities might be of use in pinpointing any additional robots. He spread a wide mental net, but came up empty.

The robot was apparently acting on its own.

Right now, the creature was attempting to run. It couldn't take to the air because Melador and company were above it, enjoying the advantage of the high ground. Sturdley caught the loudspeaker echoes of Melador's voice shouting in Argonian—a warning, apparently, as the few humans on the platform scattered. The robot attempted to join them, but was stopped as a brilliant blue flare scythed from Melador's right arm to blow off the robot's left leg.

Sturdley felt a moment of panic. The technicians were doing this on his say-so. If that turned out to be a real human being—like an empty-headed government bureaucrat . . .

Harry redirected probes, just to be sure. There was a spreading liquid stain from the downed figure's ruined leg. Relief flooded Harry as his immaterial senses assured him it was some kind of oil.

The robot tried to push itself up and got its other leg blown for that effort. Then the third technician swooped low, a gossamer-thin netting of glowing wire in his hands. This was the nullifier, a new toy Triadon had whomped up in his lab. In theory, it would yank a robot out of anyone's remote control—and also dampen any inbuilt self-destruct commands.

The sparkling mesh descended over the robot, which now lay inert.

"Looks like it worked," Harry exulted, executing an Immelman loop in the middle of Kaldoa's traffic. "The S-Force has caught itself a spy!"

Scaladon stared down from the quarter-mile-high spire—a modest structure for the planet Argon. Who would expect that it housed the headquarters of those trying to seize the planet? An early escapee from the Sphere of Exile, Scaladon had ruthlessly begun organizing the Deviants almost as soon as he'd recovered from his transit through the Rift. Now he was the supreme leader of the attack on Argonian society.

As he listened to the reports of underlings, Scaladon's mind kept overlaying the view of municipal decrepitude he now saw with his memories of a vital city of manufacturing and technology. Beneath his armor, his face tightened. The city he remembered was a thousand years gone, sacrificed by the so-called Rationalists to some doltish ideal of ease and peace, along with Argon's future, Argon's freedom . . .

Scaladon's heavy, armored gauntlet tightened on the windowsill, leaving finger-sized dents. A difficult thing, freedom. He'd allowed his research to take him where it would. The result had been physical scars, and still worse, social stigma as the Rationalist movement gained momentum. The Rationalists had branded him a freak— a *Deviant* who would never fit into the barren confines of their new society. One who would never give up the genes that gave him genius.

Till now, he'd laughed at the efforts of the dwellers in the sty to pen him up again. But the latest word from his agents in Kaldoa caused him unease. "So," he said, turning to the bearer of the tidings—a young, cocky career criminal named Emsisdin. "Our attempts to seize the manipulator of the dimensional flux and our infiltration of the Consensus computers were both foiled as the result of interference by the newcomers."

"Well, neither of those scams was going to make us rich," Emsisdin spoke up boldly.

Behind the mask of his helmet, Scaladon's lips curled. Emsisdin was a true genetic disaster—a minor gang leader with no tinge of ideology cluttering his naked greed. Still, one used whatever tools came to hand . . . "Tell me more about the newcomers," Scaladon ordered.

"There's only four of them—three with some kind of mind powers, or so I'm told," Emsisdin reported. "The one you wanted is called Jancam—Jahncam'run." The gang leader struggled with the alien appellation. "Their leader seems to be an older man called Sturdley"—another nonsense collection of sounds—"who has made alliance with Triadon and his pathetic bunch."

Scaladon frowned. "That could be trouble."

"There's only *four* of them," Emsisdin protested, to be cut off by an abrupt gesture from his chief. No sense in antagonizing the big man, though he found it insulting to report to an anonymous armored suit. Still, he'd heard Scaladon had horribly disfigured himself in a lab accident before the great exile . . .

"To this point, we, the wolves, have battled a pack of over-domesticated dogs," Scaladon said. "But these newcomers are as wild as we. They'll require . . . testing." He turned from the window to face his subordinate. After the horrors of a centuries-long exile and his struggle to seize command of the motley crew of Deviants who had escaped, Scaladon knew how to be hard. He'd be harder yet on this effete, so-called "civilization." Yes, there would be stern tests ahead for the newcomers.

"Activate all our people and machines, Emsisdin. We'll be undertaking a major offensive."

Marty Burke hammered on the table in vain. The noise level in the Fantasy Factory's conference room roared on at maximum din. It was as though the room were too small for the number of people in attendance—though, in fact, there were a few people missing.

Burke pounded again, making a mental note to get a gavel before the next meeting. This table-banging was hard on his hand.

How come Sturdley never had this noise problem?

"Come on!" Burke yelled.

The tumult ebbed, individual conversations becoming audible in the receding tide of noise. Close by, Burke made out the voice of one of the young artists in his clique.

" '— sticking to your fur?' the bear asks. The squirrel says 'no' . . . so the bear wipes his butt with him."

A knot of artists broke into sniggering laughter until they were silenced by a glare from Burke. These were the guys who were supposed to be supporting him?

"We've got a lot to get settled today," Burke said, pitching his voice to ride over the remaining hubbub. "I'm appointing a new creative team to take over *The Amazing Robert.*"

"*We're* appointing a new creative team," Bob Gunnar interjected, fighting gamely to retain the joint authority vested in them by the Fantasy Factory's board.

"Of course, Bob." Burke said with a smile. It wouldn't hurt to defer to him now. Besides, he had a couple of surprises in store for Gunnar, the last obstacle to his complete control. But those would surface later in the meeting. "It won't be easy to replace John Cameron on the *Robert* book—"

In terms of talent, that was the truth, Burke knew. But in terms of style, nothing could be easier. Everyone had commented that Cameron's art looked like vintage Marty Burke—in some cases, improved Burke.

Well, most of the Young Turks in the office credit me as an influence on their styles, Burke thought. Hell, some of them just copy me. It will be easy to keep the look of the book the same. And one more artist around here will owe me big-time.

Burke glanced at the young illustrator who'd been telling the dirty joke when he wanted silence. *He* wouldn't be the one to benefit. Zeb Grantfield was leaning forward, looking eager. He was the Fantasy Factory's current wonderkid, but Burke figured he was soon to fizzle out. Instead, Burke directed his eyes to an even younger artist. "Charlie Myers is my art choice for the book," he announced coolly. "Bob, have you got a writer?"

Gunnar nodded. "Dave Cobb," he said immediately. "He's gotten some seasoning on *The Petulant Lump*, and done some fill-in work with the *Ex-Wives*. The whole 'Brawnette Amuck' storyline was his—"

"Fine, fine," Burke cut him off. "Cobb and Myers it will be. Which brings us to the next question." He glanced at the youthful writer down the table. "John Cameron got the material for his stories from daily newspaper reports. But with the PBA's injunction keeping the Heroes off patrol, we'll need new material. I suggest squaring Robert off against Megalomanik . . ."

The room burst out in a ruckus three orders of magnitude louder than the earlier din.

"—*can't* use fictional supervillains in a Hero book," Bob Gunnar made himself heard over the wall of noise. "Our contract with the Heroes has a clause specifically dealing—"

"That clause was put in by Harry Sturdley while he was facing a very different situation. At the time, the Heroes were on the streets, preventing crime." Burke looked at Gunnar, outwardly calm but exulting in the confusion on his rival's face. "You yourself agreed to taking them off patrol when the police union got those court papers. No patrols, no new adventures."

"We've got plenty of stories from before the injunction," Gunnar insisted.

Burke gestured dismissively. "Old news."

"Well, the new news isn't all that great," Gunnar spat. "All hell is breaking loose in New York. I don't know how you could have missed it, considering your own girlfriend got hit with a beer bottle while covering the craziness. Every crook who went on holiday while the giants were out taking care of things is back in business with a vengeance. The Heroes had just about done away with illegal guns, but now there's a caravan of trucks coming up from the south loaded with enough ordnance to outfit an infantry company. In some neighborhoods, they're holding handgun flea markets, for chrissake."

He glared at Burke. "For the people in this town, the Heroes were the one hope to stem the rising wave of crime. Do you really think it's a good idea to trivialize the city's faith in the Heroes with some fictionalized villain-bashing?"

"I think it's good business," Burke stated flatly. "And as far as the contract goes, Robert has agreed to sign a rider *voiding* the reality clause. There'll be no legal impediment."

He let the words hang in a now-quiet room. As things stood, Marty Burke looked like the good steward of the company, seeking a solution to a tough problem, making the effort to arrange things with the Heroes. Bob Gunnar looked like the one who'd blown his responsibility, carping at a ready-made plan, hindering Burke's efforts.

A thin voice from down the table shattered the silence. "I hope you're not going to try foisting that nonsense on me."

Burke turned to confront a furious Mack Nagel. Mere months ago Nagel had been a has-been, an old

horrorcomics artist out of a job. Harry Sturdley had
thrown him a bone, giving him page breakdowns for Zeb
Grantfield's books. Their styles had rubbed off on each
other. Nagel's ability to draw giant, slim-hipped, busty
babes had manifested itself just as the Fantasy Factory
had launched *The Fabulous Barbara*, the first Hero title to
feature a female.

Now Nagel was riding the crest of a huge wave of fan
adulation. His stooped, storklike figure had straightened
a bit, and some of the worry lines had gone from his face.
He still dressed a bit shabbily, however. Most of his *Barbara* royalty money was spent on medical care for Nagel's
invalid wife.

"I believe this is something we should implement
across the board," Burke began.

"Hey, you're not turning *my* book into more of your
run-of-the-mill crap," Nagel told him flat out. "You may
think you're a genius, Burke, but you don't have as much
vision as Harry Sturdley had in his little finger."

"Harry Sturdley isn't around here anymore," Burke
snapped, his voice switching to intimidation mode. "And
you—"

"And I've got at least six months of reality-based stories I can still use," Nagel cut him off. "By that time, this
stupid court injunction against the giants will be history—or *would* be, if you got on the stick."

Burke glared at the grizzled man, stung. If that old fart
thinks I'm going to take this, he has another think coming.

"And as for any threats or pressure tactics you might be
thinking about, let me tell you something," Nagel went
on. "I've got a standing offer from Umbrage Comics to
come work for them. *Carte blanche*—anything I want to
do. How good are you going to look with the board if you

drive the artist on your number-two book over to the newest competitor on the block, huh?"

Marty Burke felt as if his head were going to burst as he hammered on the conference table again, trying to head off the rush of muttering that now filled the room. "I'm not wasting time on silly arguments, Nagel. Not when we all have deadlines to meet."

He promised himself that the next issue of *Barbara* would get his personal attention—to make sure that Nagel was late. Every word of dialogue, every line of the art would be dissected. It would be easy enough to find *something* to send back for reworking. *Thumbs* always required close attention. Nagel would have to redraw the offending digits, and even then, they might not pass Burke's discriminating eye.

The meeting broke up, but Burke remained seated, smiling savagely to himself as the conference room began to empty. If Nagel wanted to bust balls, he'd find himself up against a master ball-buster.

Burke glanced sourly over at editor Thad Westmoreland, who had kept quiet during the heated exchanges. That was *not* according to plan. Westmoreland was supposed to have chimed in on the advantages of bringing the Hero titles more into the mainstream of the Fantasy Factory galaxy.

"Who's editing *The Fabulous Barbara?*" Burke asked. With luck, maybe it would be Westmoreland himself. Then Burke could delegate the job of screwing Nagel to his supposed ally.

Westmoreland only shook his head. "With the rush schedule they were on, Bob Gunnar's been handling it himself."

Burke clenched his fist on the tabletop. Damnation! Another fight in the offing.

John Cameron was sitting up in a terrestrial-looking bed as Peg Faber waltzed lightly into his room, an excited smile illuminating her face. "Nice outfit," he said, commenting on the form-fitting jumpsuit she wore. "You look a lot better."

"Just what I was going to say to *you*," she told him.

He shrugged. "I'll be here another day to get my brain reintegrated. Triadon doesn't want to mess around with the 'wetware.' Afraid he'll futz up my mental powers. Tomorrow I get fitted for a suit of armor." He looked at her a little nervously. "How was it?"

"John, I was *flying!*" Her face was flushed as she plonked herself down on the edge of his bed. "It was like—well, did you ever have dreams about soaring into the sky?"

John stroked his chin in a professorial gesture. "Ah, yes," he said. "Freud tells us such dreams deal with ze repressed sexuality."

Peg made a face at him, then pressed on. "It's not as effortless as in dreams. There are controls that take a lot of attention. Those suits react to the barest twitch. I was worried about just keeping airborne. But it was . . . exhilarating!"

She glanced at John, her mood coming down to earth. "Have you noticed anything about the translating machines Triadon gave us?"

"Like what?"

"Well—" Peg drew the word out. "While I was getting fitted for my armor, I heard the head technician say, 'We'll have to recalibrate the Framistat.' "

John's eyebrows rose. "Framistat?"

"That's what I said. The technician called it the Framadon aerostatic controller—that's what fine-tunes the gizmoidal drive."

This time, John didn't say anything.

Peg merely nodded. "Yeah. They hook up the Framistat to the gizmo, and that's how they fly. Either Triadon has a bug in his translator, or he's got a weird sense of humor." She shrugged. "But they sure as hell can fly. And Harry did more than just fly. Have you heard? He caught a spy!"

"I saw it on the 3D news," John told her. "It made for a nice change. All I did today was watch the Argonian version of television."

Peg gave him a sympathetic look. Argonian broadcast technology was highly impressive—viewers found them-selves surrounded by a three-dimensional holographic image. But the content, at least to her sensibilities, was abysmal. "I watched last night," she admitted. "All I found were sitcoms—and they were all about *nothing.* It was like watching *Seinfeld* without getting any of the cultural references."

"Daytime 3D is even worse," John told her grimly. "No game shows—that would be competition. And you wouldn't believe the soaps! They have no idea of conflict, Peg. And you can't have drama without conflict. Just look at the news. The merest hint of disagreement in their government—this Consensus—and they treat it like a major crisis. When the newscasters did the story on Harry and the spy, the tone was almost titillating. They treated it as if it were something forbidden—because it referred to a fight."

He shook his head. "Harry was right to offer our help in catching these Deviants. We—*I* made it happen. All those visits I made to sketch here . . . if I had realized I was also freeing criminals . . ." His face was etched with concern. "The worst part is, the Argonians have no idea what they're in for."

Marty Burke was prepared for a long lunch. In fact, he told the gofer who'd been temporarily moved to fill Peg Faber's job that he didn't know when he'd be back. Three times on the elevator ride to the ground floor, he twitched the jacket on his trademark black suit—straightening it, then rearranging it. Burke strode across the lobby and out the doors onto Park Avenue. The glaring sunlight shafting down between the buildings of the upper Twenties was almost uncomfortably brilliant. He was glad to turn his back to the sun as he headed west toward Broadway.

Burke's destination was the largest collection of greenery in the neighborhood, Madison Square, four blocks long and an avenue block wide. As he reached the northeastern tip of the park, Burke wondered for at least the hundredth time why Madison Square was here while Madison Square Garden, where he had season tickets for the Knicks, was located more than half a mile to the north and west. This scrubby collection of lawns, trees, spindly benches, and forgotten statues and monuments had nothing to do with the sports center, at least as far as Burke could see. No, the local products of Madison Square seemed to be squirrels and derelicts. But it was an open, public space, and apparently an excellent impromptu platform for a politician who hated homeless people, unions, and anything even vaguely liberal.

Burke had heard Bob Gunnar describe New York Senator Al Demagogua's politics as "considerably to the right of the Ku Klux Klan."

But the Senator had developed an instant love for the giants whom Sturdley had dubbed "the Heroes"—for their vigilantism, their willingness, as Demagogua put it, "to sweep the scum from our streets."

The great man was using that very phrase as Burke joined the frantic crowd drawn to Madison Square by the political rally. There were a lot of new-money businesses moving into the neighborhood. New money meant yuppies, and that was a vote Demagogua wanted to court. This rally was a given crowd-pleaser, because the guest speaker was Robert, leader of the Heroes.

A twenty-foot-tall man in a white spandex suit was a sure draw, especially since the PBA injunction had stopped the Heroes from patrolling the streets. The senator busily hammered away at that point.

"We could enjoy a safer park—and a safer city—if this mighty Hero and his companions were back on the streets," Demagogua boomed into a set of microphones.

Burke knew that the Senator lived on Long Island.

"But that," Demagogua sneered, "wouldn't suit the agenda of certain *unions*."

He made "unions" sound like an obscene word.

As Demogogua raved on, Burke realized that Robert's eyes had sought him out from amid the hundreds of other rally participants.

I guess that stuff about them being able to read minds must really be true, Marty thought. How else could he pinpoint me?

Robert made a barely perceptible beckoning gesture, glancing toward the back of the portable platform Demagogua's people had erected.

Burke made his way to the edge of the crowd, working round behind the podium. Several obvious cop types—hired security, Burke figured—moved to intercept him, but stopped at Robert's low rumble of an order.

The giant turned from Demogogua and went to one knee, facing Burke. "I detect troubles," he said.

"The staff was less excited about my changes than I hoped," Burke admitted. "But I'll turn them around."

"I'm afraid you'll have to do it without me." Robert ignored the stricken look on Burke's face and nodded toward the orating Demogogua.

"The senator has invited me to Washington."

Chapter Four

The next morning, John Cameron tugged uncomfortably at the slightly baggy jumpsuit of some cottony material as he stood in the middle of one of Triadon's labs. The fit and texture of the garment he wore reminded him of an old-fashioned union suit—except there was no trapdoor in the seat. He didn't enjoy the sensation of lounging around in what felt like long underwear while everyone else in the room—including Peg Faber—wore armor.

A disassembled exoskeleton suit lay on a lab table, waiting to be fitted to him. First, the head technician had told him, they needed to calibrate his body motions to the controls. Probes had been fitted to the major muscle masses of his body, and thin wires led to some sort of computer overhead. It made John feel like a life-sized Pinocchio as he stood on a circular, raised stage, seemingly made of clouded glass.

"This is only a one-time thing," the head technician, Melador, said reassuringly as he flicked switches on a control panel.

The rounded dais beneath John's feet suddenly came to life, pulsing with a lambent glow. The glare grew brighter, and John suddenly felt his feet rising off the glassy surface. He flapped his arms vigorously, as if trying to take off but was held in the grip of invisible forces, and found himself hanging horizontal in midair feeling even more like a marionette.

John aimed a scorching glance at Peg, who, helmet off, seemed engrossed in something on the ceiling. "You might have told me!"

She burst into laughter. "It's traditional!" she assured him. "What a feeling, huh?"

"Um," he said, eying the emptiness beneath him. "Weird."

Melador took John through a whole drill manual of midair maneuvers while the overhead computer recorded and analyzed his muscle movements. He learned how to bank, how to make sharp turns, crash dives, and other aerial moves. The movements of his eye muscles were recorded for ranging and distance calculation. Then he was taught to point in an odd, stiff-armed manner—thumb and pinkie folded together to his palm, the three remaining fingers straight out. It reminded John of the Boy Scout salute, turned horizontal.

"What's this for?" he asked, holding the pose.

"That's the tridigirector." Melador's usually bland face grew serious as he answered. "It's used for aiming and firing your armor's weaponry."

"Oh." John lowered his hand, wiggling the fingers. "Sort of elaborate."

"We thought that preferable to the possibility of triggering ordnance with an accidental gesture," the technician responded.

The rest of the technical types crowded round, removing the wires and fitting John with his new armor. First, John had to raise each foot to slip on what looked like a pair of metal jockey shorts. He repressed a grin. It was the first time he'd had his loins girded. Next came the clamshell style back- and breast-plates over his head. They merged with an articulated set of strips across his midriff, allowing considerably more ease of movement than he'd thought possible just looking at the stuff. John rapped an experimental finger against the plate armor protecting his chest. Not exactly metal, nor was it plastic.

His arms were yanked out straight as the technicians applied jointed bracers and gauntlets. Then his legs were fitted with greaves and boots.

The technicians stepped back, and John tentatively moved his body until he stood spread-eagled. The armor seemed light as air, moving perfectly in synchronization with his movements, a barely-audible whir coming from the exoskeletal mini-motors.

Melador ran some sort of diagnostic device along John's left arm, then popped a small hatch to reveal the mechanical guts of the armor.

"The one thing I don't notice on this thing is an engine or any batteries," John mentioned as Melador delicately inserted a tiny rodlike device and made some sort of adjustment.

"The suits operate on broadcast power," the technician replied.

"But how can you control—?" John decided to find the answer for himself, aiming a mental probe through the opening in the armor. He detected a profusion of circuitry, cables, and servomotors, and here and there, clumps of tiny gold nodules.

Focusing his probe even more tightly, John mentally invaded one of the nodules to find near-microscopic threads of gold imbedded in some kind of silicon. "I've never seen such tiny microchips!" he gasped.

"The doojiggers?" Melador said in a surprised voice. "I'm surprised you can even see them. Jiggers, yeah, well anybody can see *them*." He opened the case of the diagnostic tool he'd used, revealing a mother board studded with what John would have called standard microchips. "But imagine being able to spot a *doo*jigger with the naked eye."

Peg stood nearby, taking in the whole exchange with a strange look on her face. John glanced down at the translation device built into the neckpiece of his new armor. "Translator," he said, "the term 'jigger' will be rendered as 'microchip' from now on. 'Doojiggers' will be translated as 'ultramicrochips.' This will go for all translating machines."

"That sounds a *little* better," Peg muttered.

Melador handed John his helmet, and they started for the door. He held the helmet under one arm, looking down at his gray and white, almost pristine armor. "We look almost dowdy compared to these other guys," he said, glancing at the psychedelic patterns coloring the technicians' armor. Melador might seem bland, but his breastplate was a virulent rush of neon orange and fluorescent blue, the colors spiraling around each other in a stomach-turning design.

"Clean armor is the local equivalent of a learner's permit in flight training." Peg glanced appreciatively at Melador's heraldic design. "Once we pass our flying test, we get to choose our own patterns. I wonder if I can sketch out some of Rick Griffin's poster art."

"Rick who?" John asked.

"He was a San Francisco-based artist who did all sorts of rock concert posters in the hippie days," Peg explained.

John still looked a little surprised. "And how do you—?"

"How do I know about him?" Peg finished for him. "How do you know about Curt Swan?"

John looked so abashed, she relented. "My mom was kind of permanently stuck in the Sixties," she said. "Got enough rock memorabilia to start her own museum."

Shaking his head, John followed her out of the lab. You think you know a person . . .

He crashed into Peg's back at the entrance to the next lab, where she'd abruptly stopped, standing stiff-legged. The servomotors in their armor stopped them from crashing to the floor. Then Peg brushed past a flat-footed Melador, storming into the laboratory.

"What do you think you're doing?" she cried at Triadon. The Argonian scientist, armor-clad, stood over a structure that looked uncomfortably like an operating table. Strapped to its surface was the limp-looking figure of Mike. A tangle of wires straggled from points all over his head to a complicated piece of electrical equipment. Mike had what appeared to be an anesthesia mask attached to his face. Through the clear plastic, John could see a thin stream of haze wisping up into Mike's mouth and nose.

John found himself in a half-crouch, his three middle fingers stretched almost into the form of the tridigirector. Only two things stopped him. He wanted to see if Triadon had a reasonable answer . . . and he wasn't sure his training armor had live weapons.

Although he seemed surprised, Triadon didn't project any guilt as he checked gauges. "Mike is breathing a gas with ionically charged molecules—molecules which interact with the vestigial vomero-nasal organ to encode information directly into the brain."

"You mean you're programming his brain with that gas?" Peg demanded, probing Triadon's brain like crazy.

The scientist nodded. "We call it *vaporware*."

John moved on to the next logical question. "What are you programming him with?"

"I was only going to give him general information—the cultural background we provide to most children as they commence their education."

"Why didn't you give it to us? I don't like the idea of you using Mike as some sort of lab animal." Peg was every inch the defending angel in her armor.

She honestly felt responsible for Mike, John realized.

Triadon, however, merely looked confused. "I wasn't testing Mike. I was responding to his special needs. He's from a preliterate culture, considerably more primitive than your own. He needed the boost."

"And we don't?" John said, thinking of the incomprehensible holographs that made up Argonian 3D.

Triadon frowned. "I would be most unwilling to introduce any artificial programming into *your* brains." He hesitated. "We have no idea how your telepathic powers work, and I don't wish to tamper with them."

The mist ceased trickling through the clear mask on Mike's face. "As a matter of fact, Mike pleaded with me to feed him higher-level programming. Otherwise, I would have left this to a subordinate." Triadon checked the monitoring equipment at the head of the table, then closed a valve and removed the mask. A second later, the electrodes were off Mike's temples. He blinked, looked around, then grasped Triadon's hand and spoke to him.

It took John a moment to realize Mike was talking in Argonian, and he was only getting a translation. "Thank you, noble scientist," Mike said. "You've opened my eyes—my mind—to so much!"

He ran a hand over his forehead, then noticed John and Peg. "This programming is unbelievable," he told them in a mixture of English and Argonian, lapsing into the alien language for the high-tech term.

Mike turned eagerly to Triadon. "Could I get one of the flying suits? I've gotten the whole theoretical background."

"I see no reason not to," Triadon said.

Mike turned to Peg with a smile. "We could go flying together, then." He stopped, peering closely at a tiny readout in Peg's breastplate. "Have you had the Framistat checked on that thing?"

John and Peg took to the air with a sense of relief, leaving the new, improved Mike to chat with Triadon and get fitted for a suit of flying armor.

How's it feel? Wasn't I right? Peg "spoke" to John telepathically rather than using their helmet radios. He couldn't see her face behind the plast-alloy helm, but he knew her big gray eyes were sparkling.

Much better than a sexual-repression dream, he teased, trying a sideslip maneuver.

Peg swooped over him, nearly kicking him in the butt. "Sure. Be a wiseguy," she said over the radio.

A discreet cough came over their radio link, followed by Melador's voice. The proximity sensors in John's armor located the technician's Day-Glo figure floating at rest about a hundred feet above them.

"If your initial equipment test and—whatever—is finished, I've been cleared by Air Control to take you to the city of Kemot. That will give us excellent cross-country practice; then, a taste of city traffic."

Melador was silent, but John could read his thoughts as clearly as if the Argonian were speaking them. *I hope you won't be as much trouble as that Sturdley character.*

The flight to Kemot passed uneventfully. Melador conscientiously put the novices through the full course of flying exercises along the way. By the time they reached the city limits, the suit felt like an extension of John's body. He'd already surpassed Peg in expertise, in spite of the fact that she'd had more practice.

It's almost as if I'm *remembering* to use the suit rather than learning the functions, John thought. He flew off to one side, moodily watching Peg practice barrel rolls.

The subject of memory was always a sore point for John. His conscious history was only two years long. After finding himself naked and amnesiac on a dirt trail near Cameron Corners, West Virginia, John had stolen some clothes, invented a name, and headed for the big city and employment at the Fantasy Factory. In all the time he'd spent getting closer to Peg, he'd battled nagging doubts. What if his missing memories hid the fact that he was a sleazebag? A criminal? What if he was already married to someone else?

His sudden facility with Argonian armor raised a new specter. What if he didn't come from Earth at all?

Of course, there were counterarguments. He'd experienced the same facility in learning to write English, and in picking up the elements of comic book art. Maybe he was just a quick study. Either that, or in his previous life he'd been an English-speaking Argonian cartoonist.

His thoughts were shattered by a tense order from Melador to switch to a different radio frequency. John did so, to hear a rattled Argonian nearly babbling out information. "A D-D-Deviant has been spotted in

Mile-and-a-Half Spire, topmost level. He is armed and has done—" the sender paused for an audible gulp— "has done *physical harm* to several citizens. Triadon party, do you copy?"

"This is Melador," the technician responded.

"And two members of the S-Force," John added, ignoring the startled look Peg gave him. "How far are we from the spire, Melador?"

"We can be there in minutes," the Argonian answered grimly. "And we'd better be. The topmost level of the spire houses the broadcast-power arrays for the flight suits. If that power is cut—"

A graphic mental image filled John's mind—thousands of Argonians plummeting to their deaths. "Let's see how fast these gizmos can go." He rocketed after Melador.

John would have enjoyed the chance to explore Kemot from the air. The towering constructions with their landing stages and terraces seemed to thrust skyward with an almost elfin grace, reminding John of cityscapes painted in the golden age of science fiction, instead of the glass-and-steel cyberpunk monstrosities of current sci-fi movies.

The air was still filled with clouds of milling armored figures as the authorities desperately tried to route traffic away from Mile-and-a-Half Spire. There were just too many airborne travelers. Some of the citizens with more initiative were landing on the tower's terraces. But how many people could those light, airy structures hold?

John thrust a mental probe ahead of himself, penetrating the uppermost stories of the spire. The top landing stage was deserted, and inside John sensed three Argonian technicians—the day-shift maintenance crew. Sending out a deeper probe, John nearly recoiled when he caught agonized pain radiating from two techs who lay wounded. The third was dead, sprawled across a control panel. He'd raised the alarm—and paid for it.

John raided Melador's mind for technical background, learning that it would take several minutes for the Deviant to disengage the power system. Yet his probes revealed no one inside the control rooms. John frowned in puzzlement—then his features froze as he flashed his immaterial senses into the heart of the broadcast array itself. There was the intruder, in a surprisingly bulky, old-fashioned flying suit—arming the detonators on a series of bombs. Why turn off the array when they could blow it up?

In a few terse words, John described the situation to Melador.

"Of course!" the technician said. "That bulky armor you described on the intruder—he's wearing a *self-powered* suit. All he has to do is fly out of the blast zone and watch us all drop like dead insects."

"Can we fly in there and try to drop *him?*" John asked, still monitoring the Deviant saboteur. The guy was almost finished, nearly ready to run for it . . .

"Use energy weapons inside the broadcast array? Even if we hit the intruder, we'd damage the structure. We may even set off the bombs." Unsaid was the logical conclusion: if the saboteur didn't set off the bombs himself when he saw them coming.

"Then we'll have to try something else." John quickly outlined a plan, then carefully began insinuating tendrils of thought into the saboteur's brain.

Inside the broadcast power array, the Deviant named Quagamor finished priming the last detonator. He climbed down from the metal gridwork where the bomb was located, moving clumsily as his exoskeletal servos labored against a weight of armor that was incredibly heavy by Argonian standards. It had to be, however, to stand the heavily charged atmosphere within the array—and, of course, to support the battery pack he planned to use in his escape.

Quagamor scrambled down through the interlocking members of the broadcast array, heading back to the control room. He cracked the outer door slightly, then stepped onto the outside platform with a smile. Although there was plenty of frantic traffic activity, no representatives of the newly created defense force had apparently appeared. Quagamor flipped open a small access hatch set in the armor on his right thigh and pressed the button that put him on battery power.

He leapt into the air, pushing to maximum speed and hugging the firing control to his chest. In three seconds, four to make sure he was out of the blast zone, he'd push—

Searing blue bolts of energy came flaring at Quagamor from apparently clear air. One speared into the control box he cradled, blasting it to atoms right under his hand. Another obliterated his radio gear. Damage alarms and proximity reports suddenly screamed into his eyes and ears. His suit was barely crawling along, and two armored figures swooped to intercept him, spreading a nullifier net to take him prisoner.

Quagamor couldn't allow that. He twisted his head inside the armored helmet, accessing the controls for the injector pack located at the top of his spine. The needle would send a fast-acting poison directly into his brain as soon as he touched the button with his jaw . . . But he couldn't trigger it. His entire body froze, his paralyzed jaw bare micrometers from the suicide control.

"Blast his armor right at the base of the neck," John ordered Melador, pinpointing the area. Sweat poured down John's face as he psychically struggled to hold the saboteur immobile. Then Melador blew away the injector, and the others wrapped Quagamor in the nullifier net. A couple of quick adjustments, and the terrorist's armor was an inanimate hulk, imprisoning the shocked Deviant.

Even through his helmet, John could feel Melador turning wondering eyes at him. "How—why—" the technician fumbled for words. "What made him fly right into our guns, out here in the open?"

John shrugged—another useless display in armor. "When he came onto that platform, I probed his mind and did a little mental editing on what his eyes were reporting to his brain. He saw what he wanted to see—a clear escape path."

"But it wasn't clear—we were right in the way."

"The image I pushed into his brain was clear. Then it was just a case of keeping him from noticing the proximity reports."

"*And* rummaging in his memories to pinpoint where the bomb control and his radio were," Peg added. "Not to mention convincing him he was zooming out of there when he was barely moving at a crawl. And holding him stiff when he tried to off himself."

"Aw—" John began.

He halted at a message from Peg on a more intimate thought channel. Keep this up, and Harry will launch *The Adventures of John* when we get home, she beamed.

Melador was considerably more respectful on the trip back to the Citadel of Silence, but still conscientious in familiarizing John and Peg with their armor.

The technician even enabled their weapons systems so the intruders from Earth could try some target practice.

After her tridigirector had vaporized a boulder, Peg commented, "A girl could get used to this."

They flew through the main gates of the Citadel of Silence, landing lightly in the hangar area where Harry Sturdley eagerly awaited them.

John had to smile when he saw that Harry had adopted native garb—that is, the clothing the locals wore when they weren't in armor. Harry was in the Argonian equivalent of a business suit, a bathrobe-like garment with matching tights and ankle boots.

"You've got to see the news!" Harry gushed, shepherding them into a huge room where Triadon and most of his followers were watching the holographic images on 3D. "The S-Force is up and running!"

As he removed his helmet, John could feel the color rising in his cheeks.

A four-times life-size talking head floated in the middle of the holographic field. "The act of this stranger to our world can only be described as true heroism," the commentator burbled. John blushed even more. "Lest there be any difference of opinion, we have this recording of the facts."

"Gee," John muttered to Peg, "I didn't think there were any cameras on us."

The face faded away, to be replaced with the image of a huge paved courtyard at the base of a totally unfamiliar tower. John and Peg both glanced at each other in puzzlement.

"This evening, the city of Valgrin enjoys its usual peace," the commentator's voice went on. "But the scene this afternoon was quite different."

The image shimmered into bright daylight. A flying platform loaded with a cargo of boxes stood by the tower. Several still bodies surrounded it, and the only moving figures were larger than human size—armed robots.

At the outskirts of the plaza, taking what cover they could, several of Triadon's technicians—John was beginning to recognize the arcane Argonian heraldry—were exchanging blasts with the killer machines.

"A gang of Deviant robots attempted to steal this shipment of ultramicrochips when they were surprised by the intervention of the S-Force. The—ah—fighting could have continued indefinitely, but was brought to a close by one of the newcomers to our world."

A figure in plain gray and black armor suddenly erupted from the Triadonian fire party, heading straight into the air. The robots all turned to aim, but the figure was already pointing both arms down in the tridigirector gesture.

Twin bluish bolts darted down, not toward the robots, but to a shiny metallic panel imbedded in the wall of the tower. Energy beams reflected off the panel to strike an area behind the loaded platform, an area occupied by an armored figure, John now realized. The figure crumpled, and the robots froze, their controller out of action.

The flying marksman came in for a landing and removed his helmet, revealing Mike's smiling face.

Enthusiastic newsmen clustered around him, and he answered their questions in flawless Argonian.

"Maybe Harry will launch the comic adventures of *The Mighty Mike*," John said ruefully.

Peg grinned and gave him a light tap on his armored arm. "Them's the breaks in the hero biz."

Chapter Five

Marty Burke wore a white shirt and a brand-new tie that looked like someone had regurgitated a hearty meal of Dr. Martin's airbrush colors. His trademark black suit was fresh from the dry cleaners—and already wilting from cold sweat.

For about the fifteenth time, Burke checked his watch. It wouldn't do to arrive too early and seem too eager. Okay. It was time. He walked down the block and pushed open the ornate gold and glass door of Le Chateau D'If.

Even worse than the unfamiliar tie was the challenge of haute cuisine. Marty Burke had grown up as a hamburger and fries kind of guy. Boone's Farm had been the first wine he'd encountered, and whenever he could, he used the line, "Hey, *any* year is a good vintage for beer."

That stance wouldn't fly here, he knew. Leslie Ann had told him all about Le Chateau D'If. It was the hippest, most expensive French restaurant in New York this season, with a star chef, an insufferable *maitre d'*, and a reputation for serving hot and cold attitude along with delicious food.

Three steps past the door, Marty found himself confronted by a blond wood podium guarded by a guy who could have played Dr. Wayne Walters, the ultra-suave human alter ego of The Petulant Lump. The factotum's hair was brushed straight back, immaculately in place. A high forehead and strong brow ridges topped flinty blue eyes, a perfect nose, expressive lips, and a carefully-trimmed beard. In his crisp tuxedo, the *maitre d'* was the exact antithesis of Burke in his rapidly wrinkling suit, and, still worse, he knew it.

He gazed at Marty as if his eyes hurt—as if Marty were the cause of the ache. "Yes, sir?"

"I have a one o'clock lunch with Stuart Silikis," Burke said.

He'd hoped for a bit of a thaw when he mentioned the name of Hollywood's latest cinematic genius. If anything, the ambient temperature went down further, and the *maitre d'*s face showed pain.

"Ah." Those mobile lips twisted, and the deep-set eyes grew more flinty. "Mr. Silikis is already at his table. If you'll just follow me . . . "

Burke followed the stiff-backed figure into the main room of the restaurant, to a table in the middle of the chamber. Leslie Ann had warned Burke of the dangers of Siberia, being stuck at a side table. Apparently Stuart Silikis was a regular here, or at least knew how to get a prime location. Marty relaxed just a tad. Hey, it was Silikis's lunch invitation, the producer's choice of restaurant.

The man sitting at the table was a couple of years younger than Burke, lighter of build but a bit more fleshy. A goatee did nothing to hide his incipient jowls, and his glasses magnified watery blue eyes.

What a nerd, Burke thought.

Then Stuart Silikis pointed to the chair opposite him and opened his mouth. "Good t'meetcha, Burke. Siddown."

The thick "Noo Yawk" accent was augmented by a vocal tone like a buzz saw encountering a steel I-beam. Wincing, Burke took his seat.

The effect was even worse on the supercilious *maitre d'*. He fled back to his podium as if all the devils of hell were at his heels.

Silikis smiled, watching the man retreat. "He tried the snooty act on me when I foist came heah," the producer explained. "I like ta shake him up."

"Whatever works for you," Marty said.

Stuart Silikis nodded. "I don't kid myself. I was born in Flushing, did the NYU film school thing, and got real lucky in la-la land. And I'm not gonna kid you, Burke. The Fantasy Factory has something I want."

Burke shrugged. "Hey, in my old neighborhood, everybody knew me as 'Mawdy.' " He didn't mention that he always hated that pronunciation.

They smiled at each other, two guys who had come to an understanding. "You guys sell more comics, but yaw competition—Dynasty Comics—always gets the cushy film deals. Y'know why?"

Before Burke could answer, Silikis plunged on. "Because Dynasty and Dirk Colby got the guys with name recognition. The guys who survived for *fifty years*. Heroes like Zenith—the Man of Molybdenum, and Ram-man—the Midnight Shepherd. My father knows them. Hell, *his* father knows them."

"We've got recognizable heroes," Burke said, stung.

"Yeah, but the Human Torpedo was out of print for fifteen years. And I may like your new characters, like the Ex-Wives, or Mr. Pain—"

Burke preened a little. Thanks to him, Mr. Pain had gone through his twenty-year update.

Silikis continued inexorably onward. "Problem is, my dad don't know them from bupkis." He raised his hands. "Yeah, I know—movies are for the youth market. But the blockbusters bring in *everybody*. And now you got blockbuster material." Silikis smiled. "After all, there are regular heroes, and then there are *giant* Heroes."

This was the offer Burke had expected. "Robert and his people are already all over the newspapers and TV," he said. "Not to mention our comics."

"I'm offering to put them on the big screen," Silikis said. "None of this 'made for TV' crap, no animation deal. I tell ya, Burke, this could be bigger than *Jurassic Park.* I'm talking an honest-to-god, big-budget feature."

"Not as big a budget as you'd need if you had to do the special effects," Burke pointed out.

Silikis shrugged, conceding the point. "No opticals, no models." He grinned. "I guess no stunt-giants, either."

"So the question becomes how big a budget you're talking." Burke's eyes became cunning slits. "How much human-size talent you can afford—and how big will their names be?"

"If we're doing a movie about giants, why do we need regular-sized people?" Silikis sat a bit straighter, his pudgy face tightening, the washed-out eyes sharpening behind his glasses.

"Why did Warner Brothers need Jack Nicholson or Michelle Pfeiffer when they were doing movies about Batman?" Burke shot back.

Silikis stared for a moment. "And who would these regular-sized people play?"

"Heroes fight *villains*," Burke said. "And the Fantasy Factory has a million villains."

Mr. Hollywood broke into a toothy grin. "I like it!" he said. "You got any villains into nook-you-lar terrorism? I think that would make a good plot."

He beckoned the waiter over. "Mind if I ordah? I know the menu in this dump."

Burke assented gratefully.

"We'll have the sea urchin mousse for an appetizer, then the bass in the potato crust." He glanced at Burke. "They do it real nice, sculpting the potato so it looks like fish scales." Then Silikis directed a stern glare at the waiter. "And don't try to screw around with any of that nouvelle crap—full plates, right? Oh, and a bottle of Mouton-Rothschild, '49." He turned to Burke as the server scurried off. "I don't know squat about wine but a foodie friend of mine ordered it once. It's the third most expensive wine on the list, but hey, we're eating on the studio."

Burke nodded with a smile. At this point, he'd have drunk vinegar with gallstones to celebrate his victory. By the time this film was over, the Fantasy Factory's villains would be inextricably mixed in the public mind with the giant Heroes. And what the public believed inevitably became what the comics portrayed. Before this movie ever hit the screens, he'd have the villains of his choice squaring off in the giants' comics.

The suburban Virginia mansion looked like something dating from the Civil War, although when Robert probed the mind of the owner, some sort of builder, he discovered the ersatz plantation house was less than twenty years old. It was a pleasant enough place, situated atop a hill with several acres of other hills blocking off the view of the developments that had paid for the estate—as well as for the owner's new status as a major campaign donor.

At the moment, the gently sloping front lawn of the mansion was dotted with graceful white pavilions shading tables of buffet food, and lavish wet bars serving a variegated crowd that numbered in the hundreds. The clothing styles ranged from understated old money to loud *nouveau-riche*. But the mental atmosphere that Robert sampled was all of a kind—something called "conservative." The giant had a hard time pinning down the term. The best definition seemed to come from a conversation their host, Lonnie Something-or-other, had with Senator Al Demagogua. "We gonna keep what we got, and to hell with everybody else."

The senator was making his way through the crowd, an oleaginous smile on his stubby features. As he spent more time near Demagogua, Robert had idly dissected the politician's mind, finding it a mass of contradictions. The strongest and most burning motivations were the senator's hates—whole classes, cultures, and groups whom he categorized as not human.

Robert wasn't particularly shocked by this outlook. It was similar to his own. For the giants on Robert's home-world, there were only two classes: the Masters, such as Robert, and the Lessers—people of Demagogua's stature. Well, almost-people.

The senator gave Robert a cheerful wave as he passed at the giant's feet. Under his buskins, Robert's soles itched to slam down on the impertinent Lesser. Instead, he summoned up a smile of his own.

One day, little man, he promised himself silently. *One day . . .*

Robert had allowed himself to be shipped to this new population center, Washington, because he wanted to see what another Lesser city looked like. This was also where the rulers of this domain—nation, Robert corrected himself—were located. He still found it difficult to concede the notion that Lessers could rule themselves, so he had come to mentally test these leaders, especially those who controlled the weapons of radiation.

Robert found that he liked Washington. The streets were wide and the buildings not quite so towering. However, there seemed to be a much higher percentage of Lesser vermin—petty criminals—on those streets. The giant could well understand now why Demagogua had invited him as an icon for a series of speeches on public safety. Even with his mental probes, Robert found the point of those orations to be obscure. Demagogua seemed to be exhorting "decent people" to form vigilante groups to fight crime. Robert found a delicious irony in a lawmaker apparently urging his followers to break the law.

But then, many of the lawmakers he had met here appeared to have extremely elastic consciences. Their greed was great, but their wills were weak. Robert had no compunction in reaching into their minds and Binding them to his service. Many of them already acknowledged several masters in secret—political bosses, interest groups, or corporations.

The giant hoped for bigger game at this party, where Demagogua had promised the "movers and shakers" would be found.

As he passed his eyes over the crowd, Robert noted the Senator talking to a man with hooded eyes and a palpable sense of power. After a brief mental prompt, Demagogua beckoned Robert over. "Meet Ben Seckert—he does something shadowy at the State Department."

Robert's research into the machinery of Lesser government told him this could be a useful contact. A few judicious probes of Seckert's memories revealed his work was shadowy indeed, dealing with intelligence, assassination, and money laundering. The State Department agent had a well-ordered, lucid, powerful mind, yet he viewed his job as game-playing on a global board.

"A pleasure, Mr. Seckert," Robert said, sinking to one knee so he only towered twice the government man's body height.

"I'd seen the pictures and the videotape, but I've got to admit, a giant in the flesh is much more . . . impressive." Seckert took him in with sharp-eyed curiosity. "The Senator here swears by you, but then, he's more interested in domestic affairs. I'd worry more about a bunch of people showing up here from apparently nowhere on Earth."

Robert eased tendrils of thought past an impressive shield of suspicion. A mind ever ready to see enemies would definitely have its uses.

"A country must be strong internally to face its external threats," Robert said, playing carefully on Seckert's thoughts. "I'd like to believe the age of the courageous individual influencing events is not quite over."

Another deeply held Seckert view. The State Department man looked up in surprise as Robert delicately bored ever deeper into his psyche.

Under cover of desultory conversation, Robert discovered the strings that controlled Ben Seckert's personality and quietly took them into his own hands. As Demagogua moved off at a mental command from the giant, Seckert thought he was merely trading conservative commonplaces with the new law-and-order symbol. In reality, Robert was quietly redefining Seckert's attitudes, bending him to respond to the giant's suggestions . . . and orders.

Robert carefully kept his face bland as he continued the process. Back home, Binding was a much simpler operation. A Master simply battered a Lesser's mental shields out of existence and imposed his own control. This delicate technique of Binding subjects without their conscious knowledge was much more of a drain.

At last, the job was finished. Robert smiled. Seckert would make a useful addition to his nascent Washington network. Even as the giant withdrew his mental tendrils, Seckert was already doing his bidding. "General!" he called to a man whose crew-cut iron gray hair gave the lie to the casual civilian clothing he wore. "General Hardesty is a member of the Joint Chiefs of Staff," he explained to Robert.

Seckert had been programmed to introduce other likely candidates for Binding, and he was immediately following through. Robert forced a smile to his face, trying to push back the incipient headache brought on by his mental tinkering. "General."

His probes already revealed a warrior's persona, raging at the lack of what Hardesty considered worthy enemies. Yes, much could be done with this mind.

"I understand you'll be in the White House rose garden tomorrow," Hardesty said, giving Robert a quizzical look.

Two Senators who happened to be passing glanced up with smiles. "Tell the President hello for me," one of them said.

Robert returned their smiles. Senators, generals, high government operatives, all would be of use in promoting a nuclear war. And a global nuclear war, he had at last decided, was the only way to advance his long-range plans.

When he'd first arrived on this world with his fifty followers, Robert had thought they would be sufficient to establish the dominance of his kind. Subsequent experience had shown that they couldn't even dominate a single human city. There were too many wild Lessers on this world, hundreds of millions of them, wielding a technology that could threaten even a Master's life. Back home, a Lesser wielding a bronze knife would be a rarity, and certainly no threat to the natural order. Raise a foot, bring it down a few times, clean off the blood, perhaps remove the blade caught in the sole of one's buskins . . .

Here, however, these unnatural Lessers could conceivably pose a danger. Therefore it was necessary to thin their numbers, deprive them of their technology. What better way to do that than use the Lessers' most potent weapons against them?

Robert's smile broadened. And tomorrow, he'd be meeting this domain's top ruler. The one the newspapers referred to as "having his finger on the button."

Chapter Six

The enormous rocky doors of the Citadel of Silence stood open to admit shafts of brilliant Argonian sunshine. But Harry Sturdley barely noticed as he strode fretfully back and forth over the vast hangar floor.

"We've been working our tails off, and the Argonian in the street still barely knows about us." His tone of voice was the same as he used at Fantasy Factory staff meetings when a comic launch had fizzled. "I don't get it! We're the *good guys* here—the civilians should love us! At least—"

"Yeah, we know," Peg Faber interrupted, her voice barely hiding her sarcasm, "*it works in the comics.*"

"It worked in real life, too," Harry hastened to point out. "Remember how most New Yorkers acted when the Heroes first turned up?"

He regretted that argument almost as soon as the words were said. How was New York doing now? What were the giants up to? His lean face tightened. Robert was surely responsible for the assassination attempt on John at the San Diego comics convention. Did the giants think he, John, and Peg were dead now? How had the Fantasy Factory board reacted? How must Myra feel?

Sturdley pushed away thoughts of wife and home, trying to concentrate on the present campaign. They had to clear things up here before they could take on the ills of Earth. "It's as if the folks here have no idea of good and evil."

"They don't—not in the sense that you mean." Triadon's craggy features seemed shamefaced as he stood with his helmet under one arm. The ruddy gold of his hair shone in the sunshine, clashing wildly with the psychedelic green and purple heraldic painting on his armor.

"And what does *that* mean?" Harry growled.

As happened quite often now, all eyes went to Mike. The mind-expanded escapee from the planet of the giants tried to explain. "You've got to remember, Harry, these people have lived in nearly perfect peace for a thousand years. To them, any conflict, *any* fighting, is a bad thing."

"Great!" Sturdley burst out. "So just the act of protecting them makes us look bad in everyone's eyes?"

Mike, Triadon, and the other Argonians nodded unhappily.

"Rationally, we know that we must fight to defend our world," Melador said slowly. "But in our hearts, well, even I have doubts about the rightness of our actions."

"We've *tried* to bring back the concept of right and wrong," Triadon said. "I asked a friend of mine—another throwback who is also a great theater director—to stage a production of *Flubadub* for *Argonian Classics*."

"*Flubadub?* Very catchy title," Sturdley muttered.

"It's a classic play from the Age of Strife," Mike went on. "The theme deals with choosing between good and evil."

"Wait a second, I saw this on 3-D," Peg said. "The guy who played the lead, Flubadub—"

"Our greatest living actor," Triadon assured her.

She sighed. "It was like watching Dick Van Patten take on *King Lear*."

"That successful, huh?" Sturdley turned to Triadon.

The scientist stood with downcast eyes. "According to the ratings, hardly anyone watched."

"Well, if we can't get their attention the classy way, I guess we'll just have to go for crass." Sturdley gave the group a crooked smile. "It's just lucky you've got a crass comic book type with you. From now on, we're going to *market* our heroes." He stabbed a finger at Triadon, at Melador, at John, Mike, and Peg. "Collectively, you're the leaders of Argon's defenders. We're going to have you out every day, patrolling."

"What about you, Harry?" Peg asked.

He shook his head. "I'll help out at first, but I think I'll work out better as the wise old guy who stays home." He frowned in thought. "We've got to have a credo— a code."

"Great," Peg muttered. "He's going to reinvent the Comics Code."

"No," Harry said, turning to her. "A hero's code. Something to distinguish our tactics from the Deviants. Those blasters in your armor," he asked Triadon, "can you change them for a weapon that stuns?"

"Stun?" the scientist echoed in bafflement.

"From here on, we go for no killing, no destruction. The *bad guys* do all that. We need nonlethal weapons, plus some way to *shoot* those nullifier nets at the villains' robots." He grinned. "The flashier, the better."

Three days later, Sturdley had a chance to test his theories. He, Mike, and three of Triadon's technicians had flown to the northernmost of Argon's spire-cities, distant Ahkeya.

"There's got to be some kind of method to what the Deviants are doing," Harry told Mike for about the fiftieth time. "Some sort of thread to all these crimes."

"They tried to kidnap us," Mike pointed out.

"That had to be part of a plan to get more of their people out of dimensional exile," Sturdley said.

"Just after we arrived, they looted several robot factories."

"And now they've got more of those killer robots."

"You stopped a spy at the Consensus computer records, there were several attempts to kill large numbers of people, and I intercepted the hijacking of a shipment of doojig—um, ultramicrochips."

"Which seem to be an integral part of Argonian technology." Sturdley nodded. "Now back in the bad old days when people still had the evil gene and were inventing stuff, Ahkeya was known as The City of Science."

"I knew that," Mike said promptly.

"Yeah, well it took me a couple of hours of digging around in those Argonian computers." Sturdley gave his hero-in-training a dirty look. "The thing is, Ahkeya still has Argon's largest science museum, with exhibits dating back to the Days of Strife."

Mike glanced over as they flew along. "You mean *weapons?*"

"I don't know," Sturdley said. "But I bet the bad guys plan to find out."

The Science Museum was housed in the lower levels of a small, aged-looking tower at the edge of the city. Traffic was light as Sturdley stood on an upper terrace, staking out the place. For the past hour, he'd mentally scanned everyone entering the museum—not that there was a great crush of humanity. A few academics had come to visit the museum's library, and a small knot of unhappy school kids had been led in and out.

Bored out of his mind, Harry glanced upward. The tarnished plast-alloy of this spire certainly didn't scrape the sky. And was it his imagination, or did it lean to one side?

"Here comes another." Mike's voice interrupted his thoughts.

Stifling a yawn, Sturdley sent out a subtle mental probe to the gray-haired figure shuffling along in a quietly painted armor suit, helmet under his arm. It would probably turn out to be another professor checking the date of Framadon's fourteenth gizmoidal experiment—that's what Argonian scientific scholarship had descended to.

Instead, he encountered no mind at all—only positronic currents swirling in a maze of wire mesh and ultramicrochips.

Sturdley whirled to the others. "That guy is a robot! We've nabbed ourselves another spy!"

He scanned the area. There were no other robots, but several human strollers were crossing the cracked esplanade at the base of the tower.

"There's nobody on the ground floor of the museum. We'll get him there."

The five S-Force members swooped down from the terrace and burst through the museum entrance, Harry quickly feeding entry tokens into the automated gates. Still flying, they crisscrossed the ground floor, finding a number of dusty exhibits but no robot. Sturdley furiously started shooting off probes. "Where the hell did the damned thing go?" he muttered to himself.

The robot didn't appear to be in any of the public areas. Harry expanded his mental search and hit paydirt. He snapped over the radio, "It's in the third subbasement, officially listed as an uncatalogued storage area."

"I don't like the sound of that," Mike said, leading the technicians to the nearest drop-shaft.

If the museum proper had been dimly lit, the lighting budget for the storage basements had been cut to the bone. Some sort of glowing strip had once ringed the shaftway, but time and neglect had left only a feeble radiance with many gaps. With a thrust of his jaw, Sturdley flicked on an infrared guidance system, warning the others to show no lights. "We don't want to warn him we're coming."

The robot had walked to its destination, leaving a trail of footprints in the thick dust on the floors. They followed the tracks down narrow aisles between vertiginous piles of sealed crates and vast, ungainly shapes swathed with tarpaulins and spiderwebs.

Harry had his outside sound receivers tuned to maximum gain and picked up a bubbling hiss from the far side of a rampart of stacked display cases. "Just beyond here," he whispered.

The technicians checked their newly-implanted stunners—useless against this antagonist—with low-voiced, nervous chatter. Two of them unslung weapons that looked like sawed-off blunderbusses. This was Triadon's answer to the need for a long-range weapon against robots. Inside the large-caliber barrel was a smart rocket that, once aimed at a robot, pursued the creature and deployed a nullifier net to take it out.

Harry sent the two gunners to the top of the piled cases, hoping they'd get a better shot. "We'll fly down this aisle and fire off our stunners like gangbusters."

"What's a gangbuster?" Mike asked.

"And what do we do if the robot shoots back?" the Argonian technician wanted to know.

"All we need is a couple of seconds' distraction so we can net the damn thing," Sturdley said. "We'll all be taking the same chance."

They floated in the aisle, Harry taking the highest position, Mike the middle, and the technician flying as low man. "On the count of three," Harry whispered into his mike. "One, two . . . now!"

He flung his hands out, going for top speed, and rocketed into an open space in the stacks. An entire pile had been brought down, the area filled with smashed crates. Harry spotted the robot kneeling on the floor beside one of the broken boxes. It was pouring a liquid over what looked like a huge, fossilized dog turd—a three-foot by one-foot brownish-gray clot.

It had to be some sort of chemical reagent, Harry thought. Wherever the liquid touched, the petrified gray-brown material bubbled away to reveal a gleaming metallic cylinder.

"Fire!" Harry yelled. He thrust his fingers in the tridigirector gesture, and pale-green stunner flashes erupted from the projectors built into his armored gauntlets. They looked pretty, he thought, but they were about as effective as throwing salad greens at the robot.

It's just a distraction, Sturdley told himself. We only need to make the robot freeze long enough—

The robot did indeed freeze, for a good tenth of a second. Then it turned back to the cylinder on the floor, tearing at the protective chrysalis.

What have we got to worry about? Sturdley thought. That thing's been in storage the past thousand years!

The robot whipped around, the gleaming cylinder—it looked like a squat, baby bazooka—balanced in its hands.

There was a glare of garish white light, and the pile of crates behind Sturdley, not to mention a ten-foot section of ceiling above him, abruptly ceased to exist.

Wish *I* could get batteries like that, Harry thought as he went into desperate evasion maneuvers. Where the hell are those guys with the nets?

The robot got off another shot, vaporizing one of the nullifier rockets. Number two, however, was right on target. Its mid-air burst deposited the sparkling, gossamer webwork over the mechanical intruder.

That should have put the robot out of commission. But in the instant before the net settled, the robot self-destructed, exploding in a gout of reddish flame. Harry found himself flung upward and through the newly created hole in the ceiling.

A shaken Harry Sturdley stood on the plaza outside the museum tower as a cluster of Argonian firefighters struggled to extinguish the flames crackling merrily in the space where the Science Museum had stood.

"You're sure you're all right, Harry?" Mike asked worriedly.

"Fine, kid," Sturdley assured him. "I regained control right after getting *whooshed* through that hole." He raised a gauntleted hand to his unhelmeted head. "Better than the tech who got smashed into that wall of crates."

"His armor kept him from getting badly injured," Mike said. "Um—I think the media has arrived."

He pointed to several flying platforms coming in for landings. All were loaded with cameras and transmission equipment.

Harry patted Mike on the back. "Go get 'em, kid. Take what I gave you—and play it the way I said."

Mike nodded and set off for the organizing news crews.

"Hey, Mike," Harry called after him.

Mike turned.

"From what you know of these bozos—will it work?"

"I think so," Mike said, a little surprised.

"Then go in there and kick some ass."

"Harry taught me a new term today," Mike said, raising a utensil full of food to his mouth. "*Damage control*."

Peg Faber smiled. "That's a very Harry-like notion," she agreed. "Especially after blowing up and setting fire to the Science Museum."

Mike raised an admonitory finger. "That was all the fault of the Deviants—and their robot. We were only there to restrain. The robot attacked."

"And the Argonians bought that?"

"According to their culture, that's exactly what had to have happened. Sturdley was worried about that, too." Mike looked at her, his handsome face twisting as he tried to put a difficult concept into words. "The Argonian worldview—it's very different from what I grew up with. And from the way you're reacting, it's very different from your culture as well."

"Well, *I* didn't think they were gods."

Color rose in Mike's face. "A point to you. Yet, even Sturdley told me that the idea of inhaling an education seemed like magic to him."

"Me, too," Peg had to admit.

"But there is also a—*logic*—to their culture, a framework. For instance, Triadon's name . . ."

"Yeah. Bizarro."

"Actually, that's a rather offensive Argonian term. The whole name-structure here ties into a complicated cultural matrix. It denotes his social status, his politics, his basic intelligence, education, class standing, his genetic background . . ."

"Hey, you could tell me it also included his hat and shoe size and whether he's left-handed. *I'd* still have to ask how the hell you can do that in just three syllables."

"And I'd have to answer—" his face twisted a little more. "You just don't understand."

Peg fiddled with the food on her plate. She knew she shouldn't have accepted this dinner invitation, but she was tired of the mess hall at the Citadel of Silence. And she had to admit that Mike looked pretty impressive in the bathrobe and tights ensemble that the well-dressed Argonian male donned for a night on the town. Argonian civvies made Harry look like Hugh Hefner's older brother.

She glanced down at the kaftan and harem pants outfit that Triadon's computers had assured her was high fashion. It seemed to fit the norm of what the local females were wearing.

But it wasn't a possible violation of the local dress code that had her so anxious. It was the sudden reversal of roles with Mike. Until he'd sniffed that vaporware, she'd been the one in charge of their relationship. Hell, she'd actually reached in and tinkered with his mind.

Now she was the one fumbling her way along while Mike held all the aces and tried to make things simple enough for her to comprehend.

He smiled at her, his dark brown eyes soft and gentle. Peg felt an odd sensation in the pit of her stomach. All of a sudden she was back in college, the naive, struggling freshman, and handsome senior Lew Irvine was coming on to her.

Her eyes went to her plate. No way do I want that to happen again. Why does he have to be so damned attractive?

"Enjoying your ludgub?" Mike asked.

Peg raised a morsel to her mouth. "Funny, it tastes just like chili con carne to me."

She glanced at the implement. "And this is the first time I've ever seen a solid silver spork."

Chapter Seven

"I've got three of them in what appears to be an unused office space," John Cameron said, acting as scout for the Kaldoa S-Force patrol. They'd been out for hours today, without encountering any Deviants. At least now he'd spotted three Deviant-built robots, apparently establishing a sniper's nest at the summit of one of the Kaldoa city-spires. The robots were heavily armed and in range of a major traffic nexus.

"Get through to traffic control and have them start rerouting everyone out there." John's face was tense. In moments, the evening commute was going to begin. If he hadn't stumbled across those robots, they'd have found hundreds of targets.

He spread his mental net, finding one more bad guy in the picture. "There's a Deviant just leaving that same office," he told Melador and the two other S-Forcers. "He must have commanded the robots."

The highest landing stage on the spire was below the Deviant's shooting blind. John turned to the rest of the patrol. "We'll come in on them from above—hopefully out of sight until the last instant."

"How are we going to get in?" Melador wanted to know. "They're not going to open the door."

"We're going in through the window," John said. "How strong are those things, anyway?"

He realized a drawback in Harry's new heroes' credo. Some of the S-Force—tested veterans, perhaps—should be packing blasters, if only to cut through the enemy's fortifications. "Could one of those rocket-powered nets break the glass or whatever it is?"

Melador assured him it would.

"Okay, then the three of you go in through the front window and take out the robots. I'll go for the human."

They all arrowed downward, John aiming for the rear of the spire while his cohorts went for the front. His audio pickups caught the sound of the rocket being fired, and the smashing of the window. A second later, an armored figure came tumbling from a window on John's side of the building.

John swooped down, thrusting his arms in the still-unfamiliar tridigirector gesture. His stunners spat pale green fire for an instant, bracketing the figure of the escaping Deviant. Then the stun-beams died.

"What the—?" Whether the rush job of replacing his armament had gone astray, or if it were sabotage, John had no idea. But now he had no weapons while facing an armed enemy leveling his blasters in John's direction.

John's instincts took over as he plunged into a wild dive, pushing his suit's gizmoidal drive to the limit. His odd, "almost-remembered" facility with Argonian armor paid off. John smashed right into the Deviant, denting the villain's armor and sending them both tumbling through the air.

Before they could bounce apart, John wrapped his opponent in a bear hug. He didn't want to give this guy a clear shot . . . better to wrestle.

Still grappling, they hit the spire's topmost landing stage, sixty feet below where they'd crashed together. The two of them tore right through the plast-alloy flooring, which didn't do their armor any good. One of the Deviant's arms now hung at an odd angle. His good hand was set in the tridigirector, sending wild energy blasts into the air as he tried to twist around to aim at John. But John maintained a death grip around the criminal's wrist and his legs wrapped around the guy's waist, while whaling away with his free hand.

Their slam-bang bout of hand-to-hand must have weakened the Deviant's breastplate. John slugged the guy again, and the chest armor cracked open and fell away. The Deviant twisted loose and dropped like a stone—his gizmoidal drive decommissioned. The man flung up his good arm, trying for a last shot. John had no time to dodge the deadly bolt. He reached out to stop the man with his mind—and discovered he didn't need to act as he read the Deviant's fury and disappointment that his blasters didn't work, either.

Then John realized their continuing plunge was about to smash them into another landing stage. He poured on the gizmo to brake his fall, reaching out to the Deviant. But this guy wasn't about to let himself get captured. He swung away—to land with a sickening *splat*.

John hung in midair over the twisted form. He might be flying, but he sure as hell didn't *feel* like a superhero.

"I'd say that went pretty well." Harry Sturdley sounded pleased as he and John stepped into the bright sunshine from the pillared portico of the Hall of Consensus, the seat of Argonian government. The building was in marked contrast to the high-flung spires of Kaldoa, being created of ancient stone and rising only four stories tall.

Both Earthers were clad in full armor, the sigil of the S-Force prominent on their chests. "Okay, now, on the count of three," Sturdley said as they reached the middle of the plaza fronting on the hall of government. Dozens of cameras were trained on the pair as Harry counted down. Then they rose in unison into the air.

"You're awfully quiet, kid," Harry said. "Did seeing all those government types get to you? You've got to say one thing for the Argonians—we might consider their government a little crazy, but at least they don't just elect pretty faces. That Boradon guy has to weigh three hundred pounds if he's an ounce. But he was very polite. I think we'll look pretty good on 3-D tonight, getting a vote of thanks from the whole Consensus."

Let's find a quiet place where we can talk, John transmitted on a telepathic wavelength.

"Something wrong?" Harry asked. "I'm getting a real angry undercurrent from your mind."

Privately!

Sturdley cast a quizzical glance but nodded his assent. They landed on a quiet plaza on the edge of Kaldoa, given over to parkland rather than manicured lawns. As they walked among a grove of trees, John removed his helmet and gave Harry a searching glance. "You really think everything went okay?" he asked.

Harry shrugged. "I'd say it was a good sign for the government to give thanks to the S-Force in general—and us in particular." Unbolting his own helmet, Sturdley gave John a look. "You know, they wanted Mike up there, but I held out for you. Figured it would give you a publicity boost."

John waved that away. "I don't care that there's a Mike fan club."

"Look, even the opposition went along with this vote-of-thanks thing," Harry said. "We've certainly helped the

S-Force's image. Even that guy Boradon was polite to us. And he's an elder statesman in the Consensus—"

"Did you read him while you shook hands?" John suddenly asked.

Harry stared at his protege, a little surprised. "I didn't think this was the time or place." He peered at John. "You mean you did?"

John nodded grimly. "He had good reason to be polite, Harry. I suppose you'd be polite, too, if you thought you were meeting a heavily-armed psychopath."

Harry's jaw sagged.

"You called Boradon an elder statesman, and he is—the same way Neville Chamberlain was. He's tried appeasement—peace at any price. One of the things I picked up from him was that he'd sent secret peace feelers to the Deviants. Complete civil rights for the Deviants already here, and negotiations for releasing the other exiles. I guess we can only be glad that the Deviants sent his envoy back in pieces."

Harry's eyes grew large at this report of a near-sellout. "The old fraud! Playing footsie with the bad guys after all we did for him—"

"We're not doing enough, Harry. After a couple of weeks on patrol, I can see that."

"The patrols *should* work. Take the *Rambunctious Rodent*. When he goes on patrol, he not only tangles with big-name supervillains, but also nails plain thug-types, too. Street crime isn't a problem here in utopia. We should have it easier."

"Harry, this isn't like the comic books! We've got maybe two hundred S-Forcers squared off against the same number of Deviants, two tiny factions lost among millions of ordinary people. The bad guys strike at will while we patrol and guard danger spots like the power grids."

"We've cut down Deviant activity significantly," Harry said.

"That's not the same as beating them," John responded. "It's not just a case of cops and robbers, Harry. Or heroes and villains. Most criminals, even organized crime, want to keep up the existing order even as they loot it. But these guys—I don't think they want to conquer and rule the world. They just want to tear everything down."

"And what do you want me to do?" Harry asked.

John looked at him wildly. Even though the kid was silent, Harry got a whisper of his thoughts. *You're the one who's supposed to have ideas!*

Harry stretched out an awkward hand, his gauntlet clanging against John's armored shoulder. "Give *Plan A* some more time to work before you start talking about total war."

"That's okay for you to say," John muttered. "You haven't killed anybody. You're trying to set up rules, but the other side won't play along."

"Kid, what happened the other day was an accident. Everybody who witnessed it—"

John nodded, his face hardening. "Sure, it was an accident. This time, at least."

"I've got them now," Marty Burke gloated, sliding on the satin bedclothes until he could sit up. "They can moan all they like at the staff meetings, but the board and the giants are on my side. And soon I'll be able to get the public working with me, too."

"*I'm* gonna start moaning if you don't turn that light off," Leslie Ann Nasotrudere said from her side of the bed, "and it *ain't* gonna be with pleasure. Come on, Marty. I've got an early doctor's appointment tomorrow. He's going to look at my face." She raised a hand to the almost faded bruises.

Oblivious, Marty pressed on with his favorite subject, the Heroes movie.

"They've gone into rewrites of the basic premise, and all sorts of Fantasy Factory villains are in the story. It all comes down to whose vision gets sold to the public. When Batman went on TV back in the sixties, the comic book went camp—"

"Because that's what the public expected," Leslie Ann parroted along with him.

"Exactly! Uh—have I said that before?"

"Only about every fifteen minutes this evening," she groaned. "Please, Marty, let me get some sleep."

"But this is important," Burke went on. "Don't you see, honey? If the movie public sees *my* idea of what the Fantasy Factory should be like, the others—the Gunnars and the Nagels—they'll *have to* fall in line."

"Right," Leslie Ann said acidly. "Now turn off that light."

"They're talking real stars to play the villains," Burke continued heedlessly. "Jeff Goldblum's people are putting feelers in for Skeletone, and Johnny Depp is showing interest in playing Megalomanik. There's even some buzz that Sean Young wants a crack at Madam Vile."

"Light! Off! Now!"

Burke complied, but he didn't shut up. "Even down in Washington, reporters were asking Robert about the movie. Free advertising!"

Under the frozen gel mask she used to soothe her injured features, Leslie Ann's eyes opened. Did Burke realize how Robert's words seemed to parrot his? Or was it the other way around?

From the moment she'd seen Harry Sturdley with those damned giants, her scam-detection antennas had been on full alert. Leslie Ann had gone out of her way to give Sturdley a hard time, convinced he was using the so-called Heroes for his own purposes.

Now she stared up into the darkness.

What if she'd gotten it wrong? What if the giants were manipulating Burke?

Chapter Eight

In the interdimensional flux called the Rift, turbulence disrupted the matrix of currents through the void. An eddy developed around a nexus in the lower levels, down to the four-dimensional substrate. Odd pressures were brought to bear on the nexus known as Earth . . .

Larry Hammeyer stifled a yawn and looked at his watch. Four A.M., on the dot—halfway through his shift. He rose from the sagging desk chair, his hands reaching around to massage his aching back.

Two steps brought him to the wooden shack's open door. South Dakota by moonlight was hardly a beauteous sight—at least here in the badlands. The shadowed gullies and tortured rock formations were downright eerie. Even the least imaginative types began to see things moving in the darkness.

But the near-moonscape outside was Hammeyer's only respite from three walls worth of instruments and readouts. The Gravitic Research Underground Measuring Project covered fifty square miles of monitors buried from one hundred feet to a mile and a half below the surface.

GRUMP. Larry wondered what academic wag came up with that acronym. Esoteric undertakings like gravity research were few and far between nowadays. Federal money had dried up for pure science experiments. Politicians who happily shelled out for pork-barrel projects could be depended on to scream like blazes at spending tax dollars to check if the force of gravity is constant at different altitudes or depths.

It seemed self-evident to a layman, perhaps—gravity was gravity, everpresent and unchanging. Unfortunately, this fact of the senses had yet to be scientifically measured. That's what GRUMP was all about, getting the data—and providing some change for impecunious almost-physicists like Larry Hammeyer. After all, why should the researchers waste federal money on minimum-wage gauge watchers when they could get physics graduate students for less?

Still, GRUMP would look good on Larry's *curriculum vitae*, as long as he didn't have to go into too much detail about what he'd actually done on the project. Not much glory in admitting he'd spent eight hours a night for nearly a year looking at gauges that never moved.

An agitated beeping noise jarred Larry out of his stupor. Stifling a yawn, he stepped back inside, then stared at the main monitoring bank with bulging eyes. The buried gravitic detectors were registering anomalies like mad. The only exterior force that could affect the probes like that would be an earthquake—and the earth wasn't moving beneath Larry Hammeyer's feet.

He leapt back toward the desk and the cellular phone. Standard operating procedure—he was to call the senior researchers if the monitors registered any abnormalities.

In his haste, he fumbled the grab for the phone. It toppled off its charging base, floated *upward* as if in slow motion, hovered for a moment, then began a leisurely descent.

Larry finally pulled himself together and captured the phone about six inches above the top of the desk. He yanked the antenna out to its full extension and dialed the number of the motel where the senior physicists were.

An unwelcome thought burrowed its way into his consciousness as he listened to the phone ring on the other end. The only thing worse than research that added no new data was research that yielded too much data—especially that of the *weird* variety.

In the open hangar of the Citadel of Silence, a fully armored John Cameron stood at ease, listening to Harry Sturdley's prepatrol lecture. "We've gotten a lot of tips about out-of-the-ordinary activity in Kemot." Sturdley smiled. That they were getting tips at all seemed to vindicate his media blitz to win the hearts and minds of the Argonian citizenry. "We're going to concentrate our forces there, with six three-person teams, plus a special team led by Mike and John."

John nodded at Mike, his facial expression unseen behind his helmet. It was bad enough that the former caveman was becoming a media sensation—although easy enough to predict, given Mike's looks and inhaled expertise in Argonian language and culture. But for Mike to gain top dog status even among the four castaways . . .

He repressed a sigh. Since their conversation a few days ago, Harry seemed to be easing John into the side-kick's position behind his first bona fide hero. John didn't know whether it was conscious or not, but he knew that Harry felt he was taking too radical a position on the war—pardon me, Harry, John thought—the *campaign* against the Deviants. He could live with Harry mentioning Mike's name first. But why did Peg have to pay so much attention to the guy?

John took a deep breath, forcing his irritation into the background. Out on patrol, their lives would depend on teamwork. He and Mike would have to work together, ferreting out Deviants and thwarting whatever mischief they had in mind.

But I'm better at finding the enemy than that overintellectualized barbarian, a little voice in the back of John's head whined.

John wrenched his attention back to what Sturdley was saying.

"We've finally found a match in the old government computers for that weapon the robot was trying to steal in Ahkeya," Harry said, fumbling with a tiny thumbpad computer. He finally entered the right code sequence, and a holographic image gleamed in midair. It looked like a short, squat bazooka, with a handgrip and sight about midway down the gleaming silver cylinder. "I'm calling it a *force cannon*," Sturdley announced.

Which probably meant it had some ridiculous Argonian name like *doo-whacker,* John thought.

Triadon stepped into the discussion, his tone grave. "The worrisome thing is that this was specifically designed as a weapon."

Mike, his helmet off, turned to explain to Peg. "The stuff they've been using in battles so far has been whipped up from civilian tools. The Deviants' red-ray weapon— that was developed from a cutting-beam device. Our blue-ray projector was originally a welding implement. The green beam, the stunner, has been used as surgical anesthetic."

Sturdley spoke up. "The thing is, the weapons in use so far aren't capable of widespread destruction. The force cannon, however, is."

He looked at Triadon. "This thing was invented right at the end of the Age of Strife, so only three prototypes were made. One wound up in the Science Museum."

"The Consensus records give no clue as to what happened to the others," Triadon finished. "But if they fall into Deviant hands—"

"You keep digging in the computers," John said. "Those of us with mental powers will probe every Deviant we encounter for information."

"Peg and I are going to question the guy Mike captured at the Kemot hijacking," Sturdley said. "If we get any information that can be followed up, we'll radio you."

Mike and the others donned their helmets, and the S-Force members who were to go on patrol checked their armor. The huge doors rumbled open, and suited figures began flying skyward.

John caught the mental message Harry sent after them: *And be careful out there.*

John, Mike, and their three Argonian backups made a leisurely orbit around the central spires of Kemot City, maintaining an altitude about halfway up the towers.

"Well, I don't *see* anything out of the ordinary," Mike said.

"We've got reports of several cargo platforms being stolen." John frowned as he watched the city's air traffic swirl around them. "But there's too many for us to stop every one to check the ownership." His frown grew deeper. What would criminal terrorists want with the equivalent of a terrestrial truck? Moving loot? A getaway vehicle? The flying version of a car bomb?

He spread a mental web across the teeming traffic, trying to isolate any thoughts that had to do with platforms or force cannons.

John found nothing—except for a heavily-laden platform whose crew didn't think at all.

"Robots!" John warned, giving his team a mental view and location of the Deviant vehicle.

"Grumadon! Moradel! Nullifiers ready!" Mike barked, peeling off with two of the technicians who quickly unslung their antirobot weapons.

John frowned at the casual way Mike had again seized command. But as they had planned, he remained with the last technician, holding back as the mobile reserve.

As soon as the S-Force team headed for them, the robots aboard the platform leapt to action. The driver brought the vehicle broadside to the oncoming team, while others shifted tarpaulins to reveal a squat, cylindrical shape that looked like a personal cement mixer.

"Looks like some kind of cannon!" Mike's voice blared over the radio. "Disperse! I'm going in!"

John, who'd continued to launch mental probes, zeroed in on another robot-crewed platform coming behind the attack team. Again, the robots were aiming one of the mixer-cannons.

"There's a second platform! They're going for a crossfire!" John warned over the radio.

Mike continued to arrow toward the first platform, committed to his attack.

"Get your net," John cried to the third technician. "We'll have to take out that other gun."

They dove down, John clutching the unfamiliar shape of the nullifier-gun in his gauntleted hands. The others all enjoyed marksman's status with the new weapon, thanks to a vaporware session that taught the niceties of firing the net-dropping rockets. John had only a week's practice on stationary targets.

His suit's proximity detectors suddenly distinguished the flight of a small rocket above and behind his right shoulder. That meant his wingman had already fired one nullifier. It swooped down to deposit its net over the driver of the platform. The robot froze at the controls, sending off showers of sparks. The crew serving the cannon-like weapon slewed it around to aim at them.

John fired his rocket, aiming not for any of the gunners but for the electronic innards of the cannon itself.

The impact of the rocket and the reaction between the gleaming net and the gun circuitry looked like the Fourth of July. Luckily, innocent passersby had already been rerouted at the first warning of Deviant activity. When the damaged cannon finally exploded, the only ones in range of the blast waves were the S-Forcers and the other Deviant vehicle.

The remaining gun platform was flung about, its crew unable to aim at the oncoming armored figures.

John and his Argonian wingman flew over to join the attack.

Moradel, a female technician, had already netted one of the gun crew. Another of the robots was aiming a hand when he was nullified by a net shot from John's wingman.

"Good shot—uh—" Damn! He'd forgotten the guy's name!

Belatedly, John realized he hadn't reloaded his own nullifier blunderbuss. As he fumbled for a new rocket, he saw two more robots go down, and a third take aim at his wing-man.

"Damn!" John knew his clumsy fingers couldn't slam the rocket home. Instead, he pegged the thing, with all the force of his exoskeletal armor, at the chest of the robot.

He knew the rocket wouldn't be primed. But it presented enough of a distraction that the robot didn't fire. An instant later, Mike landed on the platform, smashing the robot down with the butt of his own launcher. "Let's get this thing back for study," he said, making his way between downed robots to the platform's controls. "We'll rendezvous beyond the city limits, then head for home."

The S-Force's latest Deviant prisoner was not an impressive sight as he lay in a leotard-like garment across a laboratory slab. They were in the same room Triadon had used to expand Mike's mind, and the prisoner was bound spread-eagled on the same operating table-like piece of furniture.

His position and the tight clothing revealed a scrawny but leanly muscled frame, somewhat shorter than the average Argonian. The Deviant's face was ratlike. Even with the pale radiance of a soothing field flickering across them, his features retained a pinched and bitter expression. Muddy brown eyes stared up sightlessly at the field projector.

"We can keep him essentially unconscious like this, but he's been conditioned against any of our interrogation techniques, short of—" Triadon stumbled over the word— "torture."

"Well, let's see if we can try an end run around those defenses," Harry said briskly. "Peg, why don't you give it a try?"

Unvoiced, he sent her a mental message: You've had the most experience mucking around in people's heads.

Peg grasped a lax wrist and sent tendrils of thought into the prisoner's psyche. A quick brush with his ego-identification, and she reported, "His name is Emagrun."

Triadon made a little hissing noise. "Identification parameters we don't even use anymore." He hastily coded something into a thumbpad computer. "Still, I believe that was the name that corresponded to his fingerprint and retinal images."

"Has he got a record?" she asked.

Triadon frowned. "Arrested for thievery with bodily harm. Transposed to the Exile Sphere more than a thousand years ago."

Peg felt a chill crawl down her back as she looked at the slack-jawed figure on the slab. A man who'd walked this planet a thousand years ago, still alive—

Her head jerked up as she broke her physical contact with Emagrun. "How can he still be alive?"

Triadon gave a helpless shrug.

"Well, there's one way to see." Peg sank back into Emagrun's psyche, searching out his memories. His exile was a traumatic moment, easily traced. She relived the scene as Emagrun, held helpless in a force-field, faced the authorities furious and unrepentant. He spat on the floor as the hemisemidimensional paraperpendiculartronic warp enveloped his body.

Peg felt the criminal's terror as he underwent the sensation of transiting the Rift. Then Emagrun found himself in what seemed to be a gigantic soap bubble floating in the Rift's awful emptiness. The Sphere of Exile was aptly named. Like John Cameron's Grand Central Station of the mind, it was an artificial construction within the Rift. Unlike John's spanking-new version of the terrestrial commuter train nexus, however, this station was featureless—and had no way out.

There were also, Peg discovered, some odd effects within the exile zone. The periphery of the sphere—the

film of the soap bubble—somehow impinged on normal
space. If they were willing to endure the vertiginous sensation of Rift transition, the exiled criminals could see
ghostly images of life on Argon—the life they could
never regain.

Peg couldn't explain the phenomenon—she suspected
it would require a degree in physics rather than her bach-
elor's in English Lit. But apparently the deeper one
moved into the pocket universe of the Sphere, the more
slowly time progressed.

Through Emagrun's eyes, Peg saw the most homesick
exiles, those closest to the periphery, grow aged and die
like mayflies. It was like watching a life in fast forward.
For the exiles who floated in the innermost zones, the
centuries went past as years. These were the die-hards,
the ones with the most burning hatred of the Argonian
way of life.

Then, one day after numberless unchanging days, the
bubble universe had deformed. Some of the exiles were
drawn irresistibly to the periphery—and after an instant
of vertigo, miraculously found themselves back on Argon.

That must have been John's first sketching visit, Peg
thought. Unwittingly, he'd opened the door to the
exiles's prison.

She continued to probe Emagrun's memories. The
escaped Deviants had formed themselves into *ad hoc*
gangs. Some were out-and-out piratical types intent on
looting helpless enemies, like the pack that Emagrun
had attached himself to. They chose their scores carefully, not wanting to kill the golden goose. Other
Deviants were soured idealists who had resisted the
Argonian citizenry's choice of stagnation—scientists
whose aggressive lines of research had brought them
into conflict with their society. They were determined

to bring down the whole of what they considered an oppressive, effete civilization.

Other fleeting disruptions assailed the Sphere of Exile, creating more runaways, more crime—and a need for organization. A rough hierarchy had been hacked out among the escaped Deviants. As far as Emagrun knew, ultimate authority had been seized by a superscientist determined to destroy Argon through crimes against property and terror attacks on the citizens.

The main Deviant problem was their lack of numbers. Even with robots serving as the shock troops, there were not enough humans to direct them. Emagrun, for instance, had handled several robots during the attempt to kidnap John when the four castaways first arrived. His crew had been scrambled to intercept the alien arrivals. After his failure, Emagrun had been sent to Kemot to oversee the theft of ultramicrochips, only to get captured.

Peg withdrew her probes and passed on the information she'd received.

Triadon was deeply shocked. "There was no reference to time dilation or any interdimensional intersections in any of the scientific literature on the Exile Sphere," he protested.

"Well, I guess they didn't get any mail back," Sturdley said. He turned to Peg. "You're saying the bad guys *knew* we were coming?"

"My instruments detected your arrival as well," Triadon said.

"But now we know they were looking for us—and that they want John." Harry shook his head. "I think this head Bad Guy has his eye on new worlds to conquer."

Looking down at Emagrun's lax features, he told Peg, "Check out his recent memories. Maybe we can get a line on what these guys will be up to next."

She reinvaded the captive's memories, moving up toward the present. As she pulled away again, Peg gave Harry a dubious look. "I don't know if this is a reference to that cannon theft we stopped, but Emagrun overheard his boss talking to some other Deviant leaders about a major coup being planned—a new *weapon* in the pipeline . . ."

Chapter Nine

Marty Burke glanced again from the resume in his hand to the young woman sitting on the other side of the desk. On paper, she looked pretty good—secretarial school, junior college, two years' experience as an editorial and production assistant—she had everything needed to be a publisher's good right arm.

But in the flesh . . . well, that was the problem. There wasn't enough flesh on this candidate. Her modest "executive style" suit jacket covered a chest that probably measured in at thirty-two inches. Burke decided he wouldn't even waste time on a stenography test.

"I'll keep your resume, Ms. Sandoni, but we have a number of other applicants, and our criteria are very stringent."

Burke's criteria certainly were. Besides being able to type, file, take dictation, deal with phone inquiries, pick up editorial slack, and, if necessary, give a hand on the production end, his assistant had to have a cute face and big boobs. Essentially what he wanted was someone as efficient and good-looking as (or better-looking than) Peg Faber, only more stacked, and graced with a considerably more . . . accommodating . . . nature. Just the thought of Peg and her karate tricks made a twinge of pain go through his left arm. So he was probably a little more curt than he meant to be as he sent Ms. Sandoni off.

He picked up the next resume, his eyes sourly roaming the office. Even though he'd been here for more than a month now, the place was still Sturdley's. Burke felt that the long desk made him look even shorter than usual. He wanted a wide desk to keep people back, and new guest chairs—ones with shorter legs, so he could loom over visitors as he sat. Maybe he could set up some kind of dais structure so he'd have a good six inches on any seated guests.

The problem was, Burke was afraid to go on an office furniture spending spree. The board of directors wasn't in his hip pocket, after all. And Sturdley hadn't shelled out so much for the furnishings here. He'd inherited the teak-paneled office, its furniture . . . and Peg Faber at the desk outside . . . when the Fantasy Factory had taken over this floor from a defunct publishing company. Doubtless that had made Sturdley look like a good administrator.

So Burke was stuck in an out-of-scale office that made him look vaguely ridiculous—and made him feel like an interloper.

Still, there must be *something* he could do to make this his place, to bring in his own personality. Burke's eye fell on one of the framed superhero portraits that dotted the wainscotted walls. It was an old Rip Jacoby pen-and-ink rendition of the Rambunctious Rodent, autographed both by Jacoby and Sturdley as cocreators. Next to that was what had to be a twenty-year-old sketch of Mr. Pain, drawn by Fabian Thibault. Why Sturdley would display a picture by a moth-eaten hack like Thibault instead of Burke's new, modernized rendition of the character . . .

That's when it hit him. He could make this room his by displaying *his* artwork, *his* characters. He'd dump the current crop of pictures—well, maybe he'd save the Jacoby, that could be worth money, and the John Cameron sketch of Robert. Collectors would probably pay big bucks for that in a few years.

But the rest of the sketches would go, to be replaced by Burke originals. He knew there was a large-size image of Mr. Pain somewhere in his studio. He could do a companion piece of Echo, the hero's lost love. There were some works-in-progress on the Glamazon. He had a decent-sized drawing of the Petulant Lump, and there was that group picture of the Latter-Day Breed. It would be nice to let people know what those characters looked like, especially since the book—proudly announced so long ago—still wasn't completed.

Burke nodded. He might even let a few selected artists contribute a picture or two, as a mark of his favor . . .

But that could wait. First came the job of selecting, matting, and framing the artwork, which would become the first responsibility of his new executive assistant. Satisfied with himself, Burke prepared to read the next candidate's resume.

Then the phone rang.

Of course, the gofer who was supposed to be manning the desk wasn't there. Fuming, Burke snatched up the handset. "What?" he barked.

"It's Gunnar." The Fantasy Factory's head editor—and Burke's main rival—didn't sound too rosy himself. "I just got a call from that guy Silikis's people out in Hollywood. They're arranging tenting grounds as accommodations for the Heroes, and want to know what we're doing by way of getting the giants out there.

This is the first I've even heard that *we* were supposed to be doing something."

The detail had slipped Burke's mind since he'd discussed it with Silikis weeks ago. Still, he had an answer handy. "I'm sure I delegated that problem to you, Bob. In any event, I know you'll come up with the appropriate answer—and soon."

He hung up, strode over to his door, and called the next applicant. "Wendy Wentworth, please."

A compact little blonde got up, short but with curves in all the right places—and gazongas Burke could hardly believe.

He smiled. What was that line from the old movie? Oh, yeah: It's good to be king.

Several offices away, Bob Gunnar sat glaring at his phone. *The great Burke is too busy interviewing bimbos to make sure his precious movie deal works out. So the job gets dumped on me. Hop to it, Gunnar.*

The editor drummed his fingers on the desk. The only transportation the Fantasy Factory had arranged for the giants was strictly local, tractor-trailers leased from a van line as Hero-mobiles. They had neither the fleet nor the time to drive the soon-to-be movie stars cross-country. How else could they go about this?

Gunnar found himself remembering a conversation he'd had with Elvio Vital, one of the company's top artists. The prolific Vital drew the Fantasy Factory's one humor book, a superhero parody called the *Electrocutioner*. Over drinks at a convention, he'd shared an interesting theory on work. "When you do a job," he'd said, "there are three things to think about: getting it quick, getting it cheap, getting it good. Usually, though, you only get two out of three. If you get a job cheap, you might get it quick, but you won't get it good. You might get a good job cheap, but you won't get it quick. And no good, quick job comes cheap."

A slow smile came to Gunnar's face as he realized a good, quick way to respond to Burke's task. He picked up the phone, dialing directory information. Soon he had a short list of airlines—very special airlines. Bob Gunnar read the *Wall Street Journal*. He knew which major carriers were bankrupt, or nearly so. It took a few phone calls to cut through the corporate underbrush. But he soon found an executive with sufficient juice to respond to his proposal—a chance to restore his airline's flagging image with a touch of class—providing a Heroplane for the giants' air transport.

"Of course, it would require essentially gutting one of your 747s." Gunnar knew, however, that a large percentage of this carrier's fleet was out of the air and up for sale. "And, in the interest of speed, the Fantasy Factory will finance the renovations."

Good and quick, Gunnar thought, baring his teeth in an icy smile. But not cheap. These costs will take some of the shine off Burke's movie deal. . . .

After hanging up, Gunnar reworked his notes so his assistant could type them up. He winced at the prices quoted. Well, at least we're supporting the economy, he told himself sourly. With these bucks, that airline will survive for at least another month.

Still, he felt obscurely guilty. This was the first deal he'd ever made that hurt the Fantasy Factory.

Forget about it, Gunnar told himself. This is Burke's responsibility.

Burke's fault.

On the lawn of Heroes' Manor, the Westchester estate that housed the giants, Robert endured some good-natured joking from his followers about dealing with the wild Lessers down in Washington.

"What did you make of their chieftain—this president fellow?" one of the giants asked.

"I found he had a surprisingly strong and capable mind. It will take more than one session to Bind him to me properly," Robert answered. "That's why I want to finish my business here and get back to Washington."

He had assembled several of the giants on the front lawn. "As you know, filming is to begin shortly on the movie about us. I have selected five of our number to travel to California." He smiled. "You five. Most of the choices were obvious, given your already existing popularity with the Lessers." Robert gestured to Maurice and Barbara, Thomas and Ruth—comic book stars all. "And I've added Victor because I think he has a future."

He also has blond hair and a figure not unlike mine— they can use him to double for me in the long-range shots, Robert added silently.

Victor's almost pretty-boy features lit with a smile that was more like a smirk.

It was only to be expected, Robert thought. In Masterly society, loyalty was achieved only through force or intimidation. Some of his followers naturally thought two thousand miles' distance would dilute his authority.

"Thomas will be the leader for the time you are away," Robert went on, watching the smirk disappear from Victor's face. "Obey him as you would me."

Robert then dismissed the group, beckoning Thomas over. "From what I've read, this California seems an agreeable place, with a moderate climate and many pleasures." He looked his lieutenant deep in the eyes. "Some people could become very attached to such a place—but it will be a prime target when the nuclear weapons fly. Remember, Thomas, we must keep to our long-range goals, which means for the time we must keep our people on a short leash."

Thomas nodded, and Robert dismissed him. He had exercised his authority and was confident that Thomas would run the California group with brutal efficiency.

Robert frowned as he watched his powerfully-built lieutenant stroll away. Probably he would have to re-establish his authority in the near future. But Robert only shrugged. It was part of the way of things.

And he'd bested Thomas before.

I should be glad, John thought as he and an S-Force detachment swirled round the tallest tower in the city of Kaldoa. All the way from the Hall of Consensus, the air-waves had been buzzing with activity. Now the convoy of obsolete but traditional ground cars had reached the spire. When he reached the top floor, one of the main Argonian leaders would make a worldwide speech.

After weeks of discussion and soul-searching, Boradon had decided to face facts. His attempt to reach a peace with the Deviants had failed, so now he was coming out on the side of the S-Force. Boradon would tell his follow-ers in the hall—and millions of Argonian citizens tuning in—that allowing the Deviants to wreck their society was a worse evil than fighting to protect themselves. Since Boradon was revered as one of the wisest in the Consen-sus, Triadon considered this turnabout a major boost, and Sturdley was prepared to make the most of it.

John had to admit that Harry's public relations savvy had helped with Boradon's conversion. The gaudy hero image of the S-Force splashed across 3-D was in the best tradition of comic books, and it had developed a following among the Argonian public. Citizens of this placid society were so entertained by a little excitement, they ate up the armored heroes. But Boradon and the S-Force fans would have fled in horror at John's vision of total war against the Deviants. Certainly, Harry had made him downplay his beliefs. That's why John wasn't inside for the holocast. Harry and Mike would appear with the Argonian leader, with Mike giving interviews after the speech.

John's lips compressed in a tight, angry line. Rationally, he knew he should accept his job of outside security as a necessary duty. But in his gut, bile bubbled like molten lava. Once again, Mike got the glory, acting as front man for the forces of good, while John did the dirty work and kept his mouth shut.

Another thing John had to contain was his growing competition with Mike. It had begun on the day of their first patrol. Without acknowledging it, each was trying to outdo the other in the superhero sweepstakes—John using his superior knowledge of comic heroics while Mike had the better grasp of Argonian culture.

Nor was it a friendly rivalry—not when John finally realized that the prize in this competition was Peg Faber. His blood boiled when he saw Mike playing up to her. Far more infuriating was the fact that Peg seemed to be responding to Mike.

John's confusion and ambivalence had only given Mike a better shot at Peg. Gauntleted hands tightened into frustrated fists as John realized that Mike had another advantage—twenty-something years of experience with women. John only had two years of memory, and Peg was the first woman he'd ever fallen for—that he could remember. He'd found the process of getting close to her torturous, to say the least. By Peg's own admission, Mike had seen more of her—literally—than John had. In fact, the bastard had nearly—

All thought was blown away by a psychic scream, a roar of horror that threatened to swamp his mental circuits. A moment's effort strengthened his psionic shields. Then John got on the radio to his crew. "Something's wrong. We're going in."

An instant later, he was sending a mental message to Peg, who was in the outskirts of the city with another reaction force.

Come here quick, he transmitted. Surround this place, and don't let *anybody* out.

The topmost level of the tower was a single, huge room whose floor-to-ceiling crystal walls offered a 360-degree view of the Argonian capital.

Standing on a hastily-improvised dais, Sturdley inconspicuously activated his armor's gizmoidal drive, rising up an inch or two to relieve any stress on the platform.

Boradon and Mike would both be appearing in the bathrobe-and-tights Argonian business costume to emphasize their civilian status. Harry still felt silly in that getup, and clearly preferred his armor. Dressed in Argonian "civvies," he felt as if he'd been caught sneaking into the kitchen for a midnight snack. That was no way to feel if you had to confront TV cameras. No, full armor was the way to go.

Besides, it was a way to display the newly-designed heraldic seal of the S-Force. The Argonians had no knowledge of the English alphabet, and to Harry's eyes the lettering seemed a bit weird and squiggly. But there on his chest was a fluorescent blue S on a yellow blazon.

Now the cameras were on. Sturdley went into an archetypical pose: fists on hips, legs slightly apart, the planes and angles of his face set in a stern scowl as he backed up Boradon. The Argonian leader began his speech, with his most loyal adherents on hand to applaud. Harry had intended to make one more psychic security scan of the crowd, but had checked out the camera angles instead. Then, off at the edge of the assemblage, he'd noticed a striking blonde.

He also noticed that Mike had noticed. The young man had sucked in his stomach a little tighter and was standing slightly taller. Sturdley had to hide a smile when he saw that Mike had also adopted Harry's hands-on-hips hero stance.

Suddenly, Sturdley frowned. Why was the blonde bombshell heading away from all the action?

Boradon was in full cry, at his most reasoned and sincere, when the first three rows of the crowd—loyal followers all—surged forward, not in applause, but in murderous fury.

Sturdley had just one second to scan them mentally before they overwhelmed the dais.

How could all these people suddenly become Deviants?

Chapter Ten

Caught with the proverbial thumb up my ass, Sturdley grimly thought as all hell broke loose, the wave of attackers hurtling heedlessly onto the dais. It seemed like an impromptu lynch mob—old and young, male and female, representatives of all of Argon's cities. Mere seconds before they had been normal, peaceful citizens.

Now they were acting like maddened tigers, engulfing the unfortunate Boradon, pummeling, clawing, stomping. Sturdley had hesitated to use the stunners built into his armor for fear of hitting the Argonian leader. But his fate now looked to be far worse than mere stunning.

"Take out the ones at the edge!" Mike yelled, vaulting into the fray. "I'll try to protect the old man!"

At that moment the overstrained dais collapsed, sending the attackers staggering and giving Mike a chance to fling himself over the bloodied Boradon.

Sturdley began firing stun beams, at the same time shouting into his radio. Even as he did that, the crystal windows of the meeting room smashed, and armored figures came flying in, figures bearing the blazon of the S-Force. As the reinforcements' stunners spat green fire, Harry went to the aid of Boradon and Mike, who seemed on the verge of disappearing beneath a clawing mound of assailants.

The exoskeletal strength of his armor allowed Harry to pick up would-be assassins and toss them across the room where they could be stunned by the others. Sturdley hauled out a woman attempting to bite off Mike's ear and realized with a start that just moments before he'd been speaking with her. At the time, he'd considered her a gracious, civilized lady. Now she seemed to be some possessed harridan, spitting and cursing, hammering fists senselessly against his armor.

"Something has gone seriously wrong here," Harry muttered as he tossed the woman aside. He sent her rolling in front of one of the 3-D cameras and realized that they were still recording.

We may not have given them a speech, he thought, but at least they're seeing one hell of a rescue.

The disorganized, raving attackers were soon subdued, and they, along with Boradon, were rushed to the nearest hospital.

Triadon summed up the situation a few hours later in the command post they'd established in the wrecked tower room. "Boradon is comatose, but the doctors think he'll survive." The Argonian scientist was deeply disturbed. "All the people who sought to kill him have died, in spite of the best efforts of the automeds."

Harry had seen several of these huge, cocoon-like medical machines at the Citadel of Silence. John had been popped into one on their arrival. That had been the reason for his quick recovery. If the top of the line of Argonian technology couldn't save those people . . . what was wrong with them?

Harry verbalized the question and got a concerned reaction from Triadon. "We found traces of a number of exotic chemicals in the attackers' bloodstreams.

Hormones, steroids, fragments of specialized molecules from hypnotic or psychoactive drugs."

"The people were *drugged* somehow?" Peg burst out in disbelief.

Triadon gave a jerky nod. "We think it's a case of C.I.D.—Chemically Induced Deviance."

"My God," Peg breathed. Then she snapped her fingers. "That guy we interrogated—remember what we read in his mind about a new weapon being developed? At the time we thought that had to do with the big, clumsy copies of the force cannon the bad guys had cobbled up."

"This is quite worse," Triadon said grimly. "The exiles now have the ability to turn our citizens into Deviants like themselves."

"For a while," Harry quickly pointed out. "Then this 'evil juice' seems to kill them."

Triadon shuddered. "What kind of minds would develop something like that? I'd never have dreamed the situation could turn so bad." His voice was dull with defeat.

"At least one good thing came out of all this," John Cameron announced, joining the conversation. "Mike and I have been watching the news fallout. The Deviants may have overplayed their hand. Lots of people are shaken over the attack on Boradon. But many others are damned mad. We're getting much more support than we had before the attack."

"I'm glad to hear that," Sturdley said, "because I've got an announcement. From here on in, I'll be staying behind to run things from the Citadel of Silence. I don't mind fighting these guys, but the one thing this donnybrook taught me is that I shouldn't be out in the field. If Mike had been in armor, or Triadon, or Melador, we might have been able to stop this before it started. I should be giving the S-Force my best strengths—strategy and administrative planning—instead of playing the hot dog and messing things up."

He looked at his suddenly silent cohorts. "We're also going to need regular units—three-person teams. As things stand now, we've got five team leaders—Triadon, Mike, John, Peg, and Melador." John seemed about to speak, but Harry silenced him with a fierce glance. "I want you to think about the technicians you've worked with, and pass on to me the names of any with leadership potential."

Looking away, he muttered, "We don't have many troops for this scrap—but even more, we need officers."

* * *

Robert lay in the shade of a clump of trees, his chosen "office" on the estate of the millionaire builder who had hosted his big Washington reception. The leader of the giants was still essentially an outdoors person, even if he had to do business with people who spent most of their days under roofs.

Besides, even more than was usual in the Lessers' capital, his business was influence—gaining control of the military and political leaders who could plunge this world into nuclear devastation. For his plan to work, however, Robert needed the assurance that his people could survive the radiation storm he intended to unleash.

He had gotten his daily report from Dr. Thonneger, as circumspect as usual over the telephone. Robert had long suspected that the doctor might be stalling. He was loath to use a full Binding on the Lesser, for fear it might destroy some useful abilities, but. . . . He would consider that step when he returned to Heroes' Manor.

Robert's cordless link to the world now lay unregarded on the ground as he closed his eyes for a brief nap in the still-balmy Washington weather.

The bleating of the phone brought him bolt upright, scowling. No other reports were due. Thomas would be calling in with an account of the progress made on the movie in California, but that wouldn't be for hours.

He brought the handset to his ear, expecting to encounter the oft-joked-about "wrong number."

"Yes?" he said, omitting any identification.

"I believe this is my biggest friend." The voice on the other side was slightly clipped, with a trace of unidentifiable accent. But the voice itself was identifiable—Antony Carron, erstwhile gun king of New York, then hunted criminal, and finally hired assassin furthering Robert's plans.

"How did you get this number?" Robert asked.

"People can find out amazing things when they've got an incentive," Carron replied. "How come I haven't seen my money yet? We had a contract."

"The results are inconclusive," Robert responded smoothly. He had hired Carron to eliminate John Cameron, hoping at one stroke to remove a potentially powerful threat and put a salutary dash of fear into Harry Sturdley. Instead of a clean death, Cameron, Sturdley, and a girl had disappeared, probably into that bizarre place of nothingness, the Rift.

As far as the most strenuous search had been able to ascertain, the trio was nowhere on Earth. Such negative assurance was cold comfort, however. Cameron represented a dangerous loose end, a para-psychic who conceivably could exile Robert's people—or bring through the Rift enemies from their homeworld.

"What do you mean, inconclusive?" An ugly note crept into Carron's voice. "Perhaps you didn't see *Unresolved Enigmas* recently. Your problem is long gone, and I still haven't been paid."

"You won't be until I have irrefutable proof," Robert said.

"Maybe you think you're a big deal because you're down in D.C. But all those bigwigs sucking up to you might feel differently if they knew some of the things I know . . ."

Robert sneered. He'd thought this Carron was of reasonable intelligence, for a Lesser. "Threats that can't be carried out are *so* boring—not to mention potentially dangerous. You might bear that in mind," he added as he cut the connection.

Antony Carron stared at the dead phone in his hand, then turned to his chief henchman, Joey Santangelo.

"Pass the word—we're blowing this joint." Carron's *cafe an lait* complexion was suffused with rage, the nostrils of his hooked Arabic nose pinched.

Joey wasn't necessarily surprised at the sudden decision to move—Canon often shifted base, especially since the police starting coming after him. A fully-packed bag for every member of the crew was a house rule in the gang-ster's Jersey estate.

What did surprise Santangelo was seeing the boss stalk over to the kitchen and throw open the door to the cellar. "Meet me downstairs when you finish with the guys," Carron ordered.

Santangelo's broken-nosed face showed even more puz-zlement when he found Carron in the fenced-off-section of the basement. The original builders had installed the hurricane mesh and locked door for a wine cellar. As New

York's illegal armaments king, Carron kept his most heavy-duty merchandise in there.

The boss turned, a crowbar in his hand as Joey came through the door. "Come on. I want this box unloaded."

He'd already cracked the top of an olive-drab packing case, and removed a yard-long launching tube. Joey saw that the rest of the box was filled with foot-long cylindrical rockets with rounded heads, like oversized bullets—or suppositories. Joey hefted one of them in his hand. "I don't know how many of these we can load into a car. What are we going to do with them?"

Carron turned, a death's head grin on his aquiline features. "We're gonna go hunting *giants*, Joey. Maybe the big freaks are bulletproof, but I think an antitank round would give them a nasty surprise."

"We're rolling," the assistant director called. Producer Stuart Silikis leaned forward, following the action as the giantess Barbara came into the shot, heading for the three-story brick warehouse. A stuntman in a blond wig and white dress clung to one of the rusty window shutters, frantically waving an arm.

"Okay—cut!" the director's voice boomed over a megaphone. "That's the last we need of that. Arm the demolition charges."

Special effects people rushed into the old building, while a pair of riggers pulled the stuntman in from the shutter. They affixed a life-sized dummy outfitted in identical dress and wig in the stuntman's place.

Silikis glanced over at his special effects man, who was apparently carrying on about seven conversations at once over a walkie-talkie.

The director, a bearded, tanned veteran of innumerable action movies, walked over to the producer with an obviously synthetic smile. "Good to see you, Stu."

"Calm down, Steve," Silikis's buzz-saw voice interjected. "I know you'd want me around as much as you want a case of crabs. But this is our single problem shot."

The director nodded. "A one-take wonder. After Charlie here blows the charges, there won't be a building left."

"Yeah, and the bank that owns the property can put up a shopping center," Silikis said. "I could give a rat's ass about that. You're sure this will work?"

"We've talked it over with Barbara, and she's completely confident. It's a straight mechanical thing. She grabs the dummy, which is wired to the charges. As soon as the dummy is out of that window, *ba-boom!* She turns away, runs toward the camera, the building falls down, then we cut to the shot where she's holding the live actress."

"She's not worried about the blast?" Silikis said.

The director shrugged. "She tells me she's got some kind of force-field around her body. I didn't buy it until she had one of the stunt guys shoot a couple of rounds at her leg. Real bullets, not blanks. Those stories are true."

"Okay then," Silikis said, hunching his shoulders. "Whenever you're ready."

The special effects people finished their preparations, the set was cleared, and the continuity staff went into action, posing Barbara as she'd looked in the previous shot.

"Barbara, I'll talk you through the scene. We don't have to worry about the sound, except for the explosion. Okay, ready on the set."

"Cameras rolling," the photography director reported.

An assistant held up a clapper board with the scene number, clacked, and pulled it away.

"Okay, Barbara, you're running to save the girl. Now grab for her—both hands! Remember, as you pull her away, the blast comes."

Barbara ran in yards-long strides, tension showing in the play of gorgeously sculpted muscles beneath her skintight white suit.

"Looks good," Silikis muttered.

"Now grab the dummy and turn, quick turn! Remember, you're supposed to look concerned."

In a single, limber move, she leapt gracefully, cupped the dummy's torso in her hands, removed it from the shutter, and dropped lightly to the ground, turning.

At the same moment, the demolition charges cut loose. A sheet of fire blasted from the open window, tearing away the shutters.

"Too strong!" the special effects director cried in a stricken voice that was swallowed in the explosion.

The blast wave hit Barbara, who stumbled slightly, a look of anxiety on her beautiful face. She kept her feet though, despite the unexpected force, her protective aura deflecting serious harm from her flesh.

Unfortunately, the force-field was only skin-deep. Burning gases and the billowing stream of air charred and shredded the spandex top of her uniform, literally blowing it off to fall in smoking tatters.

With the supreme unconcern of a healthy animal used to bare skin, Barbara ran toward the camera cradling the dummy, a look of concern on her face, the glorious rondures of her naked breasts bobbing dramatically with her every step.

She reached her mark, stopped, and stared in bafflement at the consternation below.

"Did I do something wrong?" Barbara asked.

"C-c-c-cut!" The director finally found his voice.

Silikis slapped his forehead. "Well," he said, "There goes our PG rating."

"Yeah," the director said with an appreciative grin. "But our appeal in foreign markets has just gone sky-high."

"You look great, Peg," Mike said with a smile.

"Oh, this little thing?" she said airily, making a quick turn to display her outfit. She'd decided to try a more daring Argonian fashion, something in deep green that was almost spray-painted on top, but flowered out in petal-like panels to create a sedate-looking skirt—except for the fact that each panel was of a mist-thin lace.

Sturdley had to admit that she was one toothsome example of pulchritude. The outward signs of Peg's hormone-induced pseudo-pregnancy had dissipated, except for a glow to her skin and a bit more amplitude in the upper story.

Mike looked pretty impressive himself in a silver robe and black tights, the blazon of the S-Force embroidered like a crest. He stood by one of the enclosed flying platforms in the hangar within the Citadel of Silence. They had a date to fly in to Kaldoa and have dinner—formal recognition of his promotion to team leadership.

As the couple headed out to enjoy their off-hours, they passed a squad of S-Forcers preparing to leave on patrol. Two were Argonian techs in wildly-decorated armor. Their leader was a figure in gray-and-white flying armor, unadorned except for the S-Force sign on its chest—John Cameron.

"Have a nice evening."

Harry frowned. Either John was having a problem with his suit loudspeakers, or he was really rasping out those words. He knew he should have a talk with the kid about his attitude, but what could he say? John was doing the work of five men. He didn't take nights off, flying double shifts to bash at the Deviants as hard as he could. And the rivalry between Mike and John, superhero-wise and for Peg's affections, had become worse. Somehow it had to be resolved, or the whole team would be torn apart.

With a sigh, Harry waved goodbye both to the patrol and to the celebrating couple. What would Professor X do in a situation like this?

John had barely arrived in the environs of the city of Valmot when his immaterial senses detected someone in great pain. He reported as much to his two wingmen. "I'll pinpoint where the trouble is. You follow me in," he said.

He tried to zero in on the tortured psyche, but the personality—and its location—were rendered inchoate by the pulsing waves of agony. John had to flick probes out in a wide search pattern. His face tightened. This wasn't the pain from an injury or accident—the recurring pattern indicated torture.

The general heading he was able to determine led to the lowest levels of a nearby tower. With John in the lead, the patrol swooped down, aiming for the plaza entrance. The psionic picture was a haze of pain, like a roaring bank of flames that covered several floors. John still couldn't get a firm location for the victim, so he switched mental gears, searching instead for the torturers.

But he didn't find them—that is, he didn't find any minds enjoying the injuries being inflicted. In fact, it seemed mechanical.

Mechanical? John retuned his probes, this time finding several robots tormenting a young woman three tiers below the ground. The blasted things had been specially designed for the purpose, some sort of heat-induction coils built into their fingers as they pressed their hands against the writhing form trapped and floating in a giz-moidal field.

John was already plummeting down the drop shaft as he flung out new mental probes, scouting beyond the sickening scene. The whole torture chamber was a huge, mechanized deadfall. All four walls were wired—blasters, stunners, and what looked like a jury-rigged imitation of a nullifier net.

Whoever came in there would be nailed with the most unbeatable offensive combination available to Argonian science. There were even backup robots on the level above— the tier he'd just passed.

"Up! Up! Out!" John screamed into his radio. "It's a trap!" He was already reversing his armor's drive. The other patrol members reacted more slowly, descending farther, almost into range of the automated ambush downstairs.

Overhead, John's probes revealed the backup robots lumbering into position around the tube, bringing weapons to bear. John spun about in midair, flinging out both arms in the tridigirector. Blue blast-bolts erupted from projectors imbedded in his armor. At close range, they tore through the mechanical warriors, wrecking them before they were in position for a decent shot.

Now John was on the radio, calling for local reinforcements. The call must have been intercepted, because the whole room below them blew up, the tor-turer-robots exploding, taking their captive with them. John and his wing-men were spewn up the shaftway on the shockwave.

But John's mind was whirling faster than his body. The whole snare they'd so narrowly escaped down there had been set up to capture someone with psionic powers. The bait—pain radiating on the mental frequencies—could only attract a telepath. And he could imagine which telepath the Deviants wanted: the one who could open an escape route from the Sphere of Exile through the Rift.

The problem was, how did they know he'd be patrolling Valmot this particular evening? Harry worked carefully to keep the patrol leaders shifting randomly among Argon's cities.

John got his trajectory back under control, moving up the drop shaft under his own power now. One of the patrolling S-Forcers matched courses with him.

"Uh, sir . . ." the technician-turned-fighting-man said. "I'm glad you got us out of that." He hesitated for a second. "But I thought Sturdley had all blasters replaced with stun-weapons. His code—"

"Harry's code is a fine thing," John said. "But I don't believe in following something blindly." He stroked a hand over the blast-projector set behind his gauntlet. "Following blindly is the easiest way to go off a cliff."

The soft glow of a force-field above the outdoor terrace and the anachronistic candlelight were the only illumination in the restaurant, which Peg had already identified as a sure sign of expense, even with her limited exposure to Argonian culture.

She'd also managed to master the odder aspects of Argonian cutlery . . . beside the silver spork was a silver-hilted ultrasonic meat-cutter.

But Peg had no concept of what was on the menu. Mike had to order for her, and as she tasted her entree, she could only guess at what she was eating. The meat had a vaguely gamy flavor, but was covered with some-thing that tasted like McDonald's special sauce.

There was also wine of unknown origin and vintage, a deep red, heady liquid served in self-chilling goblets.

Peg could feel the color rise in her cheeks, both from the wine and from Mike's flirting. One thing was obvi-ous—his adopted culture suited him very well. He was totally at ease as the floor show began—a show literally *in* the floor, as the terrace beneath their feet slowly became transparent, then lit with dancing showers of tiny sparks as music surrounded them from an unseen source. Peg found herself hard-put not to gape like a yokel.

Mike simply smiled. "Like it? Several of the guys recommended this restaurant."

Triadon must pay well, if his technicians can afford to dine here, Peg thought. She glanced off into the distance. I *thought* that was Melador off by the edge of the platform, sitting with a blond babe.

A richly-dressed pair of Argonians came up to the table—an embarrassed-looking man of middle age accompanied by a wife who appeared to be fizzing.

"Excuse me," the man said, "you're ah—Mike—aren't you?"

He handles this a lot better than Marty Burke, Peg thought as Mike graciously chatted with the couple. I've seen fanboys and fangirls, but this is a new one on me. The Argonian wife gazed rapturously at Mike for several minutes, hero-worship in her eyes, then finally recognized Peg. With the aid of her translator, Peg managed some halting conversation, hoping her smile didn't look too nervous and forced.

Mike's a hero around here, she thought, while I'm defi-nitely a fish out of water.

The fan couple—Peg could think of them in no other way—took an almost scandalized pleasure in being near two people who had experienced life-threatening danger. Culturally speaking, that represented a step forward from recent popular opinion. It had really hurt when John had shared his perception stolen from Argonians in the street—Peg didn't like being considered some sort of weapon-wielding psycho.

The Argonian couple chatted a while more. They finally left when they saw the waiter coming with dessert.

Peg found a genuine smile on her face as she bade them goodbye. The waiter had taken a station behind Mike's back. Peg was glancing from the departing couple to him when something violently jarred her immaterial senses.

"Mike! Get down!" The words seemed torn from her throat.

Mike ducked before her cry ended. The ultrasonic cutter in the stone-faced waiter's hand slashed air that a moment before had been occupied by Mike's throat.

Peg could now mentally pinpoint several other people, waiters and patrons, stalking them through the semidarkness. The floor show was considerably enlivened as Mike leapt up to grapple with the knife-wielding waiter and Peg moved to protect his back.

It was obvious that the attackers were merely Deviant-drugged civilians. They had no weapons other than tableware, and no technique or training in their fighting—only a single-minded desire to cause pain.

Those that Peg didn't dispatch martial-arts style, Mike simply overpowered.

As the local S-Force detachment arrived with ambulances, the only cost they'd paid was a worked-up sweat and the broken mood of the evening.

Mike saw her home in silence. As the rocky face of the Citadel of Silence opened for them, Mike finally spoke. "I'd never have seen that coming." He gave her a pained smile. "That's the big difference between John and me—between me and you."

Peg tried to say something, anything, but Mike just raised a hand. "No. I've come very far from what I was to what I am now. But no matter how hard I try, I'll always just be a human."

Chapter Eleven

". . . so the farmboy says to the hooker, 'That may be sophisticated as all get-out, ma'am, but I don't think I can take it sixty-seven more times."

The smutty joke's punchline was told in syncopation with Marty Burke's hammer-rappings. The gavel didn't do much to quell the restless noise in the conference room, but it saved wear and tear on Burke's hand. "All right now, settle down!" he shouted. "We've got important business to discuss."

The racket moderated a little, then died completely at his next words. "After long and careful discussion with Myra Sturdley, she's finally agreed to a memorial service for Harry."

"You've only been trying to bury Harry since about a week after he disappeared," Mack Nagel mumbled. "I'm surprised she put up with your nagging this long."

"Mrs. Sturdley insisted that the others who disappeared with Harry should be honored as well," Burke continued, trying to ride over Nagel's razzing. "I've secured a nice nondenominational chapel up on the West Side, and set the date for three weeks from Friday. That should give us time to organize a guest list—"

"Give ample notice to the media, you mean." Nagel wasn't finished giving Burke the needle. "That's all you see this as—cheap publicity for your movie."

"There *will* be some mention of the Heroes movie," Burke admitted. "As a matter of fact, Stuart Silikis asked to say a few words—"

"What the hell is this?" Fabian Thibault burst out. "We worked with Harry for years! How come this Hollywood guy hears about his memorial before we do?"

Bob Gunnar frowned. "I don't think it's in the best of taste, Burke."

"Just let me finish," Marty said, trying not to grit his teeth. "Silikis is dedicating the movie to Harry and John, since in a way the giants were their creations."

"What about Peg Faber?" a voice came from the other end of the table.

"Well, Elvio, we didn't think that was quite appropriate," Burke said. "I mean, Peg was a nice girl, but she was just office help—"

"Office help who proofread the first scripts for the Hero books—by God, I know she helped *write* some of it!" Elvio surged to his feet, his heavy mustache bristling. "Peg trafficked those books, not to mention holding John Cameron's hand every step of the way. You're not going to leave her out."

Burke's gut tightened. Elvio's reputation was that of a peacemaker, an easygoing guy. An angry Elvio was a rare sight—one that few people wanted to see twice.

"If you think you can get away with ignoring that poor girl, you'd better think again." Elvio was so furious, he began swearing in Spanish. Regaining some composure, he said, "I'll tell Mrs. Sturdley myself, then you'll see what happens to your little show!"

"I bet Myra wouldn't even turn up if she heard," Mack Nagel yelled. "I know I would boycott the farce!"

"Me, too," Thibault added.

Burke scowled. Thibault had it in for him ever since he'd been ousted from *Mr. Pain*. Trust the old has-been to take any chance to stick it to him. But Marty recognized a potent threat. Even Burke's own followers looked shamefaced.

It took a little effort, but Burke managed to force a jovial look onto his face. "Okay, Elvio, point taken. For her work on the series, Peg should be memorialized in the film as well. She was a fine young woman—"

"More of a lady than that big-boobed bimbo you've got working for you now."

Burke glared at Mack Nagel. How did the old bastard make his asides audible to the whole table like that?

"Since Elvio has defended Peg so nobly," Burke went on, "I'd like him to offer something in the way of a eulogy for her. I'll say a few words about Harry."

"Yeah, you two were always having words when he was around here."

Nagel had trumped him again, but Burke chose to ignore it. "And I thought Bob here might come up with some sort of tribute to John. It's just that very few people actually knew the kid."

Bob Gunnar opened his mouth to say something, then closed it.

Marty smiled, his ends achieved. The service would bring tons of free publicity, and the ploy of dedicating the Heroes' film to the missing trio would generate tons of advance coverage for the movie. And he'd be the keynote speaker . . .

Although the ends of his mouth remained curled up, Burke's eyes darkened as they wandered down the table toward Elvio Vital. One more name on his enemies list.

Harry Sturdley sat atop one of the rocky escarpments that hid the Citadel of Silence, a chilly breeze ruffling his gray hair, his helmet beside him. It would have been an impossible climb, but it was an easy flight in his armored suit. Sturdley had taken to this eyrie of late, needing an isolated place to sort out his thoughts. Back home, he'd have had his office, with Peg guarding the door if necessary.

That thought brought a worried frown to his face. What was happening back home? How was Myra dealing with his disappearance? Was he presumed to be dead? What kind of dogfight was developing for control of the Fantasy Factory? Bob Gunnar considered himself the heir apparent, but Harry had doubts that Gunnar's personality was right for the top job. And Marty Burke would be circling around like a rabid hyena.

Harry pushed those questions away. He shouldn't even consider the problems he'd face back home until he cleared the decks here on Argon. And given the state of the struggle against the Deviants, that wouldn't be anytime soon. They struck out of nowhere, disappearing into the populace. Hell, they could even chemically convert the people to their side. Harry hated to admit it, but John had a point when he said they were fighting a war. It was even worse than the classic guerrilla situation, since Sturdley only had a handful of units to meet the enemy's thrusts.

Sure, they'd gotten some new recruits after the attack on Boradon. But it would be a while before those kids were trained and hardened. He needed some trick, some masterstroke to offset the enemy's advantages.

Sturdley's frown grew deeper as he combed his memories. Somewhere there had to be a Fantasy Factory hero who had faced this problem and won. Mr. Pain perhaps, or the Rambunctious Rodent—he was always sort of an underdog. Nothing came to mind, however. Harry was almost glad for the interruption when another armored figure came in for a landing.

From the size and the unmarked armor, Sturdley knew who his visitor was before John Cameron removed his helmet. Harry stood silent, wondering if he had to face another argument.

Instead, John said, "Could I talk to you for a moment, Mr. Sturdley?"

"What is it?" Harry asked with a sigh. He knew they were in for a serious conversation. Nowadays, the kid tended to call him "Mr. Sturdley" only when he needed mentoring.

"This isn't exactly—" John swallowed, then started again. "If I were home, I'd probably have gone to talk to Elvio."

"Something art-related?" Harry asked.

"Uh—no." John looked more embarrassed and miserable. "I used to ask Elvio for advice when I was first getting to know Peg."

"Ah." Sturdley raised an eyebrow. "Advice to the lovelorn isn't exactly my strong suit."

"Who else can I turn to?" John sank to a sitting position on part of a crag. Harry noticed dents in his protege's plast-alloy armor and realized John had been duking it out with some Deviants again. He must have come here straight from flying patrol. It came as a shock when Harry realized that John looked *tired*. He'd never seen the kid weary, not even when he was fighting the crazy deadlines to get out the first *Robert* comic.

John sighed. "Back at the San Diego Comics Convention, I thought there was hope for Peg and me. But all the stuff she went through while I was out of it on the giants' world—the time she spent with Mike—"

He shook his head. "Things haven't been the same between us since I woke up on this planet. But I can't let Mike take her . . . without a fight."

John turned pleading eyes to Sturdley. "What can I do?"

"Kid, . . ." Sturdley tried to keep his voice gentle, thinking back to his own courting days. "You haven't really followed up on what you had with Peg. Instead, you went off to war—and got yourself involved in a whole macho pissing contest with Mike." His eyes suddenly got very far away. "In a way, that's what happened to all of us. We got ourselves into a pissing contest with the Deviants, with them taking the initiative and us doing all the reacting. If we want to win, we've got to change all that."

"How?" John said.

"We're gonna have to take the ball into their court." Harry gave John a lop-sided smile. "Just like you have to pay more attention to the curvaceous Ms. Faber. Forget about Mike. Concentrate on Peg."

"I think I see what you're saying," John said. "Even if I'm not too sure about how to do it."

"Well, don't come looking to Uncle Harry for more advice," Sturdley told him. "I may not be around. There's another job this outfit needs doing if we're going to win this war."

"What's that?" John asked.

Harry tapped the side of his head. "Intelligence."

Ruth was more happy than she'd ever expected upon hearing the words, "That's a wrap."

It wasn't that the young giantess found the work of movie-making physically taxing. A typical day back on her homeworld required much more exertion.

But a typical day back home didn't call for endless retakes, excruciating waits between scenes, and the unceasing responsibility to memorize lines despite constant rewrites.

Ruth was suffering from a pounding headache and wanted nothing so much as a nice, long swim, some food, and then rest.

Instead, she got "The Director," as the California contingent of giants had come to call Thomas.

"Let's be off to our lodgings!" Thomas's words were nearly a barked order as she approached the unused sound-stage that had been turned into the Heroes' temporary quarters.

Thomas stood outside the doorway, a huge affair built to accommodate enormous flats and props for spectacles of bygone days. Robert's tough-minded lieutenant looked something like a giant idol himself. Nude to the waist, skin glistening, he'd dispensed with the spandex top of his uniform between shots in response to the oppressive California weather.

"I wish *I* could do that," Ruth complained to Barbara. What ridiculous taboos these Lessers had! Back home, simple clouts served for purposes of utility and modesty.

But the small ones here seemingly had a fear of exposed bosoms—especially Sturdley and the film leader called Silikis. Barbara had laughingly recounted the story of his reaction to her little mishap.

"Come along!" Thomas's voice grew downright testy as he led the way to the two tractor-trailers provided as transport. In comparison with the vehicles they had used on the East Coast, these were luxuriously appointed, with carpeting, plastic roof panels to let in the light, air conditioning, and countless soft pillows.

Still, none of the giants was all that fond of entering such a confined space, especially when ordered in so peremptory a manner.

"I think The Director is beginning to think he's a Master of Masters," the giant Victor grumbled, a scowl clouding his almost pretty face.

"That attitude could be dangerous for Thomas—if it were reported." Maurice was frowning, too, which made his slightly weak chin look even more ridiculous.

Barbara merely raised a perfect eyebrow. "Oh, Thomas is still loyal to Robert. Ridiculously overbearing, but loyal."

They arrived at the nearest parking area that could accommodate the huge trucks, Thomas still in the lead. The hired Lesser drivers scrambled into the cabs of the vehicles as soon as they saw Thomas arrive. He turned to give brusque orders. "Barbara, Maurice, and Victor will travel in that one. Ruth will ride with me."

"I'd rather ride with Barbara," Ruth said quietly. Warning bells were ringing in her head. She hadn't liked the look in Thomas's eyes when he mentioned her name. "Perhaps Victor would—"

"You and Barbara can have this to yourselves," Thomas interrupted curtly. "We men will ride together."

As they made their way along the California freeways, Barbara gave her transit mate an odd look. "I thought you and Thomas were—"

Now it was Ruth's turn to scowl. She brought up her fore and middle fingers tightly together. "Like that?" she asked. "It's more like this." She twisted her hand so the fingers were horizontal, the longer one on top. "You called Thomas overbearing—*overwhelming* might be a better description."

The ride to the Malibu camping ground where tents had been pitched to house the giants during filming had apparently not improved Thomas's disposition. He forbade any excursions from the camp, much to the annoyance of the other males, who had discovered a drive-in theater not too far away.

Ruth was annoyed, too, since Thomas's order also put out of bounds the swimming pool that had been rented for the giants' use. Although it barely came to her waist at its deepest point, the Olympic-sized pool's heated water was her favorite decompression chamber.

She bided her time through dinner, waiting for full darkness to fall. Then Ruth quietly made her way to the edge of the campground and set off down the road to the rented house and its pool.

If I don't turn on the pool lights, no one will know I'm here, she thought, kicking off her buskins, then slipping her spandex top over her head. She shook out her mop of russet-colored curls and slid her thumbs into the waistband of her lower garment, working it off.

Nude, she sank into the water with a grateful sigh, letting the liquid warmth unknot her muscles, her eyes closed in contentment. Then she heard the sound.

Ruth's feet scrabbled for purchase on the pool floor. Her wide eyes made out a patch of deeper darkness obscuring a huge part of the night sky.

"I thought I'd find you here when I realized you'd left the camp," Thomas's voice came from the shadows. "You disobeyed."

"I—I—" Ruth rose in the pool, the water barely coming to her knees. Her aura kept off the coolness of the night air, but she felt a chill from deep inside.

Thomas stepped closer, and she realized that the sound she'd heard had been him removing his only garment.

"I though we'd bathe together," Thomas said as he stepped into the pool. His white, square teeth showed in a cool smile. "And—perhaps you won't be so disobedient in the future."

Mike had already flown his vehicle past the bent figure in the ramshackle, mismatched armor when Peg received the mental message: *Slow him down. It's me.*

Harry? she sent in disbelief. *Jeeze. When you go under-cover, you go all the way.*

She told Mike to slow the craft, and Harry smoothly slid into the open back of the flying platform.

"You've been gone for a week," Peg said, trying to keep the worry from her voice as she helped Sturdley change into a standard S-Force combat suit.

"Get this bucket back to the Citadel of Silence—top speed," Sturdley ordered Mike, ignoring Peg's words. Then he turned to her, a tight smile lightening his haggard features. "I did it, kid. I pinpointed their headquarters. It's here in Valmot, in a slum section—if you can call a mile-high tower a slum. It's actually a complex of several interconnected towers. As soon as we arrive at the Citadel, I'm bringing back our whole rapid-reaction force."

"What about our people on patrol? Triadon's in Kaldoa, Melador is in Kemot, and John is up in Ahkeya," Peg objected.

"I'll call them in to mop up after we attack," Harry said. "But I'm not going to give these guys any warning. If you think we need numbers, we'll take along the recruits. But until we arrive, everyone but you, me, and Mike will think this is a drill."

He sat down, wishing this utopian society had something like coffee. The past week had gone by with precious little sleep as he traced his way through a labyrinthian network of interlocking Deviant cells to the top of the criminal hierarchy. In a variety of disguised armor shells, he'd gone cruising until he mentally detected a Deviant. Then he'd probed, finding the head of the local cell, that leader's contact to the next level, and so on.

Harry didn't think he'd been spotted, but he wanted to act on his information as soon as possible. One thing his spy work had shown was that Triadon's security had a number of leaks.

The attack on Deviant Central was almost an anticlimax. Harry used the recruits to ring the spire complex and prevent escape. Then he took the experienced S-Force fighters in to storm the central tower from several levels at once. When he, Peg, and Mike went in, they all followed John's example, carrying lethal blasters in their armor.

The attack was a complete surprise. Mike, as the most technically trained leader, was in charge of seizing the power array and reducing the amount of broadcast power in the area. The enemy had been forced to choose between activating defense robots or keeping their own armor and weapons operational.

Harry and Peg had led their teams in a blitzkrieg through half-paralyzed defense posts, capturing dozens of Deviants—hard-core exiles, not the temporary variety of drug-induced citizens.

At last the attack teams joined forces at the drop shaft that led to the basement sanctum sanctorum of the Deviant hierarchy.

"If we go down this thing, we'll be sitting ducks," Peg said, frowning.

"That's why we're not going down first," Sturdley said, hooking a thumb at several of Triadon's technicians refitting a trio of nullified Deviant robots.

"You're going to use the bad guys' own robots against them?" Peg still looked dubious. "Won't they be able to take control of them again?"

"Those things will have only one command," Sturdley responded. "Ready?"

The lead technician nodded, his team moving the robots to the verge of the shaftway.

"Go!"

As the robots plummeted downward, Sturdley yelled, "Everybody hold on tight!"

The blast wave from the explosion literally shook the spire to its foundations.

"We set them to self-destruct," Harry explained to Peg as he led the way into the shaft. "Any welcoming committee is out of it now."

There were no last-ditch defenses, however. Harry's raiders burst through an armored door to find what looked like a high-tech, high-cost Argonian office—an empty office, with one wall completely vaporized.

Sturdley looked through the opening, blown through thirty feet of solid rock, and saw a municipal utility tunnel. "A bolt-hole," he said through gritted teeth.

John Cameron was one of the last S-Force members to arrive on the scene, flying at top speed from distant Ahkeya. As such, his part of the mopping-up operation was restricted to the psychic search for fugitives and assembling the damage reports.

"Our casualties were remarkably low," John told the assembled leaders. "One of Harry's raiders walked into a blaster-bolt and is off to the automeds." His face grew more solemn. "And three of the recruits were killed. As near as we can make out, they blundered across the escaping Deviant leaders and were wiped out."

Sturdley shook his head at this reminder of his attack's only shortcoming. "We should have captured them," he muttered for the fiftieth time.

"In any event, we've dealt the Deviants a crushing blow," Triadon said. "Not only did we capture dozens of prisoners, we've confiscated vast quantities of their 'recruiting' drug—and secured the factory where it was made."

"My people came across a workshop where they were trying to build more force cannons," Mike said. "They must have found one of the other prototypes and were clumsily trying to copy it."

"And they must have taken the prototype with them, after they used it to burn their way to the escape tunnel," Harry said. "As soon as they find another hidey-hole, they'll be trying to reproduce it again."

"But for the nonce, we've crippled them," Triadon said, gesturing around the inner sanctum. "We even have all their records."

He picked up a pile of plastic flimsies to illustrate his point, glanced at them, and blanched.

"Where—how did they get these?" Triadon demanded. "These are my personal notes on the interdimensional flux—my experiments with the Rift!"

It was a Saturday afternoon, and the halls of the Fantasy Factory were empty. Marty Burke's laughter seemed to echo uncannily loud from his open office door.

"Leslie Ann, you've got to see some of the files Sturdley kept. I think he's got his first pay stub in here. It's dated January, 1945—and it's signed by Louis Fanchik."

"One of the famous Fan-boys who founded the company," Leslie Ann said from the desk outside Sturdley's

office, where she was going through Peg Faber's papers.
She'd heard it all before.

"I wonder if Fanchik's signature is valuable," Burke
wondered aloud.

"Marty," Leslie Ann said, feeling a mite testy, "the idea
is to finish making this office your own. You're supposed
to be gathering stuff together to give to Sturdley's wife,
not picking out the collectibles."

Instead of an answer, raucous laughter burst from the
office door. "Come on in," Burke called. "You *gotta* see
this."

Leslie Ann neatly piled the small collection of Peg
Faber's personal possessions atop the desk and headed
into the office. "Do you know if the portable radio on the
desk was hers?" she asked.

Burke gave her a *who cares?* look. "You've got to check
this out," he said, waving a fairly thick file folder. "Earlier,
I stumbled across a bunch of bills from an outfit called
Farley Investigations. Now I found their reports. Happy
Harry was paying for a surveillance job on his giants! The
old bastard didn't trust *anybody!*"

Leslie Ann, however, didn't join in the laughter as she
took the folder. Her eyes narrowed in concentration as
she paged through the contents.

Chapter Twelve

The turmoil in the Rift did not subside. New strains racked the interdimensional flax. Down in the lower-order universe of four dimensions, the eddy twisted around the nexus representing the planet Earth. A shearing force was exerted on the Rift-stuff, with the pressure generating new disruptions in the lower substrate . . .

Things get pretty boring in Flatlands, Oklahoma. They're more boring still when you have to push your pickup way past the speed limit to make it to town in under forty-five minutes. And even then, "town" refers to a two-block shopping strip.

No, in Flatlands—especially at the edges of the Greater Flatlands Metropolitan Area—the locals try to get their fun wherever they can find it. Which is why Billy-Ray Woolsey had been flipping a quarter for the past thirty minutes. The first few flips had been to kill a little time. Then he noticed he was consistently flipping heads, so he'd started counting.

And the heads kept coming.

Finally, Billy-Ray got on the phone to his pal Jesse-Bob Fargis. "I got a run of luck here you just wouldn't believe," he reported. "Been flippin' a coin for half an hour, and got—" He made a quick calculation of the Xs on the piece of scratch paper. "Shee-it! Nearly *two hundred* heads in a row."

"And you did it all by your lonesome?" Jesse-Bob demanded. "You are an idjit for certain-sure. If you had a witness, you could be gettin' into the *Guinness Book of Records.* You just sit quiet till I get over there!"

* * *

Peg arched her body gracefully, steering her flying suit out of the slow circle it had been describing around the Citadel of Silence. As she'd expected, Harry Sturdley was sitting atop the stony prominence she'd mentally christened his Thinking Rock. That's where he'd conceived his plan to crush the Deviant network. The planes and angles of his face seemed tighter than usual, more gaunt.

Harry still hasn't gotten over the effort he put into his intelligence operation, she thought. Indeed, he'd hardly contributed to the follow-up. Armed with records and equipment captured at Deviant HQ, John, Mike, and Triadon had begun making inroads on the enemy's organization. Every day, 3-D was full of the exploits of the S-Force.

But Harry sat up here.

He glanced up now, his graying hair ruffling in the breeze.

I'll have to remind him to get a haircut before the big ceremony next week, she thought.

Then she received a telepathic greeting. *Hi, Red.*

Peg swung around, aiming her feet groundward and delicately adjusting the gizmoidal drive to bring her to a flat section of rock somewhat below Harry's perch.

It took a moment to unlatch her helmet, and then she shook out her profusion of red curls. "Harry, can we talk?"

He directed a piercing gaze down at her. "You're not going to mother-hen me because I don't want to play *Gang-busters* with the other boys?"

"I think you've done more than enough," Peg said. She glanced down, unwilling to meet his eyes. "This is personal.

"I know that at first you didn't approve when John and I—" she made a hand gesture, trying to express a concept for which she couldn't seem to find the words.

" 'Expressed an interest in each other,' " Harry filled in.

Peg nodded gratefully. "And you were really worried when Mike and I—"

"Got entangled." Harry's lips quirked. "And yes, that *is* a more loaded way of putting it."

"I messed with Mike's mind, Harry," she began defensively. "I feel responsible for him."

"You know, I must be a real lucky boss to have two such responsible people on my staff," Harry said. "John felt so responsible for the mess here, he's spent all his time since he got off that hospital bed playing superhero—and neglecting you."

Peg shot him a surprised glance. "You think so?" she asked, her voice suddenly soft.

"I think it takes two to tango—or as you young moderns put it, relationships are a two-way street. If John got distracted saving the world, *you* got distracted by Mr. Muscles."

He grimaced. "I had enough problems with John not being exactly down-to-earth. But you pick a guy from another planet—in fact, after this vaporware hoo-hah, from *two* other planets."

"No," Peg said a little bitterly. "He's the one who thinks *I'm* from another planet." She related the story of their last date, and Mike's final reaction.

"So, you've got to make a choice here," Harry said. "And whichever way you go, you're going to meet a little sales resistance. I don't see where I—"

"Harry, I've got to talk to John!" The words came out in a rush. "And I—I *can't*." Peg bit her lower lip to keep it from trembling. "We were always able to talk, even be-fore—before ail this. He was the only guy in the office who'd talk to *me*, rather than moving his mouth and looking down my blouse."

"Maybe it would have done him some good to look down your blouse," Harry grumped.

"Now he just looks *through* me," Peg said, ignoring the jibe.

Harry softened his tone at the look on her face. "Let me rephrase that. If you want to talk, first you've got to get him to notice you."

Peg was surprised to find him suddenly acting like Uncle Harry, stepping down and giving her an avuncular pat on the shoulder. "You never know. He might be will-ing to meet you more than halfway."

Harry generally enjoyed ceremonies. He was a gregar-ious guy, it was a chance to press the flesh—and, of course, a chance to step into the spotlight.

On the other hand, this was the first ceremony Harry had ever attended while clad in a bathrobe. Almost unbidden, his hands checked once again that every-thing was pulled together and tightly tied. Argonian formal wear tended toward the ornate. Harry wore a deep purple robe with muted highlights. John had cho-sen basic black, while Triadon was gorgeously clad in a brocade ensemble that combined his garish heraldic colors.

Ahead of them, waiting on the reception line, Boradon's heavy frame was swathed in fire-engine red. It made him look vaguely like a Catholic cardinal.

Mike, who had become quite the Argonian clothes-horse, was clad in the most radical of local couture, *chameleon cloth*. His robe seemed a sober matte black, but unexpected flashes of flaring silver would appear in random patterns. It was rather like watching a distant sheet-lightning storm.

When the flying limo had come for them, Peg appeared in a floor-length black cape with a high collar. With her mane of red curls teased into an elaborately casual cascade of ringlets, she look like an outtake from a Dracula movie. Now, as they prepared to enter the packed banquet hall, she shrugged off the cape—an entrancing spectacle as she bared shoulders, and much of her upper body. The tan she'd acquired in their outdoor days on the planet of the giants had mainly faded, but she was still heavily freckled, and her skin yet retained some of that pseudo-pregnant glow.

Harry found himself staring at a pair of lithe, perfectly sculpted breasts, nearly revealed by a bodice that only high technology kept in place. In Harry's experience, uplift bras were generally designed to turn droopers into bulgers. Peg certainly had no problem with sag, but Harry wondered what marvel of lingerie engineering could upthrust and present warm, perfumed flesh like a gelatin dessert and still keep things decent.

When old Red goes for attention, he thought, she goes all the way.

He glanced at John, who stood slack-jawed and pop-eyed at what a difference a cape makes. The last time Harry had seen an expression like that was when an army buddy had inadvertently walked into the backswing of an eight-pound sledgehammer.

With lowered eyes and an enigmatic smile, Peg stepped out ahead of them, toward the receiving line. Taking in the back view, Harry realized something he'd never even noticed while confronted with that neckline. Peg's floor-length, hip-slit gown was also made of chameleon cloth—but of a far more daring variety than Mike's. At irregular intervals, sections of the gown would shimmer, then fade to a misty insubstantiality, revealing trim ankles in spike heels, or a flash of thigh, or—

Holy Jumping Judas! Harry found himself thinking. What is that girl wearing under there? A G-string?

He jabbed a quick elbow into John's ribs, startling him out of his daze. "Be a gentleman," Harry hissed. "Get up there and take her arm."

"W—which one," John asked, still seemingly in a dream.

"The left one. She'll want to shake hands." Among other things, Harry thought, urging his protege forward. Then he moved to intercept Mike.

"Who'd have thought our little Peg capable of that?" Harry said, deftly blocking the younger man's path. "I think she's quite stolen the evening."

"Mnnnnn," Mike said noncommittally.

Harry had quietly tampered with the seating arrangements so that he sat at Peg's right hand, John on her left, and Mike off beyond Triadon. Throw 'em together, keep them together, and see what happens. It worked in the comics.

But throughout the feast and the subsequent required congratulatory speeches, John had steadfastly kept his eyes focused on his food, the speakers, the cameras, the diners spread out below the dais—anywhere but toward Peg.

She sat with downcast eyes, idly poking the remains of her meal (had he really heard correctly? Roast loin of botk?), looking forlorn. Boradon had just finished pouring on the old oratory oil, and then it was John's turn to speak. He carefully faced the cameras, going into a speech he'd rehearsed for Harry until the older man had taken to hiding from him.

"It didn't work," Peg whispered, slumping in a highly distracting way in her seat. John briefly stumbled in his address, but managed to go on.

"You think he didn't notice you?" Harry responded. "He hasn't touched a drop of wine, and his face is as red as a forge."

Harry's breath caught in his throat as Peg's chameleon cloth gown momentarily flashed transparent. "Peg," he whispered hoarsely when his voice returned, "haven't you ever heard of overkill?"

Scaladon stared in cold fury at the assemblage of Deviant leaders sitting before him. Not only had their rebellion suffered a severe disruption of its physical assets, but a worse blow had been dealt to his prestige and viability as commander-in-chief. That was why he'd been forced into this meeting, facing the inner circle of his own faction. It was necessary to reestablish himself here before he faced the full leadership, the criminal wolves who'd hope to pull the pack leader down.

Here at least he faced kindred souls, scientists and others who valued progress for Argon—who'd fought the Rationalists in the past and were still willing to battle the grotesque stagnation that had taken over their world. There were two at the meeting who didn't fit that description, however—one being the head of the Deviant intelligence network, here to explain the lack of warning.

The other interloper was tolerated because of what he carried. Emsisdin had happened to be at the former head-quarters delivering reports when the farcical S-Force had proven not so amusing after all. By rescuing the prototype force cannon during the S-Force attack, Emsisdin had vaulted to the upper hierarchy.

Scaladon, however, had his doubts about this power-ful new "ally." The weapon that Emsisdin delivered from capture had been guarded by two of Scaladon's hand-picked followers. Amazingly, neither of them had survived the onslaught of the raiders. But Emsisdin, the only grinning face among the councilors, had brought the force cannon through. He held onto its gleaming length even here in the conference chamber.

Raising the golden scepter he'd carried since the days before his exile, Scaladon brought the meeting to order by rapping the table with the butt end. Besides acting as gavel, the scepter gave him a useful edge. Everyone in the room knew it was packed with the circuitry for several weapons systems.

"I see no need to restate the obvious," Scaladon said to the assembled leaders. "The question is where can we go from here?"

A figure rose at the table—Megladon, a brilliant sci-entist who served as Scaladon's chief of research. "With regard to material resources, I fear we can't go very far. Not only were our central labs captured, but the bulk of our fabricating facilities had been located at the—ah—prior headquarters."

"But our sources of supply are still available," Scaladon rejoined quickly. "And surely we can create new manufactories."

"The enemy also has most of our records," another at the table quietly pointed out. "This Sturdley can move to cut our supply lines at will."

"It will take time for the so-called S-Force to sort through the captured information," Scaladon said, "and still more to root out our supply network. In that breathing space, we must obtain as much as possible from our present suppliers while developing viable alternatives. We must rearm, and quickly." He swung ponderously in his concealing armor, bringing his gaze to bear on everyone in the room. "Because at the earliest opportunity, I intend to attack and obliterate this upstart S-Force."

Scaladon's eyes locked onto the potent feminine form of his designated intelligence chief. His skin crawled, as if at the tiniest stirring of insect legs across his flesh. Did the bitch have the nerve to use her psionic powers to probe and examine his disfigurement?

His voice was rough as he finished. "The responsibility of finding the time and place for our attack must fall to you, Matavi. I trust your sources will not fail us in this instance."

Leslie Ann Nasotrudere lay sprawled across the Haitian cotton of her living room couch, a file folder lying across her trim stomach. For the third time she read through the collection of surveillance reports she'd retained from the clean-out of Sturdley's office, a frown clouding her perfect features.

"When was the last time you saw the giant Gideon?" she called to Marty, who was in the kitchen in search of a bottle of sparkling water. He'd been getting pudgier since taking over Sturdley's job, and Leslie Ann did not tolerate fat lovers. She had put him on a ruthless diet, and all sweets, soda, and beer had disappeared from her refrigerator.

"Gideon? The short one? I dunno." Burke's response had a decidedly full-mouthed cast. Leslie Ann resolved to check how much bread was left. Marty was supposed to get only two slices per day.

"I remember him being part of Operation Hero," Leslie Ann said. "But after that . . ."

"Maybe they didn't think it was safe for him out on the street," Burke suggested when he returned to the room.

"He's *seventeen feet tall,* for chrissake!"

"Well, maybe they have him patrolling in the boonies. We haven't seen a lot of the giants since the PBA injunction stopped them from acting as a vigilante force. I've got to talk to Robert about a more high-profile Hero presence now with the movie coming out." Burke squinted as if he were looking into the distance. "Personal appearances, maybe. We could send them to comics conventions, state fairs—"

"Used car dealership openings," Leslie Ann muttered, shaking her head. And she'd thought *Sturdley* was crass!

"Most of the giants have been keeping to themselves at Heroes' Manor." Burke changed the subject, a little stung. "What's the big deal about Gideon?"

"It's these reports," Leslie Ann said, rustling the papers as she sat up. "From the way it sounds, Sturdley hired this detective to look for Gideon. And the private eye never found him."

Burke laughed. "Hey, you said it yourself. The guy's seventeen feet tall. Where could you hide him?"

"Where indeed?" Leslie Ann's blue eyes were hooded as she squared up the papers on her lap and returned them to the folder.

"I can ask Robert about Gideon, if you want. He's due back from Washington to spend some time at Heroes' Manor, learning his lines for the movie."

"No!" Her newsgatherer's instinct prompted the abrupt negative from Leslie Ann. "No," she said a bit more easily. "I'm sure it's nothing." She didn't want any advance warning when she began poking around.

"Got a call from Silikis today. He said everything's going great on the set."

Leslie Ann rolled her eyes. Burke got a call from Silikis *every* day. And, almost always, everything was rosy on the set.

"He got good news from those computer-retouching people. They think they'll be able to animate some sort of halter onto Barbara in that scene where she lost her top. Just for the domestic release, of course. Silikis is still debating a few more topless shots for the foreign version. The Europeans will love it!"

"Uh-huh," Leslie Ann said listlessly.

"I think Harry's request is reasonable," Mike said, staring around the conference table in the Citadel of Silence. The table, with its built-in computer terminal and 3-D projector, barely accommodated the six people around it—Harry, Mike, Peg, John, Triadon, and Melador.

The room was located at the pinnacle of the butte that housed the combination fortress/laboratory, and was enclosed by solid rock. Holo-projector wall units gave the illusion of a view. Harry looked away from a "window" exposing a vista of swaying palm trees and restated his case.

"We're all agreed that the Deviants are on the run now—their organization is shattered, their leaders are fugitives. I don't think there's anything more I can do to help the fight." He gave a significant look to John and Peg. "And I think there's a lot to do back home."

"I'd still like to finish here before we take on any new battles," John said with a frown. "We'd be better off heading home together."

"Triadon, Melador, and I could wrap up the loose ends," Mike said stoutly. "And when you speak of going home, I hope you're not referring to me." He hesitated. "I've spoken to Boradon and other members of the Consensus. They're happy to have me stay."

Sure, Harry thought, a position as hero in a world of super-science beats being an escaped slave on a planet of primitive savagery.

Mike turned to Peg. "In fact, Boradon and the others said they'd be happy to have you all stay."

Peg jerked up as if she'd been stuck with a pin. She drew a deep breath and said, "There's a lot we've got to do on our world, and we can't turn our backs on it forever."

Mike went poker-faced. That wasn't the response he'd hoped for.

"Some of us want to continue the war against the Deviants with our full forces, and some would rather all the newcomers—except for Mike—return to their world," Melador said. "By Argonian custom, we should seek compromise and consensus, which in this case, I believe, is Harry Sturdley's original proposal—that he return, with the others joining him later."

John frowned. Mike brightened—this would give him more time to work on Peg. The vote came in at four to two, Triadon joining the consensus, Peg surprisingly voting against.

Triadon turned to John. "Are there any particular preparations you must make to send Harry home?" Argonians might seem wishy-washy in their desire for consensus, Harry thought, but once a decision was reached, they were demons for execution.

"I could do it right now if you like." John sounded defeated.

The Argonian scientist shook his head. "I'd prefer to arrange various pieces of equipment to monitor the transition," he said, "not to mention implementing some security measures."

Triadon sent a grin toward Harry. "Besides, there are gifts to prepare for our departing friend."

For some reason, Peg kept thinking of the part where Dorothy is supposed to be going home by balloon at the end of the *Wizard of Oz*. There was the same sort of garishly cheerful feeling in the air, although the brass band was missing.

Too bad, she thought. Harry would have enjoyed a brass band.

Harry stood completely encased in Argonian armor, carrying several bulky packages—Triadon's gifts. He stood in the middle of the Citadel of Silence's hangar, facing John Cameron who, though armored, was not wearing his helmet. A large crowd of Argonian members of the S-Force had gathered to give Harry a good sendoff. He'd responded with a speech by loudspeaker and radio, then waved goodbye.

Peg and Mike were also in full armor. They and a squad of S-Force personnel were acting as security, ringing John and Harry, weapons ready. When John shifted Harry into the Rift, he would also be opening a conduit between the mysterious Sphere of Exile and Argon. They wanted to be ready for any unwelcome visitors.

John's eyes got a faraway look, and Peg felt the queasiness, that floor-dropping-out-from-under-your-feet feeling she associated with the Rift. Harry faded away, but the sickening feeling stayed—John had warned them it

would take a couple of minutes to complete the transit
safely back to Earth.

At first Peg thought it was a trick of vision when she
saw something move inside the security circle. But something *was* there, at first barely visible as if made of the
finest mist. But the mist-shapes resolved into armored
humans, running to grapple with the guards. John stood
unmoving, still routing Harry through the Rift.

Peg instinctively raised her arms, spitting stun-bolts
in two different directions as the spectators surged in
surprise.

Then the hangar doors disappeared in a glaring white
flash, and armored figures came storming through the
breach. The Citadel of Silence was under attack both
from inside the Rift and without!

Chapter Thirteen

Sturdley smiled as the sickening void of the Rift faded from around him and the evening skyline of New York City appeared. As planned, he found himself looking down on midtown Manhattan, atop the landmark spire of the Empire State Building.

Even as he'd gone through the Rift, his breadbox-sized burden—a gift from Triadon—had come to life. The servomotors of his armored suit whined under the weight of the gift's heavy shielding until the built-in gizmoidal drive went on-line.

After that, the combination cold fusion/broadcast power unit (or Hoozits, in the original Argonian) seemed light as a feather. Sturdley stowed the machine in an inconspicuous corner of the Empire State's antenna housing and activated the self-imbedding bolts on the underside of the box. He attached a few simple leads, and the Empire State Building's broadcast antenna had a new player—a narrow-cast power beam that would energize Argonian suits anywhere in a ten-mile radius. Maybe it wouldn't reach all the way up to the northern tip of Manhattan, but that was sufficient for him to fly to Forest Hills in Queens—or Kearny, New Jersey.

Not that Sturdley was in a hurry to visit any of those places right now. He had to find a safe harbor for his suit of armor. Next on his to-do list was locating a pawn shop where he could raise Earthly cash for some of the Argonian knick-knacks in his other bag. Finally, he needed a place to stay. His mind racing with plans, the armored Sturdley arrowed upward into the evening sky.

By the following afternoon, the ache pounding in Sturdley's head was due equally to eyestrain and fury. The eyestrain came from trying to decipher the fuzzy, scratched images from the New York Public Library's overused microfiche newspaper files. Catching up on the local news—with special reference to events at the Fantasy Factory—accounted for the fury.

Imagine that little worm Burke elbowing his way into the management of *his* company—and having the nerve to clinch what looked like a successful movie deal! By the time Harry had followed the news to the nearer past, he was fuming.

Then, in the back pages of the *Times* metropolitan section, he caught a two-inch-column story about a planned memorial service . . . for him. Damn! It was today, in about an hour and a half.

Harry bolted out of the library in search of the nearest secondhand men's store. An off-the-rack suit, some quick alterations, and then he was off to the theater district in search of a makeup shop before his final destination on Manhattan's West Side.

The ready-to-wear suit seemed to balloon around him, and he wasn't all that sure of the stitches that had gone into hemming the pants. After months without wearing one, the necktie felt like an alien growth to Harry. Worst of all, however, was the wig he'd bought as a disguise, with its matching beard spirit-gummed to his face. The blasted thing seemed glued so tight, he was afraid it would spring off if he moved his lips.

Well, he wasn't here at the memorial chapel to speak anyway—just to look and listen.

The crowd was large and respectfully silent. Harry was gratified and a little surprised at the number of people— he'd drawn as good a house as Harvey Kurtzman's farewell.

Familiar faces dotted the pews. There was Bob Gunnar, and Elvio Vital, a bunch of the young turks from the office . . . by God, they'd even gotten Rip Jacoby to fly in from California.

In the front row, chatting quietly with Marty Burke and his newscaster girlfriend, was a welcome familiar figure. Myra looked well, if a bit tired. For a wild second, Harry wanted to abandon his master plan, run up there, and take her in his arms. But two considerations kept him where he sat: his public appearance could put her in danger . . . and Myra hated scenes. If he tried pulling that "back from the dead" stunt, he'd probably find *his* life in danger—from her.

So Harry sat quietly as he could, listening to eulogies. Elvio offered a charming, even poignant, remembrance of Peg Faber. He was genuinely fond of the girl. Bob Gunnar strove manfully to pay tribute to John Cameron, hamstrung by the fact that there was so little to talk about.

I wish we could have gotten somebody who really knew the kid, the lanky editor thought as he spoke. Harry was glad his face was covered with crepe hair—nobody could see him gawking. He'd taken it for granted that his erstwhile mental powers were somehow related to the strange worlds he'd been on. But he was back on Earth— and he still had them!

While he tried to absorb this fact, some of the old warhorses of the business got up to say a few words. Harry felt a little guilty sitting there, silently taking part in his own wake. God knows, it mightn't be so long before he'd be making similar speeches at some of their funerals. Poor old Bill Schaffter, creator of the now-defunct Crimson Cape, looked like death warmed over, his hair gone from radiation treatments. Every year, there were fewer and fewer representatives from the golden, even the silver age of comics.

Rip Jacoby brought chuckles—and a bit more reality—into the room with some war stories of the young Sturdley at the height of his genius (or was that hubris?). Harry risked the integrity of his beard with a broad smile as Rip reminisced. Lord, but he'd been full of himself in the old days.

The final speech was a sample of latter-day arrogance as Marty Burke rose to the podium to deliver the eulogy.

"Thank you, Mr. Jacoby, for bringing Harry so vigorously to our memories."

Mentally, Burke added, *and showing what a royal pain in the ass he was.*

He favored the whole chapel with a smile. "And just as the stories we've heard remind us how the Fantasy Factory was in its first glory days, I'm sure Harry would be delighted to see us moving into the next great era."

Burke's mouth might have been talking about Sturdley, but his brain was almost screaming *Memememememememe!*

It was a bizarre experience for Harry as he probed into his rival's mind, like hearing the speech in stereo—the public utterances, with personality and off-color commentary from Burke's ego.

And what an ego it was! Even on his best—or was that *worst?*—days, Harry didn't think he was quite as full of himself as Marty the Genius.

For an encore, Burke brought in his new Hollywood buddy for a media sound bite. Stuart Silikis adjusted his coke-bottle glasses and said, "Although I never had the honor of meeting Mr. Sturdley, or—" He glanced at a slip of paper in his hand—"John Cameron or Peg Faber, I join with you in mourning their disappearance. So I'd like you, his family and friends, to know that we at Silikis productions intend to make the film *Heroes* a permanent memorial, by officially dedicating the movie to them."

Inwardly, he was thinking, *Who gives a rat's ass about any of these futzers, but it may mean another million's worth of gross!*

On the whole, Harry rated the experience as slightly better than some proctological exams he'd undergone. He waited till the chapel had pretty well emptied, then evaded the reception line at the door, using a side exit. He'd probed several minds to be sure he knew the next stop on Myra's itinerary—a small restaurant over on the East Side, not far from home.

During his undercover stint on Argon, tracking down Deviant HQ, Harry had perfected his surveillance technique. So his time standing in a building doorway staking out the restaurant was completely uneventful. For any passersby, he simply projected a mental message that said "homeless." Most New Yorkers then rushed along, ignoring him—though a couple of less well-off types had pressed small amounts of change into his palm. When cops passed, he sent a message that said "harmless."

Myra put up with the Fantasy Factory's elite for about an hour before making her escape. Bob Gunnar saw her to the exit. Harry eavesdropped as Myra firmly turned down Gunnar's offer to see her home. She set off at a smart pace down the block, and Harry shadowed her from across the street, tugging and silently cursing as his beard now refused to come off.

His longer legs allowed Harry to catch up with Myra two blocks before she reached home. He swallowed an applesized lump that had somehow appeared in his throat, and croaked, "M-Myra?"

Myra turned, her delicate features set in the tight mask used to deal with panhandlers, street people, and New Yorkers in general. Then, as Harry removed his wig, her eyes—those big, blue eyes he'd always wanted to go swimming in when they were kids—went wide.

"Harry?" she whispered. Then Myra hauled off and belted him a good one in the arm. "*What the hell have you been up to?*"

She tried to sound tart, she tried to sound angry, but there were tears in her eyes as she flung her arms around him. "There seems to be a lot less flab and considerably more muscle on you," she commented into his chest. "What happened? Did you get shanghaied off to Oregon to work as a lumberjack?"

"It will take a bit of explaining," Harry admitted.

They went to a park over by the East River and claimed a bench. Then Harry told Myra everything about his disappearance, including the secrets of John Cameron and the giants.

"Your *gofer* brought the giants over here? *That's* how you got the contract with them?" Myra said.

"Oh, there's more," Harry assured her. She became even more poker-faced after hearing about the planet Argon. "Before you call the guys in the white coats, let me show you a few things."

Harry reached into the inside pocket of his suit and pulled out what seemed to be a flat case, wallet-sized, made from some sort of matte-finish black metal. He placed it on the bench between them and tapped the top. Like some sort of puzzle box, the object flipped to a new configuration, now becoming an open-topped cube with three-inch sides.

"Interesting," Myra said, "but—"

Her words died as little motes of color came into existence over the box, forming a mist, then a tiny cloud of light, which finally coalesced into three-dimensional holographic figures. Scenes of Harry, John, and Peg appeared, in and out of armor, fighting Deviants, speaking at the congratulatory dinner, while a running English commentary told the story of the S-Force in a slightly tinny vocal tone.

Myra stared at this example of impossible technology that backed up Harry's story. "Well," she said with a sigh, "that beats some of the thoughts I'd been having about you and that red-headed secretary," she said.

Harry put his hand on hers. "There's only one redhead in my life." He pulled up a memory from fifty years before, the two of them on their first date, before he'd even gone to work for her dad's company, and beamed it into her mind. In his mental image, Myra had hair like burnished copper.

She raised a hand to her head, pressing fingers against her carefully coiffed curls. The years had faded her hair to a tawny gray, but errant coppery gleams still reflected in the late afternoon sunshine. "*You* did that—sent that picture—didn't you?" she said in a soft voice.

Still offering confirmation, Harry pulled out more items from his pockets—a kid's toy that floated in midair; and something for self-defense—a fountain pen-sized rod that projected a beam powerful enough to cut the edge off three of the bench slats.

"Well, either you've got very persuasive delusions or you're telling the truth," Myra finally said. "What are you going to do?"

"Letting those giants onto this world is the biggest mistake I ever made," Harry said. "I've got to set that right."

He looked at the expression on her face and added, "And don't go saying this is the first time in my life I've ever admitted a mistake."

"Well, hardly ever," she replied with a smile. "But I'll bet you've got a plan."

He smiled. Myra knew him all too well. "It's in three parts. Number one, I want to get you out of town. Once the giants know I'm back, I'm afraid they'll put pressure on me through you."

He forestalled a quick and mutinous reaction by raising his hands. "Two, I've got to get back in harness at the Fantasy Factory. Saving the world is all well and good, but there's business to be done. I'm not going to let Burke run my company into the ground." He grinned. "And let's face it, after what I've been through, I've got a trunkful of new ideas."

That got a laugh, at least.

"Third—there's the giants. From what I learned about them on their homeworld, they are *not* good guys. So I think we can take it for granted they're up to something, and I'll have to come up with ways to keep an eye on them and find out their plans."

"Couldn't you go and tell—" Myra began, then stopped.

Harry nodded. "Who could I tell? The police? The feds? The media? I've tried to come up with a way to do that, and all I see in the end is either public panic, ruin for the Fantasy Factory—or myself being committed someplace." He shook his head. "I've got a couple of aces up my sleeve, though—technology from Argon, including an armored suit. And once John and Peg clean things up there, they'll be along to help."

Creases of worry appeared on his face. "At least John will be here."

"It sounds like there's a lot more to this story," Myra said with a sharp look at him. "But I'll wait for all the juicy details. Regarding *part one* of your plan, we'll have to talk about that. Obviously, until you figure out how to deal with the giants, you're going to keep your return a secret. So I can stay and help for a while, at least."

"Especially with part two," Sturdley said. "I need a better idea of what's going on at the Fantasy Factory, stuff I can't get out of the *Wall Street Journal.*"

Myra nodded. "Well, let me tell you what I know," she said. "Then we have to figure out how to get you in there to do your mind-reading act without anybody knowing it's you."

Bob Gunnar stood in his office door, watching the shabby figure seated on the guest chair at Peg Faber's—he corrected himself—Wendy Wentworth's desk. The busty blonde alternated between ignoring the elderly messenger and being actively nasty to him, as if he were a homeless derelict.

Actually, the man's ill-fitting suit looked on the new side. His shaggy white hair needed a trim, and he had an odd, sort of patchy, beard. During the past week and a half he'd become a familiar sight in the executive hallways of the Fantasy Factory. Myra Sturdley had hired the guy to carry in files and memorabilia from her husband's home office. He'd also carted away those personal items that Burke had dismissed as Harry's *junk.*

There was a load of stuff by Wendy's desk now. Gunnar noticed the Thibault drawing of Mr. Pain topping a pile of odds and ends, a victim of Burke's redecorating program. He wondered where some of the valuable items, like the Rip Jacoby *Rodent* sketch, had gone.

Wendy hadn't yet bundled up the latest batch. She'd just put in a call to the mail room, and proceeded to type a letter on a shiny new computer, turning her back on the messenger.

Typical, Gunnar thought. And equally typical, the messenger just sat there, his eyes going unfocused as if he'd spent too much of his life waiting—or maybe he was merely waiting for death?

Gunnar pushed aside the morbid thought. Just because he was fighting for his life here at the Fantasy Factory didn't mean that death and destruction haunted everybody.

He was surprised to notice that the messenger's brown eyes had sharpened considerably and were now staring at him. "Excuse me, sir. Could I talk to you for a moment?" the old man said in a raspy, almost put-on kind of voice. Gunnar realized that he'd never heard the guy speak before.

Wendy gave her unwelcome guest a venomous look, opening her mouth to say something spiteful, no doubt. For reasons Gunnar wasn't quite sure of, he forestalled her. "Sure, old-timer. Step in here."

He ushered the older man into his office. Maybe it was that morbid feeling again. Or maybe it was just that the old guy had stirred a memory of one of comicdom's darkest secrets. Before DC Comics had finally paid out a small share of the untold wealth the company had made on *Superman*, the creators of the character, Siegel and Schuster, had fallen on hard times indeed. Legend had it that Jerry Siegel had been forced to take a job as a messenger, and had found himself delivering packages to the company whose financial future he'd assured.

Gunnar smiled. Not that he expected this poor character to turn out to be a comics genius.

He glanced over at the old man, who reached into a voluminous bag and produced a bottle of liquid with a pungent, alcoholic tinge.

Great, Gunnar thought. I've invited a wino in to have a nip with me.

Instead of drinking, however, the messenger poured the liquid on his face—and his beard began to dissolve.

He pulled off the shaggy white wig, removed a pair of trick eyebrows, and Harry Sturdley stood grinning at his dumbfounded chief editor.

Chapter Fourteen

Continued stresses distorted the lower-dimensional sub-strate around the nexus known as Earth, creating a rift within the Rift. As extrusions of the higher dimensions made themselves felt in the four-dimensional frame, what had previously seemed immutable "laws of nature" proved more and more capable of amendment . . .

In Flatlands, Oklahoma, Billy-Ray Woolsey flexed the fingers on his right hand. They looked a little swollen as he placed the quarter on his thumb. Constant use had left it so numb he couldn't even feel the coin anymore.

He flipped, clumsily caught the quarter in midair, clapped it to the back of his hand, then held it out to the lens of the video camera Jesse-Bob Fargis held.

Heads yet again.

"How many does that make?" Billy Ray asked in a slightly hoarse voice.

"Counting that one . . ." Jesse-Bob shifted his attention from the camcorder viewfinder to the scratchpad by his elbow as he made another tick-mark. "Well, I'll be dipped! That'll make *two thousand heads* since I got here."

Not only had Jesse-Bob driven over to preside as official witness, he'd brought his camera to record every moment. For the better part of a videocassette running at super-long play, and excepting only a few bathroom breaks, Billy-Ray had sat by the window, flipping that damned quarter. Behind him, clouds had roiled and rain threatened. Before him sat his buddy Jesse-Bob, immortalizing every move.

"That's *got* to be enough," Billy-Ray said, resting his hand on his lap. "I can't believe the Guinness people have somebody who'd gotten that many heads in a row."

"Can't rightly believe it myself if I hadn't seen it with my own eyes," Jesse-Bob assured him. "What are the chances against that kind of run? The whachacallum— the probabilities? You must be the luckiest man who ever lived."

For a long, pregnant moment, they stared at each other. Then Billy-Ray jumped to his feet, fumbling for the keys to his pickup. "Damn, we must've been sniffing too much powdered fertilizer or somethin'! I can't believe we spent all this time taking pictures of me flippin' a coin when we could have been halfway to Vegas!"

Jesse-Bob was slightly delayed stowing away his camcorder. He was behind Billy-Ray, closing the door of the house while his buddy had nearly reached his battered blue pickup truck.

Then Billy-Ray and the whole farmyard disappeared in a flaring blast of lightning. Blue afterimages danced in Jesse-Bob's retinas; the slam of the door behind him was lost in the most earth-shaking peal of thunder he'd ever experienced.

The bag containing the camcorder slipped from Jesse-Bob's nerveless fingers. He just sort of leaned against a wall, completely unstrung, as his vision slowly came back. A pelting rain was now thundering across the dusty yard, the drops actually seeming to dig tiny holes in the ground.

The pickup was miraculously untouched as the rain drummed on its metal hood.

But Billy-Ray lay unmoving where Jesse-Bob had last seen him.

"Hey, Billy?" Jesse-Bob called tentatively, getting no answer.

He'd just reached the porch steps when a second lightning flash blew him back.

Jesse-Bob shook his head and aimed his blinking gaze to his friend's recumbent and now steaming figure.

"Hit twice by lightning, and in the same spot," Jesse-Bob muttered. "Now what would the probabilities be for something like *that?*"

He glanced back at the camera case still lying by the door. "Coulda sold that to one of them video shows for a good figure if I'd been filming."

Jesse-Bob sighed. "Some people got all the luck."

The hangar of the Citadel of Silence rang with chaos and mayhem as swirling bodies flew and fought in three dimensions. There was no battleline, not with the attackers coming from two directions at once. The escapees from the Sphere of Exile attacked the guards circling Harry's Rifting point, engaging in power-armored hand-to-hand combat. Part of the circle disappeared as defenders were caught from behind by the weapons of the Deviant storming party. Those S-Force members who were armed and armored joined the fight. The others ran, some to find weapons, others simply to escape.

For Peg, there was no battle, merely a succession of one-on-one dogfight duels.

She dispatched another foe, killing the inertia of her dive from the ceiling as she glanced round for the next opponent. The area around her was momentarily bare of enemies. She might have won her single combats, but the fight as a whole was going heavily against the S-Force. She caught a glimpse of Mike holding a Deviant over his head and hurling the hapless criminal into three more of the attackers.

Off to one side, a helmetless Triadon had rallied a knot of fighters, setting up the beginning of a defense to keep the raiders from getting farther into the fortress. But for the most part, the S-Force was fighting badly, caught by surprise and in disarray . . . lacking the direction of its founder and leader.

How long before Harry is safely on Earth and John can bring his attention back here? Peg wondered desperately as three attackers ahead engaged a lone S-Forcer. She recognized the heraldic pattern on the defender's armor—it was Moradel, a female technician. Green stun-blasts flared as Moradel nailed one of the Deviants. The other two, however, fired bright red blast-bolts, cutting Moradel down.

Gritting her teeth, Peg extended both arms in the tridigirector gesture. *Her* armor still carried blasters, and for once, she had no qualms about using them. The two Deviants standing over Moradel went down—permanently, Peg hoped—as she looked for other targets.

A ripple seemed to pass through the very air of the hangar, and Peg felt the hairs at the back of her neck raise. Gooseflesh crawled along her arm as she aimed the tridigirector at a new attacker—a Deviant who disappeared in midair even as she fired.

The wavery feeling settled into a pattern Peg could identify—the familiar queasy sensation of the Rift in use. It hit her again, like a brief gastric attack, and then she understood.

John was back in the fight, using his unique powers. He must be popping the escapees back to the Sphere of Exile, she thought, doing it so quickly nobody can get over from the other side. The dizzy, sickening sensation struck again, making her arm waver as she fired at another enemy. The blast-bolt missed, tearing a hole in the side of a parked flying platform.

It was a lot easier dealing with the twinge of Rift transition as a single gut-wrenching swoop, rather than in fits and starts of nausea, Peg thought. She tried to reorient herself, seeking John's position in the turmoil.

He was pretty much where he'd been when it all started, except that now he wore a helmet. And there were five Deviant escapees crawling over John's armor, trying to bring him down. Even as Peg leapt forward, bringing up her arms to aim, the attackers faded, Rifted away in an even worse flaring of nausea.

"Jeeze," Peg muttered, "this is even worse than that imitation morning sickness."

The next knot of attackers coming at John was armed, members of the Deviant assault team that had blown away the hangar doors. As they brought their weapons to bear, Peg launched herself in flight, bringing both arms up to aim her blasters. The Deviants seemed to freeze, then were cut down in a crossfire of blast-bolts from Peg and Mike.

"Why'd they just stand there?" Peg asked.

Then the answer hit her. They'd frozen because *John* had used a mental attack instead of a physical one. She and Mike had cut down a group of helpless enemies, blasting them when simple stun-bolts would have served.

"You might warn us when you're going to do that," Peg snapped into her radio. She would have said more, except for the figure rising from behind the mound of moribund, spark-emitting attackers they'd just blown away.

His armor seemed considerably more lightweight than the Argonian standard, and in his right hand he carried what looked like a stubby silver bazooka—another proto-type force cannon.

Mike moved to cover John, bringing up his arms, trying to get a clear shot, but the Deviant moved with inhuman speed. Peg had only an instant's time to debate using her guns or her mental powers.

Then came a white glare of light, which briefly diminished, then reached blinding intensity.

Peg felt as if someone had suddenly spray-painted her shoulder with acid. She was flung to the side, and when she tried to extend an arm to stop her fall, nothing happened. As the defunct suit hit the concrete floor, she enjoyed all the sensations of being sealed in an oil drum and crashed into an ironmonger's shop. The bone-rattling noise finally ended, to be replaced by the faint, staticky sound of sparks crackling. The outside audio pickups must be dead, she thought. The stink of burning insulation was strong in her nose as she attempted to hit her helmet's emergency release switch with her jaw.

Instead, she sank down into darkness.

John stood in horror, staring at the tumbled forms he'd psychically bound while his friends attacked them. That wasn't the way it was supposed to be at all. They were supposed to stun them—that was Sturdley's code . . .

Of course, a small voice in the back of his head reminded him, the other side had no such compunctions.

Mike and Peg faced him, a brief tableau in the shrieking chaos around them.

"You might warn us when you're going to do that!" Peg sounded almost on the verge of tears. She'd just helped kill five helpless prisoners.

Then the new attacker popped up from behind the pile of corpses, wielding the force cannon. John found himself staring down the muzzle of the damned thing, into some sort of faceted, jewel-like lens.

It's going to kill me, he thought.

His armored arms with their built-in blast projectors were down by his sides. His brain seemed oddly numb, guilt making him unable to focus his mental powers.

The Deviant fired.

At the same instant, Mike jumped.

It was an amazing demonstration of his grasp of things Argonian. Mike used the gizmoidal drive to turn himself into a human missile. He lofted right over the pile of casualties sheltering the gunner, landing right on the force cannon, exoskeletal arms raised to pound on the mechanism.

In that moment, however, the weapon's beam cut him in two. The glare of white energy flickered for an instant as Mike's body blocked the muzzle. Then it was back at full intensity, even as the ruins of Mike's armor followed a dead man's final command, smashing down with exoskeleton-enhanced power on the gleaming cylindrical weapon.

Mike's suicidal attack saved John's life as the weapon wobbled slightly. The beam moving out of line with John's body—to catch Peg in the side.

"Nooooo!" John yelled as Peg tumbled back past him, her shattered armor sending out a pyrotechnic distress signal of sparks.

Mike's pounding must have done something to the force cannon, because the beam cut off, seeming to throw the hangar into sudden darkness. Then all the antagonists, Deviants and S-Forcers alike, screamed in distress and clutched at heads that now exploded from a wash of rage.

Lambent blue blast-bolts sent a pile of dead bodies erupting in gouts of blood and machinery. But moving with preternatural quickness, the mysterious cannoneer dodged back.

John strode among the reeling combatants like a god of war, striking down Deviant after Deviant. It was horribly easy, dispatching nerveless foes. But none of them carried the stubby silver tube of the force cannon. None of them was the enemy he *really* wanted.

The fighters on both sides began to recover their equilibrium, to separate themselves from the roaring tempest of John's emotions that had overwhelmed their psyches. And as they did so, they realized the tide of the struggle had abruptly turned. Too many Deviants had gone down in the last few seconds. The survivors didn't press their attack.

They merely retreated, running, flying—in some cases, *crawling*—for the opening they'd blasted through the hangar doors. And as John's berserker mood cooled, the other members of the S-Force plunged forward in full hunt.

John let them go. He didn't expect the enemy to attempt a stand. His brush with their minds told him they were too stunned, too terrified by his attack, to do anything but flee.

Even as he turned to scan the hangar, unarmored figures, some bearing weapons, began to examine the casualties. Harry might scoff at them as sheep, but there was a basic decency to the Argonians, a decency that would compel them to bring all the wounded, S-Force and Deviant alike, to the automeds.

Unlike us, John thought, or the Deviants who can kill at will.

He passed among the still victims of the fray. In some places, S-Forcers and Deviants lay side by side. In others, the dead and wounded had tumbled into stacks like drifted snowflakes or impromptu war memorials.

John took to the air, flying for the center of the huge room. Yes. There was the desecrated pile of dead, the grotesque ruin of Mike's torso on the top, leaking blood like some sort of obscene syrup atop a mounded dessert.

John's stomach threatened to rebel, hot bile burning the back of his throat. He flew past, searching for a smaller figure whose armor was decorated with a whimsical flying eye.

Sparks still flickered from the ruined circuitry of Peg's suit. But that little illusory movement was the only sign of life.

"Peg!" John cried into his radio.

No answer.

But even as he knelt beside her, he could see that the heavy pauldron on her right shoulder—where the radio transceiver was located—had been gouged and melted.

Almost afraid of what he'd find, John extended a probe into Peg's mind.

A breath he hadn't known he was holding gushed forth in an echoing rush within his helmet when he found she was merely unconscious.

He gathered her up in his arms and went in search of the nearest automed.

The wounded were all being sent to the infirmary, which was set higher up in the butte that housed the Citadel of Silence. But John remembered the healing machine in Triadon's biology lab, where they'd gotten their post-arrival checkup.

He burst into the empty room, the door automatically closing behind him. For a second, John just stood, trying to find a place to set Peg down. He rejected the lab tables with a shudder.

Then he noticed the couch on the far side of the lab, set under the holographic pseudo-window. It appeared to be made of some seamless leather-like material, almost butter-soft as John poked it. A good place perhaps to zonk off when experiments went on all night.

He lay Peg out full-length, hauled off his own helmet, then worked the release on hers. The helm was stuck, perhaps welded in place from that shot on the shoulder. John worked delicately, afraid to apply too much pressure—he didn't want to tear Peg's head off. Finally, after one more rasping snag, he was able to slide the thing free.

Peg's face was deathly pale, every freckle seeming to stand out with greater prominence. Her hair was a tangled, sweat-matted mass. But she was breathing, that was the important thing.

John blinked perspiration out of his eyes, then turned to the ticklish job of getting Peg free, breaking plast-alloy parts where he had to. When he finally got her upper torso cleared, he drew in a breath between clenched teeth. The union suit style undergarment was scorched and tattered at the right shoulder. The skin showing through the rents had an angry red, burnt look.

The lower armor was easier to remove. John was pulling off the last boot when Peg stirred, her breathing taking on a different note. He knelt beside her as her eye-lids fluttered open, revealing big, confused gray eyes. "Wha—the fight!" She struggled to a half-sitting position, her face tightening as she tried to use her right shoulder.

John tried to ease her back. "It's over. The Deviants are on the run. You got hit. I'm going to put you into the automed."

"The force cannon." She pulled her memories into order as she glanced at her injured shoulder.

"You were lucky. Looks like you just got caught by the edge of the beam." His face must have given something away, because she stared at him with a sudden intensity.

"Someone—is there someone else who wasn't lucky?" Peg's eyes went unfocused for a moment, and John knew she was conducting a mental search. He knew the drill. Ever since he'd discovered his own psionic abilities, the location of friends was easy—there was the barest tickle that showed which direction led to them.

Unless, of course, there was no longer a mind to be found. Peg shuddered under his supporting hands, her eyes widening, yet blind. "No Mike?" the words came as a bare whisper.

Then her eyes focused, boring into his as her mind came crashing in, grabbing for his memories. She saw what had happened to Mike, and her eyes clouded with tears. "Oh, no," she breathed. "No, no, no."

Peg's grief and desolation became a tangible presence in both their minds. John moved instinctively to the most basic form of comforting. He took her in his arms.

She hissed, and they both pulled back, feeling the pain from her shoulder. John grimaced. He might not be able to help her emotional hurt, but he knew how to handle this. A couple of probes, and he'd blocked the nerves carrying the message of pain.

Peg looked at her shoulder in surprise. John intercepted her hand before it could touch the inflamed flesh. *I just stopped the ache for a while. It still needs treatment.*

She stared at him open-mouthed. They were communicating wordlessly, their minds still intertwined, meeting on deeper channels than they'd ever shared before. He was exquisitely aware of the tactile sensation as she flung her arms around him, the tears finally flooding out.

After the sobbing ceased, they clung together for long moments in an interchange even John didn't understand, a transaction on a very basic level.

Then Peg's lips were brushing his, as she clung to him with desperate intensity. Perhaps it was like whistling in the dark, the need to affirm life against death, but John couldn't have identified such an intellectual construct if his life depended on it.

All he knew—all the two of them knew—was a rush of feeling, of need. They were both clothed, but felt a nakedness beyond any exposure as their joined minds confronted what they were about to do. John's doubts and fears of awkwardness in what for him would be a first encounter, Peg's regrets and ambivalences, all were there. So was John's love, like a bright, warming star, a star that had a twin in Peg's mind.

They were breathing faster as Peg pulled back again, her eyes glued to John's as her fingers undid the closure on her suit. An almost little-boy wonder flooded his mind as her body was exposed.

He leaned forward to brush his lips across her bared left shoulder, the hollow of her throat, the cleft between her breasts, the pale pink tips that darkened as they suffused with blood.

It was as though they had established a reciprocal circuit between their brains, the pleasure given by one sizzling through the nerves of both.

Peg's undersuit was completely off now, and John's armor clattered to the floor as they both worked to strip him bare. He sighed as he stroked a hand over the supple curve of her back, gripped the tightly-fleshed roundness of her ass, caressed the firm, sweet curve of her hip. It seemed as if beneath the smoothness of her skin he could feel the strength of every muscle, sheer vitality radiating from her.

Sliding a leg between John's, Peg pushed his undersuit down to a puddle of cloth on the floor. She'd seen John naked before—but naked and unconscious. Despite his muscular build, he'd seemed lesser than life, shrunken somehow. Now the stocky form before her seemed to ripple with power, vibrant, and oh, yes, as she planted kisses downward from the bands of muscle at his chest, rampant.

They sank to the couch, too eager for lovers' games. Peg greeted his entrance with a wordless cry, and not only their bodies, but their minds and very souls seemed to meld together like long-separated parts of an intricate puzzle, conjoining, *interlocking*, even as they danced the most ancient of all dances.

Their gasps weren't merely from tactile stimulation, but of wonder as the pleasure of one partner augmented that of the other, as they saw through each other's eyes, felt with each other's bodies.

And when they faced the little death, that moment of ultimate vulnerability and least connection with this world, they embraced it together.

A sex-flush colored Peg from head to toe. Her eyelids were closed, and she seemed to be sipping air in little whistling gasps.

And when her eyes opened to look at him with a strangely grave air, John realized they were separate—and themselves again.

"Ah—" Peg said, trying to find some kind of words.

John silently got off the couch, picked up her nude form, and brought her to the automed.

"Ouch!" he heard from the closed capsule as he psychically removed the nerve block on Peg's shoulder. Then came the humming as the cybernetic healer proceeded to examine her.

In moments, the capsule opened and Peg emerged with a glistening film sprayed across an already less angry-looking burn.

"Prescriptions being prepared," the machine announced through the translator on John's suit.

A small slot appeared at the side of the capsule revealing two plainly wrapped packets.

"The smaller package contains a spray healant/analgesic, to be used as necessary." The machine-voice paused for a second. "The other packet contains a selection of contraceptive devices, which might be advisable."

Peg froze in the middle of reaching for the bundles, blushing bright red. "Thorough machine," she muttered. "Very bloody thorough."

John managed to rustle up an Argonian lab coat for Peg to wear and donned his old undersuit.

She burst out laughing as they headed down the corridor to the living quarters. "We don't exactly look like superheroes," Peg said as they reached her room. She ruffled her voluminous garment and tweaked the saggy, sweat-stained union suit John wore.

He nodded. "The tighter the costume—"

"The stronger the hero," she chimed in to finish one of Harry Sturdley's most basic laws of comics. Peg ran a hand through her hair and made a disgusted face. "All this hero wants is a nice shower, and then bed—"

She cut off abruptly, glancing at John, the color high in her cheeks.

I'd almost rather face the force cannon than this, John thought. "Just remember to spray on that healing gunk." He took a deep breath. "If you need any help—"

Peg's color was still high as she grabbed his wrist. "I could probably use somebody to scrub my back and aim the spray from package number one." She looked him in the eye, and gave him a grin. "Play your cards right, and we may find out what's inside package number two."

Chapter Fifteen

The very stuff of the Rift buckled under the pressure as the higher-order dimensions impinged on the Earthly nexus. And down in the three-dimensional universe, larger and larger areas were influenced by forces not of this Earth . . .

Tony LaPointe had never heard of Larry Hammeyer, but he did know the name Billy-Ray Woolsey.

Even without the footage of the twin lightning strikes, the late Billy-Ray's friend Jesse-Bob Fargis had succeeded in selling his video to the local news, which in turn had passed it up the line on a slow news day. Combined with the amazing story that the exact same set of winning numbers turned up in both the Colorado and Utah state lotteries, it made for an amusing network-news wrap-up on a wave of odd luck that seemed to be heading westward.

When he'd watched the news, LaPointe had chuckled appreciatively. Luck—specifically probabilities—was his line of work. He ran the Golden Cactus resort and casino—the easternmost house of chance in Las Vegas.

As he stood now watching the bank of television monitors covering the casino floor, LaPointe wished he'd been paying a bit more attention to the news item. From the looks of things, a wave of weird luck had just engulfed his casino. The crowd on the floor was roused almost to fever pitch. At the craps table, a fat, sweaty, aluminum siding salesman from Pittsburgh continued the longest and most lucrative dice run in recorded history.

As he rolled the ivories in his cupped hand, his eyes popping, his mouth in a rictus of tension, the salesman looked like a prime candidate for a stroke. LaPointe didn't know if he should be rooting for the guy to keel over—at least he wouldn't win anymore—or if it were better to follow the gambler's creed and let him go on. He'd have to crap out soon.

LaPointe decided not to panic over what was happening at the blackjack tables either. Several part-time players who would normally have busted by now were hitting blackjack after blackjack. A casino—like an insurance company— does not make its money by paying out. The business lies in pulling money *in*. And like an insurance company, casinos depend on a very small but quite profitable set of percentages. Insurance companies bet that sober twenty-year-olds who invest in life insurance won't die before the policy is paid out. Casino operators bet that anyone who draws over a sixteen at blackjack will probably go bust.

Occasionally, of course, flukes happen and the percentages get flouted. That might happen once in a while. But when it happens simultaneously on the craps and blackjack tables . . .

People now began jumping and screaming around the roulette wheel. LaPointe whipped out a silk handkerchief and began mopping a suddenly ashen face. If the wheel turned against you, too . . .

A whooping siren-like noise echoed through the building. The $100,000 slot machine, which supposedly only paid off once every three months—and which had showered wealth on an amazed sucker only ten days ago—had just kicked in.

The house was in danger of being broken.

That's when the phone rang. LaPointe's deputy answered it and turned to his boss with an odd look on his face. "It's the Bonnie Dune up the block. Manager wants to know if anything—uh—out-of-the-ordinary is going on."

The Bonnie Dune. A block *west* of here.

"Tell 'em yeah, and get 'em off the phone," LaPointe answered, a potential way to make up the evening's catastrophic losses now occurring to him. "Then get me the racing form. I want all the long shots at Santa Anita . . ."

John and Peg were not destined for relaxation, much less rest. Within hours of repulsing the raid on the Citadel of Silence, the S-Force was deluged with reports of Deviant activity. Nowhere—and no one—on Argon seemed safe from these outbreaks.

Sighing, the couple donned their armor and went to lead the response.

"Don't bother lying to me," John told the Argonian merchant in a flat voice. "I'm one of those barbarian mind-readers—lots of evil gene in me."

Most of John's words to the terrified Argonian were lies themselves. After twenty-seven hours of constant flying and fighting, he doubted he had the strength to crack even this character's weak personality shields. And John didn't feel evil—he was more exhausted than anything else.

But he was the one who'd insisted on a counter-terrorist offensive, following up on every lead in the captured Deviant records. Judging from the reports filtering in, the S-Force was actually nailing some of these guys.

That left to him the job of running down whatever leads they could get from characters like the one he was facing—a small-time merchant who'd been funneling technical supplies to the Deviants. After innumerable similar interviews, the man was no longer an individual in John's eyes, but a type—a collaborator rather than a sympathizer. He'd let himself be used. Although he knew from the value of the goods he received in exchange for his technotoys that they had to be illegally obtained, he'd shut his eyes. The merchant was like a lot of Argonians in this war, just going along with the prevailing wind.

Well, the wind was blowing from another quarter now.

"Your contact for these exchanges—what's his name? Where does he do business? Do you know where he lives?"

John had gotten pretty good at interrogation. His "evilpsychopath-barbarian" approach worked even better than "good cop/bad cop."

The merchant babbled a name and address, his fear so palpable it ruptured any personality shields. John turned to one of the two S-Force troopers patrolling with him, pushing through the fog of fatigue to recall the guy's name. "Grumadon, this citizen has given us the information we need. Why not put him to sleep so he doesn't pass it on to anyone else?"

Grumadon aimed a stun-bolt, and the merchant collapsed. The patrol moved on to the address John had gotten.

It was the Argonian equivalent of a nice neighborhood, a medium-sized spire on the outskirts of Kemot. When John made enquiries about Domergon, the obvious alias the merchant had given him, he heard of a quiet, unassuming couple—husband and wife. So, there were two potential Deviant captives to be taken. John took Grumadon with him to the apartment door, leaving the third patrol member outside the spire, keeping an eye on the landing stages in case their quarry attempted to bail out.

The apartment entry was flush with the drop shaft, denoting the full floor was occupied by one apartment—modest luxury, in Argonian terms. Hanging in midair, John thrust his arms out in the tridigirector, blasting the door in.

"S-Force!" Grumadon blared through his external speakers. "Nobody move!"

The inner foyer was a donut of empty space, extending all the way around the drop shaft. The various rooms of the apartment split off from there in pie wedges.

Bursting into the place, John went right, Grumadon left, checking the foyer first. No one there. They met back at the wrecked door, then began to search the various rooms.

Blasters ready, John stepped into the living room, a tasteful evocation of the Argonian good life. The furniture all floated on gizmoidal fields, and the 3-D holo-projector was of the highest quality. Unlike most Argonian dwellings, however, this one had a floor-to-ceiling library of book-tapes. Few present-day Argonians had such literary tastes. John inferred that the Deviants in residence were progress fanatics rather than criminals.

Then he heard the ripping sound of blaster-bolts being unleashed. This was a bad sign—Grumadon was armed only with nonlethal stunners. John tore through the apartment, following the noise.

He found Grumadon in a bedroom. The S-Force trooper lay inert on the floor, sparks sheeting from his shattered armor. But the room seemed empty—until John glanced toward what an Earthly architect would call the cathedral ceiling. Twenty feet above was a pair of Deviants, scrabbling at a hatchway disguised as a lighting fixture. The smaller of the two boosted through the opening.

The other Deviant hung from the dangling light fixture. He wore hastily-donned armor without a helmet, and his face tightened with fear as he saw John. The Deviant brought his free arm up, his fingers beginning to curl into the tridigirector.

John's mental batteries were too low to consider a psionic attack. He didn't know if he could hurl himself at the man. On instinct, he went with his third option. His hand speared up, fingers curling.

The Deviant's blast-bolt sizzled past John's ribs.

John's bolt caught the man full in the face.

"We've got to stop meeting like this," Peg said, trying to embrace John—a clumsy job, with the both of them wearing powered armor. At least their helmets were off, allowing for a chaste kiss in one of the tiny equipment bays lining the hangar walls at the Citadel of Silence.

"If you say so," John whispered, his lips at the side of her neck. "Me, I'll take my pleasure wherever I can get it."

"Well, I'd rather not get it in the corner of a glorified industrial garage," Peg told him. "What brings you back so unexpectedly? We thought you'd be out in the field until you ran through the list you'd made up."

"We had a prisoner," John said. "And a casualty. One of the Deviants nailed Grumadon. They've got him in an automed in Kemot."

"My team rounded up an entire gang of Deviants—criminals rather than idealists," Peg reported. "They'd gathered to share the spoils when we came walking in." She grinned at John. "Want me to add your prisoner to my

batch? You look like you could use a shower and some rest."
Her expression faltered a little as she pulled back slightly to
look him in the eyes. "Please, John, don't go out again."

The masklike visage finally cracked, and John sagged
a little against her. "Okay, Peg. Take the woman. I'll wait
for you."

Peg rejoined her patrol with its twenty captives and
beckoned over the single trooper from John's unit. "We'll
take your prisoner in with ours," she said. The trooper
gratefully turned over a small matte-finish metal box and
hurried off.

Another of the marvels of Argonian civilization, Peg
thought. They don't use handcuffs, just a little disk
attached to the back of the armor that slaves all the systems to these controls.

Popping the box open, she maneuvered a small joystick
to move John's captive to the end of her line of similarly
restrained prisoners. Moving in lock-step, they headed
for the detention center the S-Force had established in
the lower levels of the Citadel.

The process of incarceration moved with typical
Argonian automated efficiency, with the prisoners being
"uncanned," as Peg considered the removal of their
armor. They were then identified by comparison with
thousand-year-old records in the population database,
and put in comfortable enough cells.

Peg's patrol had already taken off, and she herself was
about to leave when she turned to speak to the single
S-Force trooper manning the cell controls—the turnkey
of this high-tech hoosegow. He was a tallish, raw-boned
young man. Like Peg and most of the S-Forcers, he kept
his helmet off in the Citadel. His thin face showed in odd
contrast to the wideness of his armored shoulders.

"Kaladel," Peg said in a little surprise. "This isn't your shift. You should have been off hours ago."

Since the formation of the S-Force, Harry had used Peg's administrative abilities to help schedule the troopers' activities. With him gone, she'd taken over the job completely. So she knew who should be where—and Kaladel was in the wrong place.

"My relief didn't show up," the Argonian replied with a nervous smile. "With all the trouble going on outside, I don't mind the extra shift."

Peg shrugged. "If that's the way you feel," she said, turning away. But as she reached the door, Peg's dulled psionic powers, pushed to the limit over three shifts of warfare with the Deviants, registered—something—a sudden tension in the air thick enough to cut with a knife.

"Kal—?" She swung around, to see the pale-faced Argonian bringing up a blaster from under the desk. Peg stared in disbelief down the barrel of the weapon, when the world abruptly swirled sickeningly around her. John suddenly Rifted in next to her, pushing Peg aside while snatching the helmet from under her arm. He himself was half-dressed, but his breastplate was on and one arm was still armored.

The exoskeletal motors screamed as John hurled the helmet at Kaladel. It caught the rogue trooper in the chest, knocking him backward out of his chair. The blaster went off, a wild bolt blowing a hole in the ceiling. John vaulted over the console. His armored arm rose and fell.

Peg heard a sickening crunch from behind the desk. She rushed forward to find John kneeling atop Kaladel, his face as set and hard as the plast-alloy of his breastplate and bracer. Blood dripped from his ungauntleted fist as he raised his arm again. Peg grabbed John's wrist before he could land another blow, wrestling with all the strength of her armor.

"John, *stop!*" she screamed in his ear. "Read him— please!"

Kaladel lay back almost unconscious, one cheek smashed. His shields were totally disorganized.

"They got to him by threatening his family," Peg said, her voice pleading. "You can see it's the truth."

A shudder ran through John's body. His fist—and his face—unclenched. "Yesssssss." He grudgingly hissed his agreement. "I read it."

He looked up at her. "Well, we won't be leaving the Citadel for a while. Not until we've probed *everybody* in the S-Force." Then he glanced from Kaladel to the console. "Can you put him away and hold the fort down here?"

"Not until he's been put through an automed," Peg told him. "After the job you did on his face—"

"I get first dibs," John told her, grimacing. "I think I broke my hand."

Bob Gunnar stared in surprise. After removing all of his false hair, Harry Sturdley began divesting himself of the baggy suit and cheap shirt.

"No, no, it's not the naked truth," Harry assured Gunnar with a grin as he removed new clothes from his messenger's portfolio. Harry donned an expensive sports jacket, slacks, a silk shirt, beginning to appear like his old self, if a bit slimmer and trimmer.

"How do I look?" Harry asked, brushing fingers quickly through his hair.

"Like a million bucks."

A quick mental check showed that far from resenting the end of his authority, Gunnar greeted Harry's reappearance the way a besieged city looks at the arrival of the relief column. But he had a lot of questions—questions Harry preferred not to deal with right then. However, there was an easy way to avoid that. Delicately, Harry pushed Gunnar's attention to an upcoming event—the reason Harry had unmasked himself.

Gunnar smiled. "You couldn't have picked a better time. There's a staff meeting right now." Bob rubbed his hands together. "I can hardly wait to see the look on Burke's face."

A glance at his watch showed that Gunnar was already late. But he had two additional delays, courtesy of his office phone. First it rang with a call from Gunnar's assistant reminding him about the meeting. Then came a call from a rather huffy Wendy Wentworth whose package with Harry's things was now ready for delivery.

"I'm afraid you'll have to wait with that package," Gunnar told her, grinning at Harry. "I have some business with this gentleman which won't be finished for a while yet."

They stepped out into the corridor, past Gunnar's longtime assistant who sucked in a big gasp of air when she saw Harry.

He turned and put his finger to his lips. Then they were at the conference room. Even through the closed door, Harry could hear the hubbub inside. Laughter—one of the artists probably telling a dirty joke—side conversations, and the *rat-tat-tat* of a gavel punctuating Marty Burke's petulant voice. "—got a lot to discuss here, like how could our whole inventory of *Amazing Robert* Number One disappear from the storage closet next to the mailroom?"

"You blamin' the mailroom guys?" a voice burst out.

"If he bothered to manage instead of sitting in his office playing tin god . . ." Gunnar said.

Sturdley nodded. Mailrooms always bore strict watching and careful management. The staff there got the least pay—and watched the most expensive stuff pass under their noses. Pilferage was almost to be expected. It took a difficult combination of the carrot and the stick to keep them honest—a mixture Burke hadn't yet mastered.

"And what's this crap about not being able to get paper anymore?" cried another voice.

"I've discovered that staffers are taking too much of the company's art supplies, especially illustration board," Burke announced.

"I'll bet if you checked *his* studio, you'd find a couple of *reams* of the stuff," Gunnar whispered.

Burke's voice persevered against a growing chorus of complaints. "Apparently some people are even selling it to outsiders. I've gotten reports of convention dealers offering blank sheets of illustration board with our margin marks and logo. It costs money to print up that paper, people. To prevent wastage, I've established a new system—"

"Yeah, you've got some flunky sitting on the paper supply," Zeb Grantfield's voice protested. "I ask for thirty sheets for the next issue of *Jumboy*, and this clown gives me twenty-two, saying it's only a twenty-two page book. And when I ask what happens if I make any mistakes, he says, all snotty, 'Well, don't *make* mistakes.' "

"That's a little extreme, and I'll talk to Clarence," Burke said. "But really, you should be more careful. Perhaps the strain of keeping up with a big project like *Jumboy* is beginning to tell on you. Maybe you could use a little rest . . ."

Sturdley turned to Gunnar. "He really wants to take Grantfield off *Jumboy?*"

Gunnar nodded. "He thinks the kid is past his prime. And to tell the truth, a lot of Zeb's latest work has been winding up in comic store dollar boxes."

"Doesn't he know how to handle—"

"Burke has only two laws," Gunnar said in disgust. "Older artists should get out of his way, and younger artists should stay in his shadow."

The decibel level inside had gone up again. Grantfield was yelling, "You know, I thought things were supposed to get better for the artists around here once an artist got in charge. Looks like I was wrong."

Burke was trying to drown him out with gavel pounding. "If you can't take constructive criticism—"

"Like your comments on the way I draw thumbs?" the slightly hoarse voice of Mack Nagel joined the argument. "I've drawn more thumbs than you've drawn *comic books,* you little snot. And if you got your own thumb out of your ass and actually tried to manage this place—"

"Sounds like our cue to enter," Gunnar said. He opened the door.

"About time you showed," Burke said curtly, glancing at the editor-in-chief, then bringing his attention to the list in front of him. "If I had a little more *help* managing things around here . . ."

Burke suddenly became aware that the whole room had gone silent. He quickly eyed his clique of supporters, who were all staring at the door.

When he turned to confront Gunnar again, he saw that his co-manager had stepped aside, revealing Harry Sturdley in the doorway.

"Agh-ah . . . homina-homina!"

"The things you see when you don't have a camera," Harry said. "You could use a picture of your face in your photo-reference file—under surprise and fear."

"This is a typical Sturdley grandstand play!" Burke exploded. "Where have you been? Do you know the amount of extra work you've created by abandoning the company the way you did?"

"I don't know about extra work—although I hear you've put off *Latter-Day Breed* again." Harry gave Burke a cool look. "If it's such a burden, I'd think you'd be glad to see me back—unless, of course, you've been screwing up in my absence."

"I've had to run this company—with precious little help from him!" Burke pointed at Gunnar. "I didn't even have an executive assistant until just recently."

"Which reminds me," Harry asked. "Where did you pick up that dumb blonde? Bozo's Topless?"

Burke couldn't even speak. He simply seemed to swell and get pop-eyed.

"Five minutes back, and it's just like old times," Thad Westmoreland drawled. "What do we call this? Executive gridlock?"

"Nice to see you, too," Harry snapped back.

"For myself, I *am* glad to see Harry," Gunnar said. "And I'm sure we'd all like to know what happened, where he's been . . . and where are John and Peg?"

Harry glanced over at his editor and friend. Bob was smiling, but his eyes looked like a prosecuting attorney's.

You've spun lots of stories before, Harry told himself. Let's see if they buy this one.

"To be frank, I've been hiding out," he said in his most sincere voice. "After Thomas managed to get some cover for us by throwing that car—I guess he saved our lives—" Knowing his story would become public news soon enough, Harry had decided to plug one of the Heroes books.

"Anyway, we used the distraction of the explosion to run for the docks." He shook his head. "I don't know what happened to John and Peg after that. We got separated. For myself, I managed to get a ride down to Mexico on someone's boat. And that's where I've been ever since, hoping for news that the police had caught whoever was trying to kill me."

"You think someone was trying to kill you?" Gunnar said.

"Well, they sure weren't aiming at Burke."

"But the only one shot was John Cameron," Burke put in.

So they knew about John's wound? When the kids came back from Argon, they'd have to work that into their cover stories. "Yes, he was bleeding when we got away. And that was the only bloodshed I wanted. The only problem was, the longer I waited, the less successful the cops seemed to be. I'm only too aware of my responsibility to this company . . . and that's why I'm risking my life to come back and take the helm."

"Are you sure that's wise, Sturdley?" Thad Westmoreland asked.

"Afraid of getting caught in a car-bomb blast?" Harry gibed.

"So you just hid out and didn't let anyone know about your survival—even Myra." Gunnar's face was full of disapproval.

But Harry had a quick improvisation for that. "I didn't know who was after me, or what resources they had. It's really easy nowadays to intercept mail and tap phone calls."

Gunnar shook his head, his expression still sour. "Well, I'm sure the board will be delighted to have you back.

But I've got to say one thing, Harry. I expected a better story than the one you just told us."

If I announced the truth, we could sell about a trillion comics, Harry thought. Aloud, he said, "Well, it's what happened. As soon as I get some witnesses, I'll let you know." He tried to keep a straight face. "Maybe after John and Peg hear that I've resurfaced, they'll risk coming forward, too."

In spite of himself, Harry grinned. "In fact, I'd almost guarantee it."

Chapter Sixteen

John Cameron dropped lightly from the nighttime sky over Kaldoa. His target was the terrace atop one of the skyscraping spires—or rather, the remains of that terrace. Once it had been a beautiful open-air restaurant. Now armored Argonians were helping dozens of burned and injured diners in the local equivalent of evening dress.

As Peg dropped down beside him, John undid his helmet and dropped it to the scorched plast-alloy flooring, revealing sweat-slicked and tousled hair. His face was sickly pale, with dark, almost bruiselike stains under the eyes. After a few hours' snatched sleep, he'd been fighting battles and running rescues for the past thirty-six hours.

"These are the lucky ones," John said as a flying ambulance swept in to pick up another load of injury victims. "Nearly a hundred more diners are missing after most of the terrace broke up from the explosion. Falling debris nailed more people on terraces farther down. Even some passing fliers were injured in midair."

Peg tore off her own helmet as if the armor were strangling her. "How—?" she began in a shaky voice.

"As far as we can piece things together," John said, rubbing his temples, "the bomb was in an unattended package left on one of the tables. The waiter who served there and the host are both dead, so we have no idea what the bomber looks like." He sighed, looking at Peg. "This is getting dirty. The Deviants haven't used bombs before. Yesterday, when they ambushed the S-Force squad, at least they were shooting at people who could shoot back. But this—senseless violence against civilians . . ."

"It's called terrorism," Peg said numbly. "I guess it's all they can do after they took us on face-to-face—and you beat them."

"They don't look beaten if they can do this," John said grimly. "The only success we've had lately was keeping those bastards from setting their pals free." He looked tentatively at Peg. "If you hadn't spotted that guard they'd turned—if he'd opened the cells—"

"We can't be everywhere," Peg said shortly. "Although God knows we've been trying." She rubbed her eyes. With the unremitting attacks, she hadn't gotten five hours' sleep in a row, either.

The remaining leaders of the S-Force—John, Peg, Triadon, and Melador—had been pushed to the limit leading the skeleton forces of resistance. Although the enemy had lost heavy numbers in their attack on the Citadel of Silence, so had the good guys. And the ruthlessness that had characterized the Deviants' latest attacks had demoralized both Argonian civilians and the S-Forcers as well.

"They're really playing dirty," John whispered as he watched a pair of medics strap a screaming woman to a skygoing stretcher.

"Yeah," Peg said, deadpan. "It was never like this in the comics."

Stung, John swung to glare at her. "So we just let them rape and pillage their way through the planet?"

"No," Peg admitted. She turned away, replacing her helmet and flying away from the scene of devastation.

John heard her final words over his radio. "It's just that I was at this restaurant once. Mike took me."

Before she was even out of sight, John's radio was beeping with news of a new disaster. With a tired sigh, John bent to retrieve his helmet. He wished Harry were still on Argon. For one thing, he needed advice. Even more, he needed a head of intelligence. Still worse, he needed a head of counterintelligence. It seemed that the enemy knew what the S-Force was doing nowadays even before the S-Force knew it was doing it.

If only there were some way to get at the top of the Deviant organization . . .

"As you see, this will let us get at the very top of the S-Force's organization." The high council of surviving Deviant leaders stared from the holographic plan laid out before them to the icily beautiful blonde providing narration. Unlike most of them, she didn't wear Argonian armor, appearing for the briefing in extremely skimpy civilian wear instead.

She saw the ultimate leader giving her the once-over, and gave him a cold smile. "You must forgive my attire, Scaladon. After this meeting, I have a rendezvous with our mole inside the S-Force. If my plan meets with approval, I'll program him for appropriate action." She gestured to the bandoleers of tiny darts which crossed her breasts. "The chemical preparations have already been made."

"As ever, Matavi, a cogent presentation," Scaladon said, inclining his helmet. "One can see why you were renowned in the field of corporate espionage. However, your proposed plan would severely strain our limited resources."

He turned to glance at the other leaders. "Our robot-assembly capacity is extremely limited now, not to mention our manpower. And you would have us expose the results of our psionics research—no matter how much your own powers were helpful to us—"

Matavi approached the table of leaders, leaning forward to convince them—and as a further sweetener, giving them an eyeful. "A large investment, yes, but think of the dividends! Success here could well neutralize the most powerful asset the S-Force now possesses . . . John Cameron!"

At the end of the table, a lightly armored figure stirred. Emsisdin was not the most powerful gang leader in the Deviant pecking order, but he had the single most potent weapon in their surviving armory—the force cannon.

"I believe Matavi's plan is feasible," he said, a cocky grin on his half-exposed face.

"And necessary, since you failed during the attack on the Citadel of Silence," Scaladon pointed out.

"I destroyed one of their leaders," Emsisdin said defensively. "Besides, did you really want me to kill the one who operates the gateway to the Sphere of Exile? I thought the idea was to put him in our power."

He leaned forward. "And this will accomplish that end. I believe enough in Matavi's plan to volunteer my services."

"Another important asset put at risk," Scaladon grumbled.

"Consider it insurance," Emsisdin responded. "Under my command—"

Matavi whipped around. "*I* will command!"

Emsisdin shrugged. "With our joint efforts, success is inevitable."

Peg Faber stared at the holographic image floating above the recording box. The beautifully sculpted blond face reminded her vaguely of Leslie Ann Nasotrudere. But the earthly newswoman had never allowed such a look of terror on her face.

"I've followed your adventures on 3-D, and feel you're the member of the S-Force who might listen to me. I run an ortho-farm to the southeast of Kemot. It's a large place, mostly mechanized. But lately, I've noticed . . . anomalies. Air traffic has risen tremendously. I've seen lights at night in far parts of the farm. A shipment of chemicals arrived that I'd never ordered—later, on the news, I learned that these chemicals, when mixed, create a high-explosive potential. Such chemicals were used in the destruction of that restaurant."

The young blond woman shook her head. "You may think me foolishly fearful, but I've noticed odd screen patterns on my communicator. We had a problem here years ago with someone who tapped into transmissions. The same sort of patterns appeared on the screens then, so I decided to send you this recording instead of calling your information line." She looked downward for a moment, then up again, trying to control her worry. "Perhaps it's nothing, but when I heard the Deviants had been driven underground, I—well, wondered if they might truly have gone *under ground*. Perhaps at your leisure you could investigate."

She proceeded to give coordinates, and the holographic recording ended.

Peg glanced up at Melador. "This tape came in two hours ago?"

The head technician nodded. "It was addressed directly to you—I don't think you've ever received any other messages."

"I guess Argonian culture is a little too civilized for fan mail."

The Argonian's bland features showed puzzlement. Peg realized the translation device must have hit a glitch. "On my world people sometimes attempt to show too high a regard for public figures they admire. Sometimes, they even expect to have personal relationships with these public figures. It can become annoying."

"Ah." Melador seemed to find the whole idea distasteful. He gestured at the recording. "What shall we do about this?"

She shrugged, three blinks away from exhausted sleep. "Let's file it under future investigations—when we have time."

There the matter would have stayed, except that a few days later, after a hellish work shift trying to find a guerrilla sniper, Melador wakened Peg from a catnap to come to the communicator bank.

There were odd interference patterns on the screen, and the same blond woman now looking totally terrified. "Something is happening. Platforms have been landing in the farther fields, and some sort of loading process is going on. Please send—"

Something smashed in the distance. The young woman turned and screamed.

Then the screen went blank.

Peg whipped round to Melador. "We've got to field a squad immediately."

He looked distinctly unhappy. "We can't. Our Kemot squad was called for backup against the flyby shootings in Kaldoa. Even our reserve here has been deployed."

"*Somebody's* got to go," Peg said, trying to press back her guilt at not responding earlier. "Call John in Kaldoa, and ask him to send a squad—what were those coordinates?"

Melador provided them from his files. "If you can wait, I'll try to rouse some of the off duty people."

She shook her head decisively. "I'll go and check things out. Send them after me."

Moments later, she was fully armored and flying for the coordinates she'd recorded. Peg had paid little attention to the land between the spire-cities. Who'd have thought a super-science world like Argon would have a farm lifestyle?

She arrived at a set of vast fields tended by robots. There was a little domelike structure in the middle of the farm complex, shaded by a copse of what looked like cherry trees.

Not trusting the radio link, Peg cast out a mental link to John. A moment later, she felt his presence.

I've arrived at the farm, she reported.

Bafflement flowed over their connection. *What farm?* John asked.

Didn't Melador contact you? I guess he must have scraped up a reaction force at the Citadel.

She quickly passed on the report of possible Deviant activity, feeling John's mood darken deeper.

I'm on my way, John sent. *Don't walk into that place alone.*

The girl who called us might be in trouble, Peg responded.

At least be careful, John begged. *We've had too many ambushes lately.*

Flying low to the ground, Peg circled the periphery of the farm, extending mental probes. There didn't seem to be any human traces . . . no. Wait—that was an unconscious mind!

She rose higher into the air, spotting the still, half-armored form lying near the dome, half-hidden by the cherry trees. Peg made a snap decision and arrowed straight down.

She was ten feet above the body when the cherry trees came to unnatural life, whipping branches around her with inhuman speed. In seconds, she was imprisoned. Peg curled her fingers into the tridigirector, trying to cut herself free.

Even as her blasters activated, an odd sparkle shimmered through the too-supple branches that pinioned her. Peg's suit suddenly went dead, including the radio. And when she tried to send a mental S.O.S., a cloud of psionic static surrounded her head, muffling her transmission.

Peg's shock began to dissolve into fear. She saw figures moving on the ground below her, human figures besides the now not-unconscious body. But when she tried to probe them, her thought-tendrils encountered a seamless shield.

John! she called again desperately, to no avail.

Peg marshaled all her strength, calling to mind the incredible sense of oneness she'd felt with John during their lovemaking.

TROUBLEJOHNHELPME! The message was brief and, she hoped, powerful enough to get through.

The formerly unconscious figure rose gracefully to its feet. Peg found herself looking down at the classically beautiful face of the girl who'd called her here.

She has a surprisingly powerful mind, Peg caught the snatch of thought from her captor's mind. She stared, frozen in surprise within her dead armor. That woman had telepathic powers!

The female in half-armor called orders in Argonian, orders Peg couldn't understand because her translator was as dead as the rest of the circuitry in her armor.

Then the blond woman climbed into the tree, accompanied by another Argonian—one wearing

S-Force armor. As they reached her, the blonde's companion removed his helmet to reveal the bland, gloating features of Melador, his brow surrounded by what appeared to be a band of aluminum foil.

"You'll be able to understand us now," he sneered. "I've equipped this suit with a translator."

"Were you impressed by our capture trees?" the blonde asked. "Rather expensive, specialized robots. The branch/tentacles are also equipped with the circuitry from your S-Force nullifier nets. You're quite helpless."

The blonde undid the catches on Peg's helmet and removed it. Peg stared up at her as the woman reached into a utility pouch on her armor and came out with something that looked like a cross between a dart and a miniature hypodermic needle.

Peg turned desperately to Melador. "Why are you doing this?" She stared at her erstwhile comrade with wide eyes. "I thought this was your fight!"

"I, too, thought it was my fight—at first," Melador snarled. "But if it was, why did we have to bring in a bunch of alien barbarians to take our part? Triadon even let himself be bossed by you—*you*, who don't know a doohickey from a Framistat!"

Even through the psychic muffling, Peg felt his contempt. She drove desperate tendrils of thought toward Melador, trying to get some taste of his mind. "I've scanned you for security dozens of times. This isn't—"

"Deep conditioning," the blonde—Matavi, Peg got the name from Melador—explained. "And, of course, a little mind control." She frowned, obviously aware of Peg's frantic mental activity.

Peg was trying with all her might to pierce the shield around Melador's mind, attempting her own brand of mind control. She scrabbled at the psionic defenses around his mind. If she could get control, even for a second, get him to cut her free . . .

Matavi jabbed the dart into Peg's neck.

"Nooo!" Peg slurred as her whole body seemed to go inert.

"Get the platform. As soon as I slip this on her, we'll be ready to go. I'm not so sure she didn't get a message off, despite my blocking." Matavi slipped the foil circlet over Peg's forehead. "It will be—interesting—to experiment on this one."

The brow-band was in place, and for the first time since she'd Rifted to the giants' world, Peg Faber was totally alone in her head, psionically deaf, dumb, and blind.

Doubtless it would have been most distressing for her, if the blackness hadn't swallowed her up.

If John had been a few minutes later, the abduction crew might well have made its getaway. But he'd redlined his suit's gizmoidal drive all the way from Kaldoa, swooping down just in time to see a crowd of Argonians releasing Peg from a tree whose branches were strangely wrapped around her.

John took quick stock of the situation. Peg was unconscious, and all but one of the Argonians was invisible to his mental scans. The remaining Argonian, a female, had fairly powerful shields, which opened as she tried to disable him with a rapier thrust of mental energy.

He deflected it with his own psionic shields, raising his hands in the tridigirector to blast the cargo platform onto which the Deviants were about to dump Peg.

Another figure appeared from behind the vehicle, toting the silvery bulk of the force cannon. John had to go into wild aerobatics as he avoided blaster bolts, the force cannon at its widest bore, and psionic thrusts.

One of them would find him soon . . .

It was the force cannon. Its blast caught John, sending him into a tailspin, half the circuitry in his suit ruined, his helmet just . . . gone, a steady, sticky flow of blood making its way down his face.

The blond telepath down there leapt through his remaining defenses, determined to seize his mind. John got angry. In a hurricane of rage, he spewed her out of his mind, then tore right through her defenses to assail her psyche.

She collapsed like a stone, unconscious.

John knew his gizmoidal drive was failing. He didn't understand the circuitry well enough to stop his downward spiral. But he knew there was another way, a possibility. He reached out mentally, attempting something he'd tried on other occasions, but on a much smaller scale.

Psychokinesis could be used to tear things, like the time he'd disabled the robot that attacked Peg by ripping apart its circuits. But it could also be used as a push, to brake his fall.

He landed hard, but it was ten-foot drop hard as opposed to a ten-*story* drop. Even so, he lay like a man dead, his head pounding with the terrible effort he'd had to put out.

"You've killed him!" a furious voice yelled. A familiar voice, John realized. It was Melador.

"The mistress said we were to capture the girl and use her as a hostage." The Argonian stood with Peg's inert body in his arms. Now he aimed one of his wrist projectors at the side of her head, his fingers curling into the tridigirector. "No need for her now."

John didn't know where he found the strength. One moment, he was helpless on the ground. The next, he was upright, his mind reaching out to the invisible shield that protected Melador's brain, coiling around the defenses, crushing inward against them. This was a mechanical shield, inflexible, unable to respond to different pressures. Given time, John could probably have wormed his way in.

But he didn't have time. The brute strength approach was needed. John found a weak spot and loosed an eruption of unrestrained mental force, in full knowledge that doing so would fry Melador's brains.

The programmed traitor stiffened, his hand splayed, and he fell dead, Peg landing atop him.

For a few brief seconds, the other Deviant footsoldiers debated between firing at John and grabbing Peg as a hostage. John didn't hesitate. With greater and greater surety, John smashed through their defenses until all eight of the underlings were dead.

The Deviant with the force cannon made quite a different decision. He bundled the unconscious Matavi aboard the still-functioning flight platform and burned gizmo getting out of there.

John considered hurling a mental attack after them, but he no longer had the strength of emotion to power himself. Slowly, he fumbled his way out of half-dead armor and carried Peg away from the midst of the nine sprawled bodies. He'd always be glad she was unconscious for those terrible moments.

John found a dome-shaped construction nearby, the Argonian equivalent of a farmhouse. The door was open, and the communicator inside worked. John contacted the Citadel to get help. The mobile reserve had returned, and would be on its way in seconds.

Then, after leaving Peg on a floating sofa, he walked outside, back to the dead. He hated what he was about to do, but he had to do it.

John took one of the dead Deviants, propped him up, and extended the corpse's arm to point at Melador's head. Forcing a probe into the still-warm nervous system, John triggered neurons.

The hand he held twitched, formed the tridigirector, and the blaster erased the manner of Melador's death.

John's face seemed older as he left the steaming remains. What Argon needed now was heroes—living or dead—and he'd just provided another for the pantheon.

Chapter Seventeen

"I'd say the Lessers in California think much more of their pleasures than the little people here in New York," Victor told the group sitting around the campfire at Heroes' Manor. "They even heat the water in their swimming places."

All evening since his return, he'd been telling tales and answering questions about his visit to exotic California.

"What was this *acting* like?" one of the males, a handsome young fellow named Andrew, wanted to know.

"Mainly make-believe," Victor admitted with a small grimace. He'd acted in a couple of scenes as himself, but it hadn't taken him long to realize that most of his work was as a stunt double and stand-in for Robert.

The leader of the giants had flown off in the Heroplane soon after Victor had landed, going to California to film his scenes. Robert's absence allowed Victor to feel at ease and speak freely around the campfire. "Much of it was boring. They record the action scene by scene, and much time is wasted as they set these scenes up. Also, they don't 'shoot'— that's what they call it—the scenes in order." He shrugged. "I'm still not quite sure what the whole story is about."

"Did you really have to take orders from the Lessers?" another male asked.

"It was more like taking advice," Victor said. "The Lesser in charge—he's called the director—would take us aside and discuss the scene. He was most respectful, but that was his normal manner of working. I saw him act the same way with the Lesser stars."

"Stars?" a busty brunette named Penelope asked the question. Since she was a beauty who'd never paid much attention to Victor, he began to see why movie acting might be the goal of many Lessers.

"Some of the Lessers who regularly act in films have followings. Using the right *star* can result in what the Lessers call 'big box office'—much money and great success for the film."

"Among Lessers," a voice at the edge of the group noted.

"The stories *can* be interesting," Victor explained. "There was an outdoor theater showing films not too far from where we were living. I saw several different stories. Some, to be honest, I didn't understand. Others were quite exciting."

"It sounds as if you enjoyed this faraway California place," one of the giantesses said a little jealously.

"It's warmer than here, and very much different," Victor admitted. "But the Lessers have the same preoccupations. Money. Crime." He smiled. "One could easily become a hero out there."

He pointed to the pile of complimentary Fantasy Factory comic books they were using as kindling. "Have you actually read any of these? The make-believe heroes in the stories live in many different cities all over this domain. It's not such a bad idea."

Anything, he thought, to get out from under the thumb of Robert and the heavy-handed Thomas.

Victor sensed silent agreement around the campfire. "I for one," he said, "wouldn't mind taking on L.A."

"Ell-ay?" Penelope asked.

"That's what the natives call the largest city out there," Victor told her with a smile. "They seem to think it's the most important part of this whole land. For instance, because there's another great water out there, they call where they live 'The Coast,' as if it were the only coast."

Penelope shuddered a little. "These wild Lessers," she complained, "make no sense at all. The sooner we bring them to heel, the better."

* * *

"G-good morning, Mr. Sturdley." Wendy Wentworth glanced timorously over the screen of her word processor.

It had taken her a while to understand that the old coot she'd treated so badly was actually the big boss at the Fantasy Factory. Now she was terrified that she was out of a job.

She wasn't, but Harry wasn't about to tell her so.

Marty Burke could keep his little office playmate. Harry didn't want anyone handling his private phones and correspondence whose first loyalty was to Burke.

Harry had thought very hard about the Burke problem since announcing himself. He'd even done his best to help Marty the Genius save face. Today, after more than a week back, he was finally reclaiming his office. He'd discussed it with Burke, figuring that was more than enough time.

Burke would be moving to an empty office down the hall, a space kept for occasional visitors from the Fantasy Factory's London operation. It wasn't on executive row, but Marty now rejoiced in the resounding if meaningless title of "Editorial/Artistic Consultant." And, of course, he was the only writer/artist who had a secretary, the bounteous Wendy. That far Harry was willing to go in hopes of assuring some peace in the workplace. He rubbed his hands together as he headed for the office door. Now it was time to start kicking some butt.

Harry turned back to the secretary, his hand on the doorknob. "Is Mr. Burke in already?"

She shook her head. "He called and said he had a dental appointment."

Sturdley nodded. Burke would probably enjoy root canal more than seeing Harry back in place. "You know where Burke's new office is, don't you?"

Big blue eyes got wider, and her pink mouth made a little O. "Marty—I mean, Mr. Burke—told me to stay here and help out till you got a new assistant."

"I've got one of the kids ready to fill in, Wendy. You can go—what the hell?"

Harry had finally taken a look inside the office. His usually immaculate desk was overrun with what looked like a diorama of toys, four large action figures surrounded by a sea of knee-high people.

He began to distinguish likenesses as he came closer. The giants were quite recognizably Robert, Barbara, Thomas, and Ruth, all clad in shiny white spandex. They were a foot tall, while the smaller dolls were about a third their size.

Harry picked up one. It appeared to be made of clear blue plastic, with white bones inside—Skeletone. Harry frowned. The toy's face bore an uncanny resemblance to Jeff Goldblum. And here was Madam Vile, in a considerably more modest costume than she wore in the comics. Of course, when a character is drawn, you don't have to worry about such practicalities as how a costume would be kept on—or *up*, in the case of most female characters.

Sturdley now knew what these were. They had to be prototype action figures from the Heroes movie. His face tightened. Burke had left them here to rub in his success—and also to make the point about mixing the real-life Heroes with the Fantasy Factory's fictional villains.

Stepping behind the desk, Harry grabbed the wastepaper basket. He swept his arm across the table, batting the figures into the trashcan.

"Sir?" a nervous voice came from the entrance to the office.

"I'm glad you haven't left yet," Harry said, walking over and depositing the basket in her arms. "It seems that Marty was playing with his toys and forgot to take them."

Wendy nodded, hugging the wastebasket to her ample chest. "There are a bunch of guys from the mailroom—"

Beyond the girl, Sturdley heard a voice mutter a little too loudly, "Burke may be a bastard, but he's a real connoisseur of ass."

As he watched Wendy turn bright red, Harry realized things had really slipped around the office. He stalked to the doorway and stepped outside. "I don't know which of you garbagemouths just said that," he announced pointedly, scanning some very embarrassed faces with angry eyes. "But I'm sure all of you will have a bit more respect for this office—and the people who work here—in the future."

Wendy fled, and a very chastened group of mailroom types carried in the boxes of personal stuff Harry wanted back in his office.

"Sorry, Mr. S." Tony, the head mail guy, brought up the tail of the line, carrying the biggest box. "I shouldda been on the guys about their mouths long before this."

But Burke could care less, Harry thought, so why bother?

Tony hefted the extremely well-wrapped package. "Jeeze, what have you got in here, a suit of armor?" As he put the box down, it clanked loudly.

Sturdley smiled. "Exactly, Tony. I thought a suit of armor over in the corner would be a nice touch. Sort of 'A man's office is his castle.' What do you think?"

Tony laughed. "That might be a good idea. You could wear it to staff meetings."

Still chuckling, he stopped in the doorway. "Oh. You want me to leave some of the guys to help you unload?"

Harry shook his head. "Nah. I'd like to handle it myself."

As soon as the door closed, Harry set to work opening the box Tony had brought in. It did contain armor—Harry's Argonian flying suit. He quickly assembled the pieces and hid the armor in his coat closet.

He stared at the suit, silver-gray and white, with its slightly squiggly psychedelic blue S blazoned on the yellow shield. Just having it here made him feel safer, although he wouldn't have much time to get into the suit if an unfriendly giant hand came through the window.

Harry sighed and headed to the desk for a scratch pad. At the top of his "to do" list he added getting a lock for the closet door.

Marty Burke had no dental appointment that day, it was merely an excuse to come in late. He was now seated in the coffee shop across the street from the Fantasy Factory's offices, gathering his forces.

Burke took a sip of coffee and ran his napkin across his mouth, thinking a little belatedly that a jelly donut is not the thing to eat when you're plotting. He inconspicuously tried to brush powdered sugar off his chest while listening to Thad Westmoreland speak.

"So the board of directors rolled right over as soon as Sturdley came back? That's some thanks for lining up this movie deal." Thad leaned across the table. "How about the giants? If Robert backed you up—"

"I called Heroes' Manor. They told me Robert had flown to the coast to take care of his part in the movie. But when I called Silikis's people—waking them up, I might add—they said Robert wasn't expected till tomorrow."

"So you don't know where he is."

"Wherever he is, I guess it's not near a phone." Burke stared down at the tabletop. "Besides, if we're really going to stick it to Sturdley, we'll have to pick fights we can win. We've got to reorganize."

Westmoreland shook his head, a frown on his thin face. "That's easier said than done, Marty. You stepped on a lot of guys' toes while you were running things."

"I did what had to be done," Burke said. "Do you think the artists—especially the young guys—are going to be any happier under Sturdley?"

"Maybe not," Westmoreland said. "But I don't think you realize just how much you sounded like Sturdley sometimes."

* * *

"Why are we going out for coffee?" Zeb Grantfield asked as Kyle Everard steered him into the coffee shop. "We never go out for—oh."

A flush came to the artist's acne-scarred face as he saw who was sitting at the table.

"Sit down, Zeb," Marty Burke invited.

To Grantfield's eyes, Burke looked a little wired. That could be from the situation he found himself in, or maybe it was just from too many cups of coffee while he sat here talking with people. Grantfield did notice that Burke's trademark black suit had little white flecks all over it today. Dandruff?

Burke waited for Grantfield to sit, and then began what had become a standardized pitch. "I'm sure as an artist you can't be delighted to see Harry Sturdley back running things at the Fantasy Factory."

Grantfield shrugged. "Well so far, Sturdley hasn't tried to ration illustration board—or told me I was getting too tired to work on *Jumboy*."

"We've had our differences, Zeb—I'll be the first to admit that. But we're *artists*. What does Sturdley know about art?"

"Just what he's picked up in thirty years of publishing it," Grantfield said.

"Think back, Zeb. Think back to what things were like when Sturdley was running the show. Are you sure you want to go back to that?"

Grantfield kept a poker face, nodding at Burke's spiel. He may not have been a hundred percent happy with the Sturdley regime, but he hadn't noticed any particular improvement with Burke in charge. The fact was, Sturdley ran a tighter ship.

"So what do you want, Burke?" he finally asked.

Burke gave him an "1 like a man who's straight to the point" smile. "Just because Sturdley is back doesn't mean I'm going to stop fighting for what's best for the company."

"I'm sure you'll do a great job as Wartist Consultant," Grantfield told him.

Burke's face puckered. "Wartist?"

Grantfield shrugged. "Just a contraction for 'writer/artist.'"

"Well, if I'm going to succeed in helping the company, I'll need your assistance."

"Well, if it's for the company," Grantfield said, standing up.

"Thanks, Zeb."

Grantfield bought a cup of coffee to go and crossed the street. All the way up in the elevator he frowned, deep in thought.

When he arrived at the Fantasy Factory's floor, he headed straight for executive row. Burke's bimbo was still sitting outside Sturdley's office. She looked up in surprise.

"I've got to see the big guy," Grantfield said. "Now."

Harry stood in the middle of his office, a frown on his face. He'd made it his own again, but he wasn't happy about some of the stuff that was missing.

If Burke thought he could glom onto that autographed Rodent art, he had another think coming. That wasn't just a collector's item, it was a treasured memento. He and Rip Jacoby had signed the sketch of their creation thirty years ago, celebrating the height of a rare collaboration. The sketch was a piece of their lives, not an investment for Burke's old age fund.

Harry glanced unhappily at his desk. And where was the file of reports from that private investigator, Quentin Farley? They weren't in the file drawer, they weren't under the file drawer, and they hadn't been sent to Myra.

So who had them, and what were they doing with them?

Harry would have worried some more, but at that moment his intercom buzzed.

* * *

Maybe I've been hanging around the edges of comics too much, Leslie Ann Nasotrudere told herself. A store with the name Harvey's Survival World doesn't seem so weird.

Since finding the Farley file in Sturdley's office, her news-woman's antennae had been sensitized for anything giant-related. When she'd returned to work, her face healed, she'd pounced on the clipping that came across her desk.

It was from a local Rockland paper, with a headline reading "GIANT APPETITES?" The story was an inter-view with Harvey Bentziger, proprietor of Harvey's Sur-vival World, relating how he'd gotten an order for tons of freeze-dried and irradiated foodstuffs . . . and been paid with a check from the Heroes' account.

Leslie Ann had expected to find Harvey's Survival World in a rural setting—maybe a log cabin. Instead, she found her-self parking her car in front of a failed strip mall, the stores all knocked together into Harvey's survivalist emporium.

Bentziger himself was a surprisingly pudgy man for a would-be Rambo. "Where are the cameras?" he said, looking slightly disappointed in a camouflage suit that pulled across his waist.

"This is just a preliminary interview," Leslie Ann assured him. She was working alone on this story until it came time to hit up the network brass. Because some-where in this giant thing, she was sure, lurked that Pulitzer Prize she lusted after.

Still, Harvey proudly gave her a tour of the place, showing off racks of shotguns, camping gear, and high-tech, low-maintenance food that would be necessary after the fall of civilization.

"What gave you the idea that the food order was going to the giants—aside from the size of it?" Leslie Ann asked.

Bentziger shrugged. "Kinda hard to miss. The check came from the Fantasy Factory—it even had a little drawing of that Robert guy on it. Look, I even took a copy of it."

Leslie Ann frowned at the photocopy. "Can you get me another one of these?"

"Sure, I'll zox it right up."

Following him to a tiny, but well-stocked office, she asked, "Where did you send all the food?"

Bentziger glanced back from the copier. "Survivalist country," he told her. "Somewhere out in Idaho—I'll copy up the bill of lading, too."

The distortions caused by the intrusion of the higher-order dimensions extended across the Earth-nexus, both the macro-universe . . . and the micro-universe . . .

Once, Huang Dingbang had been a professor of theoretical physics at the University of Peking. Then had come Tienamen Square, and now Dr. Huang was a digger of holes in the Gobi Desert—holes used for underground testing of nuclear bombs.

Thus, the dirty-nailed, raggedly-dressed professor was somewhat surprised to be called before the officers running the latest test.

"Huang, you are a physicist," the heavy-jowled general behind the desk said.

Huang nodded.

"We need a physicist."

Huang looked at the group in white coats behind the officer. "With respect, Comrade General, you seem to have a number of them."

"An *expendable* physicist, Huang." The general looked a little hangdog. "Our bomb—it did not detonate."

Huang nodded. "It has been known to happen sometimes, Comrade General. An incomplete fission reaction—instead of an explosion, there is merely a localized shower of radiation."

"Our detectors have sensed no radiation, but they may have been damaged," the general said. He looked at Huang. "Which is why we are sending a human observer—a physicist—an expendable physicist."

Heading down the dark tunnel in a protective suit, Huang almost laughed to himself. This was the most freedom he'd been allowed in years—going to poke around in a possibly misfired atomic bomb.

The geiger counter in his hand didn't emit a single chatter as he approached what was supposed to have been ground zero. So it wasn't a misfire. Huang reached the housing, examined the warhead, pursed his lips in disbelief—and got out of there very quickly.

"Comrade General," he reported, "the two pieces of plutonium have indeed been slammed together. Critical mass was achieved."

The officer backed away. "And the radiation?"

Huang shrugged and pointed to his geiger counter. "None detected."

"Then why was there no explosion?" the general burst out.

"There are some exotic theories in quantum physics that would explain, in certain instances, how fission might not—for want of a better word—fizz." Huang frowned. "But it has never happened before. This is most anomalous."

"What do you suggest we do with this bomb?" the general asked. His tame physicists muttered nervously among themselves.

"Comrade General, the device down there could be described as a cocked revolver with a hair trigger. If you send people down there to move or unload it, the weapon may explode."

"Then what shall I do?" the general demanded.

"I'd leave it there," Huang said. "Perhaps we can study it . . . or perhaps it will go off in its own time."

"In its own time," the general echoed. He turned to the head of the official physics delegation. "Is this so?"

The scientist dithered in his white lab coat. "Possibly," he offered. "B-but we should remember, the other nine test shots went off perfectly."

"Ninety percent effectiveness," the general frowned and clenched his fingers. Coming to a decision, he fixed all in the room with a fierce glare. "This is a classified matter," he declared. "If *we* cannot be sure of our deterrent, we want no one else having doubts about it."

A week later, China declared a unilateral moratorium on nuclear testing.

Chapter Eighteen

The tractor-trailer had an open bed, edged with wooden stakes. There was also, despite the owner's assurances to the contrary, the faint smell of animal manure wafting from the floorboards. Robert had not plumbed the man's mind for the truth of the matter. Some things were better not known. Besides, this had been the only available vehicle that could accommodate his size when he had diverted the 747 to the Idaho airport.

The flight was supposed to bring him directly to California, and all through his time in the air, he'd studied the script for the movie he was to participate in. But the film people were actually expecting him the following day. Robert had carefully scheduled the time for this side journey to visit what he considered his promised land. After giving the driver a map and detailed instructions, he'd arranged himself in the spartan accommodations of the open truck and set off.

They had driven through a chill upland night, the coldest Robert had encountered since coming to this world. It reminded him of wintertime back home, a season to adjust one's aura to hold more heat against bare skin. Moving deeper into the mountains, he settled back, reveling in the magnificence of the night sky—so many of the stars were hidden by city lights, even in the giants' haven in Westchester. At last the sun rose, painting the hills with rosy splendor. Robert gazed with pleasure across the wide, grassy lands. His agents had done well. Here he could bring all his people to escape the nuclear doom he was planning. Sheltered and supplied, they would survive, to sally forth and domesticate the technologically and numerically reduced Lessers.

Now Robert looked forward to inspecting the progress in constructing the living and storage facilities of his survival compound—this place which the Lessers called the old Judson ranch.

Argonians had no organized religion, but they took their memorial services seriously—especially, it seemed, memorials for war dead. John cast a worried glance over the huge crowd in the amphitheater. This would be a prime target for a Deviant bomb—although their attacks had been petering out lately.

John's eyes then went over to Peg. If he'd had a choice, neither of them would be here. But because of their positions in the S-Force, they had to attend. Two of the honored fallen were Mike and Melador. In fact, the heroes from Earth had to give eulogies.

There was his cue. He rose to the podium, trying to ignore the thousands of eyes and the lenses of the 3-D cameras. "I only knew Melador a relatively short amount of time," he began. "But they were tumultuous times for Argon—nothing less than a new Age of Strife for this world. And in that strife, he distinguished himself as a defender—and a leader."

John felt an all-too-familiar hardness coming over his face. Probably the better to hide the lies he was about to tell, of the brave death the traitor had suffered. Not only

had John killed Melador, now he was called upon to fab-
ricate a myth to go with it. If his voice became strained,
he could only hope that it would be taken as a sign of
emotion.

He marched through the speech and somehow finished
it. That was the easy part. Now he'd have to listen to Peg
talk about Mike. She stepped past him on her way to the
podium, her face as pale as if she were about to be shot.
Peg hated crowds and speechmaking, but she'd agreed to
honor Mike's memory.

"You—" her voice cracked, and she looked down for a
second. "You know Mike as the alien, the barbarian with
the short name, the hero. I knew him from his humble
beginnings. He was a slave, you know. But he loved freedom enough to risk his life for me . . . and, here on Argon,
for you. As we all know, he lost his life saving John and
myself—"

Her gray eyes held steady on the crowd, even as tears
slowly flowed down her cheeks. "But it was for Argon, a
world that had given him a home, knowledge he'd never
have hoped to achieve, a life beyond any he'd have imagined. He had everything he'd always wanted—" Her
voice broke here, and she turned a little away from John,
who stood rigidly behind her. "Well, almost everything."

John wanted to reach out to her, but couldn't. It would
be like a desecration of what she was saying—words from
her heart, as opposed to his speech. In the weeks since the
battle at the Citadel, he'd tried not to think of the competition that had run between himself and Mike. He'd
wanted Peg for herself, not as a prize. Now the backlash
of guilt came. Mike, S-Forcers like that tech Moradel,
thousands of civilians, all would be alive if he had never
come to this planet. Not to mention the ever-growing

score of Deviants who had died by his own hand—the guy who'd fallen to his death, the one whose head he'd blown away, the victims of his berserk rage at the Citadel hangar, the footsoldiers who'd died at the farm—even Melador.

The muscles in his face tightened so hard, they ached.

When his suit radio suddenly came to life with reports of a Deviant attack on the outskirts of the city, it was like a reprieve. He left his place silently, beckoning several guards to come with him.

Better to face the blasters of the enemy than the words of his lover—or his own thoughts.

* * *

Hefting his rifle in his left hand, Elmo Forte used his right to push upward on the strand of barbed wire strung between the wooden posts. The old Judson place had gone to ruin lately, but Matt Judson always maintained good fences.

Old Matt had posted his place against trespassers and hunters, but Elmo paid little mind to that. Matt had been his friend, and had always let Elmo do a little shooting on his land. Judson was gone—the only land he owned now was a plot in the Elk Pass cemetery. The ranch had been sold, but stood empty except for some sort of construction project the new owners had going near the road. They weren't even leasing the grazing rights.

It's not like I'm hurting anything, Elmo thought as he trudged down a grassy hill in the predawn murk. There were a couple of snug, tree-filled valleys in the Judson place. With luck, Elmo would bag himself a deer.

He had followed a creek to a copse of woodland and was down on one knee, trying to make sense of some mighty odd-looking tracks, when he heard the splashing of water.

Figuring something mighty big had to be crossing the creek, Elmo brought up his rifle and began sneaking through the underbrush. It cleared quicker than he expected, and Elmo found himself face to face with a giant naked fella—with the emphasis on *giant*.

Even though the stranger was down on his knees in the creek water, he stretched more than twice Elmo's height of six-foot-one.

One look, and Elmo did what most every local boy would have done. He threw that hunting rifle to his shoulder and fired. As a member in good standing of the NRA, Elmo didn't believe in hunting with a single-shot gun. He had a full magazine, and he emptied it as fast as he could pull the trigger.

At the first blast, Robert rose from the stream where he was washing himself, leapt to his feet, and stepped back.

Fool, he chided himself. You were so sure the land was empty you failed to scan for intruders. Heavy bullets impacted against his aura, staggering him slightly as they bled their kinetic energy into the mental force-field that surrounded his body.

He stepped into the water again, heading for the figure frozen on the far bank clad in the speckled clothing called camouflage. Seen in the urban environment, he hadn't truly perceived its usefulness.

The interloper stood his ground, still trying to operate the now-depleted weapon. It wasn't courage, Robert knew, but a sort of aggressive panic.

A heavy fist rose almost of its own accord to bludgeon the little man down, the unconscious response of a Master to such temerity in a Lesser.

But second thoughts made Robert stay his hand. Elk Pass wasn't a large city, where dead bodies were an everyday occurrence. Questions would be raised, investigations started, unwelcome attention directed to what he was doing here.

No, another course would have to be taken.

Robert extended psionic probes into the intruder's brain, seizing control of the motor area, freezing the Lesser in place. The man—a hunter, Robert ascertained from the uppermost thoughts—was now safely immobilized, and Robert could step back across the stream at his ease to recover his clothing.

Returning to loom over his captive, Robert then exercised his immaterial powers in some mental surgery. This was much more demanding and delicate than the Bindings he'd performed in Washington. He was editing memories, altering conceptions. In the end, Robert chose simply to erase the minutes since this Lesser—Elmo— had stumbled across him. They would simply have a new, nonthreatening encounter.

Moving as if in a dream, Elmo reentered the underbrush. Robert stepped back across the stream, then came forward, splashing in the water. Elmo emerged to stare, his eyes growing noticeably larger. "Holy—" the huntsman yelled.

The gun was still coming up as Robert inserted a calming impulse in Elmo's mind, even as he shaped his lips in a smile and waved.

"Sorry to surprise you," Robert said, taking his cues from Elmo's mind. "I know most everybody thinks this place is empty and is going to stay that way. Well, it's not. You're looking at the new owner."

"Y-You *own* this place?" Elmo asked in a voice still on the edge of panic.

Robert gave him a smile, a nod, and another impulse of calm. "Sure do. My name's Robert. Maybe you've seen me on TV."

"That giant fella in New York City? The *Hero?*" Elmo at last was calming down.

Robert nodded yet again. "The thing is, we aren't city people. We wanted someplace to get away, some . . . country. I'm sure you can understand that."

Better, he'd decided, to establish a Masterly presence here in a friendly way, with a story that this Lesser, at least, found plausible.

A little quiet manipulation, and Elmo was now apologizing." . . . know I shouldn't be on your land, but old Matt Judson used to let me hunt."

Robert went for the light touch, shaking an admonitory finger. "But the land *is* posted. I'd sure appreciate you spreading the word." His smile grew wider. "We don't want any other hunters picking on game that's too big for their size."

He stood at the verge of the woods, waving farewell to Elmo Forte, who was heading for the property line at a fast walk, slowed only by frequent backward glances. When the hunter was at last out of sight, Robert dropped his hand . . . and his smile.

This could have been an unfortunate encounter. When they established a regular presence here, his people would have to maintain a constant watch. And this acreage would require a considerably larger defense perimeter than the one they maintained at Heroes' Manor.

Andrew's morning swim seemed a casual enough exercise, a quick dip from the lakefront Westchester property known as Heroes' Manor. In fact, it was a regular precaution taken to protect the giants' enclave.

Every day, at random times, Masters went into the water, their routes taking them close to the far shore. As they swam past, they scanned potential observation points with their immaterial powers. Depending on what

they discovered, and, of course, the giants' individual personalities, action was taken.

Andrew, for instance, was usually amused by the teen-
agers, many of them girls, who collected on the shoreline
rocks with binoculars, bodywatching. He had early on,
however, been called upon to dissuade investigators
who'd set up a telescope for surveillance. Once he'd even
paid a threatening house call when the investigators
hired a bungalow for their spying.

Thomas, on the other hand, regularly chased all
voyeurs away.

Of late, Andrew's attention had been drawn to some
newcomers on the water's edge, partly by the strange language he detected in the bungalow, odd clothing, and the
general air of hate in the neighborhood.

To the people on the lakefront, the strangers were
known as "towelheads" who would blow up buildings in
the Lessers' cities. Several times, while he'd been swimming past, people would call out warnings and invective
about the foreigners.

Today he was aware of observation from the bungalow
itself.

Andrew swam to the shallows and rose from the water,
heading for a screened back porch where he'd detected
several men with binoculars. As he approached, the
screen door opened and a man in a dark suit and gleaming
white head scarf—*kaffiyeh,* he caught the term from the
man's mind—went to meet him.

"I represent my nation's government," the suit-clad
man said in accented English. "I am told that you have
powers to discover *which* nation from my very mind."

Andrew could and did.

"If you know something of this world's economics, you
may know that my homeland is very rich, and needs a

mighty protector. We have been hoping to make this proposition to your people, but your leader has not responded."

The Arab diplomat cleared his throat. "We wish one of your males to live in our country, lead our armed forces, and of course, protect the person of our Supreme Leader." He smiled ingratiatingly. "In return, we would make such a hero's life very, very . . . pleasant."

"Making such a proposal to some of my fellows could be very dangerous for you," Andrew said, poker-faced.

"And . . . making it to you?" The diplomat was unperturbed.

Andrew remembered Victor's words around the campfire, about the pleasures to be found in faraway places. And the domain making this offer was even farther away than California. Andrew considered the advantages of greater distance from Thomas's bullying, from Robert's demands.

Now he allowed himself a small smile. "We'd have much to discuss," he said. "What sort of . . . pleasures . . . can you offer?"

Could he persuade one of the women to leave with him? Andrew wondered.

The diplomat smiled back. "Where there is interest," he said, "there is room for negotiation."

Elk Pass boasted an old-fashioned general store in its tiny business district, and the store served as the meeting place for a number of local characters. So when Elmo Forte arrived with his announcement of a giant in the neighborhood, there was a ready-made audience.

Unfortunately for Elmo, the spectators were hostile.

"A giant, eh?" Anse Chandler scoffed. "With horns and fangs? Mebbe he's one of those 'Terminated' guys."

"Naw," Woodie Ledbetter put in, "I betcha he's a 'Alien.' Jump right out of your chest next."

When Ken Tillman stopped laughing, he said, "Mebbe a buncha rabbits ganged up on Elmo while he was drunk."

Poor Elmo tried his best to convince the local gentry that he'd been stone cold sober and recognized his giant as an East Coast celebrity.

"Oh, he's a *New York* giant?" Woodie chortled. "They seem to think a powerful lot of them out there, but t'me, they just play so-so football."

"New Yorkers are always blowing stuff up," Anse said. "Buildings, prices—giants too, I 'spect."

"This was *Robert,*" Elmo tried again. "The one who was on TV—with the *President.*"

"Yeah, well," Ken said, "I always thought that president of ours was a weasely little guy—you vote for him, Elmo? Did anybody here?"

"Right," Woodie chipped in. "Most anybody would look big beside him."

Elmo got so disgusted, he went to leave the store. He was quite surprised when the others joined him.

"Got nothin' better to do," Anse announced. "So we thought we'd go up the Judson place and do some giant huntin'."

Ken's pickup had a well-supplied gun rack, and by the time they reached the fence, the outing had taken on a definite party flavor, despite Elmo's warnings.

The boys had no problem slipping through the wire and finding Elmo's trail. They followed it to the copse of trees and the bank of the stream.

"Look at all this brass here," Ken said, kicking the cartridges still gleaming against the scrub grass. "What were ya shootin' at?"

Elmo frowned, his brow wrinkling in puzzlement. He checked his gun and found it empty. "I got no recollection of shootin' anything at all."

"He *was* drinking!" Woodie hooted. "What was it, Elmo? A little blackberry brandy to chase the chill away? You never could handle your likker."

He turned to his friends. "Boys, he didn't shoot ET. He shot at the DTs!"

No laughter greeted this sally, however. Anse and Ken were silent and a bit nervous. Elmo looked smug as they stood on the perimeter of a footprint lodged in the damp soil. The length of the print was half the height of any of the boys, and wider than their torsos.

"This ain't some silly joke, is it, Elmo?" Anse clutched his borrowed rifle tighter.

" 'Cause it ain't funny," Ken added.

That was the moment the huge shadow suddenly engulfed them.

Eight scared eyes stared up at Robert.

Then the general store gang showed an interesting quirk of human behavior—the difference between complete surprise and having an inkling of what one is in for. Coming on a giant unexpectedly and alone, Elmo had fired. After hearing about the giant from Elmo, the boys gaped, gasped . . . and ran like rabbits.

"They—they wouldn't believe me!" Elmo shouted in explanation. Then he, too, set off after his friends.

For the first time in weeks, Robert enjoyed a gust of unforced laughter as he watched the quartet fall all over themselves to get back to town—or perhaps to the next county.

He felt satisfied with the work—half the storage facilities were dug, some of them even with emergency supplies stowed. The living quarters needed additional labor. Although the builders had referred to the rooms as cavernous, Robert found them on the small side.

He'd almost been ready to leave when his mental picket line had been breached. Robert was still chuckling as he tramped off to the construction site and the waiting flatbed truck serving as his limousine.

Only when he arrived back at his plane was the shine taken off Robert's day. The airline had tracked its wayward jumbo jet, and passed on a message from the Fantasy Factory.

"Someone named *Burke* called the airline, trying to get in touch with you," the pilot reported, reading from a hastily-scratched note. "Apparently he wanted you to know that Sturdley was back at the Fantasy Factory."

The pilot, who didn't collect comics and merely flew where the airline sent him, glanced from the note to his giant passenger's face. Had the guys in the office screwed up in transmitting? Or was the message in code?

A nasty-edged rumble came from deep within Robert's throat. Obviously, those few words had meant something to the big guy.

"Arrange for takeoff as soon as possible. We're still heading to Los Angeles." Robert glanced at the pilot. "My mobile phone—can I operate it in midair?"

"The airline arranged for it to be patched into our system," the pilot responded. "One of the cabin crew will help you make the connection."

As they leveled off at their flight altitude, Robert was only too aware that he was speaking over an open line with witnesses nearby.

Still worse, his most trusted lieutenants were on the wrong side of the continent to deal with this emerging crisis. Sturdley's return meant that John Cameron was alive. The oddly-powered Lesser could still thwart everything Robert had planned.

Deep in thought, he punched a complicated pattern of codes into his giant mobile phone, finally getting Heroes' Manor. He asked for Victor.

"Robert," the blond giant said when he picked up the call. "You have a message from that Burke fellow. He says—"

"I'm aware of the message," Robert cut off his subordinate. No sense broadcasting any more information than necessary. "We must be glad for the—unexpected return, and can only hope there will be more."

Would Victor understand his elliptical reference?

"You mean Jo—"

Again, Robert cut him off. Definitely, there should be no names on the air. "Yes, the others. As you know, I've always been concerned about them." He carefully accented the word *concerned*.

The contingency plans they'd made would now become operational. "Of course," Victor replied. "We'll be—ah, waiting for news—very eagerly."

Victor understood at last. The Masters of Heroes' Manor would throw a psychic dragnet over as much of New York as their powers could cover.

"Let me know if you hear anything," Robert pressed.

"Oh, immediately."

Robert cut the connection. He hoped the aircrew wouldn't be too upset at the immediate turnaround when they arrived in Los Angeles. He'd have to send a dependable lieutenant to coordinate the search for the Rift manipulator. The best choice for that job was undoubtedly Thomas. It would be necessary to emphasize that the hunt be conducted discreetly.

Thomas was only to *find* John Cameron.

Robert would deal with him.

Chapter Nineteen

One by one, the general store cowboys sifted through the collection of pictures Leslie Ann Nasotrudere showed them. Each photo showed the portrait of a strong-featured, handsome man. Five were pictures of New York models. The sixth was a shot of Robert.

"That's him," Anse Chandler said, tapping Robert's photograph.

"Which?" Woodie Ledbetter glanced over, only to have Leslie Ann step in the way. "Look at your own pile," she ordered. "Is the picture of the giant you saw in there?"

One by one, Anse, Woodie, Ken, and Elmo all identified Robert. They stared a little dazzled at the INC. cameras focusing on them. Her back to the lenses, Leslie Ann had a tight smile on her face. When the Idaho local affiliate's story came into the International News Combine's offices this morning, the staffers had chuckled and dismissed it.

All but Leslie Ann, when she realized the location of the reported giant sighting—Elk Pass—was on the bill of lading from Harvey's Survival World. She'd gone up the chain of command with this tidbit, and been rewarded with a camera crew and tickets to Idaho.

As she questioned the quartet gathered around the general store's potbelly stove, she realized that they had slipped from the first to the second stage of news awareness. The first stage, which might be called voluble hype, was the preferred condition for interviewees. They conveyed excitement about whatever experience they'd had, talked about it a lot and at detail, and were generally emotional. The mother whose child has just been run over, the man who's just escaped from a train wreck, these were generally excellent news subjects. On the tape from the affiliate, the four men had been fresh from the event, their adrenalin pumping.

In the time it had taken Leslie Ann and her crew to get to Idaho, stage two had set in. The four had gotten a chance to think. The two more intelligent ones, Anse and Ken, had begun to wonder if they were making asses of themselves with this story. Elmo, of course, had an emotional investment. He'd been the one to discover the giant in the first place, and the others were his backup. Woodie, unfortunately, was just a boob.

The essence of the story, as Anse shamefacedly admitted, was that they'd gone trespassing on posted land, been loomed over by a giant, and run like hell. Not exactly nightly news material. The giant didn't *do* anything. If he'd eaten one of them, she'd have had a lead story.

The news here, however, was not that these yokels had met a giant, but that the giant had been out here at all.

What did the Heroes want in the Idaho mountains— melting pot for America's most bizarre extremes, home of survivalists, ultra-Aryans, and unreconstructed hippies? *Why* had they bought a dilapidated old ranch in the boonies? What were they building out there? And why were they stocking it with enough supplies to weather the end of the world?

No, this story was only a wedge for a larger investigation. She'd get them on tape, although they declined to show her the giant footprint they'd found. She'd take the cameras to the construction site Elmo had mentioned. With luck, there might be prints out there as well—maybe workmen who'd seen the giant.

The hunters' story would only be a light-hearted opening gun, because the answers Leslie Ann really wanted had to come from the giants—specifically, Robert. Her only chance to get *that* interview depended on how much public interest—how much pressure—she could generate.

* * *

The California sun had just set as the giants watched the evening news. Turning from the final story of the evening, presented so amusingly by that blond newswoman who'd done a series of broadcasts attacking Sturdley, Barbara turned to Robert with a laugh. "Did you really run those Lessers off that land?" she asked. "And the buildings they showed—have you really decided we need houses our own size? And why construct them in—what was the name of that place? Idaho? It seems very far from New York."

Robert glared at the large-screen TV as if he could expunge the story—or at least change the channel—by mental effort alone.

Gods below! he swore bitterly to himself. And after I thought I'd handled the situation so well! This female Lesser, whom he knew was sharing Marty Burke's bed, had managed to focus on the giants all the attention Robert had wanted to avoid.

Robert glanced hard-eyed at Barbara's merry face. Only she, Maurice, and Ruth were seated around the television. Members of the inner circle. It was an acceptable risk to tell them.

"Its distance from New York, or any other major population centers, was the prime reason I settled on Idaho. You all know what I was doing in Washington—Binding the Lessers' leaders to cause a war of great destruction among them. That land in Idaho is to be the fortress where we will ride out the coming cataclysm in safety."

The others, not realizing how far along his plans had developed, merely stared in nervous silence.

"Our problem now is how to deal with the attention this will bring to our new domain." He frowned in thought. "When we finish the movie, Barbara and I will go there in a very public manner. Perhaps Thomas and Ruth, as well."

Ruth, he noticed, didn't look exactly overjoyed at this pronouncement.

"We'll tell the newsgatherers that we need to breathe the country air, that this complex has been built as a retreat for our kind. We'll do simple, healthy things for the benefit of their cameras. And soon enough, I expect, they'll get bored."

Unfortunately, he suspected, Leslie Ann Nasotrudere would *not* get bored. From a reference she'd made during her narration, he suspected she'd discovered something about the food being stockpiled in Idaho.

He sighed. Back home, it would be so easy. If a Lesser, male or female, discovered anything damaging about a Master, such a vexatious person would simply disappear. He couldn't do that in this world. Especially since this Nasotrudere woman was sleeping with his main ally at the Fantasy Factory.

Could he use Burke to muzzle his troublesome lover? More likely, that would break them up . . . not such a bad idea—it would limit one road of access to his people's secrets. On the other hand, Burke could be an invaluable source, revealing areas where Nasotrudere was digging.

Robert frowned in thought. His counter move could embody several strategies at once, to be developed as circumstances warranted. He'd ask Burke why his lover was distracting public attention away from the upcoming movie. At the same time, he could implant some instructions, some suspicions, into Burke's mind . . .

On the planet Argon, John and Peg lay entwined between the perfumed sheets of her bed. She held him tightly, his face in the cleft of her breasts as she kissed the crown of his head.

"Your muscles are all tense," she whispered, stroking his neck, his shoulders, his back. "And even when we were making love, you seemed distant." Her gray eyes were troubled as she held him to her.

Maybe she was being greedy. Perhaps that fusion of souls they'd achieved in their first rush of passion wasn't possible all the time.

Her lips quirked in a self-mocking smile. She'd always laughed at the idea that a single stud's lovemaking could, as the saying went, "ruin a girl for other men."

Now, though, she feared that such a thing had happened to her, with the gentle, unstudly—but very male—John Cameron. Their lovemaking had been electric, a passion reinforced by their celibacy as they'd both fought night and day against the Deviants' campaign of terror, which had slackened significantly after the failed attempt to kidnap her.

Now Peg could feel something dark in John's mind that he wasn't sharing. Something that hadn't been there the first time they'd come together. Something had happened while she'd been unconscious at that blasted farm, and he wouldn't tell her what it was.

"John," she murmured, slipping down so they were face to face.

"I'm sorry," he said finally. "It's just—it sounds silly. But I feel everything I do—*we* do—is being spied on."

"Ach, ze paranoia," she said in her best shrink voice.

But he didn't smile.

She ran a tentative finger along the barely visible scar that now extended down John's left cheek. The automeds had miraculously healed the torn flesh, but John had refused to devote the time that perfect plastic surgery would have taken.

Frankly, Peg would have preferred his face without the scar. Since he'd gotten it, well, his whole visage had changed. In all the time she'd known John, she'd thought of him as having a cute, but curiously unformed face—as if he still had to grow into it.

Peg didn't know if it was because of the physical scar or because of some mental one, but John's face now had a hard, set look. Where he'd always looked too young before, now he seemed older than his years.

They hadn't told anyone except Triadon that Melador had been a traitor. She'd gone along with John's rationale about Argon needing heroes. But she'd also participated with John in screening all the remaining S-Forcers for any signs of deep conditioning.

"It's not just Melador," John said, shifting back. "There's something else, something I can't put my finger on."

"Oh, I don't think there's anything around here you couldn't put a finger on," Peg joked.

But the moment was past. He pulled away even as she tried to hold him.

"Stay with me?" she asked in a low voice.

"I'm not good company." He rose from the bed, slipped on a light robe, and went to the door. "See you in the morning," he whispered. Then he was gone.

Okay, love is not exactly rational, Peg told herself, blinking back tears. Which seems pretty well to sum up my relationship with the mysterious Mr. Cameron.

Jackass, John reproved himself as he moved down the corridor to his own room. You wanted Peg so badly, your whole body ached. And now you're screwing it up because some tickle in the back of your mind says somebody's watching over your shoulder—some voyeur.

John opened his door, stepping into a small sitting room. The staff accommodations at the Citadel of Silence rivaled those of a four-star Earth hotel. John dropped into a hugely comfortable overstuffed chair, unwilling to face an empty bed. What was it about this hypothetical voyeur that bothered him?

Was it the psychic blonde he'd tangled with at Peg's kidnapping? What had Peg called her—Matavi? John shook his head. If she were spying on them, he was sure he could detect it and trace any probes to their source. Besides, why would a gorgeous blonde need to get her jollies watching a couple of kids make it?

No, he'd fine-tuned his shields and probed till his brain hurt, but John had not been able to find his hypothetical watcher *anywhere on Argon.*

As he closed his eyes, the phrase reverberated in his brain. So where were there watchers who weren't on Argon? Something was definitely tickling his brain.

Finally, he focused on the memory, from a briefing given by Peg after she'd questioned a prisoner. It had something to do with the Sphere of Exile.

Then it came. The homesick Deviants had gone to the outermost edges of the Sphere of Exile to catch ghostly glimpses of Argon . . . and die. An inchoate jumble of facts in John's mind began clicking together. Psychic powers could pierce the interdimensional flux—John had already proven that. The bad guys had at least one psychic— Matavi. When Harry had been returned home, the attack had been two-pronged, coming from the Argonian Deviants and those in the Sphere of Exile. *Coordinated.* The only way to do that was if there were communication between the two sets of Deviants.

They *were* being spied on—from the Sphere of Exile! That's why John hadn't been able to detect anyone. He'd been looking in the wrong places!

Now, however . . .

John relaxed in the chair, eyes closed, reaching out with his mind on a specific wavelength. He felt a slight dizziness, the precursor to the vertigo that announced an impending Rift transit.

And then he was in contact with the Deviant spy.

Although his eyes were closed, John was aware of a figure drifting in midair. The watcher was bored now, although John could still catch twinges of the avidity with which he'd spied on them in Peg's room.

Well, you won't be bored for long, John thought. Using his Rift powers and telekinesis together, John hauled the Deviant eavesdropper against the dimensional barrier that made up the Sphere of Exile—not through, but *into* the soap-bubble of immaterial force. It was extremely painful—the spy twitched like a gaffed fish.

And into that sudden, overwhelming pain John ruth-lessly thrust his own tentacles of thought, seizing control of the invisible voyeur's mind.

The Deviants aren't the only ones who can condition a subject, John thought.

So divorced from the physical world was he with this mental struggle, he never noticed the door to his room quietly opening. Peg had felt the Rift-twinge as well, and came to see if there was trouble.

What she found instead was John sitting motionless in a chair. And in the air above him, outlined in a ghastly pale light, writhed an immaterial human form.

Every body the S-Force could muster was now in the air, surrounding the semi-ruinous building set into the sawtoothed mountain slope.

"You're sure of the information you got from this spy?" Triadon asked for about the thousandth time that night. John communicated with him mentally—the storming party was maintaining strict radio silence.

It's the old laboratory of the ultimate Deviant leader—a guy named Scaladon, John responded. After the spy re-ported the information I'd implanted, the council of Deviant leaders will definitely be meeting.

But how—Triadon began.

John cut him off. He needed all his psionic powers to fuddle the Deviants' electronic detectors, as well as the exiled watchers. Throughout this night, while scrambling the assault force and making other, final arrangements, he'd spent his time probing for and neutralizing invisible lookouts. He had a flicker from the ruined complex below them—a fleeting impres-sion of inhabitants, but he hadn't probed. That might warn Matavi.

The strike force was now deployed, and John and Peg gave the signal for attack by blowing in a newly-restored plast-alloy door with their blasters.

John had gotten the layout of the place from the spy, a servant of Scaladon's in the Age of Strife. In moments, the raiders crushed through the outer defenses and were storming the main conference chamber. The room was packed—this time the S-Force had moved too fast for the leaders to escape.

Seated round a table was the brain trust of the criminal conspiracy aimed at bringing down Argonian society. John had known they'd be there, after what he'd planted in the spy's brain. Scaladon and the others would have considered it a prime threat—or opportunity.

According to the memories John had implanted, the spy had eavesdropped on a top S-Force meeting, in which John had proposed recruiting reinforcements from Earth, fighting men still contaminated with the evil gene.

That would put the Deviants up against professional adversaries. Of course they might also be able to arrange another mass jailbreak and attack, the way they'd crashed Harry's farewell party.

Whatever the course of action they'd choose, the leaders would have to discuss this development. John had suckered them all into the same place at one time.

The group was surprisingly formal as John, Peg, and a squad of enforcers burst through the chamber door. Many of the Deviant leaders weren't wearing armor.

Peg gasped as she looked toward the head of the table. Two men sat there, frozen to immobility by the stunning raid. One was short and skinny, dressed in a brocade robe. Spiky red hair burst in wild profusion over a metal face mask. He held an old-fashioned globular Argonian control device.

The man beside him would have been well built if he'd had skin. But he didn't. His flesh was an amorphous, misty outline, a sort of violet haze against which the whiteness of his bones stood out shockingly.

Peg glanced at John, her face numb. "Don't these guys look sorta familiar to you?" she hissed.

John looked on Megladon and Scaladon, the masterminds of the Deviant conspiracy, and his brain clicked to another frame of reference.

They did indeed look awfully damned familiar. With a couple of details changed, these guys were perfect twins for a pair of fictional Fantasy Factory villains—Meglomanik and Skeletone.

Peg felt as if the floor had dropped from beneath her feet—almost as if she'd fallen into the Rift. But the void here was the empty feeling of ultimate improbability. Their bitterest enemies on the planet Argon were actually comic book characters? Her willing suspension of disbelief finally crashed and burned.

She'd been willing to accept the lamebrain names for the planet's technical marvels, even as she accepted the comic book science that underlay them. That guy with the half-armor and the force cannon should have been a warning. Who had he looked like if not M-16, Weapon Supreme, the Fantasy Factory's hottest two-gun bad boy? Granted, the guy on Argon had one gun, but the resemblance was there.

And what about the blond vixen who'd seduced Melador over to the enemy side with drugs and sex appeal? Even her name—Matavi—sounded like a slurring of the Fantasy Factory's psychic femme fatale, Madam Vile.

Peg caught a flicker of movement down the table and saw that very woman, now dressed in a brief, rather sexy combination of black leather and half-armor—with a bandoleer of drug-darts slung across her shoulders. She looked like a comic artist's wet dream.

What the hell was going on around here?

She couldn't accept that the universe worked on comic book rules. Back in college, Peg had come upon a collection of science fiction stories based on the same theme: The stories that we regard as literary fiction are actually blurred visions of other realities, transcribed by Earthly writers. She'd never bought the idea of novelists as psychic mediums—at least, until now.

Just my luck, she thought. I could have visited the universe of Doctorow or Rabelais. Instead, I get the world of Grantfield and Sturdley.

Peg's skin crawled under her plast-alloy armor. There was yet another explanation for the crazy ordeals they'd undergone since the San Diego convention, the comic book life she'd been living with John Cameron. Suppose the Rift hadn't created the horrors she'd survived. What if the Rift were a creation of John's strange mental powers, a case of reality conforming to his fantasies? Fantasies, Peg realized, that had been formed in turn by comics.

The frozen moment finally shattered. Megladon summoned killer robots with his control globe while Scaladon snatched up a golden implement that looked like a high-tech scepter and fired a dazzling yellow beam at the invaders.

This was no time to debate illusion versus reality. Whatever the Deviants might be, alternate reality, phantasms, mental masturbation, they'd already proven that when they hit you, it hurt. She'd have to fight her way through this . . . and have a long talk with John when it was finished.

For now, Peg followed her part in the plan that John had proposed. The S-Forcers blocked the room's only exit, and moved to cover John. Peg again felt the ground-dissolving-under-her-feet sensation—but this *was* the opening of the Rift shivering her senses.

A quick burst of nausea, and an armored figure grappling with one of Triadon's techs disappeared. Peg's stomach flip-flopped in unnerving fashion as more and more of the *crème de la crème* of Deviant society were Rifted back into exile.

John had specifically designated three of the best S-Forcers to pin down the guy with the force cannon. Now a brilliant white glare filled the room as M-16 or whatever his name was somehow wriggled free.

The shot vaporized one of the S-Forcers—and two Deviant leaders.

"You can't use that in such close quarters!" Scaladon yelled.

"Then we'll have to open up the quarters," the cocky gunner responded, blowing out another wall.

Falling rubble took out a couple more unarmored Deviants. The pressure on the S-Force disintegrated as the leaders rushed for the new exit.

"Afraid this would happen," John muttered, surging forward.

"This wasn't part of the plan!" Peg cried, jumping after him.

"As Harry says, 'When in doubt, more hitting!' " John hurled himself over the table, where the ultimate Deviant leaders were still trying to extricate themselves.

Megladon frantically manipulated the controls on his globe. A pair of enormous robots plowed through the wall behind them, moving to smash John with fists like barrel-sized mallets.

Peg felt a pulse of psychic force that nearly lifted off the top of her skull, and watched the robots torn apart in an orgy of telekinetic destruction.

Megladon tried again. This time a golden glow emerged from his control globe, forming into a wall of energy which threw off hideous sparks as John encountered it.

"Enough of this shit," Peg muttered, aiming both of her blasters at the globe and firing. Megladon screamed as fat sparks enveloped him. He hurled the ruined mechanism at John and tried to dodge away.

But John, moving quickly despite the bulky backpack he'd insisted on wearing into battle, managed to nab the skinny mad scientist (Peg could see no other way to describe him), tossed him into the invisible-skinned Scaladon, and then landed atop both.

"Peg—here! Quick!" he called.

Peg landed beside John, blasters up, fingers ready to curl into firing position. "One false move," she snarled, "and you get a face full of tridigirector."

Scaladon writhed violently under the pile of bodies, his scepter-weapon pinned against his chest. Peg watched in fascination as his face became almost visible, suffused with a blood-red glow of rage.

"Stare at your peril, woman," the living skeleton rasped. "Many have learned the unwisdom of that since the lab accident that left me this way!"

With a near-superhuman wrench, he freed his scepter, aiming it at Peg. Another burst of telekinesis shuddered through her nervous system, and the golden weapon exploded.

Scaladon cried out with rage. But his shouts were dimmed in Peg's ears by a psychic call from John.

Peg—that drained me. Need a boost from you to open the Rift.

Taking a ragged breath, Peg opened her mind, feeling herself nearly yanked out of her body by the demand for power.

John! she transmitted in panic, I can't—

She felt the yawning gulf of the Rift drawing her in, and the horrendous sucking on her soul eased.

You remember how to move through the Rift, John's mind suddenly came at her. Push us away from Argon. I'm going to try and pull along as many Deviants as I can.

Peg's previous experience in controlling a Rift transition—the wild, tumbling ride that had brought them to Argon—seemed like a jaunt through the country compared to this passage. Before, no matter how much pitching and rolling they had faced, she was essentially steering.

Now she perceived the job as propelling them away from Argon's influence—its psychic gravity. It felt like trying to push a fully loaded Mack truck uphill, against the wind . . . singlehanded.

Doing fine, John sent. But they're resisting. And others are trying to push through.

The universe had shrunk to the interior of Peg's armored suit. She realized she wasn't in physical contact with John this time. Their connection was merely mind to mind. Even that thought was lost in the exertion of navigating the Rift. Solely on psionic power, she had to move herself, John, and the various Deviants he'd latched onto through the void—angstrom by angstrom, she feared. Peg could hear the blood thudding in her ears.

Panicked, she flailed out—and suddenly the jumble of Rifting bodies was free of Argon. She had a momentary impression of a construct, a bubble in the Rift. Then she heard a wild mental wail as the Deviant leaders were consigned back to their dimensional prison.

John took over the steering, sending himself and Peg across an immensity of emptiness.

We're not going back, John told her. Our job is done. The backbone of the Deviant leadership is dead or exiled. For the rest, they can be handled by Triadon and the S-Force.

That's why you packed a bag, Peg thought muzzily. She found herself drifting away.

Peg! John's mental voice was sharp as he gathered her mind-stuff to himself in a clutch that was like a full body caress. Stick with me. I don't want you getting lost!

Yeah. There's a lot we've got to talk about, she responded. This was the longest she'd ever been in the Rift. Did John know which way to go?

I'm taking us home, he assured her, but we're bucking the Rift currents. Think of it as flying against a strong headwind.

They continued for perhaps a hundred pulsebeats, then seemed to *pause* somehow. Peg felt a discharge of psychic energy.

What's going on? she asked.

Checking our landing zone, John said briefly.

Then the Rift was fading, to be replaced by the faded walls of a pokey, narrow room. On one side was an army cot and cheap dresser, the other wall was lined high with comic boxes. A drawing board stood by a window that had been painted shut generations ago. Every surface was covered with a thick layer of dust.

They'd reached John's rented room in Astoria, Queens, New York . . . New York.

Peg laughed and activated her suit radio. "When you said you were taking us home, I didn't realize you meant *your* home."

"Easiest spot to find," John returned with a grin. "That's the first rule of Rift navigation."

They undid their helmets. "Welcome home," Peg whispered, giving him a kiss.

Then the two of them rebounded with a muffled *clunk*.

John looked down ruefully. "I'm glad I chose some-where private to arrive, dressed like this. Luckily, after I got the first check for doing the *Robert* comic, I gave the Putniks six months' rent in advance."

Peg had already encountered the immigrant family who were John's landlords. "Most people would have cleaned this room out and rented it again," she said.

John shook his head. "Not the Putniks. With their kind of pride, when they make a deal, they stick to it."

"I guess it's kind of useful to be able to read your land-lord's mind," Peg said.

You should know, she caught John's thought. *You've been doing it long enough now.*

Peg's eyes went wide. "You mean—" she began in words, then finished her sentence psionically. *I'm tele-pathic here? I thought that was just on the Riftworlds.* She paused for a second, then went back to speech. "So Harry and I—"

"Looks like it," John said. "I guess Harry's done well so far. He must have gotten the broadcast power unit up and working, or we'd be having a lot of trouble with these suits."

He slipped off his backpack and began divesting him-self of his armor. "We're in luck, by the way. Nobody's in the apartment."

Peg stared at him in consternation as he stood before her, peeling off his baggy undersuit. "God!" she exclaimed. "Is that all you can think of?"

He rolled his eyes. "There's a change of clothes for both of us in my backpack. And there's nothing here you haven't seen before. We can dress and quietly go out—unless you want to walk down Astoria Boulevard in that get-up."

"Oh," she said in a small voice, getting to work on her armor.

John grinned. "I mean, we've got a lot of work to do. Is that all *you* can think of?"

Two figures shimmered into being on the roof of an apartment building in the working-class enclave of Astoria. Matavi's hair was matted with sweat as she nearly collapsed onto Emsisdin. "I told you I could do it," she gasped in Argonian. "It was just a case of hanging onto their psychic coattails, close enough to transit through the dimensional flux, far enough away not to be detected."

"I had doubts," Emsisdin admitted. "But even at the cost of you blowing a few circuits, this beats the alternatives. Just think of the great Scaladon, once again consigned to ignominious exile."

He looked at the drooping blond head resting against his half-armor. "Are you all right?"

"Just a little rest," she said, running a shaky hand over her forehead. The transit had taken more out of her than she cared to admit.

Emsisdin helped her to a sitting position against the rooftop parapet. "Where are we?" he asked.

"The aliens' homeworld," Matavi answered, her eyes closed. "I get conflicting identification-images. This is either Astawya or Nooyok."

"Well, it seems to be a major population center," Emsisdin said, looking off across the vista of brick apartment houses to the distant towers of Manhattan.

"Rather primitive." He coughed, shifting the weight of the force cannon in his hand as a cloud of truck exhaust wafted up.

"There are possibilities, though," he said. "A worldful of possibilities."

Chapter Twenty

John Cameron felt distressingly earthbound as he and Peg Faber walked the Queens streets down Astoria Boulevard toward Thirty-first Street and the elevated trains. Maybe he'd gotten too used to the high technology of the planet Argon. In the time it took them to walk to the Hoyt Street station, they could have cruised to Peg's Manhattan apartment in their suits of flying armor.

"Sorry about taking the subway," he apologized for the fifteenth time. "I scoured the house, but all I could find was a couple of bucks."

"Too bad I left my bank card on the world of the giants," Peg said. "Now that things are back to normal, we've *got* to get you set up in the legitimate economy."

"*We.*" The word had never sounded sweeter in John's ears. Home again, a future ahead of them . . .

They climbed the steps to find that someone named JO-JOE had decorated the station with repeated spray-painted renditions of his name. Persons unknown had used the stairwell for a toilet. Everybody on the platform seemed slumped and pale-faced.

"Welcome back to New York," John muttered.

After a change of trains, an hour's ride, and a five-minute walk, they finally reached Peg's apartment building on Amsterdam Avenue.

"I don't have a key, of course," she sighed. "Luckily, the super lives in the building."

Peg scanned the intercom buttons. "Good. His name is still on." She buzzed, and a growly voice with a heavy accent demanded to know who it was.

"Gergely, it's Peg Faber. I need to get into my apartment—" Peg's words were drowned out in an outburst of *Mitteleuropean* language. She buzzed again, apparently to an empty apartment.

A moment later, a short, hairy man in paint-stained slacks and an athletic undershirt burst into the lobby. His eyes went big, as if he were seeing a ghost. "Peg!" With his accent, it came out more like "Payg." Gergely raised a shaking hand. "You dead! I see on TV."

"I'm not." Peg rapped sharply on the glass of the lobby door. "See? I'm solid. I've got to go to the bathroom. And I'd like to do that in my own apartment."

Gergely shook his head. "No."

"What do you mean?" Peg demanded.

"Not yours anymore," the super said nervously. "When you die—" He decided to amend that. "When everyone *think* you die, we send all your things back to Pennsylvania."

"Pennsylvania?" Peg repeated, her face looking numb.

"To your parents. Everything sent back. Apartment went to new tenant."

Peg didn't seem to hear anything after the first sentence. "My parents think I'm dead?" She turned to John, who retreated a step at the fury in her eyes. As she stalked off, he trailed after, trying to contact her mentally. His tentative probe bounced off a beefed-up psionic shield. John blinked. It seemed as though her latest passage through the Rift had strengthened Peg's immaterial abilities.

"Um, Peg?" John ventured. "If you need a bathroom, I bet whatsisname will let you use his."

That earned him yet another baffling glare from Peg. "Right now, I'm more concerned about a bedroom than a bathroom," she snapped. "I've lost my apartment, everybody seems to think I'm dead, and I don't have any ID or money. Where am I supposed to stay?"

"I don't have the money for a hotel," John said, unhappily checking the change in his pocket. "We could call some of your friends, or we could head back to Astoria." He squirmed at the look on her face. "I know it's not the most beautiful place . . ."

"I'm not spending the night with—in there." Peg looked away.

John wished he could get an idea of what was eating Peg. But her shields were impenetrable. Throughout their trip to Manhattan, all he'd caught was Peg's need—more like a hunger—for normality. He could have Rifted them to her apartment with no expense at all—although their sudden appearance might have scared the new tenant to death. Using his powers, he could probably sneak her into any vacant hotel room in the city. But judging from her mood, that wouldn't be a wise plan.

"So what do you think we should do?" he finally asked.

Peg frowned. "Have you got enough bus fare to get us over to Harry's?"

Harry Sturdley was just settling down to the ten o'clock news when the doorman rang him. "Send them up right away!" he yelled after hearing the identities of his visitors. After warning Myra about late-night company, he pulled a robe over his pajamas and waited eagerly by the apartment door.

At first glance, the kids looked almost aggressively normal, dressed in jeans and cotton sweaters. Then he saw the look on Peg's face—and the scar on John's.

The scarring wasn't that noticeable—a barely detectable seam of keloid tissue spanning his left cheek from nose to jawline. But it marked a subtle alteration in John's features. He looked as if a knife had pared away all traces of youthful softness—a knife that perhaps had slipped on the kid's cheek.

"I expected the pair of you weeks ago," Harry said. "What happened back there on Argon?"

"We weren't goofing off," Peg replied in angry tones. "It was no vacation—and definitely no day at the beach."

Harry listened in growing shock to their account of the bloody warfare his departure had precipitated. "Mike . . . dead?" he echoed, trying to come to grips with the facts. "And the Deviants?"

"We finally beat them," John said. "I managed to jam their leaders back into the Sphere of Exile when Peg and I Rifted out of there."

"So we won the war," Harry said in satisfaction. "And maybe it did some good, shaking a little life into that zombie-world—"

"You weren't there," Peg interrupted, her voice rasping. "You never saw the worst of it."

Harry stared at her in silence for a moment, then finally nodded his head. "Okay," he said. "I wasn't there. But I *have* been *here* for weeks now, so let me bring you up to date."

The pair sat on the couch as Harry began reporting on the situation he'd found on coming home. But the older man had barely started the recital of his actions before John began shaking his head.

"You're only telling us what's happening at the Fantasy Factory. What about the real problem—the giants?"

"I've reestablished surveillance on Heroes' Manor—at a far enough distance so the giants can't read the minds of the watchers," Harry said. "No way was I going to take on Robert and company by myself. Besides, there are other considerations. The Hero books are still one of the bestselling Fantasy Factory lines—"

"We've got to get rid of them," John interrupted flatly.

"I agree," Harry said. "Now that you two are here, we can begin coming up with a plan. Something that will get rid of the giants with a maximum of safety for us, the people of this world, and, of course, the Fantasy Factory."

"Harry—" John bit back the impatience in his voice. "I've only been back a few hours, but I'm getting a sensation of—wrongness—in the air."

"Bad vibes, man?" Harry tried to joke.

"Whatever the giants are up to, it can't be good for anyone under fifteen feet tall—and it will be a lot worse for the Fantasy Factory than the loss of a few titles." John leaned forward, the scar snaking down his face suddenly catching a gleam of light. "We've got to start fighting them. Remember what happened the last time you made us fight with one hand behind our backs? You didn't do the planet Argon any favors."

"Look—" Harry bit off the second word he'd been about to say—kid. The face confronting him was not that of a kid. It was that of a warrior, demanding immediate action.

Harry tried again. "I admit it, John. I messed up on Argon. But that was because I had no intelligence about the enemy. We won't make that mistake again. I want to know what Robert is up to before I start a total war. So, unless the giants start trouble, we lay low while we scope them out."

John didn't even have to voice his disapproval. It flooded the mental airwaves in the room, making both Harry and Peg stir uneasily.

"Now that you two are back," Harry went on, "we can take a more overt hand in checking out the giants. I'm not saying we should do nothing. I'm just saying we should be . . . circumspect."

John looked as though he were trying to swallow a large, very bitter pill. "All right," he finally said, begrudging every word. "But I think pretty soon we'll be taking *direct* action."

"When the time is right." Harry decided to change the subject. "You two look well. Any problems here on the home front? Do you need money? A cash advance?"

"I need a place to live," Peg's voice was a little unsteady. "John kept his apartment, but mine got rented out, my stuff sent back to Pennsylvania—Harry, my parents think I'm *dead*."

"We'll fix that," Harry soothed. "You can stay here, and we'll make a phone call to your folks pronto."

He wondered what Myra would say to having his curvy red-headed assistant as a house guest. There was one advantage, though. "I'm keeping my armor in the office. Maybe you should keep yours here—as a security measure." That would put some miracle Argonian technology to work protecting the house—and Myra.

"I'll get it," John said. He closed his eyes, and both Harry and Peg felt the tug of mental vertigo that indicated the Rift at work.

A second later, Peg's armor swam into existence on the living room floor. It lay just as Peg must have divested herself of it, the long john-like undergarment draped over the segments of plast-alloy.

"We changed at John's place," Peg said, a little color rising in her face.

Harry chose not to comment on that. Instead he excused himself to tell Myra about their new tenant and to get the guest bedroom squared away.

"Guess I'll be going," John said. "Do I see you in the office tomorrow, or do we stay invisible?"

"Come to the office," Harry said. "If anybody asks, you got away on a boat owned by a doctor and hid out in Mexico."

John nodded, then stepped forward to kiss Peg good-bye. She shifted position fractionally so the kiss landed on her cheek instead of her lips. John's face tightened, but he didn't say anything. Instead, he vanished into the Rift.

Harry looked at his erstwhile assistant until the silence became uncomfortable. Peg's color heightened. "It was just a good-bye kiss, Harry."

"From the looks of it, he was expecting a bit more from your end," Sturdley said. "What happened on Argon after I left?"

Peg let out a big breath. "A lot of things." When she didn't elaborate, Sturdley headed for the door, only to stop when she spoke again.

"Harry. This whole crazy—*whatever*. Does it remind you of something?"

"Remind me of what?" he asked.

"It's like something you would have scripted." Peg frowned, and Harry noticed that little lines had engraved themselves between her brows.

"Not me." Sturdley raised a disclaiming hand. "You know Sturdley's Law: When in doubt, more hitting. But I don't do wholesale bloodshed, Red. There's been too much of that on this adventure."

Peg shook her head. "I just meant it feels like we're trapped in a comic book. Giants, for chrissake. Those cheesy science fiction worlds. As for what's happened on them—no, it's not your kind of story. But it is the kind of blood-and-guts storyline you'd fight about at staff meetings. The kind of story the young guys might write—the k-kids who don't know anything but comic books—"

She broke off.

"Peg, what are you trying to say?"

She stared at him, apparently gathering courage for what she had to say next. "We know John has an incredible mind, with powers and abilities—"

"Cut it out," Harry interjected. "That's copyrighted, I think. But, granted, the kid can do amazing things. We just saw him warp your armor here."

"Maybe he's warping reality," Peg said in a small voice. "We don't know what he can do—I'm not even sure John knows. It's too bad you weren't there for the end on Argon. When we squared off against the head Deviants, I recognized them. They were *comics* characters, Harry. Skeletone. Megalomanik. And a half-dressed blonde who looked like Madam Vile."

"What?" Now it was Sturdley's turn to stare.

"The adventure didn't just *feel* like a comic book anymore—we were actually fighting with super-villains. It made me wonder. Suppose they were projections of John's subconscious? What if this whole disaster—all we've suffered—is coming out of John's head? The two of us—the *whole world*—may be trapped in a blood-soaked daydream triggered by too many comic books."

"You're beginning to sound like old Doc Wertham," Sturdley said.

"Harry, I'm serious," Peg insisted.

"More than that, you're scared," he said. "I sure as hell can't explain what's happened to us. The giants' world was like no comic I ever wrote—or wanted to. And if you saw Fantasy Factory villains on Argon, well, I don't know what to say. Maybe the next world over has Dynasty Comics characters running around. Maybe we'd have met Ram-Man, Herowena, and the Straight Arrow. What we've gone through doesn't seem to have rational rules. But I'm sure of one thing. John would never let anything happen to you—not even subconsciously. He may be spacy, but he's solid that way."

Peg looked dubious, but she didn't say anything else. She began assembling her armor—her only luggage—as Sturdley went to tell Myra about their new living arrangements.

John Rifted his way to the roof of the Astoria apartment building he called home. He went down the stairs and knocked on the door of the Putnik apartment, to find that Mama Putnik was now home. Her response ranged around the subjects of his inconsiderateness in disappearing and how thin he'd gotten. But underneath, John's immaterial senses noted a certain gladness that he was still alive. Probably something to do with the difficulties in finding a new tenant, he thought.

Filled with some surprisingly spicy Balkan stew—a corollary of the "too thin" tirade—John finally retired to his room and lay on the thin confines of the surplus Army cot. He'd gotten too used to more luxurious sleeping accommodations—not to mention company in bed.

John closed his eyes, trying to ignore the prickle of thought teasing its way through his brain. What was the reason for Peg's coldness on the train ride to Manhattan?

Why had she turned away when he'd kissed her at Harry's? Had she been embarrassed that their boss might see their new intimacy? Or was that intimacy over?

"Now that things are normal." John had been so excited to hear Peg say that when they'd first arrived back home. He'd thought it meant they had a future. But maybe it meant that what they had was in the past. They weren't on Argon anymore. Peg now had a world full of *normal* men from which to choose.

John pushed the thought away, lying with his eyes closed. His attention wandered. When he sensed the harsh *klick-chack!* of the pistol's action being worked, it took a moment to realize it was a mental rather than auditory stimulus.

Sitting up in the bed, John sent probes to zero in on the sound.

It came from a housetop almost a block away. Three young thugs stood on the roof. One was working the action of a newly-purchased 9 mm pistol. The others were setting beer bottles on the cornice overlooking the street, creating an impromptu shooting gallery. Each punk reveled in the weight of new pistols tucked into the waistbands of their pants. None of them seemed to care that their planned target practice would send stray shots flying through the neighborhood.

John rose from the bed and donned his armor, then Rifted out of his room, taking a position high over the rooftop. He dropped a few yards before the gizmoidal drive took hold. Maybe he could knock out the punks before they really saw him. If not, to hell with Harry's call for circumspection. John knew what he had to do.

The guard at the jewelry store's receiving entrance stared at his video monitor in puzzlement. The blonde standing outside the door was easy on the eyes. But she was nearly falling out of an outfit that would have looked more appropriate in a sleazy sci-fi movie than late-night on Fifth Avenue. Maybe she'd been at a costume party—

The woman's face on the screen took on an intent expression even as her eyes went unfocused. And suddenly the guard's will was no longer his own. Moving as if he were a puppet with tangled strings, he tottered to the inches-thick steel door and opened it.

Even as he moved, the guard's mind was being raped for details of the store's security system.

By the time the Argonian Deviant named Matavi stepped into the store, she already knew about the security cameras covering the entrance and the control center up on the fifth floor. As quick as thought, mental tendrils shot for the guard manning that desk. His hand was halfway to the button that would call the police as Matavi exerted control.

Trying to control two minds at once strained her talents beyond the breaking point. The nearer guard's mind began to break free. He turned to her, features distorted with terror, his hand fumbling for the crude weapon on his hip. Putting all her power into holding the more distant guard still, Matavi plucked a dart from the bandolier she wore and flung it into the would-be attacker's face.

Instant oblivion. The guard dropped, his eyes rolling up into his head. At the same moment, Matavi's Deviant partner Emsisdin burst through the door, the heavy force cannon in his grip swinging to cover the collapsing security man. "He won't even remember what happened," Matavi said. Her voice sounded distracted. Lines of effort appeared on her perfect face. "But I perceive that everything is being recorded. I'll have to take care of that."

In the control center, her new mental slave began turning off cameras. Although firmly in Matavi's mental grasp, the guard's fingers fumbled over the controls for the recorders—fine motor control was difficult from a distance. Soon, however, all the video evidence had been erased. Then the guard slumped at his desk, his own memory expunged.

Freed of the need to focus for control, Matavi spread wide her psionic nets. "There are four other watchmen in the building." She compared the mental picture to the map she had extracted from the guards. "None are near the vault we want."

The two intruders rose silently on Argonian gizmoidal drives and flew through empty corridors. Soon they reached the destination Matavi had chosen—a vault door whose steel in earlier days might have been used to armor a battleship.

Neither of the guards she'd questioned knew the combination—in any event, the vault had a time lock. But no matter on Earth could resist the destructive power of the force cannon.

Emsisdin quickly blasted a human-sized hole through two feet of steel. Unfortunately, he also cut a number of circuits attached to the door. Alarms began to scream.

"Take what you can," Matavi ordered curtly. "I'll monitor the approach of the other guards."

Her heightened web of psychic probes detected not only the approach of guards, but of the police. "That will have to do," she told Emsisdin. "We don't want them to see us."

Emsisdin came out of the vault and followed Matavi's path upward. The forces of law were gathering to surround the building. They wouldn't expect ordinary jewel thieves simply to fly away.

In moments, the store and the converging guardians were hundreds of feet below them. Matavi moderated her upward motion and banked eastward, in the direction of a towering hostelry. Earlier, she had sifted the thoughts of passersby on the streets, pinpointing this "Walldoaf" as a desirable place to stay. A few mental commands to the staff had arranged for a luxurious suite to remain vacant, even for a window to be opened.

She flew through the open casement and landed on thick carpeting. Emsisdin followed a moment later, force cannon in one hand, a bag of loot in the other.

"Sorry about those alarms," he apologized. "These Astawyans are so primitive, I have a hard time not underestimating them."

"Nooyawkas," Matavi corrected him. "In this area, they call themselves Nooyawkas."

"Well, how do Nooyawkas turn on the lights?" Emsisdin asked, running a hand over an obvious lamp, then snapping a finger at it. "It doesn't respond to power pulses—"

Matavi reached out with her mind. Most of the occupants of nearby rooms were asleep. She caught the tide of their unconscious dreams. Ah, several floors below there was a couple awake in bed. Very awake. Very busy. Just as well. They were so bound up in their rutting, they didn't even notice her mental intrusion.

Withdrawing her mental probe, Matavi went to the lamp, found the switch, and then there was light. Emsisdin removed his helmet and gave Matavi a cocky grin. Treasures glittered around the lamp's base as he dumped out the loot.

"This was just what I could get my hands on," he told her. "I don't think it's even the very best. But once we get acclimated here—take on some local help . . ."

His self-satisfaction was so strong she barely needed a probe to catch his thoughts. A new, improved gang, with a technological edge over this world's barbarous security systems. A mind reader to spy out opportunities, ensure gang loyalty—and, inevitably, warm the gang leader's bed. Emsisdin was sure it would happen. After all, he was the only Argonian on this world.

Emsisdin stretched, unclasping his armor. "Ah. Now time for rest."

From the images flickering in his brain, his idea of "rest" matched that of the couple downstairs.

"There are several bedchambers in this suite. Choose whichever you want," Matavi said coolly. "I'll choose one of the others."

For a second, Emsisdin's cocky grin faltered. All right, not now, his thoughts whispered. He could play along. Sooner or later . . .

True to form, he chose the largest bedroom. Matavi chose the one farthest away. Before she stripped for the night, she set up psychic triplines at door and window to warn her of intruders. To make sure Emsisdin got the message, she also imprinted a psionic aversion pattern into the bedroom door.

Matavi sighed as she slipped between the crisp sheets. Emsisdin's expectations could become a problem. *"The only Argonian on this world."* Matavi had no fond memories of Argon. Even among the Deviants she had been an outsider, a mind reader, a gene-tinkered freak. There had been all too few telepaths among those consigned to the Sphere of Exile. Most of them had died rather than endure the thoughts of those around them. Matavi had survived, but she no longer thought of herself as Argonian.

In the Sphere of Exile and during her subsequent escape, she had merely been *genus* Survivor. Now, however, she could transfer her allegiance to a new race. Not the stunted normals of Astawya or Nooyawk. Matavi's race was the small circle that could use mental energy.

They'd have to make sure the powers bred true.

Matavi fell asleep wondering how it would feel to breed with John Cameron . . .

Chapter Twenty-One

Marty Burke took a sip of coffee, grimaced, and stared blearily at the television set. It used to be easy to make coffee in his house—two spoons of instant, hot water from the tap, and there you were.

That was before Leslie Ann Nasotrudere came into his life. Now there were boxes of gourmet beans in the kitchen, a grinder, a drip-filter pot—and to Burke's palate, the coffee tasted like asphalt. Maybe it was the reheating—Leslie Ann had brewed the pot at five A.M. and flown out of his apartment soon thereafter. He'd lain in bed half-dead, his usual response after a night with the voracious Ms. Nasotrudere. Now was the 6:55 newsfeed, and Burke had learned from painful experience not to miss watching so he could comment on Leslie Ann's big story.

She appeared on the screen in her network news blazer, looking perky and perfect, her full lower lip pressed tight in a puzzled frown.

"I'm standing in front of the main vault at Tiffany's—two feet of armor-grade steel. But that wasn't enough to deter thieves in the early hours of the morning, as you can see . . . " The camera panned to her right, revealing a hole large enough for her to crawl through.

Burke woke up a bit more, leaning toward the screen to study the image. It didn't seem as though the vault had been blown into. The edges of the opening seemed melted, but there wasn't enough runoff to account for the size of the hole. It was as though solid steel had vaporized . . .

The phone rang as Leslie Ann went into new details about unconscious guards and alarms scaring off the burglars. Without even considering the odd hour of the call, Marty picked up the receiver. "Burke here."

"Report fully, Lesser scum," hissed the voice on the other end.

All trace of conscious thought vanished from Burke's mind. He sat silently holding the phone until the voice asked, "Are you alone?"

"Yes," Burke answered flatly.

"You will tell me all the details of the stories Leslie Ann Nasotrudere is presently working on."

Burke rushed into a rapid monotone, revealing everything Leslie Ann had told him in the last few days. "She's been preparing an undercover piece on the treatment of women at local unemployment offices. There are a couple of allegations of political corruption. And it seems she's now involved in the investigation of a jewel robbery."

"Has she continued making inquiries about the beings you call giants?" the caller asked.

"She hasn't been asking me as many questions since Sturdley came back," Burke said. "Although she did want to know how much influence Robert had on business decisions I made."

"You will, of course, tell her there was no such influence," the voice said. "Deflect all inquiries she makes, but do not seem evasive. Continue to gather as much information on her work as you can, especially any investigations on the giants. You will forget this call and the conversation until the next time you hear the trigger phrase, *Report fully, Lesser scum.*"

Burke hung up the phone and stared blankly for a second. Then he blinked his eyes. He was watching a commercial—breakfast foods dancing on the screen. What happened to Leslie Ann's story?

"Must have dozed off," he muttered, rubbing his face. He'd have to ask her for more details of the story later. Burke smiled to himself. That would be nice. Leslie Ann liked it when he showed an interest in her work.

The giant Thomas disconnected his portable telephone, an impressed expression on his slightly florid features. He'd been dubious when Robert had spoken of the new binding he'd applied to the Lesser Marty Burke, especially when he heard that Robert had discovered the technique from one of the Lessers' fanciful movies. Fantastic or not, however, the binding had worked. Burke had responded like any brain-burned Lesser.

One more example of Robert's already impressive mental abilities, Thomas mused. *He seems to find new uses for his powers every day. It leaves me a very poor second. Second in command, perhaps. Third in influence, after that bitch Barbara.* A fist clenched involuntarily. *Certainly not the position my strength deserves.*

His hand relaxed, and Thomas sourly put the portable phone away. *Physical strength just wasn't enough in this situation. But situations change . . .*

Harry Sturdley caught an early shuttle flight to D.C.'s National Airport, then took a cab to the downtown studio that housed *A Capital Morning,* Washington's premier local morning show. Luckily, a glimpse in the taxi's rearview mirror showed the stony planes and angles of his face.

I'm never going to crash my way onto the show with a mug like that, he thought. But even a more benign expression wasn't enough to get him past station security.

The door guard was a big, burly black man whose muscles stretched his blue uniform shirt in all the right places. Sturdley touched the guard's mind and caught the mental tag "crazy old grandpa" being attached to him when he asked to see the show's producer.

A little mental tweaking changed that to "distinguished elderly gentleman." The guard reached for the studio phone.

Before the producer even appeared through the studio doors, Harry could sense her fury at damn-fool guards and pushy comics publishers.

It required considerable psionic prodding and readjusting on Harry's part before she came up with the brilliant idea of slipping him onto the show as an amusing surprise for the guests of honor—Robert and Barbara. Harry was surprised at the effort it took to keep a smug smile off his face as the woman led him to the open-air atrium where the giants were about to go on the air. The segment would be hosted by the station's media reporter.

The producer waited for the inevitable first couple of questions and answers to pass, letting Robert get into his well-rehearsed public relations rap. Then she spoke into the headset she wore, which was connected to the unobtrusive receiver tucked in the reporter's ear.

The decorative young woman out in the atrium smiled and said, "We've got a little surprise for you this morning."

Since Robert was scanning the reporter's mind, he knew immediately what the surprise was. Both he and Barbara wore their best company faces as Harry stepped out into the atrium.

Harry had a smile on his face, too. They looked like one, big, happy family.

Aiming her face at the camera, the reporter said, "Let me introduce Harry Stirling, the editor in chief of the Fantasy Factory, the comic company which makes up the Heroes' comic book adventures."

Harry had to fight to keep his smile intact, but he'd had lots of practice with the media. "That's Harry *Sturdley*, I'm *publisher* of the Fantasy Factory, and very soon, we'll be printing more real-life stories of the Heroes' adventures. In the meantime, of course, we'll have the Heroes movie to enjoy. The story may be fictional, but one thing's for sure: these kids did their own stunts—unless they managed to find twenty-foot-tall doubles."

Robert's own smile thinned at the way Harry had both insinuated himself and taken command of the interview.

"It's a shame Harry was gone when the plot was being thrashed out," the giant said, turning to the reporter. "I'm sure you remember the big disappearance this summer. Harry and two other people vanished at the San Diego Convention Center when some criminals got out of control."

At the word "control," Robert lashed out with mental probes, aiming to seize Harry's mind even as they sat in front of the TV cameras.

Robert's look of bland superiority cracked, however, when his psionic tendrils ricocheted off a hurriedly erected mental shield.

"My story is unimportant." Harry struggled to keep the strain from his voice as he fought off the attempted mental coup. "But I've got some good news. The young couple who disappeared that day have also turned up. I was contacted by them just last night."

That little shocker disorganized Robert's attack, allowing Harry to riposte.

"Ah—" Robert found himself a little too involved to speak and fight at the same time. The psychic tension produced a static-electric charge which sparked in the air over the reporter's head.

Luckily, the young woman didn't have the mental circuitry to detect its source. Barbara did, however, and elected to cover the sudden silence by nervously launching into a story about how she'd done a stunt and gotten her costume blown off. It was better suited for late-night than morning audiences, but it filled the air as both combatants retired behind their psionic shields.

Harry capped Barbara's story with a hearty, carefully sincere laugh. "Sounds like you got a bit more than you expected that time, Barbara. Though I don't expect we'll show that take in the official Fantasy Factory movie tie-in comic."

The reporter chuckled, her eyes on the set director, who was making slicing gestures at his throat. "Well, for one reason or another, I guess we'll all be waiting for that movie, which will be out soon. I'm afraid that's all the time we have, so I'd like to thank Robert, Barbara, and, ah, Harry—"

The cameraman retreated, trying to catch all three guests in his viewfinder—a difficult job when two of them towered three times the height of the third.

Harry waved jovially as he added, "And don't forget the comic book!"

Then the red eye on the camera went dead, and the reporter pulled out her earphone. Rising from the director-style chair she'd been sitting in, she thanked the guests again and headed back into the building. Harry walked with her, aware of the poker-faced glare Robert directed at him every step of the way.

"I think that worked very well," Harry said, beefing up his psionic shields just in case Robert tried another hostile takeover. He gave the hulking giant a shark's smile over his shoulder. "They sure looked surprised, didn't they?"

Maybe I gave away more information than I got, he thought, stopping in the studio to thank the producer once again. But I served notice that these big lugs can't push us around anymore.

The amount of higher-dimensional energy radiating from the mental duel at the Earth-nexus "Washington" was infinitesimal compared to the forces roiling in the flux known as the Rift. But as a lightning rod offers a superior circuit, the small energy expenditure drew a vortex of extrauniversal force—a vortex capable of warping the three-dimensional norms of space, time, and energy.

The smiling salesman watched as Judd Corcoran signed the sales contract, the finance contract, the extended warranty contract, and the rider that insured that the finance payments would be made even if Judd dropped dead. Lots of dotted lines to be signed, all outlined in bright yellow by the salesman's highlighter pen. And every dotted line boosted the salesman's commission a little higher.

"That was work," Judd said, shaking out his wrist after pressing down on the ballpoint to imprint the multipart forms. The salesman let him keep the pen with the Metro Motors name and logo. Five cents apiece when buying twenty-five hundred.

"But look what you're getting," the salesman said, jingling the keys between his thumb and forefinger. "This year's MC^2 is already acknowledged as the industry's hottest car. You don't know what I had to do to reserve you one."

Actually, all he'd done was see what was available in inventory, but it didn't hurt for the customer to think that he'd gone the extra mile. The overpowered, under-sprung MC^2 could use all the favorable word of mouth it could get.

The keys dropped into Corcoran's palm, and the young man almost ran out the door to his new purchase. The salesman trailed behind with an avuncular smile.

Corcoran wedged himself behind the car's wheel—a slightly clumsy operation, thanks to one of the car's many design faults—and slipped the key into the ignition.

"Happy motoring," the salesman called, raising his paper-free hand to wave good-bye.

As Judd Corcoran turned the key, the laws of physics changed in that section of the three-dimensional universe occupied by the hood of the car.

For a split second, instead of delivering twelve volts to power the electrical ignition and spark plugs, the battery instantaneously delivered one hundred percent of its power potential.

The engine exploded up and outward, sending Judd Corcoran through the rear roof of his new MC^2 on a soaring trajectory that took him a good twenty feet into the air at its highest point. Were he still alive, he'd have been most impressed at the way the battery lived up to the car's name.

Chapter Twenty-Two

"Turn that shit off!" Antony Carron's usually cool, precise voice was more like a snarl as he walked into the tenement living room. His current hideout was a far cry from his suburban mansion. This was a depressed area in one of the Hudson County river towns, and the building stank of urine and scents from cuisines of many lands—all of them poor.

Carron pinched his fingers against his high-arched nose. The smell had been choking him for days, but it was the picture on the television set that made him want to vomit—the smug, almost inhumanly handsome face of Robert, shot as usual from a worm's-eye view. The big bastard—with the accent on *big*—was chatting with some Barbie-doll bimbo about his new movie.

At least he *was*, until Joey Santangelo shot up from the swaybacked couch and mashed in the *off* button on the plastic portable. The wire coat hanger used as an antenna fell down with a rattle.

"They were going to show his woman—Barbara," Nildo, one of the other bodyguards, suddenly spoke, complaint in his voice. That was another indication of the sorry state of things. Once upon a time, no underling would have dared to speak to Carron in that tone.

The former gun-running king of New York considered the 9 mm pistol holstered under his fleece running jacket. Eliminating Nildo might shore up his authority, but it would further erode morale.

Like a good lieutenant, Joey Santangelo leapt into the breach. "Whaddaya want with her?" he asked.

"She a *chica linda*," Nildo said, gesturing exuberantly toward his chest. "Got good *tetas*."

"She's too big for you," Joey-boy mocked.

"Nobody too big for Nildo." That wasn't only Latin machismo speaking. Carron had shared a john with Nildo once. The bodyguard was justifiably proud of his size.

Joey simply laughed, his eyes inviting the other guards in the room to join the joke. "She's almost twenty feet tall—*veinte*. No matter how happy you might get, it will look—" he extended the smallest finger on his right hand, and made a chopping motion with his left—"like a pinkie to her."

Harris, a tall black thug, and Sam, the blocklike fourth member of the team, added their own indelicate riffs on the general theme. Nildo sank down on the couch, humiliated.

Carron smiled approvingly at Santangelo. Sometimes there were better ways than a bullet to cut someone down to size. His eyes flashed a sneering glance at the blank TV screen while one hand went to the single out-of-place element in the shabby room—the olive drab cases of anti-tank rockets stacked behind the couch.

And sometimes, what you needed was a bigger bullet to cut a foe down to size.

"I've got to get out of this place," Carron announced suddenly. "I'm going for a drive."

The bodyguards rose almost as one man.

"Alone," Carron told them.

Joey Santangelo looked dubious. "Are you sure that's—"

"It's what I want," Carron said.

Like a good subordinate, Santangelo sat down.

Carron held his breath on the stairs. One hand held his keys, the other was tucked unobtrusively under his hooded sweat suit jacket. Nobody paid attention as he walked down the block to his car.

Hiding out in neighborhoods like this one had dictated the demise of Carron's Porsche. The car awaiting him at curbside had a ten-year-old body, a faded paint job, and lots of dents and dings. Under the hood, however, it boasted the most powerful available production engine with all of the E.P.A. modifications removed.

It was a car meant to run, and Carron appreciated the low, throaty rumble that sounded when he turned the key in the ignition.

Carron took the bridge into Manhattan, intending to meet with some uptown business associates. The gun-running trade had suffered a brief downturn when the giants began intercepting shipments using some kind of mental x-ray vision to see which vans were carrying what loads.

But the Police Benevolent Association had quickly moved to stop any competition in the law and order field. They'd gotten an injunction barring the Heroes from stopping crimes. With that legal restraint in place, the neighborhood armaments merchants were going gangbusters.

Carron should have been right back on top again. Instead, he was being forced into the position of peripheral player, dealing from across the river. The city had gotten too hot for him after he'd tried to arrange a trap for the Heroes, where their interference should have triggered a massacre of innocent bystanders. That had made him *persona non grata* in Manhattan.

Time would have taken care of that problem—the cops always have new crimes to deal with. But he'd thought he could move ahead of schedule when the head Hero— Robert—had offered him a contract to waste the Fantasy Factory's comic book artist, John Cameron. It had required a trip to California and a shoot-out at a comics convention, but he and his people had done the job.

Except Cameron hadn't died, he'd just disappeared. Robert had refused to pay off on the contract, and then gotten ugly when Carron tried to apply pressure. That ugliness is what kept Carron undercover, while Robert moved from one publicity triumph to another.

Carron viciously jammed on the brakes as he passed a playground. Even up here, the damned Heroes were playing up to the crowds. They weren't doing crime fighting anymore. Now they were into social work. A nearly twenty-foot-tall redhead with a spectacular figure was refereeing a basketball game. And astonishingly, the gangbangers on the court were behaving themselves. Carron glared with pure hatred from behind his steering wheel.

The giantess stirred, as if she were smelling something on the wind. Her eyes left the game and briefly went vague. Then she turned to look straight in Carron's direction. The redhead squinted, then her eyes went wide— with recognition.

Panic gushed through Carron. She knew his face— Robert had his freaks out looking for him!

The giantess put fingers to her mouth and gave vent to a piercing whistle, stopping the game. Then she began taking yards-long strides toward Carron. He goosed the gas on his car and roared out of there, jolting down a pot-holed street toward Broadway. In his rearview mirror, he saw the giantess vault over the twelve-foot cyclone fence surrounding the park.

Instead of providing an escape route, Broadway was jammed with traffic, not to mention hordes of school kids heading for the subway. The giantess was coming on. Carron stopped the car, flung the door open, and joined the moving crowd of kids. He compelled himself to match their pace and pulled up the hood on his sweatsuit jacket.

Not daring to turn around, he checked the view behind him by taking a glance at a store window. The giantess had halted at the edge of the crowd, peering down in confusion.

Carron felt a spark of triumph which he quickly pushed down. Keep it calm, he told himself. Don't give yourself away now. The freaks aren't invincible. You can move up on them.

He gratefully scrambled for the safety of the subway.

The next question is—can we hurt them?

* * *

"Don't look at *me!*" a thoroughly frustrated Peg Faber burst out at her boss. "If you can't keep him in line, how do you expect me to do it?"

Harry Sturdley had returned from Washington in a bad mood. Peg knew he was probably going to vent off a load of steam when he called her into his office, but she was not about to suffer a Sturdley tantrum tamely. After falling through a hole in reality and living through attempted rapes, kidnapping, and murders, a tiff with her boss was the last thing in the universe to worry her.

"If he won't listen to me, we'll just have to double-team him," Sturdley said. "I'll try to talk sense into him, and you can keep him distracted from playing real-life Silicon Savage."

"Don't bet on that, Harry," Peg warned. "Things are tough enough between John and me right now. What you're suggesting—"

"I'm suggesting you help keep him out of trouble!" Sturdley shouted. "Is that too much to ask?"

Peg looked troubled, then her face set in firm lines. "I think it is."

Sturdley strode around his office. "Great!" he growled. "I can't keep John out of the superhero sweepstakes . . . so I'll have to figure some way to use him."

He glanced at Peg, whose expression was still unfriendly.

"I mean, we need some way to divert him from reveal-ing all the cards in our hand." Harry sighed. "I showed off enough to Robert and Barbara this morning. What we need is a peek at what they're up to—"

His voice trailed off, then Harry was abruptly every inch the decisive executive. "Give Quentin Farley a call. I want him to bring everything he's gotten on Heroes' Manor." Sturdley raised a hand, stopping Peg's progress for the door. "Especially any maps and reconnaissance photos of the place he might have taken."

Peg's expression went from unfriendly to wary. "What are you up to, Harry?"

Sturdley made whisking motions at his assistant. "You'll see. Just get a meeting set up for today. And when you know the time, tell John I want him here then, as well."

Quentin Farley arrived two hours later loaded for a complete briefing, which was just as well. That's what Sturdley had in mind. He sat with John Cameron on the office couch while the detective set up an easel with blown up photos and maps.

What Harry hadn't counted on was Peg striding into the office and sitting in a chair.

"What—?" Harry began.

Peg quickly held up a steno pad. "I thought you'd want notes," she said in a demure voice.

Sturdley shut his mouth with a click, knowing Peg didn't really take shorthand, but unwilling to lace into her for insubordination with Farley present. "Ah. Ah-hum. Yes."

The room went quiet, and Farley began his presentation. "I'm not sure what you're looking for in this briefing," the detective said. "Your assistant wasn't exactly clear."

"I want you to run over the approaches to Heroes' Manor, and as much as you know of the present physical layout," Harry said.

John gave him a quick look, Peg's eyebrows rose, and Quentin Farley gave an uncomfortable cough.

"Sir, right from the beginning of this surveillance, I tried to infiltrate people onto the grounds. The giants' security—"

Sturdley no longer tried to correct the terminology to "Heroes." He simply waved a hand. "I believe I've got a way around that, which is all you need to know."

Farley now turned to John. "We've already tried experts—recon professionals. The dangers—"

Cameron looked at the detective. "I can handle myself," he said.

Whatever Farley saw in John's face, he stopped arguing. Instead, he went into a detailed presentation on what he'd observed and learned of the present state of affairs in Heroes' Manor.

When the detective finished, John stepped up to the large map of the property resting on the easel. "From the sound of it, your best approach was on the water," he said. "That brought you closest to the place."

Farley shuddered. "It also resulted in some very nasty things being done to my head," he said.

John ignored the warning. "Maybe coming in *through* the lake . . ."

"You think the water would block their mental detection?" Farley said. "I wouldn't bet on it."

"I can handle it," John assured the man again. "The question is, where could I come out of the water without being noticed?"

His finger fell on a structure delineated on the map, a structure right by the water. "What did you say this was?"

Farley dug out a large telephoto shot of a ramshackle building. "It's an old boathouse."

"Right." John nodded. "That might make a good point of entry."

John and Harry continued to pore over maps and photos as Farley left, bearing considerably less than he'd come in with. Peg held the office door for him, but didn't return inside as Farley set off down the executive corridor.

"Excuse me," she said, stepping round to her desk. "Could you spare me a few more moments?"

"Yes, Ms.—" he paused for a beat, retrieving her name from his mental memory bank—"Faber?"

Peg opened a desk drawer and withdrew two things—a checkbook and an envelope. "You're the only investigator I know," she said. "I'd like to hire you."

"My firm's services don't come cheap," Farley warned. He quoted some rates. "If you'd like a referral to someone less pricey—"

Peg shook her head and began cutting a check. The re-tainer would eat into the months of back pay Harry had passed along to her, but she could pay for a couple of weeks. If more were needed, she'd turn to Sturdley—or to John.

"I want you to try and trace somebody," she said. "I don't have a name. All I can give you is a place, a face, and the possibility that it may be a case of amnesia. It's all in here."

She handed over the check and the envelope. Farley opened it and scanned the neatly typed two-page report, the boiled down version of Peg's own attempt to check John Cameron's background. "Kokomo, West Virginia. Formerly known as Cameron Corners," the detective read. He glanced at the photo enclosed. It was one of the first publicity shots Sturdley had ordered when John start-ed drawing the *Amazing Robert* comic.

In the picture, John looked very young and just a bit scared.

Farley's eyes went from the photo to Harry's office door. "This is the young man in there . . .?" The faintest interrogative lilt entered his voice.

Peg nodded again.

The detective replaced the material in the envelope. "He's changed considerably."

Once more, Peg nodded. "That was taken before—" She cut herself off. "I think that picture would be closer to his appearance two years ago," she finally said.

"I've got a contact in Charlotte," Farley said. "I'll fax this information and see what he can dig up."

"Yes," Peg said. "Do that."

Thirty-five blocks north and west, Leslie Ann Nasotrud-ere yanked the flimsy sheet of fax paper from her desk and smiled. Then she caught her reflection in the newsroom window. Just a shade *too* predatory—this particular smile made her pearly, even teeth look awfully sharp.

Schooling her expression to broadcast standards, she scanned the fax message. Leslie Ann had known where Robert and Barbara would be this morning—at the Washington INC affiliate. She also had a contact there, who had waited until the publicity flack from Silikis Productions had been distracted by Harry Sturdley's unannounced arrival. Then Leslie Ann's friend had abstracted the giants' Washington itinerary.

One fax later, and the schedule was now on Leslie Ann's desk. She didn't intend to act immediately on the information, she just wanted a look at who the giants were seeing during their Washington stay.

Her lips pursed in a silent whistle as she read. Four senators, a newspaper owner, two names known for generations as advisors to presidents, and three names that would mean nothing to the proverbial man in the street. Leslie Ann, however, recognized them as movers and shakers inside the Beltway.

Quite a few engagements before the giants sped away to the next stop on their publicity tour.

Leslie Ann flicked a finger against the schedule, baring her teeth again in that predatory grin. She'd have to ask Marty Burke about the connection between his gigantic proteges and these national bigwigs. That would be easy enough—Marty had been downright sweet lately, always asking about her work. It was as if he knew he was on borrowed time with this relationship. He had been ever since he'd lost out at the Fantasy Factory.

Marty had proven a blunt weapon against Harry Sturdley. So, for the nonce, Leslie Ann kept Marty around because of his useful connections to the giants . . . and because nothing better had come along.

"I can't believe I'm doing this." Peg Faber shook her head as she slowly drove the rented van down unlit West-chester byroads.

"We needed someone to get me close, someone whose mind wouldn't be detected," John Cameron said from the back of the van. He was climbing into his suit of Argonian armor, which boasted an ungainly addition on the back, another piece of supertechnology he'd carried to Earth in his backpack.

"I guess that means me," Peg groused. "My mind hasn't been detectable since we got back here."

"I meant, a person with the mental shielding—" John broke off, his apology as ungainly as his appearance. "Look, I appreciate your help," he said. "We're beyond the range of Harry's power broadcaster up here, and this Argonian battery we wired into my suit doesn't have such a long operating life."

"What I can't believe is that you don't know how to drive," Peg said.

"Something else we'll have to work on now that we're back home," John said.

All of a sudden, Peg didn't have a word to say from behind the driver's wheel. John finally cleared his throat. "I guess you should kill the lights now."

With the headlights off, the darkness of the night became impenetrable—at least to normal eyes. Peg, how-ever, had immaterial senses to guide her along. Even so, she used them sparingly, keeping her mental shields up and ready. The van slowed even more, rolling almost silently down the hillside to the lake that marked one boundary of Heroes' Manor.

Peg brought the vehicle to a stop on the stony beach. John fiddled with the dome light. When he opened the side door, the interior of the van stayed dark. Peg twisted in her seat, extending a hand toward him. "You be careful in there."

John yanked off his gauntlet and gently took her hand in his. Her shields were up at full power, but he could still feel her anxiety through the clasp of flesh on flesh. John didn't know whether to feel annoyed at the attempt to hide something or to be touched at her concern.

"You be careful, too," he finally said.

"I've got Harry's magic wand of death," Peg said, producing the fountain pen-sized rod that spat a stream of deadly fire. "Any giants come reaching for me, I'll cut their fingers off." She managed a half-smile, which faded as she looked at John. "You remember this is just a scouting expedition." The smile was completely gone as she gave him a pleading look. "Don't try to be a hero."

Peg removed her fingers from John's grasp, and he finished fastening his suit. He stepped from the van, activated his gizmoidal drive, and glided silently through the air until he plunged through the surface of the water.

John hadn't tried much underwater travel on Argon. The lake's early fall chill mucked up his infrared sensors. He focused on the giants by mental means, then set off at a sedate pace toward Heroes' Manor, keeping as deep as possible to avoid leaving a wake.

As he got close to the far shore, John cast about for a few moments until his armor's diminished sensors finally detected the pilings that marked the boathouse.

He rose up inside the enclosure, still submerged but sweeping with a psionic probe to ascertain that the structure was empty. For a second, he got a hint of a contact, but when he tried again, the boathouse seemed empty.

John rose above the surface. The lake water dripping from his armor sounded unnaturally loud in his audio pickups. Unhindered now, his infrared sensors brought the shadowy room to crystal clarity. John's breath caught in shock as he discovered the antiseptically modern hospital setup, so at odds with the ramshackle exterior of the structure.

And then he saw the giant patient. The raw-boned, almost homely features were distinctive amongst the conventional prettiness of the giants. This was Gideon, the one who had tried to warn Sturdley of ulterior motives among his Heroes, then promptly vanished.

Considering the battered aspect of Gideon's body, even after months of healing, John had no problem accounting for the smallest giant's disappearance. He'd been savagely beaten into a coma, clinging to life with so tentative a grasp that John couldn't contact Gideon's higher mental functions.

John prowled the improvised infirmary until he found the file cabinet. Riffling through months of doctor's notes, he had to credit the unknown Dr. Cedric Thonneger for a painstaking approach. Heart rate, breathing, temperature, all of Gideon's physical signs had been charted. John came across a mention of semen samples being extracted, and nodded in grudging appreciation of Robert's "waste not" approach. The head giant would want as much genetic diversity as possible in his little colony.

The more recent notes took a different turn, detailing odd experiments. John read of tests on how much protection the unconscious giant's psychokinetic shields offered against radiation, of carefully inflicted radiation burns and how long they took to heal.

John frowned, an involuntary shudder running down his back. His hands clenched into fists at the thought of using a helpless invalid as some sort of laboratory animal. For one mad second, he considered confronting the giants, forcing them to see what their leader had done. Then John remembered Peg's words. "Don't be a hero."

Silently, he returned the papers to their appropriate folders and closed the file drawers. With a final look at the huge, still form on the gigantic air mattress, John stepped back to the water and submerged himself. His scouting expedition had encountered more than he'd expected on his first probe. He didn't like the implications of the Nazi-style research. This was a case for older and wiser heads.

Like a human torpedo, John arrowed toward the far side of the lake.

In this case, the only older and wiser head available was Harry Sturdley's.

Chapter Twenty-Three

Harry Sturdley shifted his lean frame on the understuffed seat of the hotel chair. It was bad enough that he'd been up half the night listening to the bizarre report of John Cameron's reconnaissance mission up at Heroes' Manor. To add injury to annoyance, however, he was now trapped in the armchair answer to the torture rack.

The blasted thing looked impressive, with its white and gilt frame and tapestry upholstery. Too bad it hadn't been designed for human spines.

However, Sturdley was not going to lose his chance to catch Stuart Silikis. He'd spent weeks trying to speak with the producer on the West Coast, but Silikis never returned his calls. Then he read in the *Hollywood Reporter* that Silikis was visiting New York to sign an option on a Broadway play. Peg had been given the job of finding Silikis, and had tracked him to an expensive show biz hotel on Fifty-eighth Street.

Sturdley found Silikis in his suite, but was left sitting in the living room while the producer hid out in the bedroom. Too bad the bathroom was on the other side of the door.

After leaving Harry to cool his heels for an hour and a half, Silikis was apparently convinced that his unwelcome visitor had no intention of leaving any time soon. At long last, the producer emerged.

"Harry!" he said, trying to make his buzz saw voice sound bright and cheerful. "Sorry about the delay. I had—er—something." He gestured vaguely toward the bedroom.

Sturdley gave him a hard look. "That could be anything from a long-distance call to a brace of hookers." He shook his head. "Look, let's get down to cases, Silikis. Robert and Barbara have been traipsing around the country for the better part of a month, banging the drums for this Hero movie. But we still haven't heard anything about a release date."

"Right," Silikis said. "That."

"Maybe it's just a little detail to you," Harry said, "but I'm supposed to be scheduling a movie-tie-in book. I've got a final script, I've got writers and artists running with the project. You don't have any post-production work to do, so why don't you have a release date?"

"Well, actually, I was going to tell you about that," Silikis said uneasily. "I knew we had initially considered a general release—"

"*Considered?*" Harry barked. "That was in the contract you signed with Marty Burke—in black and white."

"Literally speaking, that's true," Silikis admitted. "The problem is, we don't have the green."

"Green?" Sturdley repeated blankly.

"As in money." Silikis looked a bit shamefaced. "Burke thought he made a good deal with me, and I thought I had a good deal with the studio. The only thing I didn't count on was the entertainment habits of the distribution execs. They pissed away most of the budget for our film in a Beverly Hills cathouse."

"I can't believe this!" Sturdley exploded. Then he said, "I take that back. After what I've heard about Heidi Whatser-name, somehow it sounds all too likely."

Silikis shrugged. "We're screwed."

"There's no money at all?" Harry asked.

The producer sighed. "We've got enough for a very limited premiere—say, ten cities."

"New York, L.A.—where else?" Sturdley wanted to know.

Silikis went back into his bedroom and came back with a slip of paper. "Here's the list my people made up. The studio just dropped a big bomb with that supposed comedy sequel about the half-wit. We can slip into a few of those slots in ten days, get some momentum going, and move to wider distribution in a week or two."

"What can we do to help?" Sturdley asked.

"Well, those giants of yours kinda draw crowds," Silikis said. "If you could get a few to each of the premiere cities, that might help our numbers."

Sturdley frowned, thinking it over. After hearing of the bizarre doings at Heroes' Manor, he wasn't sure he wanted the giants spreading their tentacles farther around the country. On the other hand, less giants around New York might open new opportunities for some undercover action against Robert's plans.

"Okay," he finally said. "My staff will get to work on it."

The lobby clock at Harry Sturdley's building was just striking ten when the elevator arrived for Peg and her boss. She stifled a yawn, then glanced over at Harry, who seemed almost asleep on his feet.

"I'm getting too damned old for twelve-hour days," Sturdley muttered, holding the door for Peg.

"That goes for both of us." Peg squinched her big gray eyes shut, then opened them wide. "All I'm fit for is bed."

She stretched until she noticed Harry staring at her— or rather the interesting things she was doing to the sweater she wore. "Sorry," she said, blushing. "I really am out of it."

"The two of us have spent more than a week making travel plans for thirty giants to reach nine destinations. That meant hiring planes and trucks at a cost that wouldn't break us and arranging food and lodgings once they got there—not to mention stopovers along the way for publicity purposes." Harry grinned. "It's a lot easier when your characters are just on paper. If we want the Rodent to turn up at six conventions, we just hire a model in each city and FedEx the costumes."

Peg didn't respond to Harry's feeble joke. She was in a brown study as she waited for Sturdley to unlock the door to the apartment.

"I guess Myra's not home from her bridge game," Harry said, glancing at the phone machine in the vestibule. The LED on the machine flashed the red numeral one at them as they entered.

Harry pressed the "message" button, and Peg moved on to the living room. She stopped when she heard John Cameron's voice come from the speaker. "Mr. and Mrs. Sturdley, this is John—Cameron—leaving a message for Peg." The voice stopped for a moment, then went on, trying to sound casual. "Uh, Peg, if you've got a minute, give me a call at 555-1463. That's um, 718 area code. Hope to hear from you. Bye."

The machine's mechanical voice came on to give the day and time of the call. Peg didn't turn even when Harry asked, "You want me to erase it?"

"Um, yeah . . . please," she said.

She heard Sturdley tap the "rewind" button, and the subdued chatter as the tape ran over John's message.

Peg was heading for the guest room when Harry spoke. "Maybe I'm sticking my nose in where it's not wanted, but I can't help noticing that this is becoming a nightly occurrence."

She ran a hand through her mop of red curls—getting kind of long, she thought. Then she tried to phrase some sort of answer for Harry. "I'm just too tired to call him tonight. Tomorrow—"

"Tomorrow you'll be too busy, and chop him off at the knees when he calls you," Sturdley said. "You've been doing that all week. It's gotten to the point where I think John's afraid to come into the office, after getting turned down five days in a row for a lunch date."

"I don't have the time," Peg began.

"Pardon me, but we both know that's baloney," Harry interrupted. "Even when we were tearing our hair out getting the first *Robert* issue on the stands, you still had time for John. He's the only guy on Earth who could take you to Paris for lunch and get you back two seconds after coffee and dessert."

Peg didn't respond. Harry stepped into her field of vision, his hands jammed into his pockets. "It's just that I saw the two of you getting closer. Hell, you both asked me for advice on Argon. And when you came back . . . well. I'm not blind, you know."

He paused for a second, but Peg had nothing to say. "There's been something wrong between you two. You're avoiding John, barely letting him come near you."

"I can't touch him!" Peg burst out, dropping herself onto the couch. "You know how touching boosts the contact between minds? Well, when we—uh, got close, it was as if we were one person. It's too easy to pick up his thoughts, even from a casual contact, like brushing his hand." She hunched her shoulders miserably. "I don't want him to know what I'm thinking—what I suspect about him. And I don't want to know if I'm right."

She turned to Sturdley. "Harry, what if everything that's happened really *did* come out of John's brain? That would make him responsible for all the crappy stuff that happened to us." Peg bit her lip. "It would mean he's responsible for killing Mike."

"That's a lot to hold onto," Harry said. "I think you're wrong, by the way. If the giants were wish-fulfillment, why wouldn't they be real heroes? Why would the giants' world be such a pit?"

Peg opened her mouth to reply, but Harry raised a hand. "I can't tell you why Fantasy Factory look-alikes were there on Argon. But I wonder again—why only villains? Why no heroes?"

"Who says a daydream has to make sense?" Peg asked.

"Well, if you want to make sense of it, you should have a talk with John."

Peg shook her head so vigorously, curls bobbed around her face. "That's just what I can't do."

"Why?"

She raised worried eyes to Harry. "What if he writes me out of his dream?"

Sturdley stood stock-still for a moment, giving her a thunderstruck look. Then he finally said, "I've heard all sorts of reasons from guys about why they can't commit to someone. But, girlie, this one takes the cake! If you think there's something more between you and John than some nice bouncey-bouncey, the two of you have got to talk!"

"That's easy enough for you to say," Peg complained. "You've been married for years—what's kept you and Mrs. Sturdley together for so long?"

"That's easy." Harry sat beside her on the sofa, an odd gleam coming into his eyes. He leaned close to Peg, his voice going low. "Myra has done things for me that she's done for no other man."

Peg shifted uncomfortably on the plush upholstery. This was like having your trusted old grandpa suddenly start chatting about his bedtime practices with grandma.

"Yes," Harry's voice drew the word out into a whispered hiss. "She's washed my dishes. She's picked up my dirty socks—and *cleaned* them. She's even been known to bring me a beer without my asking."

Peg had been so prepared for awful revelations, it took a moment for Harry's words to get through. Then they both began laughing.

"Along the way," Sturdley said, "I learned a little about give and take—like picking up and washing my own socks and doing the dishes sometimes. Myra's not so much into beer, but she enjoys it when I make the occasional pot of tea. Give and take, Red. That's how people stay together."

Peg nodded, but added nothing to the conversation.

"You should give him a call," Harry insisted. "Hell, *I'll* get in touch with him."

Harry frowned, reaching out psionically. It took a bit of effort, finding John several miles away in the mental babble of the metropolis.

"There he is," Harry muttered. As he made contact, the imagery invading his mental circuits was so intense, it spilled over to Peg's consciousness.

She caught only an instant of emotion—a furious John in armor, smacking down a burly looking creep with a gun. The fleeting contact came just as John's fist crashed down on the gunman's wrist. Peg winced at the *crunch* conducted through John's nerves to her brain.

Harry broke the connection and turned, pale-faced, toward Peg. "Maybe we should give him a buzz tomorrow."

Peg shook her head. "Somehow," she said, "I'm not sure he'll be in an answering mood."

Peg brought the list of comics-related media people back to her desk to make sure they were on the invitation list for the movie premiere, only to find someone had been there while she was gone. Atop the usual clutter lay a neonorange envelope marked PEG in large red letters.

Frowning, she tore it open. The envelope contained one thing she'd been expecting—her own invitation to the premiere screening of *Heroes*. But the words "and guest" on the invite had been underscored in red. There was also a slip of paper—apparently an itinerary. It seemed that the remainder of this afternoon was to be spent in an expensive hair-cutting establishment. Tomorrow was marked in blocks labeled "WORK," "GETTING READY," dinner at a restaurant she'd only read about, and the premiere, followed by a post-screening party at a famous club.

While the list was mysterious, Peg recognized the handwriting. She headed straight for Harry's office, to find him in the act of hanging up the phone. "Just finished arranging the limo for tomorrow night," he announced.

"You're taking a limo?" Peg asked.

"And so are you." Sturdley's eyes went to the envelope in her hands. "I see you got my schedule."

Peg rattled the paper. "What's it all about?"

"Today's activities are so you'll look your best tomorrow. You're getting a little shaggy, Red."

Peg pushed back her hair. "And the rest?" she demanded.

"I took the liberty of making some arrangements for you and your escort."

Now Peg was staring. "My *escort?*"

Harry gave her his most avuncular smile. "That was one of the arrangements I made. *I* couldn't take you, but John agreed with just a little arm-twisting."

"*John* is taking me?" Peg shook her head. "I'm beginning to sound like an echo—and a particularly dim one, at that." She glared at Sturdley. "You've got some nerve, just dropping this in my lap."

In the face of her annoyance, Sturdley's Uncle Harry facade faded. "Well, *you* weren't going to do anything. So I figured I'd push you two together. A romantic dinner, the movie, a hot party, and after—" He didn't look at her— "well, there's a hotel room available, if need be."

When his eyes finally met hers, they were filled with concern. "Come on, Peg, give it a chance. It'll be an evening to patch things up."

"Oh, all right," she flared, heading back to her desk. "But don't blame me if it busts things up instead."

By the next evening, Peg was glumly aware of her prediction. The silence in the limousine was thick enough to slice and package.

It was a shame, really. John was looking the best she'd ever seen him. His hair was freshly cut and styled, and he wore a designer suit with a crisp white shirt and a dark silk tie.

Peg tried unsuccessfully to hide a smile, recalling her first vision of John "dressed up" in fresh jeans and a too-small corduroy jacket.

"What's so funny?" he asked.

"Remember the last time you wore a tie?"

An answering grin appeared on his face. "I had to get Elvio Vital to tie it for me." In his first days at the Fantasy Factory, the suave Mexican artist had often served as John's mentor.

"And now?"

John's smile grew wider. "I finally got him to teach me how to do it."

No longer quite the innocent he used to be, Peg thought as they arrived at the restaurant. The maitre d' fell all over himself to seat the young couple. Peg immediately detected the heavy hand of Sturdley. The mood in the place was almost aggressively romantic—the alcove they were led to was quiet and out-of-the-way. The lighting was almost as soft as the banquette they were seated on.

John handled the wine order without even consulting the proffered list. Another hint from Elvio? Peg wondered. The menu was an unwieldy monument to haute cuisine, with dishes even Peg's college French couldn't decipher.

Again, John took the lead, offering to order for both of them, requesting dishes that brought a hint of awe to their waiter's eyes while John's perfect pronunciation brought a smile to the Frenchman's face.

As the man hurried off, Peg stared at her companion. "John?" she finally whispered in disbelief.

"I almost shouldn't tell you, and leave you impressed." John tapped his forehead. "I took a look inside the guy's brain and ordered what he considered the top of the line—staying away from the stuff like snails."

He paused for a second, waiting for Peg to laugh. "Hey, I'm not the office goof anymore," he said, his smile fading. "Do you miss that John so much?"

"Sometimes . . . yes," Peg said.

John's eyes filled with shadows. "To tell you the truth, at times, so do I. He was a lot more—innocent."

His use of the word she'd just been thinking jolted Peg. She beefed up the shielding around her mind. John must have caught the psychic reverberations. "Why do you keep pushing me away?" he asked. "I used to think it was just a temporary thing—the whole shock of coming back to the city. But it's not, is it?"

"I want things to be normal—at least as normal as they get at the Fantasy Factory." It angered Peg to hear how defensive she sounded. "Is that so much to ask for?"

John's face grew tight. "But we're not normal, are we?" he asked in a low voice.

"Speak for yourself." The words were out of Peg's mouth before she could stop them.

John forced a tendril of thought through Peg's shields even as she tried to strengthen them.

But we're not what you'd call normal—or you wouldn't be able to receive this.

Peg flung him back with a blast of raw fury. *Get out of my mind! Out!* She glared at him in silence, her shields up to maximum, her hands clenched on the silverware as if she intended to stab him.

"Oh. don't get excited," John said. "Remember Harry's low profile. Let the giants do whatever they want—beat their own kind into a coma, torture them . . . what do you think they're going to do to *us*?"

"You and Harry can argue over how to save the world," Peg replied. "I don't feel the need to dress up in my armor every night to play Zorro."

"Maybe you and Harry live in a nicer neighborhood." Peg bridled at the scorn in John's voice. "I live closer to the streets—near the projects. And when I see trouble out there, I try to stop it."

"While turning yourself into a whole new UFO phenomenon," Peg shot back acidly. "Did you know that armored figures have been spotted in Georgia and Alabama as well as Manhattan?"

"That's not me," John said. "I've kept in Queens. And I try to stay out of the public eye. Nobody's even gotten a picture of me."

"Yet," Peg interrupted.

John shook his head impatiently. "Look," he said, "we aren't just plain civilians anymore. We have powers. And with power comes responsibility."

"Where'd you get that gem of wisdom?" Peg gibed. "This month's issue of *Zenith*? Or the Harry Sturdley Book of Comics Aphorisms?"

John drew back. "Actually, I found it in a biography of Theodore Roosevelt. His full quote is, 'Power invariably means responsibility—' " he paused—" 'and danger.' "

Peg looked at him for a long moment, trying to come up with something to say. In the end, she could only sigh. "I'm afraid I come down more on the side of Ralph Waldo Emerson. He said, 'You shall have joy, or you shall have power . . . you shall not have both.' "

Over John's shoulder, she could see the waiter hovering in the distance, holding back their food until the argument was over.

John followed her eyes. "Tell Harry I'll pay him back for whatever the tab comes to." He rose to his feet, yanking his carefully knotted tie askew. "Enjoy the movie. I've got business in a different suit tonight."

Chapter Twenty-Four

Harry walked into the restaurant to find Peg sitting before a barely-touched plate and an empty chair with a full dinner spread before it. One glance at her eyes told him the whole story.

"The jerk *left?*" he said.

Peg nodded numbly. "He said he had business in a different suit."

Harry scowled. "Forget it, Red. He's not worth worrying about. Anyway, you've got a new escort for the evening."

Peg came out of her misery long enough to look around. "Where's Myra?"

"Home in bed with some version of the flu. She's doing a rather rude imitation of Mount Vesuvius every forty-five minutes, and decided to pass on the premiere. I was going to stay with her, but she said this was my night." Sturdley's voice was baleful. "More like Marty Burke's night—or Robert's. But I'm stuck now—just as I'm stuck with the giants. Making a deal with Robert—that was the worst mistake of my life."

He glanced at Peg, but she was busy contemplating other mistakes.

Sturdley cleared his throat. "I suppose we should head over to the theater," he said. "Your limo or mine?"

That got at least a ghost of a smile from his assistant as he paid the bill.

After five minutes of stop-and-barely-go traffic, Harry came to the sad conclusion that they'd have been better off leaving both limos behind and walking to the premiere. His mood didn't improve as they got closer to the theater, and he realized that the congestion was all his own fault.

Harry had wanted the kind of movie premiere he remembered from the days when he was a kid. Stuart Silikis complained about added expenses, but had finally given in. The result was limos, searchlights, rubbernecking traffic, and jammed pavements on Sixth Avenue. Not only were reviewers, guests, and celebrities from both the comics and entertainment worlds arriving, the sidewalk was thick with gawkers.

The reason for the crowds was an attraction that hadn't existed in Harry's boyhood. Approximately 120 feet of Heroes stood outside the theater. Clad like his five colleagues in an immaculate white Hero uniform, Thomas shepherded his fellow giants while smiling and waving to the crowd.

The big stars of the production, Robert and Barbara, were out on the Coast with the human-sized stars for the Hollywood premiere. The lesser lights—Thomas, Ruth, Maurice, and Victor—were in subsidiary, though no less important, markets.

Of course, Thomas was used to crowds. He had his own comic book, *The Terrific Thomas*, and had made the rounds of comics conventions. In fact, Thomas's exhibition of strength at the San Diego Comic Convention had been the setup for the assassination attempt on John Cameron—the start of John, Peg, and Harry's odyssey through the Rift.

As their car pulled into the line of waiting limos, Sturdley stared up at the sandy-haired giant. The first time he'd seen Thomas, he'd been impressed by a muscular form straight out of a classic comic—"Murphy Anderson abdominal muscles" had been his initial thought. With Thomas's handsomely rough-hewn features, that had been enough to start Sturdley thinking in terms of an addition to the Heroes titles.

Now Harry wished he'd paid more attention to the cold eyes, that incipient sneer on his lips. Oh, Thomas was smiling and waving, but Harry had a cold feeling that the giant could just as easily be slaughtering the adoring masses who barely came up to his knees.

* * *

Matavi repressed a sigh as she stared around the Diamond Exchange. Over the last two weeks, her existence with Emsisdin in New York, as she had finally learned the place was called, had settled into a certain routine.

Matavi would use her mental abilities to scout various locales where wealth was stored. She located the guards and security devices that might bar their path—after the debacle at Tiffany's, she'd learned to invade minds for security information before entering. Some of the alarm devices she could handle psionically. Others she'd had to describe to Emsisdin, who had proven surprisingly adept at using primitive Earth technology to circumvent guardian systems in unexpected ways.

"Don't look so surprised," the cocky Argonian gangster had told her as he assembled circuitry out of crude-looking components. "As the Rationalists gathered power back home, they started many programs to uplift less advantaged sectors of society. I learned a bit about all sorts of useful trades—" his lips twisted in a sneer as he looked down at his busy fingers—"and some I thought not so useful. But even that course in restoring antique technology is coming in handy."

Antique or not, Emsisdin's little creations seemed an order of magnitude ahead of New York's available alarm technology. Matavi suspected they could live better selling antisecurity devices to local criminals than stealing and fencing valuables. But Emsisdin wouldn't hear of it. He even wired his contraptions to self-destruct after they had served their purpose.

The raid on the Diamond Exchange had been par for the course. Matavi had seized control of a guard's mind to allow them entrance. She'd used another mind-controlled security officer to incapacitate the security control room. Then it had been a case of psionically pulling the guards toward her one by one to be darted. Six "renta-cops," as they identified themselves, had slumped blank-faced—and blank-minded—at her feet.

Meanwhile, Emsisdin deployed his high-tech arsenal to defeat wires, cameras, motion detectors, even beams of coherent light. He happily ranged the silent halls of the exchange, looting jewelry from anything that had a lock. From a glimpse at his mind, Matavi knew he was trying to show his usefulness in their partnership.

Emsisdin was painfully aware that Matavi had done the lion's share since their arrival. She had created their identities as Finnish business travelers, seeking a nationality that matched their appearances and also provided an obscure, impenetrable language barrier.

She had warped minds to arrange for everything from food and shelter to financial services. They had a bank and a checking account, an office where they kept their armor, and a pleasant sublet. Even the man who fenced their loot had been discovered and brainwashed by Matavi.

They had a command of English thanks to her mental thievery. Emsisdin had been rigid with anxiety when she implanted the necessary knowledge in his cerebral cortex, fearful that she would tamper with his mind. For a brief second Matavi had been tempted. But over the long term, controlled minds proved to be blunt weapons. She reminded herself of what happened with Melador back home on Argon. Besides, what was the purpose?

Purpose . . . from the first, her only purpose in life had been to survive as a valuable commodity—the successful survivor of a gene-meddling program. Working telepaths had been relentlessly exploited. But Matavi had learned to exploit back, becoming a premier corporate intelligence operator. Then the Rationalist movement had begun, determined to banish certain genes—and Matavi's abilities. Even after the fighting was over, she'd managed to survive several years, living underground. But in the end, she'd been caught and sent to the Sphere of Exile. Her millennium of incarceration had been another lesson in survival among snarling, vicious, sometimes insane personalities.

Then . . . she'd perceived the shift in the roiling flux-stuff around them, the passage of the traveler John Cameron. Matavi had taken immediate advantage of the possibility of escape. As more escapees utilized the disturbances in the void, she'd become prominent in the Deviant underground, until she alone ran the rebels' intelligence operation.

Matavi had emerged from this struggle with two imperatives—her personal survival and the perpetuation of the powers she'd developed.

As Emsisdin approached with a jingling bag of choice loot, she had to admit that their recent activities had laid a foundation for the first imperative. But the long-term question remained. What were they going to do on this strange new world?

Mere moments into the ride home, John Cameron knew he had made a mistake taking the subway. He'd wanted to calm down after the confrontation with Peg, wanted—his expression went sour—to get home *normally*.

Rush hour was long over, and John was the only one in the subway car wearing a suit. And even though he'd removed his tie, his affluent appearance seemed to imprint the word WITHDRAWALS on his forehead.

After dealing with three beggars in as many stations, John became aware of the scrutiny of a nasty piece of work peering at him from the other end of the car. The scrutinizer was big, but a lot of his bulk came from fat. He also had a sharpened screwdriver jammed in his back pocket. After taking stock of John up Broadway and across Fifty-ninth Street, the thug made his move as the train thundered through the tunnel between Manhattan and Queens. He'd already taken a seat beside John. When the train hit a rough spot on the rails and the lights flick-ered, the hood whipped out his screwdriver, aiming to place the sharpened tip at John's throat.

But John was aware of the move even in the dark. He grabbed the shaft of the screwdriver, trying to deflect it. The body-warmed metal was greasy and slipped between his fingers.

A new fury exploded in John's mind. Couldn't he even handle a garden-variety mugger? Rage blazed in his eyes as he glared through the darkness. It ignited a dull red spark in the metal shaft of the sharpened screwdriver. Changes occurred in the metal as the ferocity of his emotion attacked the crystalline lattice of the tempered steel. The spark briefly brightened, and the tip of the screwdriver twisted away as the metal shaft bent as though it were made of warm taffy.

The lights resumed, and a thoroughly discomfited thug stared at the *objet d'art* his weapon had just become. He turned suddenly fearful eyes toward John, who abruptly rose and exited at Queensboro Plaza.

John found an empty stairwell, started down, and Rifted home to Astoria. He felt no triumph at scaring the hoodlum. Even the strange new wrinkle in his powers—could it be telekinesis?—barely interested him.

All John wanted to do was get out of the monkey suit he wore and into his armor.

Why? he asked himself. Was there that great a need tonight to kick ass and take names? Or was he just running from the mess he'd made of whatever delicate bond he might have shared with Peg?

It's better this way, he tried to assure himself. Now she's free to find some stud—I mean, some nice, everyday guy without weird powers.

John wadded up his designer outfit and tossed it in the corner. Although, he wondered, what would that potential new boyfriend make of Peg's suit of armor in Harry Sturdley's closet?

The traffic on Sixth Avenue had broken down to an almost complete standstill. But even in the back seat,

Antony Carron could feel the power of the big V-8 engine throbbing through the floorboards of the car he had reclaimed after escaping the giantess.

Joey Santangelo sat hunched over the steering wheel as they crept through Rockefeller Center at a rate that could only be called agonizing. He barely looked at the searchlights, crowds, and hoopla in front of the huge theater on the right. "Are you sure this is okay?" he asked his boss. "I mean, if these guys can read minds . . ."

"They've got hundreds—maybe a *thousand* minds around them," Carron pointed out. "That's a lot of reading to do."

Privately, he wondered how the multitude surrounding the giants must feel to a telepath. Was it a dull roar impinging on the consciousness? Or something more like the chittering of insects?

In the final analysis, he didn't care, as long as it kept the giants' early-warning systems overloaded.

Even so, Carron didn't take chances. He kept his mind off what he intended to do, taking refuge in Zen. Zen archery: The archer is the arrow. The arrow is in the target.

He kept his mind on pseudooriental mumbojumbo until the seeming clunker made its way past the knot of giants. The snarled traffic began breaking up. Carron glanced from the huge figures to the opening spaces ahead. "Windows, Joey."

Santangelo stabbed a finger at the power window controls. The two rear windows smoothly slid out of the way.

Antony Carron brought the olive drab tube resting on his knees up to his shoulders. He squinted through the attached scope, searching for a target.

There—the brunette with the ample top.

The crosshairs centered on her head, then her chest, and finally, her knee.

Carron squeezed the trigger. A yard-long plume of flame gushed from the rear of the tube, and an antitank rocket arced from the front.

When Joey heard the blast of the propellant, his foot came down hard on the gas. With a squeal of tires, the rust-bucket took off like a bat out of hell.

Chapter Twenty-Five

Penelope's ample bosom rose and joggled entrancingly as she stood outlined in the glare of the premiere search-lights, waving to the crowd. With a figure outstanding even by Masterly standards, Penelope was used to turning heads. But then, the simultaneous adulation and lust of hundreds of minds was an experience she'd never encountered before. On her homeworld, her appearance usually generated fear among the Lessers who saw her—fear and a bit of strangu-lated desire. In this strange new world, however, the males were much more open in their appreciation.

Normally, Penelope would have become furious at being ogled at by mere Lessers. But here, the unabashedly hormonal response to her body, amplified by the multi-tude of minds, felt like basking in warm sunshine.

As Penelope smiled and waved to the crowd, Thomas nudged her, indicating a pair of Lessers exiting from a limousine. "Harry Sturdley," he whispered, a sneer shad-ing his tone. "And his red-headed slut."

With her eyes on their enemies, Penelope never noticed the flash from the window of the passing car. Only the surprise and alarm she detected among the Lessers made Penelope turn her head.

By then, the antitank rocket had almost struck the telekinetic shields that supported her body. This was no mere baseball bat or bullet. A 9 mm slug weighs a little more than a quarter of an ounce. The warhead aimed at Penelope's knee weighed more than five and a half *pounds*.

Penelope's shields shredded under the impact. They absorbed some of the kinetic shock, slowing the warhead slightly, then failed. The metal tip of the rocket struck skin, then turned the kneecap and the delicate joint it protected into a red ruin. Penelope's leg buckled, her eyes going wide with shock, terror, and pain.

The giantess tried to grab onto Thomas's shoulder, but her hands were clumsy, fumbling, not quite in synch with her brain. Down she went, twisting to make a desperate grab for the lip of one of the searchlights. Overheated metal sizzled against palms no longer protected by psychic shielding. Penelope lost her hold and fell to the ground screaming, the agony of her burns and fractured leg broadcast to all telepaths in the vicinity.

Thomas, his fists clenched, gazed with such concentration at Sturdley and Peg that he didn't realize anything untoward had happened until the blast of pain assailed his mind.

He turned in shock, able to offer only a stupid stare as Penelope's hands groped feebly at his shoulders. Then she toppled, shrieking in anguish. Thomas tore his eyes away from the sight, shooting out mental probes, trying to find the perpetrators.

Almost instantly he pinpointed a combination of malice and triumph in a car screaming away. A momentary image came—Antony Carron. Recognizing another member of the enemies list, Thomas charged forward, but had hardly taken a step before he found himself blocked by a throng of curious Lessers.

"Back! Get out of my way!" Thomas roared. But the damnable fools refused to clear out, surging forward to gawk at the bleeding Penelope.

The giant had no patience. He had to get through. And if the Lessers wouldn't move, he'd *make* them. When Thomas reached the tightly-packed mob, he lashed out with his right foot.

Cries of confusion abruptly turned to screams of pain and terror as Thomas waded into the crowd, lashing out right and left with his legs. Buskin-covered feet half as large as a normal human body smashed into onlookers with sickening thuds or the muffled crunch of breaking bone.

But a path began to open as people along Thomas's course clawed at the bodies behind them to escape those relentless, crushing kicks. Still others fell to the ground in the panic-stricken scramble, only to be trampled by members of the crowd.

Thomas could move more quickly now, needing only the occasional kick to clear the way of crouched or dazed figures. He felt the psychic stir as Kevin, one of the better mindcasters among the giants, tried to reach out and dominate the driver of the car.

Kevin apparently tried to force the driver back to the theater. Unfortunately, his control wasn't complete. The escaping car turned, swerved onto the far sidewalk, then proceeded south causing new mayhem.

Thomas attempted to cross the avenue, now forced to deal with standstill traffic. He was nearly incoherent with rage, screaming for the cars to give way. When they didn't, he snatched up a slow-moving cab. Brakes shrieked as he raised the vehicle over his head.

From the crowd below came a sudden, sharp sense of *déjà vu*. Thomas looked down at the swirling confusion at his feet to lock glances with Harry Sturdley. Of course.

During the attack in San Diego, he'd been entertaining the Lessers by picking up cars.

Effort and rage made the veins pulse in Thomas's neck. He could feel the pounding of his blood. Here was a chance to do away with one of Robert's bitterest enemies on this world . . .

Sturdley seemed to recognize his danger at almost the exact same moment. The Lesser's hand dove to an inside pocket of his suit. A second later it emerged, clutching a stubby metal rod. A pen? What did Sturdley expect to do with that?

But just as Thomas was about to heave the cab down, a beam of light streaked from the rod. It was pallid, barely noticeable in the extravagant blazes of the searchlight. But it sliced unimpeded through Thomas's shields, his uniform, and into his flesh.

The sting of sudden pain upset Thomas's grasp on the taxicab. It cartwheeled out of his hands to smash into other cars on the avenue, creating an instant roadblock.

Thomas caught an odd odor, like scorched cloth and overcooked meat. He twisted his arm to see where the beam had hit it, feeling a sudden burning twinge. The immaculate white spandex of his uniform was now marred by a charred brown line across his left bicep. The fabric had split and curled away, revealing angry burned skin around a razor-straight trench seemingly seared through his flesh. There was no blood—the heat of the bolt had apparently cauterized the wound. It was merely a graze—the proverbial flesh wound.

But that beam could just as easily have continued to slice through flesh and bone until it had amputated his arm. The world around Thomas began to dissolve in a red haze. In the space of seconds, Lessers had dared to assault Masters *twice*. Still worse, they had succeeded in inflicting pain!

Thomas yelled orders, his voice bellowing across the crowd noise. "Kevin, get that car! Camilla, take care of Penelope. Everyone else—*punish these vermin!*"

His followers, already burning with fury and fear, didn't need any more persuasion. In seconds, pandemonium quadrupled as four giants rampaged into the crowd.

Harry Sturdley felt his gorge rise as he saw a woman fly over the crowd, propelled by a particularly vicious kick. Her body was as limp as a rag doll's, but her mouth was open, emitting a keening wail of pain that cut over the confused, frightened roar of close-packed humanity.

Harry gripped the weapon in his hand more tightly. The metal rod had been warmed by contact with his flesh, but it felt slippery in his sweat-dampened palm.

"So much for scaring off Thomas," he muttered to Peg, who stood pressed against him in the crush of people. The sensation might have been pleasant if they hadn't been in danger of getting stomped to death.

Peg didn't answer, her face pale with nausea, the features screwed up as if she were in physical pain.

"Boost your shields," Harry advised. "I think you're tapping in to what's coming from that giantess."

Another inhuman shriek came from a distance in the crowd.

Or maybe into what's coming from the people around us.

Peg straightened a bit, some of the lines disappearing from her face. "I—I think you're right," she croaked. "That—the pain was really getting to me."

"What we've got to figure now is what we can do," Harry said. His face tightened as he looked around. It was like gazing into a painting of Hell by—what was the painter's name?

"Bosch, maybe," Peg mumbled, picking up his thought, "Or Doré'."

"Now I know how it feels," Harry said.

"What?" Peg grabbed his arm as the Brownian movement of the crowd suddenly threatened to pull them apart.

"I've written it a million times. The superhero gets caught in some crisis while in his secret identity. How can he save people without giving himself away?"

"Except our problem is that we left our superpowers in our other suits," Peg said, nearly getting flung on her back as the crowd began a new scramble.

A new giant—not Thomas—was storming in their direction. Harry brought up his blast-rod, hoping for a clear shot, hoping no one would see, wondering just how long the batteries lasted on the damned things.

"You know what this is?" Harry muttered as the stampede of people carried them along with it.

"What?" Peg was trying to keep cool, but the strain showed in her voice.

"I'd say this is a job for John Cameron."

"We're . . . not . . . getting . . . outta . . . here."

Joey Santangelo's voice was hoarser than usual, his tight vocal cords reflecting the struggle being waged for control of his body. Quite simply, his hands and feet felt like wood, unresponsive to his own will. They moved to someone else's orders, turning the escape car around, back toward those damned giants.

"Joey, what the hell do you think you're doing?" Carron yelled, pulling a pistol from under his jacket as the car lurched onto the sidewalk.

"Not thinking. They—they're *makin'* me come back," Santangelo croaked. He could say no more. All his will had to be devoted to the struggle *not* to turn the ignition off, *not* to take his foot off the gas.

His only weapon was his enemy's ignorance of how to operate a car. The giants could never fit into the vehicles, and had no notion of how they worked. The mind trying to control him had to fumble for technical knowledge. Joey, on the other hand, was operating sheerly on instinct, swerving the big clunker from side to side in an attempt to hit as few bystanders as possible.

At last, however, Joey's psychic antagonist dug out enough knowledge to sabotage any escape attempt.

A harsh whisper of "H—hang on!" was the only warning Santangelo could offer as his own hands sabotaged them, turning the wheel to send the car careening into a taxi held motionless in the Sixth Avenue traffic jam.

Joey managed to avoid a head-on crash with the stuck cab, turning the impact into a sideswipe instead. The muscle car bounced off, only to get hung up on the pole of a streetlight instead. The windshield dissolved in a tracery of cracks, and Santangelo was flung against his seatbelt. In the rear of the car, Carron had no constraints and was thrown upward into the roof. He sprawled on the back seat, half-stunned.

As if the crash had dispelled the mist in his mind, Santangelo suddenly found himself free of giant mind control. He shook his head, glancing around. His front view was useless, more like a kaleidoscope than a windshield. Then he looked out the side window and saw why the control had dissipated. One of the giants was striding toward them.

At once, Santangelo began clawing at his seatbelt buckle. He kicked a way out of the twisted door. His boss was just pushing himself up, groaning.

Joey desperately scanned the back of the car. Hadn't Carron brought more than one of those rockets?

"Boss?" he called through the still-open window, "one of the freaks is coming for us. Do we fight or run?"

"F—fight," Carron muttered, grabbing for an olive drab tube jammed under the front seat.

Then the mental mist rolled in again. Carron suddenly began moving in slow motion.

Santangelo turned, staring up without hope at the handsome, ruthless face glaring down at them.

The only thing that could save us now is Zenith swooping down from the sky, Joey thought.

Then, behind their advancing nemesis, he saw a pair of flying figures.

"—the hell?" Joey mumbled.

"— in the name of seven hells do you think you're doing?" Emsisdin's voice crackled in the earphones of Matavi's half-armor. She smiled at his reference to pre-Rationalist religion, but didn't respond otherwise. Since their arrival on this world, she'd done pretty much what he wanted, except for warming his bed. Now there was something she wanted, and he'd have to follow along.

Matavi wanted to track down the source of the telepathic outcry that had blasted through her mind as she stood in the Diamond Center. If Emsisdin hadn't finished sorting through his loot, too bad.

She flew the few blocks to the site of the mental disturbance, pursued by an angry Emsisdin. They arrived to find a company of three-story-tall humanoids wreaking havoc on a large crowd.

Matavi hung in the air, almost too surprised to throw out mental probes. The appearance of the giant humanoids took her by surprise. Matavi had gotten some mental impressions of giants from the minds she'd raided. Some seemed to refer to a sporting team, others did not. She'd basically ignored them, as she had the television coverage of the movie called *Heroes*.

Now she regretted her ignorance, because the giants apparently had psionic powers. Matavi was interested, but couldn't deny her disappointment. Oversized telepaths wouldn't help *her* notions of a breeding program . . .

Emsisdin's urgent voice cut through her thoughts. "Stop staring and let's get out of here," he said. "We're being noticed by more and more people."

Matavi was aware of the people on the ground staring upward even as they jostled each other to avoid being stomped. Arms rose to point. Voices screamed. Already too many minds had seen them—too many to have the memory erased. Matavi shrugged in her half-armor. Well, it had to happen sometime.

A flare of mental power focused her attention on a giant stalking across the wide, traffic-snarled road below. The giant was using a crude compulsion construct to keep a pair of humans frozen beside a wrecked land-transport vehicle. The huge stalker's intentions were all too evident.

"Come on," Emsisdin transmitted yet again. "Let's leave—what are you doing?"

Matavi checked her wrist blasters. "Teaching a bully not to choose victims smaller than he is," she replied.

She swooped down, her fingers forming the tridigirector.

Chapter Twenty-Six

"This way!" Peg Faber yanked on the lapels of a semi-famous soap star's suit jacket. The actor's usually expressive face was blank with fear.

Peg pointed him toward an inconspicuous indentation in the wall of the movie theater. "That's an entrance to the subway over there. Head down the stairs."

The actor must have been a bus-and-cab New Yorker. "Is—isn't that dangerous?" He dragged his feet as she tried to shove him in the proper direction.

Peg glared at the guy as if he were out of his mind. "More dangerous than that?" she asked, gesturing to the carnage along Sixth Avenue.

Below the screams and yells of the terrorized moviegoers, the whimpers and moans of the injured rose in muted, hellish counterpoint.

They may be the lucky ones, Peg thought. Some of the huddled, bloody forms littering the pavement made no sounds at all. They didn't move. They didn't appear to be breathing.

Peg forced her attention away from them. There were still plenty of warm, mobile bodies with their brains apparently disconnected. A vengeful giant appeared on the left, so they ran to the right. Heavy stomping feet crashed down on the right, so they veered to the left—at least the ones who survived did. Chickens with their heads cut off.

A few of the more with-it crowd members had stormed the entrance of the theater. But as soon as they were safely indoors, they'd stopped, jamming the lobby to watch the show outside—and blocking that route for any other fugitives.

Would-be escapees had congregated at the locked doors of nearby office buildings, trying to get in. These clusters had proven very attractive for the rampaging giants. Still bodies and vast smears of blood marked places where fleeing patrons had failed to win entrance.

A plate-glass window had shattered inward under the pressure of another surge of frenzied fugitives. It offered a possible haven—if one had the nerve to navigate between the red-stained shards of plate glass that rose up like fangs in the windowframe.

Peg hauled again on the dithering actor's jacket, wishing for about the fiftieth time this night that she were in her armor. Harry was wrestling with another lost lamb, trying to steer him toward safety and nearly being pulled along in a new terrified stampede. It would be a lot easier if the cool heads in the crowd were backed up by exoskeletal muscles . . .

The resistance in the soap actor's frame dissolved as he stared upward, his mouth falling open. "Look! Up in the sky!" he said.

Peg was about to reprove him for using another company's tagline when she caught movement from the corner of her eye. She glanced skyward to see a human-sized armored figure floating over the maelstrom of violence on the avenue.

For a second, her chest tightened and she found it hard to breathe. John had come to the rescue!

Then she saw the stubby bazooka-like weapon in the figure's right hand and squinted harder. That wasn't John's armor. It was the M-16 look-alike who had tried to kidnap her back on the planet Argon!

Perhaps later she could think about what the airborne Deviant's presence portended. Right now she had more pressing problems closer to the ground. Another god-damned giant was lurching her way. With a sound of disgust, she hurled the actor toward the available bolt hole, hurrying him along with a kick in the butt.

Then she joined Harry in moving the crowd member he'd buttonholed. Maybe they should head for the stairway themselves. She glanced over her shoulder. The giant was coming closer.

Yes. Better claustrophobia than ending up a jellied smear on Sixth Avenue.

John Cameron was in his armor and in the air, moving as if he'd finally found his native element. His armor was a damned sight more inflexible than the blue wool designer suit he'd doffed in his apartment. So why was he so much more comfortable flying patrol?

The image of Peg, carefully done up for the *Heroes* premiere, rose in his mind's eye. Lead weights seemed to sink in John's gut. He tried to leave the mental picture behind, flying in a lazy spiral that left Astoria far below him. The only thing to watch out for was the occasional plane taking off from La-Guardia Airport. Now the whole of Queens lay like an intricately wired relief map, tiny glittering lights representing individual homes. Astoria was now a neck of land jutting out from Queens proper. The highways sewing the county together gleamed like looped diamond and ruby necklaces created from the glimmer of headlights and brake lights.

New York truly did look like a city of dreams when seen from on high. Closer to the ground, a depressing reality became visible. John saw the graffiti on the expressway overpasses, the dog crap at the base of the gleaming buildings, the human flotsam in search of the evening's victims.

At least he could take care of the last category. Perhaps punching out some urban terrorists would loosen the steel straps that seemed to have wrapped round his chest since he left Peg in that restaurant. At least it might distract him . . .

With a flick of his jaw, John activated the radio receiver in his suit. He'd calibrated the apparatus to sweep the news and police frequencies—a useful adjunct in pinpointing local crimes and gauging the uniformed response.

" . . . out of midtown," a traffic helicopter reported. "Sixth is completely clogged, and the riot at Fiftieth seems only to be getting worse."

Fiftieth and Sixth—the location of the theater where *Heroes* was to premiere. What was that about a riot?

John flicked to the Manhattan police frequencies. "We've sealed off the area, but I'm not going to send in the riot squads," a nervous voice argued. "Even fully-armed, they'll be no match for a bunch of berserk giants. Those suckers are bulletproof, and I don't have much hope of stopping them with tear gas."

As John listened, he threw his body into a midair tumble, reorienting himself on midtown Manhattan and redlining his gizmoidal drive to get there as soon as possible.

The voice in his earphones paused for a moment. "Any luck on getting the National Guard to release some of their antitank missiles? We think that's what the drive-by shooter used to zip the giantess— "

John had left Harry and Peg to handle the rigors of the film premiere. But they were as vulnerable as the other innocent bystanders if the giants had run amuck.

I told Peg I had business tonight in this suit, John thought. Looks like I'll have more business than I expected.

Then, too, there would be newspeople, photographers, camera crews on both the local and network levels. John's business would be public and high-profile.

He began checking his weapons systems. Maybe if he saved Harry Sturdley's butt there'd be less discussion about proceeding in a circumspect manner.

Thomas paused in midkick as a new wave of pain attacked his immaterial senses. This wasn't the unfocused pain-yammering of the terrified Lessers beneath his feet. It was the sending of a psionically gifted mind, which in Thomas's book meant a Master was in pain.

Yes. Kevin was suffering burns. Then Thomas's mind-connection was abruptly snapped. Psionic warfare! He drove probes back toward the embattled giant's mind, but Alexander was already unconscious.

Thomas spread a mental net to find the pair of attackers Kevin had gone to dispatch, but Carron and his damnable Lesser assistant were already fleeing on foot, vanishing into the mental hum of the big city.

Changing course, Thomas headed for the giant casualty, only to be intercepted by another of his cohorts. Andrew had obviously been carried along on the tide of anger following the attack on Penelope—ominous red stains on his buskins showed that. But it seemed as though he now had second thoughts.

"Thomas," he said uneasily, "maybe you should rein Walter in—tell him to stop chasing the crowds and send him to Kevin."

"Why?" Thomas gibed. "Are you feeling squeamish about teaching a few Lessers their proper place?"

"I'm worried that those damned picture-takers are recording what we do," Andrew replied. "Is this really what Robert would want?"

Hearing their leader's name struck Thomas like a bucket of cold water. The whole point of appearing in this Hollywood charade had been to lull the Lessers while Robert worked out his plans. To put it mildly, Robert would not be pleased by tonight's turn of events.

"Gods below," Thomas swore. "We can't let Robert see this—the Lessers, either."

"How are you going to do that?" Andrew asked worriedly as his temporary leader marched wrathfully off.

"Those little boxes the Lessers carry hold the pictures," Thomas said. "I'll just have to break them and let the pictures out."

* * *

Marty Burke was happy now that he'd worn a black outfit to the movie premiere—not because it made him look slimmer, but because there'd be less physical evidence if he messed himself.

He'd been standing with Leslie Ann and her camera crew for the pre-premiere festivities, adding a little color commentary to her coverage of the arrivals of the great and near-great. Then the tone of the evening had abruptly changed with the drive-by rocket attack and the giants going berserk. Burke's first inclination had been to .get indoors somewhere. But Leslie Ann had rallied her cameraman to record the worst of the carnage, charging perilously close to crushing giant feet.

Burke had stayed beside her. His brain was telling Marty that he was doing a very brave thing. Unfortunately, a couple of his sphincters seemed to have other ideas on the matter.

Leslie Ann seemed to have no conception of the danger into which she so blithely thrust herself. She interviewed injury victims, or rather, stood looking concerned while they moaned and sobbed for the camera. She buttonholed fugitive crowd members, including several movers and shakers. An ex-mayor nearly knocked her down when she tried to stop him for a few words.

Burke had been frankly astonished by their luck in surviving. The street scene had started to clear. Everyone who could move had run for whatever cover was available. The only people still standing around were the camera crews, all now broadcasting live details of what Leslie Ann had christened "The Slaughter on Sixth Avenue."

The cameraman panned across the avenue, following Thomas as he disrupted another network's crew. Leslie Ann snapped off her microphone and turned to Burke. For a brief second, her broadcast face disappeared and she frankly gloated.

"Got the bastards now," she said. "Ever since the first time I saw those overgrown freaks, I *knew* there was something wrong about them. I just couldn't prove it. Now they're showing the world that the precious 'heroes' aren't all sweetness and light. They're doing it on tape . . . and they're doing it in every living room across the country."

For a second, Burke wanted to argue with her. After all, the giants Leslie Ann was attacking were *his* heroes—his supporters in the battle for the Fantasy Factory. But one of those supporters—Thomas—was presently punting a cameraman the length of a city block. The camera shattered on impact. Burke turned away to avoid seeing what happened to the technician.

"Great coverage," he managed to say. "But are you sure this is the way to get it? Out here in the open? Maybe you should go for a bird's-eye view—up in one of the office buildings— "

He pointed to the glass-and-concrete towers surrounding the scene of carnage. From the corner of his eye, he detected Thomas heading for them.

"We'd have to go off the air to get up there," Leslie Ann said flatly. "And no way are we going off the air."

She flicked on her mike, resumed her plastic face, and stepped back into the camera frame with new commentary. Burke wondered how the cameraman felt, watching Thomas grow larger and larger through his viewfinder. Maybe the guy's job depended on doing what Leslie Ann said. Burke's job didn't.

Marty stepped forward, pointing desperately over Leslie Ann's shoulder. She glanced at Thomas, but continued speaking. As Burke came closer, threatening to come on-frame, Leslie Ann gestured for the cameraman to pull in for a tight shot on her face. Then, still talking, she used her free hand to fend Marty off while keeping most of her attention on the camera.

Burke pulled away, then stepped behind Leslie Ann, heading into Thomas's path. Maybe she'd see what he was doing and wake up to her personal danger. Maybe Thomas would recognize him, and Burke could talk him out of this attack. That would make Marty Burke a household name.

Thomas loomed over Burke, not a trace of recognition in his face.

Or maybe, Burke thought, I'm about to get squashed like a bug . . .

John Cameron flew over a cordon of police to find the area around the movie theater pretty much empty of activity. Two giants were down, two more knelt over the stricken titans, tending them. In the distance, another giant seemed to be involved in waving his arms over his head. John ignored him, at least for the moment. The only giant engaged in anything like a hostile act was Thomas. He was advancing on a lone camera crew.

As John came closer, he saw a figure detach itself from the crew and move to intercept the giant, waving its arms. It was either the bravest or most stupid thing John had ever seen. Then he recognized Marty Burke, which seemed to answer that question.

Two more figures came dashing onto the scene—Harry Sturdley and Peg Faber. They began arguing with the news crew. From INC, John noticed. Could that be Leslie Ann Nasotrudere down there?

John focused his attention from the byplay to the main action. Thomas wasn't going to stop. He was raising his foot, apparently determined to stomp Burke flat, when John revved his drive unit and aimed himself straight for the giant's jaw. At the last moment, John cut the drive and flipped end for end, arrowing in on momentum alone.

His impact smashed back Thomas's telekinetic shields until John's armored boots impacted against the point of the giant's chin. The effect was as if Thomas had been slugged with a particularly robust punch.

The giant, caught offbalance, staggered back, nearly falling to the pavement. John ricocheted off Thomas's jawline, cutting in his gizmoidal drive to hang in midair at his adversary's eye level. Down below, Marty Burke darted away, heading back to the INC camera crew.

Thomas shook his head like a prize fighter trying to come back from a good shot. He glared around, trying to spot what had hit him. John waved until Thomas caught the motion. His usually florid face went red with rage, and he lunged forward, aiming a roundhouse swing.

John boosted gizmo and floated above the punch, dodging right and then left to avoid subsequent empty blows. Poor Thomas, John thought. He looks like his friend a couple of blocks away.

Flying beneath the giant's fist, John looped around to strike with both feet just at the solar plexus.

Thomas folded, stumbling back.

How does it feel, bully? John sent mentally. How does it feel to be on the receiving end of pain instead of dishing it out?

The giant tottered over to the microwave mast rising from one of the network vans. The transmission tower rose nearly as tall as Thomas. His face was no longer red. It was pale and pinched.

Thomas seized hold of the mast at its base and yanked it free. Holding the metal pole in both hands like a quarter-staff, he jabbed at John. With a banking motion, John sent his armor swooping under the thrust.

But Thomas wasn't through. He twirled the mast in a wide loop, then chopped downward as if he were swinging an ax handle.

Thomas had a good eye. The metal spar connected, jolting John out of the air.

John's plast-alloy armor withstood the blow, but he had the air knocked out of him as he crashed into the ground with bruising force. Thrusting up with his arms, John twisted on the pavement to look up at Thomas. The giant was raising the microwave mast for another shot. His face was florid again, his lips pulling away from his teeth in a rictus of anticipation.

"Robert will be glad to hear that I disposed of you, Lesser scum."

John tried to activate his gizmoidal drive, but all he got was sparks and a stench of burning insulation. He had no escape—physically. John brought up his hands to blast at Thomas, but the giant was already swinging.

So it all ends with me being pounded into the ground, John thought, while I fry Thomas.

The mast slashed down, suddenly intersecting with a glaring burst of white radiance. Solid metal flared and disintegrated, leaving Thomas with only a small stub of his weapon. The rest of the metal mast flew off to land with a clatter. Thomas faltered to a stop, staring in disbelief at his amputated staff. That hesitation saved Thomas's life, as John's blast-bolts crashed past his ears. The giant took off toward his wounded friends.

John went to fire again, but his aim went astray as the realization crashed through his brain. The beam that destroyed Thomas's weapon could only have come from an Argonian force cannon. And that only existed on the Planet Argon.

Perhaps surprise made John broadcast his thoughts, because they were answered by a flirtatious mental projection: *Don't complain about it, handsome. We saved your life, didn't we?*

John pinpointed the sender, whirling to find two figures floating overhead. Both wore Argonian armor, both were familiar. The thug with the force cannon had once blown him out of the sky on another world. The blonde in the revealing armor suit had tried to bend his mind. Both had tried to kidnap Peg and use her as a hostage.

As recognition came, John's hands seemed to rise of their own volition, forming the tridigirector. Blast-bolts flew upward, but the pair of Deviants were already swooping off.

The blond psychic sent him a parting message. *Maybe some other time.*

John was too busy shooting to pay much attention— not to the blonde, not even to Peg when she began sending frantic mental messages. Finally a psionic roar from Harry Sturdley got his attention.

KID! Sturdley broadcast. *You'd better get out of here, unless you want to be the interview-du-jour with that Nasotrudere broad.*

John turned to see Leslie Ann determinedly dragging her cameraman forward to get footage of the new phenomenon on Sixth Avenue. Through his external audio receptors, John could hear the newswoman yelling all the typical questions—who was he, where did he come from, why had he and his armored associates stopped the giants, why had he shot at the other two armored people, could he please open his visor and give an interview.

For a brief, crazy second, John considered acceding to the last request. It would be interesting to see how Leslie Ann would react to a complete surprise.

On the other hand, he feared that Harry's response might be a coronary.

Instead, John resorted to the best traditions of his chosen genre. He executed an airy salute with his right hand, raised it straight over his head in a fist, cocked his left leg, and engaged his gizmoidal drive to fly out of there.

All he got was the smell of burning wires.

Damnation! He'd forgotten that the drive had been knocked out of commission. The silence around him grew longer. John realized he couldn't just walk away now.

There was only one way out.

Focusing all his mental energies, John went into psychokinetic mode.

His takeoff was a little wobbly, but he managed to gain speed and height. It wasn't as though he had to go far. All he needed to do was get something between himself and that damned camera.

John cleared the roof of the building that housed the movie theater. With his last bit of strength, he boosted himself toward Fifth Avenue.

At least he was out of frame by the time he thumped ingloriously to the rooftop.

Groaning from a new set of bruises, John quickly pushed himself to his feet and Rifted out of there.

Chapter Twenty-Seven

Nature abhors a vacuum. And as time went on, the once nearperfect emptiness of the Rift drew in currents and eddies composed of the stuff of higher dimensions, creating a maelstrom of constructs, pocket universes whose "laws of nature" did not conform to the basic working concepts of the four-dimensional world.

Sometimes a facet of one of these miniature universe-constructs managed to interact with four-dimensional reality, fitting, in momentarily—and cataclysmically—with a four-dimensional matrix on the nexus known as Earth . . .

The streets of New York City were far away—both physically and psychically—from the green campus that housed the Vigilance Foundation. One would have to traverse four counties before coming to the city's northernmost border. The upstate business center that housed the Foundation was large on open spaces and short on sidewalk. Modernistic buildings arose on a bucolic plot of land larger than Central Park—and its greenery was immaculately manicured.

A conservative think tank, the Vigilance Foundation monitored all threats to the American dream, from urban unrest to foreign terrorism.

Dr. Lowell Carswell, Ph.D., loaded his pipe while reading the coverage on last night's disturbance in the *New York Times*—ideologically unsound, but still the newspaper of record. "This may require rethinking several urban parameters, not to mention an entire new threat assessment."

"We had initially processed the Heroes as containment factors in the urban equation." Dr. Thayer Birch, Ph.D., took a sip of coffee. "Despite the police injunction restraining their activities, they nonetheless remained a deterrent *in esse*—a threat to street crime."

"And, of course, they established an almost immediate alliance with Senator Demagogua," Benedict Scheer pointed out.

Scheer only had a Master's degree, and his contribution to the coffee break discussion gained him only superior looks from the two doctorate holders.

"Demagogua is no true conservative," Carswell sniffed.

Birch nodded. "He's merely an opportunist riding the conservative groundswell."

"Well, certainly those giants didn't turn out to be dependable compatriots for the superpatriot," Scheer hastily agreed.

"Mmnnnn," Carswell said in quelling tones. "But I think we should table any discussion of the import of the Heroes' actions for a more formal venue—like the weekly status meeting. Scheer, you get back to quantifying the megadeath potential of the Brazilian atomic arsenal."

"The *hypothetical* Brazilian atomic arsenal," Birch added.

Scheer bent over the keyboard of the office computer—neither of the Ph.D.s was computer-literate. "A Master's degree, and they treat me as a blasted errand boy," he muttered.

Those were his last words. As he tapped into the Foundation's computer network, a loose vortex of tenth-dimensional space—a pocket universe—made a conjunction with the Foundation's electronics system. For a brief instant, electrons were turned into positrons, negative matter that reacted explosively with the normal matter around it.

The computer, the scholars, the Foundation buildings, and most of the green-swarded campus disappeared in an incalculable flare of energy.

John Cameron bit his lip as he applied a pungent potion to his bruises. He'd moved so creakily when he came out to breakfast that Mama Putnik had pressed a jar of her homemade remedy on him. The smell was enough to bring tears to the eyes, but as John gingerly spread the stuff, it felt as though he were taking a blowtorch to his bruised ribcage. Apparently the burning surge overwhelmed his pain receptors—the tightness eased.

If only my armor could be restored as quickly, John thought. He picked up the clamshell plates that protected his chest and back. That was where the damage had been done. The stink of burnt insulation mixed with the spicy tang of Mama Putnik's embrocation.

John extended hair-thin tendrils of mental force, following the circuitry embedded in the plasteel. He frowned as he detected a number of electrical connections that had been sundered—some of them in the irreplaceable Argonian ultramicrochips.

No chance of taking this thing to the shop, he thought. Argon and its technicians were on the far side of an increasingly stormier Rift. He'd have to find some way to repair this damage himself.

Then John recalled what he'd done the evening before, deforming the screwdriver that subway thug had used to threaten him. If he could combine his circuit tracing and psychokinesis . . .

He wormed a psionic tendril along electronic pathways until he came to a break in the circuit. Then he focused his psychokinetic talents on the crystalline lattice of the circuit's metallic elements, literally turning it momentarily molten to seal the gap. It was like manipulating a microscopic arc welder. Again and again he operated, throughout the entire suit, until every system was whole.

John sat back on his cot, a fine sheen of sweat on his face.

Well, he thought, my body is okay, and my suit is excellent. Of course, my *head* feels like it's just been kicked by a mule . . .

* * *

Robert made a graceless, awkward exit from the specially-outfitted 747 after it rolled to a stop on the LaGuardia runway. He had spent the past six hours flying from California, abandoning the West Coast movie premiere when newscasters began asking about the riot in New York in a near feeding frenzy. Robert had forgotten to take his Hero-phone, so he spent the entire flight incommunicado. He hadn't gotten a wink of sleep. His eyes felt as if there were pebbles caught under the lids.

He strode across the tarmac, bypassing the terminal he'd never fit in. Passengers from other flights gathered at the floor-to-ceiling windows. Robert was familiar with that phenomenon. He was even familiar with the fear rising off the Lessers like a stinking fog. What he'd never experienced was the hatred he now detected in the glaring crowd.

Months of painstaking work building the trust and respect of these pissant creatures, destroyed by one of Thomas's temper tantrums. A delegation of newsgatherers crowded against the cyclone fence at the edge of the runway.

"Robert! Are you aware of what happened on Sixth Avenue last night?" a reporter asked.

Hoping he didn't look as haggard as he felt, Robert replied, "I returned as soon as I heard. This is a terrible situation—a cowardly attack, an angry response . . ." He sighed. "And all too many innocent bystanders caught between."

The newscasters were on him like a pack of baying hounds.

"We have reports of people being kicked to death!"

"Would you have allowed that, Robert?"

"Do you feel your people's response was appropriate?"

"Thomas actually attacked news crews. Do you think that was a good idea?"

Robert forced back the response he'd have liked to give, that he wished all Lessers—especially these reporters—dead.

Instead, he exerted his mental powers to the fullest, trying to dissipate the fear and distrust among the news people. "I feel for *every* victim of this tragedy—those who were caught in my people's response, and poor Penelope. Does anyone know where she's being treated? Do we know if she'll be able to walk again? All I heard was that she'd been shot in the leg by some sort of heavy weapon—"

He continued in that vein, picking up information from the minds and voices of the media crowd. Robert's next move was to arrange ground transportation. Luckily, he had some Lesser money on hand, which allowed him to rent the use of an open-bed tractor-trailer. His first move was to visit the midtown hospital where Penelope and Kevin were resting uncomfortably in improvised quarters—a circus tent roofing over a small atrium. Kevin's burns didn't give Robert much concern. With minor wounds, Masters were fast healers.

But the sight of Penelope's face, pale and drawn with pain, filled Robert with conflicting emotions. Foremost was rage at the Lessers who'd committed the atrocity. Underlying his fury, however, was the uncomfortable admission that without this world's medical technology, Penelope wouldn't survive. Back home, despite the support of their telekinetic shields, giants' legs and hip joints were the first to go. And there was no such thing as a crippled Master. As their limbs began to fail, older giants were pushed to the periphery of Masterly society, off into the woods where they finally fell, took additional damage, and never got up again.

Robert took it as a fact of life that, barring the vagaries of power, most Masters were dead by their early forties, giving him a life expectancy of barely twenty more years on the outside.

Had Penelope suffered this damage on their home-world, the only decent thing to do would be mercy killing, out of sight of Lesser eyes. The broken bones and injuries from her fall couldn't even have been addressed by the level of medicine available.

Here, however, Penelope lay if not in comfort, at least in woozy acceptance of her pain, her leg encased in an enormous swathing of plaster.

"It was Carron," Kevin said, "one of the Lessers you'd told us to look out for. I pinned him and his toady mentally, but before I could finish them I was attacked by more Lessers. These were covered in metal shells and could fly. One burned me—" He looked a little shamefaced—"while the other got into my mind. That's all I remember."

Robert frowned. More vermin with mind powers? "The Lesser who attacked you mentally—that wasn't Sturdley?"

Kevin shook his head. "That one was down on the ground when the trouble began. He'd just come out of—what is that name for a fancy car? Lemon?"

"Limo," Robert said. "I'll leave you now. Rest, heal quickly. As soon as possible I'll have you moved to Heroes' Manor."

Although, he thought, only the gods below know what I'll find there.

Robert's truck was stopped a good mile from his destination. The whole area around the home of the giants had been evacuated and cordoned off. Hundreds of Lessers in the mottled green outfits this domain issued to its warriors bustled about, setting up heavy weapons and metal war machines.

A little mental spying reassured Robert somewhat. These were not professional fighters, but members of something called the National Guard. The local chief, or governor, had called them out to contain a perceived threat.

The commander of the troops was a short, grizzled man whose growing stomach strained his uniform shirt. "I'm glad to see you," the Lesser said. "We've allowed no one out of your compound since your people came back, and no one has come out to talk to us. I'm glad someone with authority has returned. The only leader we know to be inside is Thomas—and he's the one who started the problems." "Yes," Robert said as he poured soothing thoughts into the colonel's mind. "I'm sure that between us we can restore order."

He turned to see another crop of the ubiquitous news crews turning their cameras on him. Reporters asked questions just as inane as those of their urban counterparts.

Robert ignored them, walking up the path to the iron gates of Heroes' Manor. Well, he thought, things could be worse. At least there's a sentry out.

The giant stood behind the cover of one of the trees arching over the front drive. It was Quentin, one of the older members of the group. From the look on Quentin's face, he wasn't there as a sentry—more as a lookout.

And it seemed that Robert was what Quentin had been looking for. "You're barely in time." The faint wrinkles at the edges of Quentin's eyes and lips seemed deeper. "It's as bad or *worse* than when the old Master of Masters died. Everyone has formed cliques and factions. The arguments are just about to break into real violence."

"And what faction claims you?" Robert asked.

Quentin smiled without mirth. "The older and wiser heads. I expected you'd be along sooner or later. The only problem is resolving the doubt and panic among our people without letting the little ones outside know about it."

"And *my* main difficulty?" Robert pressed.

"Thomas," Quentin said flatly. "We just barely persuaded him to stay inside the walls. He wanted to go out and break the Lessers' picture-boxes, thinking that would let the pictures out." The older giant shook his head. "Though his plan certainly didn't work so well last night. That blond-haired vixen you're so fond of caught Thomas on something called 'tape.' We all saw it on the Tee-vee."

"And how did Thomas respond?"

Quentin shrugged. "He wanted to break the Tee-vee, too."

"Always good to have some advance warning," Robert said, heading onward. "I'll remember you, Quentin."

Quentin trailed after him, but well to the rear. He might believe Robert would win the coming confrontation. Nonetheless, he hedged his bets, not following the leader too closely.

The grassy slope of lawn leading from the mansion to the lakefront beach was the giants' usual meeting ground. As Robert came around the building, he could see his followers bunched in three knots, all glaring among themselves. Factions, indeed.

A bare handful clustered around Thomas—the most heavy-handed and arrogant. Robert ignored them, turning to the largest group.

"I leave you alone for a few days, and you undo all my work," he said.

"The Lessers attacked us!" Thomas protested. Robert still paid him no heed.

"They crippled Penelope!" Katharine cried from the second largest group. "That could never had happened at home! This is a bad place for us. We'd be better off going back. The fighting in the old domain must be over by now. We could make a deal with the new Master of Masters—at the worst, there's always the woods."

"Oh, you'd become a woods runner now?" Thomas taunted. "And what of them out there?" he hooked a derisive thumb in the direction of the National Guardsmen. "You'd allow those Lesser vermin to harm a Master—and live?"

Robert forbore from pointing out the logical flaws in both positions. John Cameron, not Robert, had brought them to this world. Robert had just led them. And Robert had no intention of taking on the Lessers' artillery to gratify a quick impulse for vengeance. His long-term plans would take care of that . . .

He continued to look at the largest group of his erstwhile followers, still waiting to hear their position. "And you?"

"We want to leave." Camilla's voice was nervous, but emphatic. "Since we arrived here, we've acted like clowns for the Lessers. Those picture books for Sturdley. Your film. There's a whole world out there—we see it on the Tee-vee. But only a chosen few have been allowed more than a day's travel from here. We think we could make our way out there, as Andrew probably is . . . "

"Andrew?" Robert directed mental probes through the compound.

"Gone," Camilla told him. "We think he swam out through the lake after he, Thomas, Walter, and myself returned here last night."

"You think it's so easy to walk away from here?" Robert asked. "Warriors surround us. The Lessers fear us now."

Camilla gave a cynical grin. "We know what to do to make them like us again. You showed us how."

"To the pit with making them like us!" Thomas shouted. "They *should* fear us! They should feel our wrath!"

Robert swept forward and knocked Thomas to the ground with one blow. "These others I can forgive because of their ignorance. But you knew my plans—and nearly sabotaged them with your temper!"

Thomas lay crouched on the grass. One hand cradled the side of his head as he cringed under the mental outpouring of Robert's wrath.

The giants' leader turned on his people. "So, some of you fear these Lessers, others want them to pay, still others wish to lose themselves among the Lesser hordes. I have not been merely entertaining the vermin out there—I have been working to lessen their numbers by using their own vaunted technology against them!"

He outlined how he'd been Binding Lesser leaders, preparing a global holocaust.

"You'd kill them all?" Camilla asked.

"Not all," Robert assured her. "There'll be some Lessers left—breeding stock for the new order."

"And we'll survive?" Quentin demanded.

"The tests I ran on Gideon indicate that we are considerably tougher than the Lessers in resisting the deadly aftermath of the bombs—this radiation."

The giants took heart at this validation of their superiority, seriously battered after the kneecapping incident.

"We will have a haven—the structures I arranged to be built in Idaho. All we need to do is stay together."

"If we hang together," Harry Sturdley desperately raised his voice over the hubbub of the staff meeting, "we can overcome even this disaster."

"Is it true this Silikis character is trying to pull *Heroes* from the theaters?" Thad Westmoreland demanded.

"After the incredible success of the New York premiere, it's hard to imagine why," Sturdley said tartly.

"Hey, maybe we should look at it as an enormous publicity stunt," Marty Burke suggested. "Remember when those poor jerks imitated that football movie and got themselves run over? People were falling all over themselves to see the flick."

"There speaks the man who drew the movie tie-in comic," Sturdley said.

"Hey, one way or the other, I expect that sucker to become a collector's item," Burke insisted.

"Like the *Famous Serial Killers* card set?" Mack Nagel inquired nastily.

Burke ignored the jibe, his allies continuing the attack. "It seems as though Sturdley's Heroes comics weren't such a great idea after all," Westmoreland sneered. "I've heard that dealers and distributors are dumping orders like crazy. You got another brilliant idea up your sleeve?"

Nagel shrugged, looking at Harry. "Unless you want to revive the horror comics genre with the giants as villains."

"For one of them, that might work," Xan Ximenes, the artist on the book starring Thomas, sighed. "We could change the title from *The Terrific Thomas* to *The Terrorist Thomas*."

"That's one plan." Sturdley stared around the table. "But maybe we can come up with some other alternatives."

At Dynasty Comics, Dirk Colby had a very different idea of what constituted a staff meeting. Artists, writers, and editors need not attend. Colby dealt with his marketing and trafficking people. And there was no brainstorming. These were meetings to pass orders onto the working talent.

"So," Colby said, "The *Death of Zenith* cycle seems to be reaching an end of profitability. Just one more publicity angle."

Jerry Barnum, head of marketing, nodded. "Where he's reincarnated as a female and we rename the series *Zenithe*."

Barnum's assistant, Chuck Sutton, chimed in, "Maybe it will get the libbers off our backs to see a broad in Zenith's suit."

"I want sketches from three artists for a new Zenithe costume—briefer," Colby abruptly said. "Our market research says the buyers want four things: small heads, big muscles, clenched teeth with lots of blood on them, and busty babes in small costumes." He fixed the assistant with a piercing glare. "Why do you think we put Zenith through a sex-change? No decent broads in that book. Ram-man has Vulpinette, the villainess in the little fox costume."

"Well, not lately, since Ram-Man got that stroke after the killer robot Nemesystem beat his brains out," another assistant pointed out.

"How is that developing?" Colby wanted to know.

"Ram-man has trapped his worst enemy in the ram costume, after jamming the horns full of plastic explosive," Barnum said. "He needs a stand-in since half his body is paralyzed. But he always holds the detonator in his good hand."

Wendell Piltdown, one of the traffickers, raised a logic problem. "You mean the Jesticulator has been stuck in that costume for weeks? It must stink."

Colby turned to Barnum. "Make a note. Maybe they can use it in a plot." His grin was more like a baring of teeth. "I'll show 'em gritty."

As Barnum scribbled away, Colby roved the rest of the table with his pale eyes. "So, what other ideas do we have to make our Silver Age heroes more attractive in today's market?"

Carlo Ponzi, a lesser marketing staffer, held up a crude action figure. It was the Aquabat, Dynasty's underwater hero. But the figure's legs had been chopped off and shiny metal cylinders glued on.

"How's this sound for a scenario? The Aquabat has his legs bitten off below the knee by a mutant shark, and replaces his lost feet with jet-skis."

"I like it," Colby said. "Blood, pain, and high technology. And it makes him more of a human torpedo than the Fantasy Factory's hero."

"Besides," Barnum chimed in, "the Aquabat doesn't need to stand—he's always swimming around."

"Not to mention the merchandising aspects," Ponzi went on enthusiastically. "This could make a fine bathtub toy."

"Other characters?" Colby went on.

"I talked to one of the editors about your idea of making Herowena pregnant," Walt DeMara of trafficking said. "He said there may be trouble with the Comics Code if we go with Zeus as the father. Zeus is the father of Hercules, and since Hercules is supposed to be Herowena's father . . ."

"Right. The mother thought he was a traveling salesman."

"Which brought us code problems forty years ago," Colby said, tapping a forefinger to his lower lip. "Is the publicity value worth the trouble?"

"Actually, the editor had a useful suggestion," DeMara offered. "Why not make the whole thing a mystery? The story arc will feature Herowena figuring out who did the deed."

"And will give us more time to decide on a final answer." Colby nodded. "I like it."

"I guess that means we hold off on her costume redesign," Alf Orton of marketing sighed. "I mean, it's awful small—and if she's going to be pregnant . . ."

"She'll keep her figure the first few months—even get bustier," Colby said. "Then we can cover her up." He shot his glance around again. "Any more?"

"The Red Scepter," Vic Lustig, another trafficking guy, spoke up. "Suppose he loses his mind . . ."

"Like Ram-man did last year?" Ponzi asked.

"And Herowena right before her last hiatus?" Barnum added.

"Sort of," Lustig admitted. "But this would be different. He'll turn nasty—bloodthirsty—after we kill off everybody he knows by blowing up his hometown."

"Blow up Lake City?" Colby inquired. "How? An asteroid strike?"

"I was thinking a tactical nuke," Lustig said.

"Awful lot like the plot of the Fantasy Factory's Heroes movie," Barnum objected.

"But meaner," Colby said. "The terrorists there failed—here they'll succeed. What else do you have in mind?"

"Changing the crimson scepter to a battle-ax."

Ike Kruger of marketing roused himself from the end of the table. "Another one turning into a broad?"

Colby skewered him with a look that didn't bode well for Kruger's future advancement.

"I mean the scepter itself," Lustig clarified. "It turns brainwaves into energy. But when he goes nuts, his brainwaves transform the scepter into an ax—more bloodthirsty, you see."

"Too subtle," Colby complained. "How about we change it to the *Blood-Red Battle-ax of Death*?"

"Is that too close to *Doom's Blood, the Black Death*?" Baraum asked.

"Or *Death-Hawk's Bloody Claw*?" Ponzi added.

Colby shrugged. "One more won't hurt. Anything else?"

Silence fell over the table.

"Okay, that's the end of old business." Colby picked up a newspaper from the tabletop. "Here's the new business." He pointed to a fuzzy picture of a flying armored figure on the front page. "Sturdley and the Fantasy Factory have been beating our brains out for months with his real-life giants. Well, it looks like there are new real-life heroes in town. I want 'em. *You*"—he pointed at Bamum—"will find them, and get them under license."

Colby then turned to Piltdown. "You'll have the job of setting up a wholly-owned subsidiary company to turn the comics out."

Piltdown blinked. "A whole new company?"

Colby nodded. "Yes—a small one. It's bait, you see." He gave his people another thin smile. "But I'll bet it will be enough to get the guy I want to run things."

For a brief moment, John Cameron became aware of a flash of emotion far below. He broke off his search pattern and swooped downward to find a young kid lying flat on a rooftop, his eyes the biggest thing in his face.

John reversed gizmo and regained altitude. He wasn't looking for kids, he was looking for the pair of Deviants who'd appeared the night before.

But, as he resumed the painstaking survey, his quarry remained hidden under the mental murmur of eight million minds.

Nonetheless, John kept circling.

Chapter Twenty-Eight

"It's like something out of a Fifties monster movie," Peg whispered, staring at the television set installed in Harry Sturdley's office.

The screen showed a phalanx of nervous-looking National Guardsmen fingering their M-16 rifles—weapons of proven uselessness against giants. A few of the citizen-soldiers appeared more confident. They were holding olive-drab tubes that were now familiar to TV viewers. Ever since the giantess had been cut down on Sixth Avenue, pictures of rocket launchers and the rockets they fired had been all over the tube.

Of course, the most cheerful faces in the military cordon were the ones poking from the hatches of the tanks. Not only did they have cannons to shoot at any errant giants, the crews were behind one to four inches of armor.

Sturdley sighed, turning away from the image. "Those poor, dumb bastards. All they lack is Godzilla coming over the hill at them."

John Cameron, slouched in the corner, soberly shook his head. "Godzilla might scare them, but they'd stand up to him. The giants can invade their brains."

He glanced at Sturdley. "We knew they were dangerous long before they proved it to the man on the street."

His hands clenched on the arms of his chair. "And we still have no plan for dealing with them."

Up at Heroes' Manor, Robert walked the walled perimeter of the compound. Standing behind a tree was Quentin, no longer a watcher and waiter, but a sentry placed by Robert's command.

"Anything to report?" the giant leader asked.

"Their leaders are all congregated opposite the gate in something called a 'command post,' " Quentin said. "They're in a defensive posture, waiting for some response from us."

Robert sighed in relief. "So they still aren't coming in to take Thomas?"

"It doesn't look that way," Quentin said. "Although I'm sure we could take them if they made the attempt."

After setting up the defense of the compound, Robert had no doubt of that. The crew of each tank had been targeted by the strongest mind benders of the giants' colony. At the first sign of attack, mental commands would cause the tanks' weapons to be turned on each other. The second line of defense would be to eliminate the warriors armed with rocket launchers by mental and physical means. That would leave the mass of Lessers with their ineffective rifles and low morale. If required, the giants might have to kick a few officers to death, but any attack would undoubtedly dissolve.

No, the Masters could defend themselves. But Robert sincerely hoped that wouldn't be necessary. Thomas and his escapade on the streets of the city had caused enough damage to Robert's plans. Destroying these National Guardsmen would mean war with the Lessers—a battle of forty-nine against millions.

Much as Robert would love to send the curs lurking at his doorstep yelping back to their kennels, he had to keep his larger purpose in mind. He didn't want to massacre a few Lesser warriors . . . he wanted to exterminate the majority of the troublesome dwarves.

To achieve his long-term goal, he must have freedom of movement. He wouldn't have that with troops surrounding his compound. Thus, Robert must somehow resolve the tense situation of the past few days. His impromptu speeches to the media and his visits to his injured people had made a start. Sound bites had appeared on the Tee-vee, pictures of Kevin and Penelope as victims . . .

Robert smiled to himself. These Lessers loved to see victims. It was just unfortunate there were so many Lesser victims from Thomas's riot.

But it would take more than fair words and sad pictures to win the Lessers back. Robert needed allies, Lessers themselves, to speak out for his people. Since his return to New York, he'd called Senator Demagogua's office several times. The local office had referred him to Washington. The Washington staff had assured him for the last few days that the Senator was unavailable. Even over the long-distance connection Robert had detected the lie. The politician was distancing himself until this affair reached some sort of conclusion.

Robert could easily call on the Washington figures he'd bound to his will, but doing that would expose part of his master plan. He didn't want to move those pawns until it was time for Armageddon.

Sourly admitting he had no option, Robert got out his giant-sized cellular phone, dialed the Fantasy Factory, and asked for Harry Sturdley.

Sturdley was astonished to hear his enemy asking for help in damage control with the public. "And why should I do this?" he asked.

"Your company has invested considerable money in the Heroes comics. I should think you'd leap to protect our good name." Those, at least, were the words he used on the open airways. His subtext came as a psionic message. *You daren't tell the truth about us, or your fellow Lessers would tear you limb from limb.*

After a brief silence, Sturdley finally said, "What do you think I can do?"

"Talk to the media . . . intercede as you did when we first came here, when our cultures clashed initially. You can explain how shock and anger overcame Thomas's judgment, that he was instinctively trying to clear a path to pursue the attackers."

And then kicked the hell out of a few hundred people because he was in a snit, Sturdley sent telepathically.

Aloud, he said, "No matter what the extenuating circumstances, Thomas will have to face trial, at the very least."

"Of course," Robert said smoothly. A trial would be no bother, with his immaterial abilities to influence prosecutor, judge, and jury. "We'll all happily commit to community service, and if Thomas must suffer more, that will be the price we pay—as long as we can enjoy freedom of movement."

"I don't know, Robert," Sturdley drawled. "I sort of liked having the National Guard all around you guys."

Matavi schooled her face into a smile as she stared into Dirk Colby's reptilian eyes. She was handling the negotiations with Dynasty Comics, just as she was the one who'd detected the operatives searching for herself and Emsisdin.

Matavi had researched the world of comics, dressing in Earth-type clothes and visiting a nearby comics shop. She'd been amazed at the reaction of both customers and staff. The young males had clustered around as if they'd never seen an attractive woman before. Matavi was aware of her body—the genetic tinkerers who'd constructed her had developed a comely package for the psionically gifted mind they'd created. It had been simplicity itself for Matavi to obtain mental data as well as samples of comic art. She had then used her intelligence-gathering abilities to infiltrate both the Fantasy Factory and Dynasty Comics.

One thing was clear. By having their adventures rendered into comics, the giants she'd recently fought had established a comfortable base on this world—both politically and financially.

When Emsisdin heard all this, he was amused and interested. "What exactly are you suggesting?" he asked.

"I think we should deal with this Dirk Colby," Matavi said. "The citizens of this world know of our existence. This will bring us a position—and a profit."

Emsisdin sat on their newly purchased sofa. "We're making a good enough living as we are." His argument wasn't exactly heartfelt, Matavi noticed. With the ease of their jewel robberies, his delight in that activity had begun to pall.

"Still," the young thug said, "to go over to the law—even this primitive world's law. . . . Do you really see us playing S-Force?" Emsisdin finally asked with heavy skepticism.

"For a while," Matavi said. "Think of it as eliminating rival gangs. And getting paid for it."

"And then?" Emsisdin demanded. "What about our own gang?"

Matavi gave him an entrancing shrug. "We'll see."

Thus it was that Dirk Colby got to enjoy an eyeful as Matavi leaned over his desk in her revealing half-armor. She carefully kept her face blank as she picked up the agreement memorandum. Colby had some dark places in the corners of his mind, and she did not like the images of herself appearing in those corners.

"Speed is of the essence." Colby's voice came out as a wheeze until he got his eyes back to her face. "I want to get a book about your exploits against the giants on the stands as soon as possible." He had been delighted when the lush blonde appeared in his office to negotiate without a lawyer.

Matavi was about to change that attitude. "The royalty percentages are acceptable," she said, looking at the paper. "They're industry standard. But your upfront money is inadequate."

"That's as high as I'm willing to go on an untested commodity," Colby responded.

"It's considerably less than Harry Sturdley offered the giants," Matavi said.

Her knowledge shook Colby, but he came back quickly. "That was a deal for fifty potential licenses. I can't go much higher than the figure I outlined." In his head, however, Matavi discerned an outlay twice as high.

Calmly, she leaned over the desk again, snatching pen and notepad. As Colby gawked, she scribbled an amount twice as high as the one in the publisher's mind.

The negotiation was furious, but Matavi was relentless. In the final draft of the agreement, the payment was halfway between Matavi's note and Colby's mental top figure.

Colby sucked his breath through his teeth. "You're a tough one," he admitted. "And you've left me considerably less budget to get the artist I wanted."

In the newsroom at INC, Leslie Ann Nasotrudere pored over an untidy pile of research. Copies of police reports lay interlarded with newspaper clippings, faxes, and a couple of videocassette boxes.

Gemma Donelson, a fading star on the network's news team, stopped by the desk. "What's this supposed to be?" she inquired cattily. "A model of the Matterhorn?"

"Is that a smile, Gemma," Leslie Ann responded, "or is your facelift acting up again?"

The brunette newswoman ignored Leslie Ann, riffling through the pile. "Flying figure, possible UFO—" she glanced up. "This isn't the Silly Season, honey. You won't stay on network news with flying saucer crap."

"It's not flying saucer crap," Leslie Ann replied. "I'm trying to get a line on those armored types who intervened in the Sixth Avenue thing."

"And saved that slightly expanding ass of yours," Gemma finished. "You're getting to that dangerous age, Nasotrudere. Secretary spread sets in real fast."

Leslie Ann ignored the comment, but the donut in her hand abruptly fell into the wastepaper basket. "That stuff there is the manure pile. I've gotten reports of flying figures from all over the country." She picked up a small sheaf of papers. "These, however, are all coherent, consistent in their details—and they all come from here in New York."

She frowned. Somewhere, somehow, there had to be a connection she could exploit to find these flying figures. Because, until she could speak to them, she had no story at all. Who were they? Where did they come from? Why did they intervene in the Slaughter on Sixth Avenue? And why was one shooting at the other two?

Leslie Ann noticed Gemma Donelson craning her neck to get a look at the papers in her hand. Instinctively, she crumpled them, then put them out of sight in her desk drawer. She wasn't about to share this story.

Nor was she going to share the odd split in her "good" sighting reports. Half the accounts put armored figures near the sites of major robberies. The rest described a figure in armor nailing criminals.

John Cameron slipped his helmet on, donning the final piece of his Argonian armor. He felt a little conspicuous gearing up in the morning daylight. All his crime fighting excursions had been at night. Still, it wasn't as though he'd go flying out his window and be spotted by all Astoria.

He concentrated, feeling the familiar vertigo of transit into the Rift, frowned, and abruptly broke the spell. John bent to pick up the duffel bag on his cot. Then he went back into the Rift again.

Moments later John landed on the carpet in Harry Sturdley's office with an audible thud. Peg Faber knocked on the closed door. "Harry? You all right?"

"Fine, fine," Sturdley replied, motioning for his protege to get up off the floor. "What do you think you're doing?" he demanded in a hiss.

John removed his helmet, revealing a pale face. "I got caught in something in the Rift."

"How do you get caught in a dimension full of nothing?"

"You know there are currents in the Rift," John said.

Harry nodded. Those currents had dragged the three of them off to the homeworld of Robert and company. A very unpleasant place. "Yes, I've felt 'em."

"This wasn't exactly like a current," John said. "It felt more like a tornado."

"Well, you're here now," Harry said, cutting him off. "And you brought your armor as I asked."

John nodded, working off his breastplate. "I figured this would be the best place to keep it. Those Deviants know who we are—we didn't exactly hide our identities on Argon. And I guess you figured they'd have an easy enough job finding us."

He tapped the weapons set in the armlets. "There are two of them, so I figured it would be good to have two sets of blasters on hand in case they show up."

"You haven't found them." Sturdley made it more a statement than a question.

"Not even a trace," John admitted. "There's just too many minds out there. I had a lot better luck on Argon—the cities were smaller."

"And there were more Deviants to find," Sturdley suggested.

"I've got to find these two." John's voice was flat, and he could feel the muscles on his face tightening. "They were part of the squad that tried to kidnap Peg. In fact they were the leaders—"

"Peg told me all about it," Sturdley said. "Ten Deviants tried to kidnap her, but you and Melador came flying to the rescue, scragging eight of them. Melador got a posthumous medal."

"Yeah. Right." John did his best to remain stone-faced as Harry told the story. Peg had been unconscious at the time. She'd never seen John blow out the brains of the eight foot-soldiers with a mental attack after killing the turncoat Melador. Then he'd had to arrange a heroic death for the traitor.

It would be such a relief to talk to Harry, to get the massacre off his chest . . .

No, John decided. Not with Peg right outside.

He had to find the two Deviants and deal with them. The one with the force cannon had killed Mike, and who knows how many others. He and the blonde had been at the top leadership meeting of the Deviant commanders, murderers all. The blonde must have somehow managed to tag along when John Rifted for Earth.

Of all the Deviants to escape, it would have to be the only two survivors of John's worst secret.

"Well, I gave you the time off to go searching," Sturdley said, opening a file drawer in his desk. "Now we've got to get down to cases. Whatever those two were doing on Argon, it looks like they're going into the superhero game here in New York. Do you know Dirk Colby has people out looking for them, trying to sign them up for Dynasty Comics? That's why we need . . . this!"

Sturdley brought a large, square radio up onto the desk. He switched it on, but neither music nor happy talk came out of the speakers. Instead, constant murmur of voices emerged amongst bursts of static.

"One-Adam-K," a female voice suddenly made itself heard. "Three-oh-one East Nineteenth Street. Possible ten-thirteen."

"What *is* that?" John said.

"Police-band radio," Sturdley replied. "I figured we'd need it with a superhero in the office."

"*What?*" John forgot Peg's presence outside, his voice rising.

"I'm not going to ask you to draw, or write, or anything." Sturdley raised placating hands. "Although a book done directly from the hero's point of view . . ."

"I don't believe you!" John burst out. "We start out discussing the appearance of two dangerous killers, one with a superweapon, the other able to twist people's minds—a pair at least as dangerous as Robert—and all you can think of are the comic book possibilities!"

"Hey, don't tell me my responsibilities," Sturdley said. "I've got a bunch you apparently don't think of. Like a responsibility to keep all the people here—including Peg—employed. And then there are the stockholders."

"Oh, yeah, all the relatives of the people who founded the company—Cousin Louie and Cousin Louise," John couldn't keep the disgust from his voice. "Thinking they should run things because they're a Fanchik, Fanciulli, or O'Fanahan."

"Don't make fun of the Fan-Boys," Sturdley shouted. "They gave me my start."

"And you gave me mine," John said. "I'm sure you'll wind up reminding me of that all too soon."

Harry tried to lighten things. "I've hired artists, writers, editors, even marketing people. But this is the first time I've actually taken a hero on board."

John clambered out of his plast-alloy armor, depositing it in a pile in the middle of the floor. Then he opened his duffel to slip on jeans, a flannel shirt, and a pair of running shoes.

"So what's my origin supposed to be?" he finally asked. "Are you going to put Silicon Savage through some major plot change?"

Sturdley shook his head. "Actually, I was thinking of creating a character from scratch."

"Not exactly from scratch," John pointed out. "After all, Leslie Ann Nasotrudere caught me on videotape. I guess we can't change my look."

He gave Harry a sour, "I-don't-like-this-but-I'm-going-along" sort of glance. "That means we're stuck with the big, squiggly S on my chest. Do you intend to revive the S-Force and send us all flying around?"

"I don't think so," Sturdley said. "The longer we keep our armor a secret from the giants, the better."

"So, I'm just a lone, armored hero with an S on my chest." John's tone grew sarcastic. "I've got it! *The Super-human!*"

Sturdley was bent over the police scanner, turning it off. "Copyright infringement," he said seriously. "Even if that was the name on your birth certificate, we couldn't use it."

Chapter Twenty-Nine

The conference room at Dynasty Comics was crowded with media people. Dirk Colby didn't usually resort to press conferences. Publicity was, in the main, handled through releases and interviews by selected journals. But this was a big story, bigger even than Zenith's death and transsexual resurrection. Not merely journalists interested in the comics field were on hand, but business reporters and general-assignment types from local newsrooms and the national newsweeklies. Even a network camera crew had wangled a spot.

The crew was led by Leslie Ann Nasotrudere, and she had come because, of all the newspeople in that room, she'd had a breath of a hint on what was to come. All the other media types had merely been told that they'd have a chance to meet two people they'd very much like to interview.

Dirk Colby stepped to the podium at the head of the room, his usual expensive suit hanging from his skeletal frame. After identifying himself and greeting the ladies and gentlemen of the press, he said, "While my company will make an announcement of serious import to the comics business—"

A rustle of annoyance came from the reporters.

"The more newsworthy story is the introduction I'm about to make. Meet Emsisdin and Matavi, the heroic team soon to be known as the Deviants."

Leslie Ann had to give Colby credit for showmanship. A pair of armored figures suddenly hung in midair outside the conference room windows. Dynasty Comics staffers opened the windows, and the couple made a spectacular entrance.

The room was a chaos of journalistic pack madness, with reporters wildly yelping questions. Colby tried to make himself heard over the podium microphone, but was drowned out. Then the impressive-looking costumed blonde made a hand gesture, and the room grew still.

"We will make a brief statement," the woman said in a slightly accented voice. "I am Matavi, and this is Emsisdin. We are strangers to your world, having arrived by way of a freak space-warp."

She smiled at the reporters. For some reason, the questions Leslie Ann had been about to shout were stilled on her tongue.

"On our homeworld, we fought for freedom against a repressive and stagnant government, and were branded with the title Deviant. Now that we live in exile on your world, we intend to continue our fight for freedom and justice against any who would use their strength or size to dominate the weak."

After the giants' riot, that got a groundswell of response, which Matavi again quelled with a gesture. "We must also warn you that agents of the stagnant society we escaped have apparently followed us to this world."

Leslie Ann remembered the armored figure that had fired on the two Deviants, the figure with the odd-looking S on its breastplate.

"These Stagnators, as we call them, will no doubt attempt to depict us as criminals," Matavi said. "We only ask you to judge us by our actions on your world."

With that, Matavi ended her statement and turned back to Dirk Colby. Again, the room thundered with volleys of media questions. Once more, Matavi gestured, and the room went still.

How the hell does she do that? Leslie Ann wondered.

From his podium, Colby announced that his company had signed a license agreement to present the true-life adventures of these new heroes. To do so, Dynasty Corporation was creating an entirely new subsidiary line, Deviant Comics. And to run this line he had acquired the services of a talent whose name was well-known in the field . . .

The door behind him opened and Leslie Ann's advance source stepped in.

Marty Burke's entrance was not as impressive as that of the Deviants. For one thing, he was jostled by a group of general-assignment reporters taking the quickest way out of the room. For another, hardly any of the journalists knew him. One of the cognoscenti, however, made up for that.

"Holy spit!" yelled the freelancer covering the event for the *Comic Purchaser's Weekly Intelligencer*. "That's Marty Burke!"

Unfortunately, he rather ruined the effect by calling, "Hey, Marty, you looking for writers?"

Burke stepped up to the podium, glancing over the media people he was about to address on the direction of his new line—and his new career. He gave Leslie Ann a little smile and a bow.

Leslie Ann smiled back as she leaned over to whisper in her cameraman's ear. "Forget him. Keep the camera on the two new heroes."

Harry Sturdley lifted out of his chair as if he had rockets attached to his fundament. "That sonofabitch Colby!" he howled, pointing at his office television.

Peg Faber quickly entered to see what the commotion was about. She froze when she saw the two Deviants on the screen.

"Now that they're standing there, I can see what you were telling me!" Sturdley was nearly dancing with rage. "He's almost a twin for M-16, Weapon Supreme, and she's a ringer for Madam Vile! Even their names sound like our characters' names! Colby isn't going to get away with this!"

Sturdley dialed Frank McManus, the head of his legal department, with stabs of his forefinger. "Frank! Have you got a TV in your office? Switch to INC. No, it's not just Nasotrudere. Wait till you see what Colby is pulling this time."

He let McManus watch for a few minutes, giving a running commentary of the costume and name thievery the Deviants represented.

"I want to sue Colby's ass," Sturdley told his head lawyer. "And I want to sue him big-time. Screw the budget on this. Bring in whatever experts you need."

"There's a law firm that specializes in copyright and trademark infringement," McManus said. "Maybe we should bring them on board. They've got the name in the field: Mohe, Lorenz, and Kirley."

"What's the name again?" Sturdley said.

McManus repeated the names, with spellings, as Sturdley scribbled on his notepad.

"Okay, Frank," Sturdley said, "you get those people on it right away. Draft a letter to Colby, telling him to cease and desist. Meanwhile, I'll see if we can't come up with a way to steal some of the bastard's PR thunder."

He hung up the phone. Without even looking at Peg, he said, "Get John in here. *Now!*"

Even as he spoke, Sturdley dug the police scanner out of his desk.

John dashed down the hallway to Harry's office at a speed that would appear unseemly for the Fantasy Factory's executive suite. But whatever was up, Peg had certainly made Sturdley's summons sound urgent. If he hadn't been standing in the middle of the artists' bullpen, John would have Rifted in.

As it was, he outpaced Peg in the race for the door. Without knocking, John threw the portal open, then skidded to a stop on the carpet.

His armor, which had been quietly stacked in Harry's closet, now occupied a pile in the middle of the floor. Sturdley sat behind his desk, frantically operating the police scanner.

"Looks like the biggest thing right now is a botched bank robbery in Chelsea." Harry glanced at his notepad and rattled off an address. "Should be easy to spot. The building is surrounded by cops. There are just two robbers, but they've taken hostages."

"What?" John tried frantically to get up to speed. "What's happening?"

"Dirk Colby has signed those two Deviants to become the new heroes at Dynasty Comics," Harry explained tersely. "You're going to show them up—*and* show how heroing is done."

He glared at his protege, pointing to the armor. "Come on! I gave you the address. Get your stuff on! Get going!"

Moving almost in a daze, John began to pull his sweater over his head.

"Speed it up, kid!" Harry yelled. "Kick off those sneakers. Peg, get his pants down."

At that order, both of the young people froze.

Sturdley made a sound somewhere between a cough and an *ahem*. "All right. Peg, help get his sweater off. John, drop your pants."

In seconds, John was down to his underwear. He quickly donned the armor's loin protector and the clamshell breast and back plates.

"Come on," Sturdley said, crouching over the scanner for the latest reports. "They'll negotiate an end to this before you're dressed."

John and Peg bent simultaneously to get the leg guards and greaves. Realizing he was about to butt her with his helmet, John pulled back, inadvertently triggering his gizmoidal drive. Although all the circuits weren't complete —several components were in the still-to-be-donned arm and leg armor—the field was enough to send John swooping off his feet and into a barrel roll.

Peg dove to the floor, just missing getting kicked in the head by one of John's flailing heels.

"John?" she said, rising, then throwing herself flat again as his body swooped in a circle in midair. The out-of-control gizmo took him in an orbit that brought him within a foot and a half of the ceiling, then the same distance from the floor.

"This is a hell of a time to be fooling around," Sturdley barked.

More ready this time, Peg ducked then leapt, grabbing John by the leg. Her weight wasn't enough to bring him down. It merely unbalanced the orbital equation, sending them both zooming around the room.

"Yike!" Peg yelled.

Now it was Harry's turn to duck as the two flew at an angle across his desk. Peg nearly smashed her knees against the edge of the desktop. She managed to bring them up. Instead, they caught the scanner, sending it smashing against the wall. The radio hit the framed picture of the Rambunctious Rodent drawn by the legendary Rip Jacoby. The frame fell to the floor, its glass front shattering.

A knock came at the door. "Everything all right in there?" Bob Gunnar asked.

"Fine! Fine!" Harry was struggling to keep his voice calm. "Just a little mishap."

To Peg, he hissed, "Let him go!"

She did, timing her release so she could land with a roll and recovery in the best karate style.

Something's wrong with the controls! John sent the message mind-to-mind.

Peg relayed it to Sturdley. He used his psionic ability to Pace circuits. "Of course!" he burst out. "All the armor is supposed to work together! We've got to get the rest on him!"

The next few minutes passed like a high-tech Keystone comedy. John spun through the air in wild somersaults as Harry and Peg tried to help him don the remaining armor. Peg got taken for another wild orbit, clinging to John's waist with one arm while helping him into his leg armor. Harry nearly got brained when a boot went flying off.

With all his armor finally on, John was able to regain control. He hovered about a foot off the floor as Sturdley collapsed into a chair. Peg leaned, panting, against the desk.

"Go!" Harry wheezed, pointing toward the window. He had no breath for anything more.

The flight to Chelsea was short enough that John didn't feel it necessary to Rift. It was just a case of getting up enough altitude not to crash into any buildings, then burning gizmo to reach the robbery site.

Even from roof level, it was easy to spot the bank. Police cars and news vans blocked the street. A crowd gathered behind a phalanx of blue uniforms, facing the place.

But as John arrowed down, he also caught the flash of plast-alloy coming out of the bank. He put up the magnification on his facescreen and boosted the gain on his exterior mikes.

Emsisdin and Matavi stood proudly facing TV cameras as police handcuffed a pair of thugs who looked much the worse for wear.

"Matavi pinpointed their location," Emsisdin said. "All we had to do was wait on the floor above till they got close to each other. Then—" He aimed the force cannon in his right hand at the sidewalk and made a circle—"we dropped the ceiling on them!"

Reporters gabbled questions, but John was no longer hearing. When he'd agreed to play hero, Harry had said it would be best to avoid conflicts with the Deviants if they bumped into each other.

That suggestion was the farthest thing from John's mind as he continued his dive. Without conscious thought, he activated his external speakers. "Deviants!" he yelled, his voice thick and savage.

Emsisdin and Matavi boosted off the ground immediately, trying to deprive him of the high ground advantage. John nearly crashed into the blond witch, prompting a mocking mental message: *If you want me that badly, there are easier ways.*

The ground came up with frightening speed. Working sheerly on instinct, John managed to haul himself around and head skyward once again. The Deviants were above him now, silhouetted against the sky. John twisted to aim for Emsisdin, his fingers curling into the tridigirector. Blast-bolts leapt for the Deviant, but the range was too extreme. He managed to evade them.

Emsisdin brought up the force cannon, but Matavi intervened. Even from a distance, John caught the mental overtones of their wrangling. At last Emsisdin put the weapon down.

John and the Deviants flashed past each other. Now John was the higher one. He looked down. On the ground below the Deviants the crowd had expanded, everyone looking up. Some had seen Dirk Colby's press conference. The mental opinion of the crowd was that they were seeing a publicity stunt.

Emsisdin was again aiming the force cannon, this time upward. Matavi tried to stop her partner, but Emsisdin fired anyway. The thick beam of destruction had knocked John from the sky before. He flung himself back in a looping bit of aerobatics, and the blast missed.

That is, it missed John. The force cannon's beam went on to take a neat slice off the corner of a building. Brickwork and weathered copper cornice began to slide downward . . . down to the crowd below.

A little belatedly, the audience in the street began to realize this was no stunt show. This was the real thing.

Swinging desperately around, John drove for the collapsing corner of the building. His blasters were useless in this situation—they couldn't disintegrate enough of the falling stuff.

There was, perhaps, another way. John swooped below the deluge of debris. Resting his chest against the main piece of masonry, he increased the push of his gizmoidal drive. Then, reaching out with his mind, he caught the rest of the deadly avalanche in a psychokinetic net.

He couldn't hope to stop it altogether. But maybe he could slow it for long enough . . .

"Clear the street," he yelled. The message boomed out from his exterior speakers. "Get out from under—"

Then he had to save his breath. Holding back a body this massive was the greatest test he'd pitted his powers against so far.

They were still going down, despite his efforts. Red dots swam before John's eyes. The periphery of his vision went gray, then black. He couldn't hold on any longer.

John slid aside, and the landslide of debris thundered to the ground.

He shook his head, afraid of what his returning vision might reveal.

Dust still rose from a huge pile of shattered masonry. But there was very little damage, as though the bricks and metal had fallen perhaps one story instead of twelve. And the gawkers who had crowded the impact spot were a good half-block away, behind a wall of pale-faced police.

All was well on the ground. John turned his attention to the sky. But Emsisdin and Matavi had disappeared.

Chapter Thirty

The autumn wind coming off the water had traveled two thousand miles across the cold Atlantic. It was just short of bitter. But the giant called Andrew didn't mind. He just tempered the shields of immaterial force around himself to retain more body heat, and felt just as comfortable as if he were strolling the East Hampton beach in midsummer.

Both the private beach and the oceanfront mansion that hid it from the landward side were part of a diplomatic compound, operated by the Arab state whose shadowy agents had contacted Andrew months before. They had continued negotiations, and the debacle at the premiere of the movie *Heroes* had finally convinced Andrew to sever his ties with Robert, Thomas, and the other would-be world conquerors.

Despite the watch around Heroes' Manor, it had been childishly easy to swim the lake, avoiding the patrol boats and troops on the far side. Mental control of the guards had caused heads to turn at the right moments so that he slipped by unnoticed. Then came the work of establishing communication with his contact, and the humiliating string of truck trips and safe houses—actually warehouses—until he had reached this compound. It was to be his jump-off point to leave the domain called the United States.

Tonight, an oil tanker would pass the point of land that housed this estate. It was run by the national oil company of his new hosts, and entirely crewed by his new employers. An unremarkable radio message would be sent to the compound, but it would actually be the signal for Andrew to start swimming. He'd rendezvous with the ship and then sail off to an opulent existence as military commander and personal bodyguard of the foreign domain's Supreme Leader.

Andrew stretched out full-length on the sand, lazily gazing out to the line where sea and sky met. He'd gain much luxury, and be out from under Robert's thumb. But there were things he'd miss—pleasures that would be denied him.

Closing his eyes, Andrew thought of a young giantess named Veronica. Honey-blond hair, blue eyes, a slim figure, but lithe, and full enough for him . . . he wished he could have taken Veronica along. But that would have meant revealing his secret negotiations, and no Master would ever let another of his peers acquire so dangerous an advantage.

Still, it would have been pleasant to carry off Veronica to a faraway land where they could establish their own domain.

Andrew opened his eyes and blinked in astonishment. Was he still daydreaming? There, in the water, not so far away, bobbed a swimmer's head. A blond head.

He shook his head, a wry smile forming on his face. The owner of that shining hair, was swimming in the wrong section of sea. He'd have to reach out and eliminate all memory of seeing a giant lounging on the beach.

Andrew extended a mental probe just as the swimmer rose from the water—way too far out at sea for a mere

Lesser. A giant—blond hair—but it wasn't the delectable Veronica.

Robert strode his way ashore, clad only in a traditional Master's clout. "You led me quite a chase, young Andrew. I'd probably have lost you, except your new paymasters made a mistake. Instead of pulling out after you disappeared, they left an agent to maintain watch."

Andrew managed to get his mouth to work. "I told them—"

"I'm sure you did." Robert's lips twisted. "But they disregarded your warning. I caught up with the agent. He wasn't hard to break."

Robert looked down at his hands, but Andrew knew he was referring to the power of his mind. Now his erstwhile leader was looming over him. Andrew tried to scramble up, but Robert stopped him by the simple expedient of shooting out a heavily callused foot. It caught Andrew in the temple, and he dropped to the sand, his senses reeling.

Then Robert knelt, grabbing Andrew's head in both hands and twisting it so their eyes met, Andrew's blinking and watery, Robert's as cold as two stones.

"You were quite enterprising, reasonably clever, and brave enough in choosing where, how, and when to desert us." Robert's voice hissed as he spoke. "Those qualities also make you dangerous. I can't have any other of my followers taking your example. Which means I'll have to make an object lesson out of you . . ."

Pinions of mental force suddenly encircled Andrew's mind. He tried to resist, a stifled whimper coming from between his clenched teeth.

Perhaps Robert would be out of practice. In his recent travels, he'd only bound Lesser minds, Lessers who were unaware of what was happening. It would be much more difficult to bind a mind in active revolt. Harder still to bring a Master's mind to his will.

Even as Andrew clung to those comforting thoughts, he felt his mental shields begin to crack. Frantically, Andrew tried to shore them up, to bolster his defenses. The pressure inexorably increased. Andrew contracted his shields, letting Robert into his brain circuits.

The smaller shield was stronger and should have been easier to maintain, but Robert was stronger still, crushing in, forcing a new contraction, and another.

With each retreat, Andrew lost a bit of himself. Memories, likes, dislikes, even control of voluntary muscles. Still the relentless pressure was exerted on the shrinking shields.

By this time, Andrew didn't even remember why he was resisting. All he knew was that the pressure was a danger, a deadly danger, a threat to everything that was Andrew. The retreat continued until all that was left was a tiny seed of Andrewness nestled down in a slack body's lizard-brain.

But the wringing mental grasp continued, squeezing until that little seed flickered, then died.

For long moments, the being that had been Andrew was kept alive by an exterior power operating the circuits that controlled heart and lungs. Probes streaked along brain neurons, selecting certain sections to revive, ignoring others.

At last, the former Andrew's eyes blinked open. They stared for a moment, not quite focused. At the sight of Robert, there was no alarm. There was nothing, no sign of intelligence at all.

"You," Robert said. The vague eyes looked downward. Enough language centers had been retained in the newly-cobbled circuits for the newborn mind to recognize a reference to itself.

"Get up."

The recumbent form clumsily rose as if the body were new and the owner's manual not yet read. Which was quite literally the case. Where once there had been a cognizant entity called Andrew, there was now a mental caretaker somewhere between an infant and a zombie.

"Come," Robert ordered, and the Andrew-creature shambled after him into the sea. Now came the difficult part of the capture. Swimming was almost beyond the caretaker-mind. Indeed, the caretaker was swimming in the considerable volume of Andrew's brain.

Robert helped until a distraction arose in the form of kaffiyeh-wearing guards firing AK-47 automatic rifles. The bullets were deflected by Robert's shields, and he had to admit to himself that he was glad there was no more major ordnance on hand.

Of course, Andrew nearly drowned before they got away. But Robert kept his zombie follower above water. He didn't want to lose Andrew's contribution to the already-small gene pool of Earth's Masterly colony.

Then, too, there was the horrible example Andrew would provide for the others in the group.

After a strenuous swim, a circuitous truck ride in a Hero-mobile whose driver then had his memories wiped, and yet another swim to reenter the compound by way of the lake, Robert was back in Heroes' Manor. He had just enough time to dry himself, don a fresh Hero costume, and meet the media people he'd invited to the estate for a press conference.

Robert actually conducted the interview from the gate of the estate, facing a ring of reporters backed by a cordon of heavily-armed National Guards.

"My statement will be brief," Robert said to the phalanx of cameras and microphones. "I am as shocked and horrified as anyone at the cowardly attack during our celebration of the new Heroes film. And I cannot condone my people's response, angry as they must have been—and eager to capture the attackers as well as ward off further assaults."

He'd hoped for a better response to the "cannot condone" line, but psionic sampling showed the newsgatherers were old hands at detecting "weasel wording," which is what they considered his comments on the mental state of the rioting giants. Obviously, he'd have to sweeten the pot.

"The result has been such public concern—" a better word than *fear*—"that a military cordon has been established around our home." Robert sighed, doing his best to look concerned, too. "I won't attempt to offer justifications. I merely ask the people of this city and state to weigh the good we've done for the community against the results of one unfortunate excess."

He was losing the media, he felt it. Time for the big announcement. "But the damage done requires recompense. I request that the City of New York commence formal charges against those involved in the disturbance on Sixth Avenue, including my deputy, Thomas."

That caused a buzz of excitement from the reporters.

"Since there are no proper facilities for incarceration, I further offer that all of us will sequester ourselves in the recreational compound we built in Idaho—after paying an appropriate bond and signing agreements to waive extradition."

He leaned forward, projecting sincerity with all the force of his personality. "We have always known that our size and powers require more than ordinary responsibility. And if some of us are perceived as a threat, it would be irresponsible to keep us here so close to a major population center. Better by far my followers confine themselves to the wide-open spaces of Idaho than an urban megalopolis while I consult with the nation's leaders in Washington."

Where I will light the fuse to let nuclear fire clear this world of most of you Lesser scum, he thought.

Marty Burke glanced up in surprise at the female standing beside him in the empty photo studio. "I heard Robert was holding a big press powwow up at Heroes' Manor," he told Leslie Ann Nasotrudere. "That's where I thought you'd be—asking pointed questions."

But his newsgathering inamorata replied with a toss of her blond hair. "Old news," she said dismissively. "The backlash against the giants has too many people jumping on the bandwagon." She had new questions now. Had the Deviants really cut a piece of building off so it fell on a crowd?

Leslie Ann smiled, running a massaging hand along his shoulders. The muscles were tense. Jumping from his job at the Fantasy Factory to take this assignment as "creator" of the new Deviant comics had him on edge.

She wasn't sure exactly what Burke was creating if he merely visualized the activities of real-life characters. But he thought the title impressive, and she was willing enough to indulge him.

"Besides," she said, making her voice a purr of promise, "I want to meet these people you'll be working with."

"No interviews," he said, raising a hand. "We're here to work, after all."

"What exactly will you be doing?" Leslie Ann asked, glancing around.

"I'll be shooting pictures while they pose," Burke said seriously. "Colby wants a book ASAP, so I'll need a lot of photo reference—getting their faces and costumes right."

"Sturdley says they look just like a pair of his characters—Superweapon and Vile Girl?"

"That's M-16, Weapon Supreme, and Madam Vile," Burke corrected her. "The Deviants don't look at all like them. But that's another reason for the pictures. Colby wants to make sure I emphasize the differences."

He directed suspicious eyes at Leslie Ann. "You still haven't promised not to interview them."

She responded with her most innocent gaze. "Do you see a camera around? I'll just chat in between your work."

And get the contact and background for a killer personal interview, she promised herself silently.

The Deviants almost disappointed her when they arrived. Leslie Ann had expected a dramatic entrance through the studio skylight. Instead, they knocked on the door, like ordinary mortals. Burke started to make introductions when the female Deviant, Matavi, interrupted.

"You were at the news gathering yesterday, weren't you?" she said, pinning Leslie Ann with glittering blue eyes that seemed almost frighteningly perceptive.

"Right. I'm Leslie Ann Nasotrudere of INC." As they shook hands, Leslie Ann had the oddest sensation. She'd spoken with rock stars, big-time political figures, hell, she'd even gone on camera with giants. But this woman made her feel . . . small. She'd be a tough interview, indeed.

"Leslie Ann is a . . . *friend*," Burke said, dropping his voice the half-octave necessary to indicate "significant other."

Matavi gave them a bright smile and indicated her companion. "This is Emsisdin. I believe you'd call him 'the strong, silent type.' "

The alien male's smile was just short of cocky as he took her hand. Then Burke bustled both Deviants off for picturetaking on a grand scale. First, he shot them together, flying, fighting back-to-back. "Just move the usual way you do when in a battle," he advised. Both aimed their wrist-blasters. Emsisdin hammed it up with the bazooka-like weapon he carried, while Matavi snatched a dart from her bandolier and prepared to throw it.

"Okay," Burke said. "Now, Emsisdin, you move to cover Matavi."

"Cover?" the two Deviants said.

"Protect her," Burke elaborated. "Then maybe we can shoot the pair of you in a clinch—uh, kiss—celebrating the vic—"

"No," Matavi said flatly. "Our relationship is not like that."

Leslie Ann's eyebrows rose. Really?

"We work as partners," Matavi went on. "Emsisdin does not protect me. We do *not* 'clinch.' "

"I did carry her once," Emsisdin said with a gleam in his eye.

"I was unconscious at the time." Matavi said coolly. "The next time it happens, I will be dead."

Giving in, Burke then decided to try some pictures of Matavi alone. "I can see great possibilities in that armor."

Like how it stays up, Leslie Ann thought.

Emsisdin came over, sweat showing on his half-revealed face after a stint under the hot lights.

"Could I get you something to drink?" Leslie Ann offered.

"If I could have some soda," he said. "The sweeter the better. We used to have drinks like that in my home, but—" he fumbled a moment for a word, reminding Leslie Ann that this was an alien speaking. "The . . . government . . . did away with them."

"Your government did away with soda?" Leslie Ann couldn't believe this. "Why?"

"It was decided that it was . . . bad . . . for the citizens."

Leslie Ann continued digging more tales of his home-world from Emsisdin. She shuddered as she listened. The place sounded like *Star Wars* as written by George Orwell.

"So your rebellion was crushed," Leslie Ann said. "And as far as you know, you're the only two to escape."

"Yes, thanks to the freak space-warp." Emsisdin got that off very glibly, she thought, as though he'd been coached.

"And now you and Matavi are alone on a planet of strangers. It must be a difficult life—especially if you have no relationship."

"We are partners," Emsisdin said. "And now, perhaps, we are not so alone."

His eyes in the slits of his half-helmet grew bold as he spoke.

Leslie Ann didn't mind. In the course of her career, she'd enjoyed several bold-eyed men of mystery.

"*Oy,*" Harry Sturdley said softly to Peg as they looked around the reception area for the law firm of Mohe, Lorenz, & Kirley. "That paneling will probably put another thousand bucks on our legal bill."

Although the midtown office building had probably been constructed while Peg was still in college, the satin-finished cherry paneling looked as if it had been there since colonial times. Conservatively dressed men and women strode along the thick, dove-gray carpeting as if each stride were vital.

In his silk jacket and dark slacks, Harry felt vaguely underdressed. Peg's navy "interview suit" seemed cheap and third-world next to the understated outfit of the female functionary who came to fetch them. They followed the woman's well-tailored rump through a warren of offices, then past a sort of upscale bullpen.

It was a large open space with dozens of word processors. The operators of the computers, however, sat a good twenty feet away, typing on keyboards with enormous extension cords and peering at the computer monitors through what appeared to be high-tech spectacles.

"Could I ask what that's about?" Peg said.

The young lady leading them shook her head. "I'm afraid it has something to do with a product-liability case," she said vaguely.

At last, the woman stopped outside a glass-walled office with a magnificent view of Central Park.

Inside, a man with handsome if sharp features and an Oliver North haircut sat at a desk, dictating into a microcassette recorder in his hand.

". . . and, since the deceased was known to deposit wagers in the neighborhood of ten dollars per week on the state lottery, we estimate a further sum of at minimum fifty thousand dollars in potential winnings lost due to this wrongful death . . ."

He turned around and smiled.

Peg goggled. "Lew?" she said in disbelief.

The young man clicked off the recorder. "Peg! I knew your company was in on this case, but I didn't expect to see you!"

"You know each other?" Sturdley said.

"Harry Sturdley, Lew Irvine," Peg said. "We knew each other in school."

Sturdley decided not to ask if there were a Biblical connection in that knowledge. Instead, he said, "I had expected to meet with one of the partners."

"Yes, sir, you will," Lew Irvine said. "They thought you'd merely be sending data first. The firm will of course bring the whole of its copyright experience to bear on this case. I'm merely the litigator."

"When did you leave Fein, Besser, and DiRita?" Peg asked.

"This past summer," Irvine replied. "I got a better offer."

"Well, I've got your case right here." Sturdley dug into his briefcase and came up with a sheaf of papers. "Here are photos of these Deviants, and comics featuring our characters M-16 and Madam Vile."

Irvine looked from one set of pictures to the other. "The male doesn't look as heavily-muscled as his drawn counterpart, and the lady's costume seems—a bit more practical." He glanced at Sturdley. "I was thinking of contacting the owner of the building that got damaged after the bank standoff. I understand the Deviants were responsible—"

"You want to talk about damage? Look at this? Here's what Colby and Burke intend to do to us." Harry pulled out a creased sheet of paper. On it was a photocopy of a pencil drawing. Sketchy flying heroes, dressed like the Deviants, were blasting back a giant in a Fantasy Factory

Hero suit while on the ground a sketchier armored figure directed bolts up at them. "They're not merely stealing two characters, but using other trademarked Fantasy Factory heroes as *villains* in their stories."

"The giant and the other person were present at the Slaughter—er, incident—on Sixth Avenue?" Irvine asked.

"Yes, they were." Sturdley pointed to the picture of the giant. "That's a very bad likeness of Thomas. And the guy with the S on his chest—" He cut Irvine off before the young lawyer could speak. "No, not *him*. He's trademarked by another company altogether. Nor does the S stand for Stagnator, as Colby said in his press conference. Can we sue over that, too? Vilifying a hero?"

"What *does* the S on the man's chest represent?" Irvine asked.

Sturdley smiled as he tapped the figure of John Cameron in armor, savoring his latest brainchild. "The S, my boy, stands *for Stalwart*."

Chapter Thirty-One

John Cameron muttered something vulgar and obscene as he struggled with the final fastening of his armored helmet. Among the things he'd learned as an official Fantasy Factory crime fighter was to put his helmet with its gizmoidal drive controls on last—thus avoiding any spontaneous side-trips. He'd also learned that Argonian armor was designed for long-term wear, not with quick changes in mind.

Since taking over Marty Burke's office, John at least had a reasonably private place to change. But unless he wanted to sit around in his armor, there was still an embarrassing gap between Harry Sturdley's telephoned alerts of promising action gleaned from his new police scanner and the Stalwart going up, up, and away. On several opportunities, John had been upstaged at crime scenes by the damned Deviants.

John's hand unconsciously tightened, and he hurriedly let go of the office drawing board. One corner was already suspiciously crumpled.

Harry's proposals to improve the Stalwart's response time had verged on the ludicrous. The most recent suggestion was that John stay in his armor, with very loose clothing over it. Of course, people might wonder over how John had put on about 200 pounds over the weekend. And where would they find quadruple-extra-large clothing on quick notice?

John opened the window, which overlooked Twenty-eighth Street. At least the sidestreet was a little less conspicuous, he thought as he scanned the area with his suit systems and mental probes. With the ever-worsening currents and eddies in the Rift, he'd decided against that mode of travel, choosing instead to exit by way of the window when no one was looking. John was good with his hands. After a bit of sanding and oiling, the window now moved soundlessly.

He hesitated at the window just one more moment to cover all possible watchers, made sure heads were turned, then leapt out and burned gizmo to attain the highest altitude in the shortest time.

From high above the metropolitan area, John spread his mental net, seeking feelings of anger, terror, violence . . . signs of crime.

There—down in Queens. John banked and headed downward, zeroing in on the feelings of fear. It was an outdoor automatic teller machine with a woman backed against the controls, a creep confronting her with one hand outstretched and a knife in the other. John swooped down, grasping the blade with an armored gauntlet. Metal snapped, and the mugger was now weaponless. One blow, and the thug lay senseless at the shrieking woman's feet.

Then John took off.

The next sign of trouble was a burst of rage. John burned gizmo to find a guy in upper Manhattan trying to smash down an apartment door with a sledgehammer. Inside, a woman and children were screaming.

John tapped the homewrecker on the shoulder and got the sledgehammer in the face—or rather, on the faceplate of his helmet. He staggered back a step, recovered himself, and spoke on his exterior speakers.

"You took your best shot, now try mine."

Again, all it took was one punch to send the guy off to dreamland. John heard the snarl of approaching sirens and neatly arranged the man beside the door with the hammer in his hands.

See what they make of *that*, he thought as he flew out the hall window.

Attaining a respectable altitude again, John flicked on his radio. The Queens police frequencies were dull. John flicked again, trying a new adjustment to his Argonian controls. In moments, he'd accessed Harry Sturdley's portable phone.

"Harry," he said, "I thought I'd check in with you. Been listening to the radio?"

"Actually, I've been fooling around with a police scanner," Harry responded in an offhand tone. After all, they were speaking on a connection open to the world. "Nothing much is happening. The cops are chasing some guy who ran a stoplight. He's driving an old red Impala, and just pulled onto the East River Drive at Fourteenth Street, heading north."

"Sounds fascinating," John drawled. But even as he spoke he was reorienting himself. "Nothing else to report?"

"Nothing that can't wait till tomorrow. I'm heading to bed."

John streaked downward till he was over the highway in the Twenties. An old gas guzzler—an Impala nearly as old as John—was careening up the road, pursued by three police cars.

What am I doing here? John wondered. I've spent the whole night out and fighting, and for what? When you come down to it, I stopped a few piddling crimes.

Maybe he'd saved several people from being hurt, but that was not his immediate goal. Given a free hand, John would have grabbed the Deviants and shoved them through the Rift back to Argon. Then he'd be out picking off giants and shipping them back to their homeworld, as well.

But there were Harry's plans to consider, people to protect . . . the Deviants had once almost succeeded in kidnapping Peg. And that Emsisdin guy's indiscriminate shooting with the force cannon had shown how little he valued the safety of New Yorkers in the street.

Then, too, there was the new instability in the Rift. Could he even penetrate to the worlds where the Deviants and giants came from?

Instead, John battled street crime and chased probable drunks who'd run red lights. He fought back a wave of disgust. If this kept up, he'd be New York's first armored dog-catcher.

Keeping pace with the speeding car, John dropped down to the point where he could hear police sirens. The Impala sideswiped a Volvo that didn't pull out of its way quickly enough. Behind the wheel of the big car, the driver waved something. John kicked up his visor magnification. The object in the driver's hand was a MAC-10 submachine gun.

Great, John thought, when the cops get close enough, he'll spray them with bullets. The stakes were now an order of magnitude higher than they'd been a moment ago. Previously, John had given some thought to the question of how to stop speeding cars. He believed plast-alloy armor could survive a ninety-mile-an-hour impact. But he wasn't sure whether the occupant would survive the concussion.

Plan B was a bit more ambitious. He swooped in over the Impala's left fender, went lower, and grabbed for the exhaust pipe. Using his exoskeletal strength, John squeezed, hoping to close up the pipe and choke the engine to a stop.

Instead, he wound up with a handful of rusty debris.

John's third plan was a bit more risky. He rose up, making sure he'd be seen in the rearview mirror. The driver swerved wildly, one hand on the wheel, the other trying to aim his gun, his eyes turned away from the road ahead.

The guy was speeding right up the rear of a little Ford Escort that seemed determined to maintain its forty-five-mile-an-hour right of way.

John had to make his move.

The back windshield blew out in a hail of glittering shards as the driver opened up with his gun. John shrugged off the bullet impacts, boosting his speed so he came right through the gaping hole where the glass had been. One armored arm wrapped around the driver's neck. John grabbed the steering wheel with his left hand. He activated his exterior speakers.

"We're going to pull off the road and stop. I'll steer, you apply the brakes."

John began twisting the steering wheel to the right, to the slow lane and the concrete retaining wall that overlooked the East River.

The driver neither slowed nor stopped. He kept the gas pedal to the floor as he tried to wrestle the wheel to the left. He was no match for John's exoskeletal armor.

In panic, the guy smashed his gun butt on John's hand, with no effect. He aimed the gun and opened fire. Bullets tore out the front windshield and ricocheted off John's armor. One errant round bounced off and tore a path across the gunman's cheek. Screaming, the driver planted the gun flush against John's faceplate and fired.

The plate went black against the muzzle flare. John couldn't see, and he'd run out of patience. He tightened the grip of his arm around the driver's neck, and the shooting stopped.

Either the driver was unconscious or had been hit by another ricochet. John could care less. When his vision came back, the Impala was headed into a sharp turn, aiming straight for the retaining wall.

John saw only one way to avoid a crash. He let go of the sagging driver—at least the man's foot was now off the gas—and boosted the lift on his gizmoidal drive. John's back pressed against the roof of the car.

Well, he thought, here's where we see just how strong they built 'em way back when.

With a definite wobble, the Impala took off from the highway, just barely clearing the concrete wall. Its forward momentum took it yards out over the water. But without more gas being fed, the engine's revs dropped. Fighting two tons of dead weight, John swung around in a wide curve, heading back onto the highway.

The pursuing police cars slowed down, blocking the road and opening a space for him to land. Behind them, frustrated drivers began to honk their horns. One guy was already leaning out his car window, aiming a camcorder.

John brought the Impala in for a bouncy landing, down-shifted, and turned off the ignition. When the car came to a stop, he flew out through the wrecked windshield and waved to the cops. He turned to the amateur cameraman, made sure the S on his chest was visible, then flew off.

Peg Faber stared in shock when John rounded the corner of the corridor leading to Harry's office, swinging his portfolio. The figure stumping forward to his eleven o'clock meeting was as far as possible from the John she thought she knew.

His skin was sallow, his eyes red and squinting from obvious exhaustion. Still worse was the tight, frustrated set of his lips and jaw.

She wished there was something, anything, she could say that would relax the clenched set of his muscles.

"I hear Stalwart did a real job last night," she said. "That Impala he saved from crashing was loaded to the gills with drugs. And the driver had three murder warrants out on him."

"Um-hm," John responded. He barely seemed to be listening.

She lowered her voice. "Couldn't you sleep at all?" Peg herself had suffered through a rotten night, with bizarre nightmares about being suffocated and squashed in invisible bands of force.

"Sleep?" His lips twitched in something more like a rictus than a smile.

Bad question for a guy you used to sleep with, Peg suddenly thought.

"You ever read about earthquakes?" John suddenly asked. "They say that dogs start to act strangely weeks before a tremor actually hits. That's how I feel. Restless barely begins to cover it. I don't sleep."

His voice dropped to a whisper. "And the Rift is almost closed to me. There's too much weird shit going on in there."

Peg turned away from the torment in his face. "I—I'll see if Harry's ready"

Sturdley immediately appeared in the doorway and waved them both into his office. "Close the door, please, Peg," he said pleasantly. "How's it going, champ?"

"Like hell," John replied flatly. "I can't sleep, I've got a headache that makes a trip through the Rift feel like a Spring day, I'm wasting my nights playing undercover superhero for you, and by day I pencil goddamn comic books featuring 'Heroes' that I know are villains."

Peg watched Harry's face go from forced joviality to outright testiness. "Look, kid. Nobody's got a bed of roses around here. I'm having lousy nights myself—"

"Tell him about the Rift," Peg interrupted, looking at John, who shook his head.

"What about the Rift?" Sturdley asked in alarm.

"That's not what we're here to talk about now." John opened his portfolio. "Here's the pencil work for the *Amazing Robert*. I've finally wrapped up the story are that Burke stuck us with. The problem is, where do we go from here?"

"I've been thinking that maybe you, Ximenes, Grantfield, and Nagel might put your heads together, get a crossover story running through *Robert*, *Barbara*, and *Thomas*. How about an antigiant assassination plot that Robert and Barbara discover and thwart out in California, but in New York, the bad guys manage to get a shot off with an antitank rocket—"

John surged to his feet, staring at his onetime mentor. "Are you for real?" he demanded. "We're supposed to be fighting these guys, but you want me to help concoct a whitewash for what happened on the night of the premiere?"

"It would let us portray the Deviants as the villains they are, and it would make a great introduction for the Stalwart."

"No. No way." John shook his head as if he were trying to get something unpleasant out of his ears. He glared at Harry. "Are sales *that* bad?"

"They're leveling off after a bit of a decline," Sturdley admitted. His face tightened. "A bit of a *steep* decline."

"Then why not let me off *Robert?*" John said. "Put somebody else on. Someone who'll let you rewrite history."

Sturdley raised a placating hand. "Kid, I know how you feel about the giants. Hell, I feel the same way. But the comics—they're something else again. I've got a responsibility—"

"To the company and everyone who works here," John finished for him. "So if you've got someone who can't stand working on them anymore, you *should* let them go."

"Actually, I agree."

Both John and Peg gawked at Sturdley in surprise. Peg knew John had been trying to get off *Robert* since his return from Argon. What had suddenly changed Harry's mind?

"Let's face it, *all* the Heroes titles will probably become losers. They're not selling the way they did even with big guns working on them. So, logically, I should let them go, move in second-line talent, and allow the books to wither—"

"Like what happens with Glamazon every time we give the character her own book," Peg couldn't help saying.

Sturdley shot her a dirty look, but returned to his discourse. "I mean, that's the best thing to do for the company. The books die out—"

"And we finally move against the giants," John said.

Sturdley nodded. "Of course, we still have our obligations. We want the company to be healthy. That means we've got to develop new ideas, and have I got a development job for you: *Stalwart!*" He gave John a big smile.

"Is this a natural, or what? All the reference you need is in the mirror. We'll go with the real-life adventures angle, and this time we'll get it right! The whole story can be told from Stalwart's point of view—and we already have the beginnings of great stories! That bit you did with the car last night will make for spectacular art. And we have to include your run-in with the Deviants. The collapse of the corner of that building—that will look good, too. It will also help establish them as the series villains—"

John stared at Sturdley as if he'd never seen him before. "You're serious," he said slowly. "The whole blasted world is in trouble. We've got a hostile force of twenty-foot-tall aliens who hate people our size in general and us in particular. They're ruthless and up to something about which we haven't got a clue except that it's almost killed one of them and certainly won't be good for us. To top it off, we've got a new set of aliens—those damned Deviants—who've made a career out of trying to wreck the planet Argon. Lord knows what they're trying to do here—except, again, I don't think it will be good."

The longer John spoke the louder his voice became. "There's a food shortage developing in the city because the truckers who are supposed to supply the stores aren't moving. They claim their big rigs are blowing up for no reason whatsoever. And on every streetcorner, people are passing along the latest rumor about some unlucky bastard who had some modern convenience turn on him. People aren't riding the trains, and when they buy something, they ask nervously, 'Is it electric?' New York City, America . . . *everywhere* is going to hell in a handbasket."

He stabbed a forefinger at Sturdley. "And what's *your* big concern? Launching another goddamned comic book!"

"That's the business we happen to be in, kid." Harry's voice was loud, hot, and angry, too. "And it's been damned good to you. I'll thank you to keep a more civil tone. You weren't pulling this holier-than-thou crap when I gave you your first break. Remember, I *made* you—"

"But now you just make me *sick!*" John broke in. He dumped his portfolio on Sturdley's desk. "Use anything you want in there, but I don't want to hear from you again. I *quit!*"

He left and slammed the door. In the silence that followed, Peg took a step after John, but stopped at an abrupt hand motion from Sturdley. He sat at his desk in white-faced fury for another speechless moment. Then he broke out in a barrage of cursing and swearing. Peg watched, fascinated by his inventiveness in stringing together the same old Anglo-Saxon terms into whole new forms of opprobrium.

At last Harry remembered she was in the room and subsided, turning from pale to bright red. "Sorry about that, Peg," he apologized. "I don't usually—"

"I know," she said. "Even Marty Burke never generated an outburst like that."

"I never trusted Burke," Harry growled. "But the kid— talk about *ingratitude!* He'd be nobody if I hadn't—"

"If you hadn't been pushed by me into giving him the chance you promised him." Peg matched glares with her boss. "You might be brilliant at writing comics, but you've got a bad habit of trying to rewrite reality."

"What is this, *dump on the boss day?*"

"You're going to listen, because I'm not going to quit on you, and I don't think you're going to fire your first assistant to last more than six months."

"Does that include our luxurious vacation on the giants' world and Argon?" he asked.

"As a matter of fact, it doesn't," Peg replied. "But I think our time there is the problem with all of us."

Now Harry was the one staring as she went on. "We've gone through some pretty bizarre adventures—being hunted, fighting to pry John loose from that computer-run hell, getting dumped into the middle of a high-tech civil war. I know the one thing that kept me going was the thought that if I held on, I'd manage to get back to a normal life. Now we're home, and the problem is, *nothing* is normal. We've got giants, we've got Deviants, and you must be hearing the same weird rumors I have."

She took a deep breath. "But we both try to *act* as if everything is normal. You're back running the company . . . and I—I sit on my thumbs wondering if this is all John's fault."

Peg brought her chin up. "So what are we going to do about it?"

Sturdley sat in mute concentration for long minutes. Finally, he spoke. "I think maybe we should try the jobs we proved ourselves best at. I'll go back to Intelligence—not just spying on Colby, but trying to find out what all the bad guys are up to." He looked at Peg. "And maybe you should start suiting up and going out with John when he's on patrol."

Her jaw dropped. "Jeeze, Harry, where did you get that? Out of the *Superheroes' Manual*? Or is it an old *Ex-Wives* plot? We're in too deep to try something just because it worked in the comics."

Sturdley shook his head. "I wish I had a plot that fit this situation, but I don't." He sighed. "We'll have to wing it, Red. That's one reason why I want you keeping an eye on our boy John."

His face was grim as he looked at her. "We've just lost control of him at work. I think it might be a good idea to have someone riding herd on him when he puts on that damnfool superarmor."

Peg gave him a suspicious look. "This isn't some cheap ploy to create a new superteam? The Stalwarts?"

"Now that's an idea," Harry began enthusiastically. Then he shook his head, hard. "Sorry. Old habits. Look, I know you're not wild about dressing up and playing superhero. But that won't be your real job. You'll be out there for damage control in advance."

An image of John, bitter, angry, and backed with all the might of Argonian technology, flashed through Peg's mind. "Damage control," she assented, "for a loose atomic cannon."

Chapter Thirty-Two

More and more, accidental interactions occurred between the four-dimensional nexus called Earth and the universes swirling through the Rift. Sometimes a brush with the alien physics embodied in the higher-order cosmic fragments caused minor annoyance. Other times, even the merest connection meant catastrophe.

"All right," Leslie Ann Nasotrudere said through clenched teeth. "Sound check—*again*."

She spoke into her microphone, glaring at her cameraman. If this were an actual take, it would be disastrous for her career. Network newswomen were not supposed to look like bitches on wheels.

But this was just another test run, the latest in an apparently endless cycle as either the microphone, the camera, or both would act up.

"Well?" she directed a frigid glance toward the technical part of her team. "Did it work this time?"

"Your voice isn't tracking on the tape," the young video technician said in bafflement.

"Maybe you should put a fresh tape in," Leslie Ann suggested.

"I've tried three new tapes already," the technician replied. "It shouldn't—"

"We're out in the middle of East Armpit, our Suffolk County office is miles away, and you stick us with bum equipment. Why the hell didn't you check it out before we left Manhattan?"

"I did check it," the technician said in injured tones. "The equipment tested out fine."

"So we have fine equipment, okay videotape, and no damned audio," Leslie Ann's voice was scathing. "What do you think the problem is? Were the laws of magnetism repealed to discriminate against my voice?"

The cameraman shrugged. "Or maybe we got a touch of whatever happened in there."

He nodded toward the suburban house they'd parked outside. The INC news van wasn't the only visitor. Police cars, a firetruck, an ambulance—all the emergency services were on hand. At the moment, however, Leslie Ann and her crew were the only representatives of the electronic media. But Leslie Ann was willing to bet that the battered station wagon blocking the driveway across the street had been left there by a local newspaper reporter.

"Let's try it one more time," Leslie Ann sighed, speaking into her microphone. If her tone were any more frigid, she'd have flash-frozen the sweating technician in his tracks.

"B-better," the video tech said. "But we're still having problems with the audio pickup—"

"Screw it!" Leslie Ann said decisively. "As long as we can get some decent video, we'll be okay. I can always loop in some commentary back at the studio."

She shoved the door of the van open and hopped nimbly down. "Start on the establishing shot," she ordered the cameraman while she straightened her news blazer and applied a little lip gloss.

The home they stood outside was a typical suburban dwelling, a single-story ranch house less than twenty years old, sprouting on what used to be a potato field. It was virtually indistinguishable from the fifty other buildings in this cheap development.

Leslie Ann could almost predict the interior decor—plastic slipcovers over gold velour. And in the backyard, there'd be an above-ground swimming pool.

Now that she was ready for the camera, Leslie Ann led the way up the walk, to be confronted by a Suffolk cop at the front door. He blocked the entrance, but she got a glimpse inside over his shoulder. Okay, so she was wrong about the furniture. It was red velvet.

"What can you tell us, officer?" she asked.

"Female Caucasian." Conscious of being on-camera, the policeman checked his notebook. "Tiffany Dawn Mascaretto—a teenager. There was a fatal fire in her bed—"

"It was the telephone!" A squat, heavyset middle-aged woman burst out the doorway. "That damned cordless telephone! She kept at us and at us to buy one. We used to have a nice princess phone in her room, but she always used the cordless. She was talking to one of her friends, and I heard a sort of *fwoosh* from her room, I go in, and the bed's all on fire. Her hand where she held the phone—gone! And her head—what was left—"

The woman burst into hysterical wailing.

Leslie Ann glanced at the policeman for confirmation. He nodded, then gestured that the camera point away.

"I can't let you in," he said in a low voice to Leslie Ann. "But essentially, that's what happened."

"Have you had similar appliance-related accidents in the vicinity?" she asked.

"Not like this one." The man looked a little sick.

"You're sure we can't get some footage of the scene?" Leslie Ann pressed.

"Lady," the cop said, "you don't want to see the scene. And nobody would want it on their TV. Real crispy critters time. Imagine a bed with a big scorched circle and a dead teenaged girl lying in the middle, half of her cooked, the other half—charred."

"Are there arson investigators on the scene?" she asked. Learning that there were, Leslie Ann continued to stake out the place. A little more interviewing and some sweet talk to the fire investigator, and she got one of his Polaroid snapshots.

It *was* too grisly for television viewing. In fact, when the technician caught sight of it, he lost his lunch out the back of the van.

"Well, I can see *you've* never covered any airline crashes," Leslie Ann said. "Gimme the keys. I'll drive us back."

She was working to compress that long outburst from the girl's mother when the phone rang in the editing room. "For you," the guy working the console said.

"Leslie Ann Nasotrudere," she said into the handset.

"Save the pleasant tone," the voice of her producer came over the line. "I'm not a news source."

"So what's up, Curt?"

"This telephone thing in Suffolk—we're not running it."

"Don't tell me that!" she burst out. "I've tracked down three cases of people getting killed by appliances in the last week or so, but this one I got while it was hot!" Even though Curt couldn't see, she gestured to the editing monitor where the image was frozen on the woman's anguished face. "You won't believe the speech I got from the mother!"

"Leslie Ann—"

"Just come and see," she begged into the phone. "One look, and I'll bet you change your mind."

"It's not my mind that's the problem," Curt said. "This came down from Corporate."

"What?" Leslie Ann's perfectly modulated voice roughened to a snarl. "They running a little short of lead for their pencils up on the top floor? You can't tell me they're afraid of the phone company."

"They don't want people afraid of their televisions," Curt said gently. "After all, those are electrical appliances, too."

Leslie Ann was back at her desk in the newsroom, muttering words that were seldom if ever heard on television—except for certain cable channels. With the demise of her "Revolt of the Appliances" story, she'd lost a week's work.

She glanced through the typed transcript of her conversations with the Deviants at Burke's photo session, recorded on a microcassette hidden in her purse. She'd promised not to interview them then and there, but it didn't hurt to start collecting data.

Leslie Ann reached into her desk and got out a transcript of the Dynasty Comics press conference. Odd how both Deviants used almost the same words to describe their transit to Earth—discussing it with Colby and his minions must have worn the story smooth.

Emsisdin, however, had given some more personal anecdotes of life under the repressive regime of his homeworld. What a gray, grim place it must have been, attempting to stamp out all creativity in an effort to construct the ultimate conformist state. If I ever get hold of him for an exclusive interview, I'll have to mine that, she thought. If he hasn't been interviewed to death by then.

"One cent for your thoughts," a deep voice said from over her head.

"That's a penny," Leslie Ann automatically corrected. She glanced up, but there was no one in front of her desk. Then she looked higher, to find Emsisdin floating above her.

The whole newsroom ground to a complete halt as people stared in surprise, shock, and, in some cases, pure journalistic jealousy. Leslie Ann smiled upward, doing her best to project her personality and annoy those onlookers. "I'm surprised you even knew the idiom."

"Matavi is very skilled at translating languages," Emsisdin responded.

Leslie Ann felt a moment's trepidation. "I suppose, then, that she would be the one who talks to reporters."

"Most reporters, yes," Emsisdin agreed. "In fact, she's talking to one now." His cocky grin came back. "However, I convinced her that we need a . . . friendly reporter for our first major interview."

"Major?" she almost whispered.

"What is the word?" Emsisdin said. "Explicit? No. *Exclusive.*"

Leslie Ann had to keep her smile from going predatory. After all the ups and downs of the past year, that elusive Pulitzer was finally in her grasp. The first exclusive interview with the mysterious Deviants!

"When?" she asked.

"As soon as possible," he replied. "If you are available now, we could start making preparations."

With no hot story on hand, she was definitely available. Leslie Ann opened her desk drawer, tossed in the papers, picked up her phone, and dialed Curt. "Can't say much now. But I've got a big story—*definitely* not electronics-related. See you later."

As she picked up her purse, Emsisdin swung round to land on the floor. They walked out together.

Emsisdin had to hide a smile at the reporter's disappointment when he led her to a luxury hotel. "You were expecting us to have a headquarters hidden in a cave?"

Matavi had briefed him on the stereotypes of comic books, as well as on what she had read in the mind of Leslie Ann Nasotrudere. The ambition there could be used by both of them. But what he'd seen in the woman's eyes was something he intended to enjoy privately.

He indicated the couch in the sitting room of the suite. "Why don't we sit down, you can take out your recording device—yes, we knew about it—and we can talk."

For the next hour and a half, their conversation moved in a fascinating give and take. Emsisdin told stories about life on Argon, suitably edited to play up the freedom fighting aspects of the Deviants' campaign of terror. In return, he asked questions about Earth, about the practice of journalism, questions that slowly turned toward the personal.

"I act," he admitted frankly, "and in the midst of action, I certainly don't take time to reflect. Your chosen career—reporting and reflecting—is very hard for me to understand."

"While you men of action are the meat and drink of my profession," Leslie Ann said with a smile. "We make a living supposedly understanding and explaining the things you do."

"It's nice to make a living. But don't you wish, some-times, to *do* instead of listen?" He gestured to the recorder whirring away on the arm of the couch.

Leslie Ann pointed to the hotel room's TV set. "I can have more influence speaking from that little box there than many men of action."

"I'm sure of that." Emsisdin took off his half-helmet and the clamshell breast and back plates.

He smiled as Leslie Ann stared. "Oh, you think I should keep this on? Retain my secret identity?" Emsis-din shrugged. "I have none. I have no history on this world. I have no connections."

Leslie Ann met his eyes and slowly removed her blue news blazer.

"What are you doing?"

"I'm taking off *my* armor," she replied.

Emsisdin didn't need to be a telepath to feel the vibra-tions in the air. Leslie Ann stepped into his arms. He ran a hand over the satin blouse she wore, enjoying the warmth and firmness of the flesh beneath. "Ah," he said quietly, "you *can* act."

"Mmmmmm," she said as their lips met, then turned away to turn off the recorder. "I think this should be off the—aaaaahh!—record."

Matavi's press contact was more circumspect. She flew through some low-lying clouds over the borough of Brooklyn, keeping mental tabs on a car rolling along Flat-bush Avenue below. Inside the car was a newspaper reporter. His destination was the apartment of a security guard—or rather, an ex-security guard, who had once worked at Tiffany's. Now the man was collecting unem-ployment and considerable suspicion as the inside man for a spectacular burglary.

While Matavi knew the man was innocent, she could not allow this interview to take place. She felt exhausted. Being a superhero as defined by Dirk Colby was strenuous work. But in addition, she had to maintain the psychic trip-wires that warned of interest in the rash of jewel robberies.

This reporter was especially dangerous. From some-where, he had managed to make a connection between armored figures and the Tiffany robbery. Matavi was sure the guard would not help him make more connections—when she suppressed memories, they stayed suppressed.

But this journalistic investigation would have to be ended, and that meant she would have to deal with the reporter—something she couldn't do in the middle of a crowded avenue.

Carefully working her way into the reporter's mind, she augmented his annoyance at the slow-moving traffic, then inserted the idea of a shortcut. He turned off into a maze of one-way streets, and it was easy to influence the man's steering until he found himself on an empty, dead-end street surrounded by abandoned buildings.

Although the area appeared desolate, Matavi moni-tored the buildings to verify they were indeed empty. Then she landed.

"Why don't you get out of the car, Mr. Simms."

The reporter blinked as if coming out of a daze (he was) then moved to confront Matavi. "Glad to meet you," he said belligerently. "I've got some questions—"

"Yes," Matavi said, "I see."

Casting psionic tendrils inside the reporter's head, she did indeed perceive his questions, and more importantly, his sources. There was a late-shift office worker who would soon receive a visit to have his memories of flying armored figures fuzzed. It had become a regular operation of late. Matavi had hit upon the trick of inserting the image of a passing helicopter. That was usually enough to confuse the subject's memory.

Adjusting the reporter's mind, however, was more ticklish work. She couldn't merely suppress his memories and suspicions. The key here was to temper his enthusiasm for the story.

Of course, she already had a start here, with Simms's frustration at getting lost. Building on that emotion, she introduced doubt about the guard. Was it worth the effort going to talk to a guy who'd probably wind up in jail?

Next came doubt about his eyewitness, who would now be doubtful himself. Was the guy as certain as he seemed?

Matavi then turned up his concern about other deadlines. Was he taking too much time away from better stories for a wild-goose chase? How was his editor going to react?

After having done similar jobs on the brains of three other reporters sniffing around the same story, Matavi had an excellent working knowledge of a journalist's fears and paranoias.

In this case, she had one more disincentive for Mr. Simms. Leaving him in trance state, she searched the street until she found a broken bottle, which she rammed into his left rear tire. In Matavi's flights over the roads of New York, she frequently encountered enraged motorists trying to repair this problem. Personally, she was glad she could fly.

Now came the memory-wipe, so Simms would never remember confronting her. But before she pulled out of his mind, Matavi raided the reporter's mental files for any references to telepaths.

She frowned in disgust. Another dead end. The only entry in Simms's "telepath" file was something called a stage magician, whom Simms dismissed as a charlatan.

It had been the same with the other three reporters whose minds she'd invaded. They either had no idea what a telepath was, or dismissed the idea of mind-to-mind communication as a fraud.

Except, of course, for that one journalist from *The International World Weekly Evening Star*. Her memories had included references to *hundreds* of telepaths, some of whom she'd dated. Unfortunately, none of them had been genuine. The journalist had participated in several frauds herself.

Shrugging, Matavi directed Simms back into the car and behind the wheel. Then, after flying well out of sight, she let him out of his trance, inserting the memory of a swerve to the curb.

She grinned to herself as the reporter began swearing at his flat.

But the smile faded as Matavi had to face the apparent facts. It seemed that telepaths were even more rare on this world than they had been home on Argon. There were the giants, of course, but it was evident that many local news-gatherers were not even aware that the giants had mind powers.

Nor could the giants help Matavi with her long-range goal—propagating a race of telepaths. As far as she could determine, there were only three people on this planet with psionic capability.

One of them, Sturdley, was too old to take to stud. Another was the female, Peg Faber. She'd be no help to Matavi in terms of fathering a telepathic child. And

considering the way John Cameron had rushed to the rescue during the abortive Deviant kidnap attempt, there
was an obvious relationship between the two.

No, this Peg would be a definite hindrance to any
experiments in eugenics with John Cameron.

Matavi smiled again.

No matter how enjoyable they might prove to be . . .

Chapter Thirty-Three

Marty Burke's eyes went from the photograph taped on his drawing board to the face he was sketching on the fourth panel of the thirteenth page of what would become the first issue of *Deviants!*

This was no *Latter-Day Breed*, a project that was now years in the making. He couldn't afford to dawdle over this artwork. Dirk Colby had been emphatic enough on that point. Burke's deadline was ridiculously short, especially when he was still feeling his way in terms of rendering the characters. For instance, if he wasn't careful here, Matavi would end up looking perilously close to the Fantasy Factory's Madam Vile.

The photo reference was at least useful—all he had to do was copy Matavi's face. If the crunch kept up, he might even wind up lightboxing features or projecting them with his camera lucida for tracing. Too bad the physical poses didn't work out. Why the hell did comic book perspective have to be so much more exaggerated than the real thing?

As his left hand busily wielded the pencil, Burke's right hand pointed a compact remote control at his television set. The TV was large, high tech, and full of the latest bells and whistles.

But even when all he'd owned was a battered black-and-white portable, Burke had always used channel surfing to help stay awake on all-nighters.

Of course, he hadn't worked *all* last night. Leslie Ann Nasotrudere had turned up at his door about two A.M., looking tired and frustrated. Something about covering a fire that had been started by someone's electric blanket . . .

Anyway, she'd been surprisingly affectionate, as if she were going out of her way to be nice to him. And all work and no play . . .

But after she'd dropped off to sleep, Burke had returned to his drawing board. Then disaster struck. The remote control died on him. And the damned thing required those really tiny batteries! Where could he find them at five in the morning?

At that moment, an ad for beepers came on the screen. Of course! Leslie Ann carried one of them—and they used the same tiny batteries.

Burke rifled through Leslie Ann's clothes until he found the tiny device, then switched batteries with his remote. When she got up two hours later, she'd collected her stuff, given him a kiss, and regretfully told him she'd be working all night again.

"I'll see you lots later," she'd said, heading out the door. For a long second, Marty debated telling her about the batteries. But why ruin the moment?

Burke sorted through his reference files, looking for a decent shot of Thomas's face. At the same time, his finger tapped the channel select button on the remote. What went best with drawing a fight scene? *The Flintstones?* A rerun of *Bewitched?* No, here it was. *Tom and Jerry.*

Peg Faber glanced at her watch. Where the hell had the time gone? She'd been tracking and coordinating the preparation of legal exhibits for the copyright suit—Harry's anti-Deviant crusade, as she privately called it. Now it was suddenly well after lunch.

She reached for the phone to order something from the deli downstairs when her eye fell on the open door to Harry's office. He was out, schmoozing a newspaper editor in the hopes of getting a few column inches printed about Dirk Colby's treachery. For a brief instant, Peg desired to do something more concrete on the Deviant problem. Harry was still pestering her to don her armor. It was just inside, locked in his closet . . .

Peg had just risen from her seat when the room seemingly made a sudden, vicious orbit around her, lurching not merely around, but downward. Peg dropped weak-kneed back into her desk chair, her hands gripping the chair's arms. The whole unpleasant experience had a sickening similarity to her jaunts through the Rift. But this time, John Cameron wasn't around to initiate the transition.

She huddled over her desk, all thoughts of superheroics driven out of her head. Unless the weird stuff going on in the Rift was beginning to affect her . . .

No longer was the Rift an interdimensional void. It was now more of a dimensional soup, with fragments of the higher-order cosmos tumbling around in ever-growing profusion. More and more pocket universes began jostling each other. If the realities they contained were sufficiently antithetical, such a collision resulted in complete destruction for the two bubbles—in some cases, vaporizing all the universe-bubbles unlucky enough to be nearby.

In other cases, the impacting fragments might be of sufficiently similar cosmography to join together and form yet a larger bubble-universe. When these superfragments interacted with the Earth-nexus, they affected larger and larger areas in the four-dimensional realm.

On the floor of the New York Stock Exchange, Terrill Saunders III felt the blood drain from his face as his colleague Sean Chapereau passed on the news. Three airliners had suddenly plummeted from the holding pattern around O'Hare as if they had all simultaneously forgotten how to fly. That was bad enough for the Chicago-bound passengers. But for Terrill Saunders, the news spelled ruin.

In moments, stocks of airlines and plane manufacturers would go into a free-fall as disastrous as the crashes had been. And not only had Saunders steered his brokerage clients into the transportation sector, a good deal of his own money was tied up in the airline stocks that would take a big hit.

He frantically initiated selling procedures, but the hum of incipient bloodbath was already invading the exchange floor.

"Gonna be a hell of a day," Chapereau said, his eyes gleaming with excitement. Saunders hid the wash of WASPish contempt he suddenly felt. His family had maintained a seat on the exchange since his great-grandfather's day. They'd weathered panics, depressions, recessions, and black weekdays of every stripe—and they had done so stoically. But this outsider, whose father's name had been Shapiro, was acting like a spectator at a bullfight.

"You see," Chapereau leaned forward, wintergreen-laced breath puffing in Saunders's face, "I found a safe haven."

Saunders glanced around and leaned closer. "What? Where?"

"Look at the market. Automotive's gone to hell, with cars and trucks blowing up. Most of the manufacturing sector, especially electronics, are getting slapped with productliability suits for appliances that killed people. Retailing's getting sued for selling the damned things."

Right, Saunders thought. The whole consumer ethic—the economic engine that had made America great—was unraveling.

"So we've got to go back to the basics—back to what made America strong. I'm investing in crafts companies, horse and mule farms—hell, I even found a buggy maker."

Galvanized, Saunders turned away to a computer and frantically began scanning the issues. He might be able to save only pennies on the dollar, but he was going to invest in the immediate future, in the form of America's past.

Unfortunately, even as he depressed the keys on his keyboard, anomaly engulfed the Exchange—physical anomaly, not financial. Every device carrying electricity—telephones, computers, fax machines, even the building's wiring and the phone lines—suddenly turned to white-hot plasma. Saunders, Chapereau, and every broker, runner, and tourist at the Exchange abruptly died in flaming agony.

And the building that housed the Exchange swayed, rumbled, and disintegrated from the ground up.

Leslie Ann Nasotrudere was in a van heading downtown seconds after word of the disaster reached her newsroom.

"What is it—terrorists?" her cameraman asked as they battled their way through traffic.

"From what I heard, it sounds like all their electronics blew," Leslie Ann said grimly. "This is one they can't shove under the rug and cover up."

She joined a throng of media people milling around at the police cordon blocking people off from the Exchange building—or rather, the site where the building had been. Concrete dust still hazed the area, but there were beams of sunlight piercing through the space where a cathedral of commerce had risen only hours before.

Leslie Ann spotted a familiar face—a young cop she'd half-flirted with at other crowd scenes. "Hey, O'Brien," she wheedled, "give us an idea what's going on behind the lines."

He only shook his head, looking sick. "This one makes the World Trade Center look like a day in the park."

"What do you mean?" one of Leslie Ann's rivals, a print reporter, asked.

"With that, we had a hole under the building and a lot of people to get out." The cop swallowed hard. "This dropped a building full of people on a street full of people. Every chunk of debris they pick up has somebody squished under it. Hell, they're evacuating people in other office buildings who got hit by stuff falling through walls and windows."

He glanced significantly at Leslie Ann's camera crew. "They're not gonna let you in there. It's too damn ugly."

"Can you tell us where we can get a shot of the people being evacuated?" Leslie Ann asked.

"Even that ain't too photogenic," the cop said. "A lot of the people are minus arms or legs." He lowered his voice. "And with the body bags, the best they can do is load in whatever pieces they can find."

After a frustrating tour of the area trying to find something to film that wouldn't make the viewers throw up, Leslie Ann took her crew to the official briefing.

The police commissioner did the talking while the mayor stood by looking appropriately serious beside a representative of the Exchange, who looked frankly dazed. Leslie Ann surmised he'd been out for a late lunch and missed the catastrophe by sheer luck.

The statement was short and sweet, a masterpiece of stonewalling. Bad enough the tourists were afraid of crime. If the big companies began to suspect that Con Ed was blowing them to bits . . .

"We are working on the assumption that the explosion was an act of terrorism—and that, in time, some extremist group will take responsibility," the commissioner intoned.

A virtual invitation, Leslie Ann thought. But there were lots of media types beside herself who weren't ready to accept that explanation.

"Mr. Commissioner," one of her network rivals asked, "what about the reports of strange effects from the electrical systems—"

"We have no such reports," the top cop plowed over the question.

"Really?" the reporter pressed. "I was in the hospital talking to several survivors—people from outside the building. They said the lights, including the streetlights, gave off what one called an 'intolerable glow.' "

The commissioner looked as if he'd been on the receiving end of a kidney punch, but he made a game response. "Perhaps if you helped us identify these people, we could question them."

His words sounded jovial enough, but the gleam in his eye made it clear that such inconvenient witnesses might spend their hospital stays incommunicado.

Leslie Ann had her own question prepared. Prompted by what the cop on the line had told her, she'd made a few phone calls for professional advice. She raised her hand and was acknowledged.

"Mr. Commissioner," she asked, "could you give us an idea of how much explosive was used to destroy the building? We know the terrorists used a truck full at the Trade Center to blow a hole in the parking garage and cause a fire. How big a bomb would they need to bring a whole building down? How did they manage to position it to achieve the amount of structural damage that was done here?"

The commissioner assured her that such details would be discovered by further investigation, but he sounded more like Porky Pig than a police officer and leader of men.

Leslie Ann came out of City Hall enjoying the taste of a little blood on her teeth. Sooner or later, the blanket would have to come off this burst of electrical mishaps. And she wanted to lay the groundwork . . .

Her thoughts were interrupted by a leather-lunged voice coming from City Hall Park. "It is up to us, my friends, to stop this new plague that is upon us. It is judgment, friends, a judgment upon godless, soulless machines!"

Leslie Ann peered into the park to find a rally in full swing. A heavyset bald man stood on a makeshift rostrum haranguing the crowd through a bullhorn. It was the crowd, however, that caught Leslie Ann's attention. Graying secretaries stood by brawny mailroom clerks. Street people stood by men in executive suits. It was as wide a range of people as one could hope to find in the city. But there was one similarity. Every person in the assemblage had frightened eyes.

"Is he making a Monckey out of you?" a bored, superior voice inquired. It was Garstairs of the *Gazette*, married but still trying to add Leslie Ann to his collection.

"Monkey?" she asked.

"That's the Reverend Judah Moncke—with a CKE at the end. He's quite particular about that antiquated spelling, but that's the man in a nutshell. Fellow's a neo-Luddite, wants to bring everyone back to nature or some such. Equates the Industrial Revolution with Original Sin. All technology is sin—using the bullhorn to get out his message must be a venial sin."

Garstairs was so busy scoring wit off the speaker, he paid no attention to the audience. Leslie Ann cold-shouldered the newspaperman until he finally went away. Then she beckoned her crew over. "Park the van right here on the sidewalk and light up the microwave mast," she said. "I want to go in and get some footage of this rally."

"What for?" her tired-looking cameraman asked.

"To show Corporate that people are already frightened about machinery blowing up—and they'll only get more scared if they don't get accurate information."

In moments, she was poking her way through the back of the crowd, clearing a path for the camera. The Reverend Judah Moncke was launching into a new topic. "The Lord in His infinite mercy was willing to stay His hand when we went against the natural plan," his hoarse voice boomed out. "But then we embraced *alien abominations!* I have heard otherwise sensible people refer to the giant freaks thrusting themselves uninvited on our world as 'guardian angels'! And now we have metal-clad flying demons in our skies. If the good Lord had wanted man to fly, He would have given us the wings of angels, not a diabolic metal suit."

Leslie Ann had reached the front of the crowd. With a camera and lights, her crew was not exactly inconspicuous. While the reverend worked on his listeners' emotions, she kept the tape running, interjecting no comments. Moncke was a persuasive speaker. One of the stockroom boys in the crowd tore off his Walkman and threw it on the ground. It was crushed by dozens of eager heels.

Enthusiasts began closing in on the news crew, but Moncke spoke to forestall them. "Let the technology-worshipers be!" he thundered. "They will help us spread the word—I will use Satan's tools against—awrp!"

Leslie Ann's cameraman gave a yell as a fat blue spark crackled from the camera to the bullhorn in Moncke's hand. The hand-held loudspeaker blew up, and Moncke fell backward, his face a red ruin.

Screams and yells rose from the park, echoing off the building fronts. Leslie Ann and her people were hemmed in on one side by Moncke's makeshift stage, and on the other three by a scared and angry crowd.

"They killed him!" somebody yelled.

A louder voice cried, "Look! Look over there!"

The microwave mast on the INC news van was haloed with a spectral glow, like a multicolored St. Elmo's fire. A couple of hardy types from the edges of the crowd ran over and began rocking the van, ignoring the protests of the technician inside.

Things were getting out of hand, and Leslie Ann knew the time had come for a quick exit. The problem was, she and her people were still surrounded, although those near her were shying away, since Leslie Ann's microphone was now giving off the same eerie glow. She tried to use it as one might use a torch against beasts, and cleared a path a little ways into the crowd. They were trapped in the midst of the press of people when the glow abruptly faded.

As she stood holding a useless microphone, Leslie Ann had an instant's memory of a picture from her childhood, an old lithograph of Custer's Last Stand, the blond-haired Custer brandishing his six-shooter against a pageful of enemies.

Then came the true cry of a mob. "Get 'em!"

The crush of bodies increased. Rough hands grabbed Leslie Ann. But their grasp suddenly slackened as heads glanced upward, responding to a low, warbling noise. Gasps rose from the crowd when they saw the armored figure floating above them—one of the enemies Moncke had warned about.

"Goddam freak-monster!" somebody yelled.

"Demon!"

Leslie Ann recognized the figure as Emsisdin.

Rocks and clods of earth flew up from the crowd, as well as a few bottles and somebody's briefcase. The fusillade proved useless, the impromptu ammunition either missing or rattling off Emsisdin's armor. Then it fell on other members of the mob, not improving their tempers.

When the briefcase came flying up again, Emsisdin extended an arm and vaporized it. That took the fight out of the crowd. It began dispersing—fast.

Emsisdin flew low over the news crew, covering them from above. Before Leslie Ann got in the van, she beckoned to the Deviant.

"I have to handle some things before tonight's newscast," she said. "But I should be free after eight o'clock."

"And?" Emsisdin said.

Leslie Ann smiled. "A lady in distress is under a debt of honor to . . . *reward* anyone gallant enough to rescue her." The smile became sultry. "I prefer to honor my debts as soon as possible."

Peg Faber sat quietly in the den of the Sturdley household, braving doom by listening to a radio through a set of ear plugs. The local news station droned through its hourly schedule. She glanced down at the notepad lying on her right thigh. Four bizarre stories of mechanical mishaps in as many hours, the major one occurring at a rally in City Hall Park that had apparently become a near-riot.

That story got updates. The others had not been repeated. A man in Westchester trying to use an automatic garage opener had been left with a bloody stump when the remote exploded in his hand. A woman in a tanning parlor had been killed when the machine she'd been in seemingly imploded. And a telephone operator had a whole lot of stray voltage leave the lines and enter her head by way of her earphone . . .

Peg resisted the desire to pop the plugs from her own ears and roam around the room. Yes, listening to the radio this way might be dangerous. But Peg had heard of people getting electrocuted nowadays merely by trying to turn on a light.

Besides, her restlessness stemmed neither from the news nor the rumors she'd heard about murderous appliances. It was more like the way her grandmother had predicted the onset of thunderstorms. Gram could just feel them in the air.

Peg wasn't expecting thunderstorms. But some primitive, gut-level detection system was warning her that *something* was on the verge of occurring.

For just a moment, she thought of her armor, still locked away in Harry Sturdley's office closet. *That* technology, bizarrely enough, seemed to be working perfectly.

Which job would make Harry happier—maintaining the media watch he'd requested, or flying out on patrol as he kept asking her to do?

Peg shook her head. She was an administrative assistant who'd started out in publishing and wound up in comics. That was bad enough without acting like the characters in the comic books.

Resolutely, she readjusted her earplugs and turned the radio dial to the competing news station. What appliance stories were they covering?

Peg tapped her pencil against her notepad. She wished Quentin Farley would get back to her with whatever he'd found on John Cameron's origins.

John flew out on his evening patrol, feeling vaguely distracted, as if his skin or his brain were prickling at . . . *something*. Luckily, the evening seemed to be fairly routine. John swooped down to thwart a carjacking, three fistfights, and a basketball game where the score was about to be settled with guns.

As he gained altitude to resume his circling of the city, John shook his head inside his helmet. As far as crime busting went, he was racking up a score more like an old-time beat cop than a superhero. The Rodent, Silicon Savage, and the Human Torpedo always managed to stumble on far more significant action.

Of course, if their adventures were running daily instead of monthly, maybe their patrols would get a bit more humdrum, too.

Ah! John detected a large group of men gathering around the back of a Cadillac. Focusing a mental probe, he got images of a score of weapons and spirited bidding. The Caddy's owner, apparently, had just made the run from out of state, and was auctioning off his latest shipment of smuggled weapons.

As John plummeted downward, he set his priorities. First, the auctioneer. Then the weapons. The bidders were a distant third. Without guns, they would be basically harmless. And even if the auctioneer had a loaded sample, it would be useless against Argonian armor.

Appearing over the car, he cued his exterior speakers to the word that was sure to scatter the buyers. "Freeze!"

The auctioneer swung a sawed-off shotgun from under the oversized raincoat he wore. But he used his weapon to cover his stock, not John. Instead, the man yelled, "Yo, Wally!"

From the back seat of the Caddy popped a short figure—Wally was little more than a kid. But he was toting a Stinger hand-held antiaircraft missile. Reluctantly, John brought his hands down in the tridigirector. But Wally was already triggering the rocket.

Unfortunately, the auction's protection system was electronic. John felt a ripple run through reality—a sensation of *otherness* attacking his Rift-heightened senses.

The missile blew up on the ground, killing Wally instantly. The explosion ignited the car's gas tank, destroying the guns in the trunk, the auctioneer, and several slow-moving bidders. John boosted gizmo, soaring off ahead of the expanding blast wave.

It never happened this way in the comics.

* * *

The image on Marty Burke's television shifted, again, and again, and again as he tapped on the remote. Tap—a dumb sitcom. Tap—cop show. Tap—dumber sitcom. Tap— some T&A show about models.

He left that on, always happy to get some new figure reference. Too bad he was in the midst of working on a male giant. Burke felt a little groggy, having spent the whole day at the drawing board. He carefully began touching up his rendering of the giant.

The phone rang four times before he put down his pencil and answered. "Burke here."

"Mr. Burke, this is Kimberly Knudsen at INC?" Kimberly had an odd lilt to her voice that turned every sentence into a question. "I'm trying to get hold of Leslie Ann Nasotrudere? She's not answering her pager, and she left your number as a backup?"

Burke blinked his eyes and glanced around his studio as if to find Leslie Ann hiding. Then he shook his head. "Wait a minute. Leslie Ann is working for you guys tonight. She told me this morning."

"Um, sir, I don't think so?" Kimberly lilted in reply. "She worked very late last night, so she'd have gotten tonight off?"

"Well, Leslie Ann isn't here. You want to leave a message in case she calls in?"

"Just that we're looking for her?" Kimberly said.

"That's Kimberly Knudsen?" Jeeze, Burke thought, she's got me talking in questions now.

"That's right. Thank you!" Kimberly almost cooed as she broke the connection.

Burke glanced over at the television. The models were gone, replaced by a car ad. He picked up the remote, preparing to go surfing again, then abruptly turned off the TV.

Tossing the remote aside with a frown, Burke bent over his drawing board.

Chapter Thirty-Four

Peg Faber was stifling a yawn as Sturdley came down the hallway to his office. "A matched set," he said, putting his hand over his own mouth. "I don't think I got a wink last night—and I saw the light coming from under your door about five A.M."

"I gave up pretending to sleep." Peg set her jaw against another yawn. "And pretended to read, instead."

"Maybe a little exercise," Harry said, scanning the hallway for possible listeners. "I understand John Cameron goes for midnight runs."

Peg gave her boss a dirty look. Harry was trying another shot at getting her out on patrol and after John. "Right," she snorted. "I should have jumped up in my PJs, and come down for—"

She caught a flicker of movement at Bob Gunnar's office door.

"For, uh, special equipment," Peg finished as the chief editor stepped into the corridor.

"Harry, Peg," Bob greeted them. They both yawned in reply. "I'll leave you insomniacs in peace," Gunnar said. "I'm seeing a print broker with Yvette Zelcerre."

"Must be the excitement of the case," Sturdley said sheepishly as his number-two man marched off to the elevators.

"Case?" Peg repeated.

"We go to court today!" Sturdley burst out, dumb-founded. "Where do you think I was this morning? Down at Mohe, Lorenz, & Kirley, dotting the I's and crossing the T's. I'll be at the courthouse this afternoon. Don't you look at my desk diary?"

"Harry," Peg replied, "I look at your diary every day. You haven't written anything on it in the past week."

"Busy," Sturdley harrumphed.

"The wheels have certainly been spinning, but have we been getting anywhere?" Peg looked hard at her boss. "Those appliance accidents have gotten people crazy. They've just about turned that Moncke guy who died into a martyr, and antitechnology groups around the country are calling themselves *Monckeys* now. Cities all over have had *Monckey* demonstrations turn into food riots. There was one over in New Jersey last night."

She took a deep breath. "And what are we doing? I'm charting the number of appliance accidents being report-ed, and you're starting a new comic and suing Dynasty over stealing some characters."

Sturdley's face tightened to a collection of planes and angles. "I suspect this must be leading somewhere."

"I just get this weird feeling that something very wrong is about to happen, and I'm wondering if we're paying attention to the right things. What if John was right—"

"Oh, sure you'd think Mr. Studmuffin is right," Sturd-ley snarled. "Too bad he quit when we needed him to help take care of business."

Peg felt as if she'd just taken a punch to the stomach. It took her an instant to get her breath. And when she finally did, she was in no mood to be conciliatory. "Sure, Harry.

Gotta build up that business. That'll be a great help when giants come smashing our way, or Deviants come with blasters, or a starving mob starts to burn the place down."

Silently, Sturdley stepped round her desk and into his office. A few minutes later, he came out. "I'm on my way to court," he said, making no reference to her outburst. "It may take a little longer than usual to get downtown." He disappeared down the hall.

Muttering words that would never find their way into any Fantasy Factory publications, Peg shifted piles of paper from one side of her desk to the other. Then the phone rang. Peg picked it up. "Harry Sturdley's office."

"That you, Peg?" She recognized Lew Irvine's voice on the other end of the line. "I thought I'd give Harry a buzz and suggest he get an early start. Cabs are a little thin on the ground today."

They certainly were, she thought. A lot of cabbies had quit *en masse* when several of the yellow vehicles had exploded for reasons unknown. Then, too, several *Monckey* mobs had overturned cabs farther uptown.

"He's already on his way," she said.

"Oh. Good." Lew's voice took on a more seductive note. "You know, I've been thinking it might be a good idea for *us* to get together on this case. Maybe dinner and whatever sometime this week? I think I could benefit from your input."

It was the same confident tone he'd used in their college days, the senior talking to the naive freshman girl. *Yes*, a cynical voice mocked inside Peg's head, *he always enjoyed inputting with me.*

"I don't think so," she said.

"What?" Lew's voice didn't sound confident now—he seemed in shock.

"I don't want to wind up as a research expense on Mohe, Lorenz, & Kirley's bill," Peg said coolly.

"I, ah, was thinking of something a bit more informal." Lew stumbled over the words.

"And on the personal side, I'm not in the mood for any . . . 'inputting,' however you want to call it."

"Hey, it's just—well, we had such a nice time the last time we got together—lunch—I thought. . . . You're not going out with somebody, are you?"

Once upon a time, she might have been amused at the spectacle of Lew Irvine, master of the spoken word, reduced to babbling drivel. But his words did strike home. Peg's eyes widened. Why was she acting this way? Was she still hanging on to what she'd had with John? But even over the phone, Lew's come-on suddenly seemed just too damned transparent.

"I think we both have work to do," she said crisply, "and I don't want that messed up by some old-time's-sake grabass."

Peg heard a long breath being taken over the phone. "Yes," Lew finally said. "I see."

What a rotten thing to do to him, she thought, right before he has to go to court. "Good-bye, Lew," she said.

The phone went dead in her ear. Peg gave the handset a sour smile as she put it down. She'd have bet her next month's pay that from here on, all calls to Harry would come by way of a Mohe, Lorenz, & Kirley secretary.

She shifted a few more papers, then smacked one pile with her outstretched palm. She had nothing to do here. Almost without conscious thought, she stepped into Harry's office, locking the door behind her. Peg stepped up to the closet behind Harry's desk, the one with the shining new keypad on it. She input the combination, and the door opened. Two sets of Argonian armor gleamed in the office's indirect lighting. One was Harry's. The smaller one was Peg's, smuggled in piece by piece.

Peg began slipping out of her clothes. Whatever this restlessness was, she felt there was only one way to stop it.

She pulled on the long john-like undergarment, then started donning the rest of her armor.

Sturdley arrived at the courthouse in a bad mood. He'd had a struggle getting a cab, only to end up with a driver who spoke absolutely no English. Perhaps that's why the guy was still driving amid all the antitech hysteria.

And the gremlins that seemed to be infecting all machinery were still hard at work. As they headed down the East Side drive, the taxi meter had made a belching sound and dropped four dollars from the fare. But then, just before they pulled up at the courthouse, the box had made a ruder noise and added twelve bucks to the total.

The cabbie had silently pointed at the unwinking red numbers, and Sturdley had paid.

He'd rendezvoused with a rather subdued-looking Lew Irvine and several partners from Mohe, Lorenz, & Kirley and they set off for the courtroom.

Sturdley had expected something large and imposing in dark wood with lots of room for a jury box and seats for interested parties. Instead, the courtroom was small, brightly lit, and starkly modern. The judge's bench was little more than a modestly raised desk, and a video camera took the place of a court stenographer. Microphones sprouted from the judge's bench and from the pair of tables facing it.

Sturdley and the team from Mohe, Lorenz, & Kirley took the right-hand table. One of the partners glanced over at the people seating themselves behind the other and nodded. "Fein & Dante have brought in some big guns. Mr. Colby will be paying heavily."

Sturdley was disappointed in the judge. He'd never have sat behind a bench in a Fantasy Factory comic. The guy didn't look judicial at all, a middle-aged nonentity with a fringe of gray hair. One of Rip Jacoby's background characters would have had more presence.

Lew Irvine rose and began making lawyer-noises about precedents, citing National Periodicals Vs. Victor Fox and the Captain Marvel litigation. "A straightforward case of copyright infringement," one of the partners whispered to Sturdley.

Blowups of various artists' treatments both of Madam Vile and M-16 were supplied. The villainess had joined the Fantasy Factory's universe in the early Seventies, in the initial burst of public interest in psychoactive drugs. M-16 had been a creation of the big-gun boom of the early Nineties. Copies of various comics were entered, proving the characters' appearances in print years before the coming of the Deviants.

A smooth-looking character rose from the other table and told the judge that there was no basis for a copyright, that far from creating new characters, Dynasty Comics was merely recording the activities of real people.

From the looks on his lawyers' faces, Sturdley got the notion that Fein & Dante was earning its pay. The smooth character beckoned, and a team of technicians wheeled in a high-tech version of the old high school AV cart. This gleaming implement bore a large-screen TV with connected VCR. After being arranged for maximal view and plugged in, Colby's lawyer operated a remote.

The screen filled with the image of a pair of flying figures—Matavi and Emsisdin. Colby's lawyer quickly pointed out that neither Fantasy Factory character flew. He was about to point out the few minor differences in costume—Matavi was a bit more covered up than the latest incarnation of Madam Vile—when the picture suddenly froze. The pair of Deviants turned bright green, then brown, then black, and then the screen dissolved in snowy static. The pungent smell of burning videotape filled the room. Smoke began to pour from the VCR.

At the defendant's table, a sweating lawyer hit various buttons on the remote. "Your Honor, I don't understand what happened here. We tested this equipment not half an hour ago in our offices—"

Finally, he whisked a finger in a cutting motion across his throat. One of the technicians pulled the plug. As the wire left the wall, a large blue spark leapt from the plug to the socket. The technician jumped back, and the smell of ozone replaced that of burning tape.

"Counselor, do you with to SQUAAAAAAAAAWRK! WHEEEEK! SQUEEEEEAL! RIZZZZDIZZZZDIZZZZ POOOOOOOM!" The judge's amplified voice disappeared in a cacophony of electrical noise and feedback. He tapped his microphone, creating a sound effect reminiscent of the Crack of Doom. Sturdley noticed that the electric clock on the wall overhead was now running backward.

The amplification abruptly cut off, and the judge's normal voice, weak even for the small room, began to launch into an apology. He was cut off, however, by the shower of sparks from the recording video camera.

Fein & Dante's technicians managed to get that mechanical difficulty under control, one of the men yanking off his jacket to wrap around the camera.

There was a brief recess as a court attendant brought in a new camera, then a longer one as that machine promptly blew up on being plugged in.

In the end, a hard-faced older woman with a stenographer's pad sat in a borrowed chair, scribbling away as the proceedings began again.

"Your Honor, in addition to our abortive action presentation, we also have photographic representations of the protagonists of Deviant Comics." Sturdley had to admit that the man from Fein & Dante had managed to retain his smoothness despite the technical problems besetting his initial address. "For purposes of illustrating our case, we suggest a simple comparison between these photos and plaintiff's *drawings.*"

Sturdley burned at hearing his evidence made to sound like something childish.

The lawyer went on. "First, allow me to point—"

"Hold it," the hard-faced stenographer intervened.

Some of the smoothness left the lawyer's delivery. "Pardon?"

"You're going too fast," the woman said. "I'm only up to 'comparison,' and you're already pointing things out."

"Your Honor—" The man from Fein & Dante turned to the judge.

"While I regret the various exigencies, we face a full calendar, and must try to conduct this case as best we can—with whatever recording process available. Therefore—"

Throughout the judge's speech, the lights in the courtroom began to fade. With no windows, the place quickly became pitch-dark. Whatever the judge had to say was lost in a buzz of rattled voices until the sharp crack of the gavel rang out.

"Court's adjourned until tomorrow morning," the judge barked. "Now somebody find the damned door."

John Cameron blinked, wondering how sand could have gotten into his eyes when he'd spent the past twenty-two hours sealed inside his Argonian armor. Of course, he thought, that might have something to do with the grainy state of his eyes.

Never would he complain about the boring nature of New York City street crime. The action of the last few days had shown him there were far worse alternatives. *Monckeys*, the adherents of the growing antitechnology movement, had established control over huge tracts of the cityscape below. In the evening, their enclaves were easy to spot—they were the areas devoid of lights except for the large bonfires.

The areas without lights *and* bonfires were probably suffering from one of the periodic blackouts that mysteriously afflicted every developed country on Earth. The darkness had nothing to do with power availability. Whole districts just went out, with no rhyme, reason, or detectable sequence. Sometimes the blackouts encompassed a single house, a couple of blocks, or square miles. The outages were bound neither by local boundaries nor by power grids. The lights and everything else electrical simply went out.

John suddenly spotted flames rising in an area he'd noted as being blacked-out. When he flew down to investigate, he found a group of torch-wielding hardies robbing a supermarket. These characters weren't after the store's money, although that was probably easily available in the electronically locked safe. No, this was a new sign of the times. The thieves emerged carrying food.

For those living in big cities, the first sign of unraveling technology came when they were put on an impromptu diet by the failure of food deliveries. Exploding trains and big rigs meant no foodstuffs were getting into town. Some enterprising New Jerseyans had made a good buck (and a nice picture for the declining TV audience) by organizing a horseback cattle drive across the George Washington Bridge. But for the most part, Manhattan was short of vittles.

Things were even worse on Staten Island, because food shipments destined for that borough were hijacked in Newark and Manhattan.

It was hard for John to drive off people who were stealing food they couldn't afford anymore. What really chilled John, however, was the fact that several of the looters appeared to be wearing police uniforms.

His appearance caused the forceful shoppers to scatter, firing epithets, bricks, and a couple of bullets at him.

"Gidatta heyah, yuh gawdam freak!" yelled a husky type with a pillowcase full of canned goods.

"Howcum his machines work and ours don't?" another guy asked around a mouthful of Twinkies.

John had pondered that question himself. When the blackouts hit, even battery-operated items like flashlights and transistor radios went dead. But the Argonian technology John had imported, in some perverse twist, was operating better than ever. The Hoozits, the broadcast power source Harry Sturdley had planted atop the Empire State building, had mysteriously cubed its output, according to the readouts in John's armor. That meant, if necessary, he could fly hundreds of miles. The suit's visual scan, radar, and weapons systems were performing above standards.

Unfortunately, so were his audio pickups.

"Go back where ya came from," an empty-handed running figure screamed. "This is all your fault!"

Streetlights suddenly began throwing a sodium glare on the looters. Windows glowed as lights inside received power again. The store's burglar alarm cut loose with an ear-splitting blare. In the distance, John heard the approach of sirens. He pulled up into the sky. The police had a tendency to fire indiscriminately at armored figures. The PBA had a court case in hand to ban Stalwarts and Deviants alike from vigilante activity. But technical difficulties had slowed it as badly as Harry's crusade against Dynasty Comics. And more than ever, citizens needed *someone* to protect them.

But as he soared above the clouds, John felt more sick than satisfied. Despite the fact that he was on patrol day and night, his efforts were little more than a cup of water thrown at a forest fire.

The final looter's cry, flung over a shoulder, seemed to echo in John's mind. What if this growing mess were indeed all his fault? There seemed to be some sort of connection between the Rift and the anomalies of natural law occurring on Earth. As things declined here, the Rift had become more tempestuous—downright dangerous to enter.

Had his travels to other worlds—and bringing aliens to Earth—upset some sort of cosmic balance?

John oriented himself toward the north and began burning gizmo. There was one way to find out. Heroes' Manor was now well within the flight range of his armor. He'd go up there, start exiling giants back home through the Rift, and see if circumstances began to improve here on Earth. If they did, he'd move out the rest of the giants.

In his exhaustion, John thought this a good strategy. He didn't consider what it might mean if conditions remained the same or declined further. And he ignored how much effort it might take to navigate through the Rift's turbulence.

John felt he had to try *something*. And if Robert and his people resisted . . . John's armored fists clenched. He'd blast them.

High in the sky over Riverdale, John's mental receptors suddenly detected psionic activity. John swooped down to find Matavi standing in the midst of a hilly park. Before her, hands on each others' shoulders, moving in lockstep, were the local thugs who'd used the place as their base of operations. John could read that much from their minds. Matavi laughed as she marched them out of the park and toward the nearest police precinct, where she intended them to confess all their crimes.

John felt a familiar blast of anger at the Deviant, but it was tempered by—what? Jealousy? His superheroing had definitely been of the physical sort, the kind trumpeted on the pages of Fantasy Factory and Dynasty Comics. Matavi's approach, while it would mean very few fight scenes, was actually more effective, John's tired brain realized. This is how he should have handled the looters, rather than buzzing the store and making them scatter.

But then, he hadn't had much chance to observe how the Deviants worked. Ever since the start of Sturdley's case against Dynasty Comics, Fantasy Factory staffers had been cautioned to avoid contact with Emsisdin and Matavi. John had gotten the official letter from Mohe, Lorenz, & Kirley, but the subtext was straight Sturdley. If the Stalwarts did damage to Dirk Colby's pet heroes, Dynasty would countersue the pants off Happy Harry.

Now, however, John was acting as a free agent, having quit in front of Sturdley. He could . . .

Hello, handsome, Matavi sent a thought his way. *Why hang around up there when you could come down and join me?*

John snapped at the arrogance of this Deviant. He seized on the idea of marching her into the Rift as docile-ly as she manipulated her criminal conga line and hurled a psychic attack at her.

The thugs broke step, stumbled, then ran for it as Matavi redirected her mental resources from controlling them to defending herself. But John found the weak spot in every shield she raised, piercing, piercing, piercing . . . until suddenly he realized his psionic spearhead had somehow been deflected. He should have penetrated to Matavi's personality centers, to the circuits of her brain. Instead, his immaterial senses transmitted the perception of lunging into something quite physical—warm, yielding flesh, like—

The realization of what he seemed to be thrusting into brought John out of attack mode and into acute embarrassment. What was going on here? It was some sort of psionic construct . . . he tried to pull away, but instead got the sensation of a very erotic plunge into a damp, inviting, very private place . . .

His thoughts felt very far away, but sensual information seemed to storm through his body. A tremor of sheer, ani-mal need rocked his form.

A trap! a yammering part of his personality warned.

A very tender trap. Matavi's mind was somehow en-twined with his. *You have a powerful mind and a powerful body. But I have more experience, handsome. A thousand years caged in that bubble, and nothing to do but hone my mind.*

His consciousness thrashed in her immaterial trap, merely intensifying the carnal sensations—not merely for himself, but for her.

Ah! Yes, this will be good . . . Matavi's mind messages became stronger as she came closer. John suddenly felt cool air against his face as the female Deviant removed his helmet. She took her gloves off and pressed her hands to his face.

John reeled. He had never felt anything as exquisite as that simple touch of flesh against flesh.

"Now we'll have to find one of those quaint motel places," Matavi whispered. "You'll impregnate me for the good of the race we'll create—a race of natural telepaths."

He felt her smile like a brand against his skin as she looked into his memories. "Yes," she said. "You know how it can be when one meets mind to mind as well as body to body. Though there can be certain . . . refinements."

Her lips barely brushed his, but undreamt-of carnalities rushed through John's mind. He quivered like a hound begging to be released, panting.

Then a furious mind intruded. *WHAT THE HELL HAVE YOU DONE TO HIM?*

Matavi glanced skyward. "Ah. Your little red-haired friend. And she doesn't seem in a mood for discussion."

Blast-bolts blackened stretches of grass, but Matavi unconcernedly used John for cover as she undid the psychic construct that had held him captive. "I could have left you trapped in that cycle of lust. But I don't want *her* to enjoy it." Matavi's voice grew caustic. "Nor do I want a novice messing up the job of getting you free." She patted John's face. "Save yourself," she said, "until we meet again." For a second, she also caressed John's mind. *There'll be another time.*

Matavi released John, who tumbled to the ground. At the same minute, she boosted her gizmoidal drive, heading straight upward.

Both John and Peg could hear her laughter in their minds.

Chapter Thirty-Five

"We should remember," the eminent physicist said, steepling his hands at chest level, "that widespread ownership of electronic appliances is a fairly recent development—a mere century for electric lighting, seventy years for radios, less than that for refrigerators."

"A hundred years sounds like a long time to me," the reporter said.

"But it's merely one-fiftieth of recorded history," the physicist replied. "We can add in another hundred years for serious scientific examination of electromagnetic phenomena."

"So you're saying we wouldn't know if much could go wrong with a television because they've only been around sixty years?"

The physicist's hands unsteepled so he could point a finger. "Exactly. How long have we known about sunspots and their effect on broadcasting?"

"You'll have to tell me," the newsman admitted. "But you think this is the same sort of thing? A—what did you call it?"

"A temporary fluctuation in the electromagnetic spectrum," the physicist said smoothly. "The Earth may have encountered them before, which may explain certain accounts of 'miracles.' The sun standing still at Jericho—light, after all, is an electromagnetic phenomenon."

"They just didn't have telephones to explode," the reporter amplified.

"That might be a little more colorful than I would put it, but it's essentially the case." The physicist frowned significantly. "The important thing for the public to realize is that the situation is undoubtedly natural and *temporary*. We can survive this fluctuation, study it, design safeguards for the future, if we all keep our heads . . ."

His lips twitched in annoyance as he interrupted his speech. "Pardon me, but I notice you're not writing any of this down. I thought this conversation was for attribution."

"Certainly, Doctor," the journalist reached into the open case on the table between them. "This recorder is getting everything—"

"Turn that goddamn thing off!" The professor's voice rose in a screech. "What are you trying to do, get the two of us killed?"

Outside, the reporter's car wouldn't start. He wound up walking a mile and a half until he found a working pay phone. Using the tip of a fallen tree branch, he poked the number of his office on the keypad.

Pinning the handset in the crook of the branch, he yelled, "You there, Pete?" until his editor responded.

"We can scratch the Nobel Laureate interview," the reporter shouted into the phone. "He's not as calm about this whole thing as his letter to the editor suggested."

"Don't worry about it," the editor responded. "Looks like everything goes on the spike for the time being, until we get the printers on-line."

The reporter sighed. "This is a hell of a time for the union to go out."

"Oh, it's not the printers going out," Pete replied. "It's the presses themselves. They went up in about a million little pieces. We don't have a printing plant anymore, just a hole in the ground. Bet you this will have a bad effect on circulation."

"Yeah," the reporter commiserated, "and right when so many people were giving up on TV news."

The sun had come up unnoticed in Marty Burke's studio. The blinds were still drawn, the lights on, the television muttering in the corner. Burke wasn't channel surfing this morning. His remote lay on the corner of a supply taboret, right beside his electric eraser.

He'd been using the eraser rather liberally through the night. For some reason, despite his photos, despite his light box, in spite of his other tracing equipment, Burke could not seem to get Emsisdin's face right whenever he appeared in the story—a major problem when one is dealing with the title character of a book.

But there it was. The eyes were wrong, or the head was cocked at an odd angle, or, most often, no matter what expression Burke set out to draw, Emsisdin's image smirked on the page.

This was the fifth version of a closeup panel, and the Bristol layout board had been erased in some spots down to tracing-paper thinness. Burke was trying to rerender the eyebrow so it wasn't raised, and instead managed to run his pencil point right through Emsisdin's eye.

"Damnation," he muttered, ripping the heavy paper free. The panel was useless with a hole torn in it. No amount of whiteout would fix that. Tossing the paper atop a growing pile, he turned on his lightbox and positioned the original, offending picture with a sheet of layout board on top.

Then the phone rang. Burke groped for the handset and picked it up without even looking. "What?" he demanded impatiently.

"*Report fully, Lesser scum.*" The voice on the other end sounded rushed, but Burke didn't notice. He sat glassy-eyed, falling into the trance of Robert's binding.

As was standard, the voice of Burke's controller asked if he were alone.

"Yes," the artist intoned.

"What stories is the woman Leslie Ann Nasotrudere working on?"

Burke plodded through each story Leslie Ann had discussed or mentioned in recent days. The voice interrupted. "Has she been working on any stories in relation to *giants?*"

"No," Burke replied tonelessly. She—" He stopped.

"What is it?" the controller on the other end of the line demanded.

"She has not—" Burke's voice broke again, a hint of emotion showing through.

"You are to report fully," the controlling voice said impatiently. "Any and all details that may be of interest."

"She—" Strain still showed in Burke's voice. This information was not something of which his conscious mind was aware. It was something repressed to the subconscious, something Burke didn't want to think about.

The binding won. "She has shown very little interest in the giants lately," he said in a tight voice. "Her attention is all on the newly arrived aliens called Deviants. This may be because she is having a sexual liaison with the one known as Emsisdin."

The voice on the other end was silent for a moment, then broke out in a laugh. "Listen well, cuckold," it ordered coldly. "You will continue to associate with the

Nasotrudere woman. Make yourself pleasing to her. Keep her in your company, and keep her in New York City. Continue to gather information on her work, especially as it pertains to giants. And you will forget this call and this conversation until the next time you hear the trigger phrase, *Report fully, Lesser scum.*"

The contact was broken.

A second later, Marty Burke cried out in agony. The handset of his telephone lay grasped in his left hand, its body cracked, shards of plastic piercing the skin. Blood trickled in thick tendrils down his wrist.

"Damn!" Burke muttered, dropping the ruined handset onto the cradle. He plucked ineffectively at his wounds. "Why'd I even pick that thing up? I guess it must have blown."

He took a moment to deal with the fact that he might have died. Then there were more urgent concerns. "Damn," he muttered again. "And my drawing hand, too."

In Heroes' Manor, Thomas took one more moment to chuckle over the spectacle of a cuckold unconsciously reporting his own shame. Then he dismissed the report as unrelated to his efforts. There were not enough hours in the day to accomplish all he had been ordered to do.

He punched in the number of yet another interstate trucking concern and asked about the availability of their units. The call had finally come from Washington. Robert had arranged for his people to remove themselves to the remoteness of Idaho, far from big cities, disturbances—and the destruction targeted on the Lessers' dwelling places.

Coordinating this hegira had been a nightmare as the Lessers' vaunted technology had apparently begun falling apart. After a few trips—barely enough to establish a housekeeping presence at their haven—the Heroplane had fallen from the sky. Thomas thanked the gods below that it had happened on a return flight. The only loss had been the crew of Lessers.

Thomas then had turned to ground transportation, which had also proven unreliable and dangerous. After leasing a fleet of twenty big rigs to carry the bulk of the Masterly colonists, a third of the vehicles had broken down before even leaving Heroes' Manor. Twenty-eight giants, mainly females, had left on the remaining transports while Thomas strove to find wheels for the ten who had to stay behind.

The trucks he'd managed to find for the second wave were inferior in space and cleanliness, but at least all of them had moved out.

This success hadn't ended the problems for Robert's deputy. Reports kept coming back to him, both psionically and by mobile phone, of disasters on the road. Trucks had blown up, killing their drivers. Masterly casualties had been kept to a minimum thanks to the giants' protective fields of immaterial force, but some were wounded. And those more gifted in mind powers were wearing themselves out controlling the drivers who survived.

Where he could, Thomas tried to arrange for replacement trucks at various towns along the way. But it seemed an endless task, aggravated by the Lessers' low cunning and treachery. Thomas was not the Master to deal with the genus of Lessers known as "biznizman." Too often, he'd wire enormous sums of money—when that system could be used—for the use of nonexistent trucks. He began to hope that when Robert's promised fire-from-the-sky fell, it would land on all those Lesser rats.

Lessers were also making nuisances of themselves by attacking the caravans, thinking they held something worth stealing. In cities, the cargo was imagined to be food. In the open spaces the trucks were thought to contain big-city valuables. In all cases, the would-be thieves got a big surprise before they were eliminated.

Between wrecks and raids, many of the travelers found themselves stranded. By the latest count, almost a fifth of Robert's people were making their way westward by foot. The only advice Thomas had been able to give was that they should avoid large cities and show restraint in acquiring food—i.e., try not to kill too many farmers.

Thomas had remained in Heroes' Manor with two male giants as brawny as he was. For the public at large, they were supposed to be his guards. In actuality, the pair was on call as a strong-arm squad and as backup in the process of closing down the giants' base.

At last the call had come from Robert, giving Thomas the code words for immediate retreat. With the thought of imminent sky-fire over his head, Thomas had negotiated the use of three big tractor-trailers, now en route. That left only a few loose ends to dispense with.

Thomas found Dr. Cedric Thonneger in the boathouse/infirmary, where the turncoat Gideon still lay comatose. Lying beside him was the brain-blasted Andrew. Thomas sneered as the white-coated Lesser labored to get another sperm sample from Andrew, but, per Robert's orders, he didn't interfere.

Waiting for the Lesser to finish his antics, Thomas mentally called to one of his companions, Frederick. He'd been chosen specially for his well-exercised abilities in binding.

When Thonneger finished putting the samples away, he froze, his mind seized. Stumbling slightly, he went to the charting area, picked up a blank sheet of paper, and began to write. Robert had dictated the suicide note. It mentioned actual past misdeeds the doctor had committed, ending with the phrase "I can't go on."

Frederick then lifted his control. Thonneger read the note before him and went pale. Thomas did it quickly—there was no fun to be derived from breaking this one's neck. Frederick had already prepared a noose. He took the body and carried it through the darkness to a tree outside the manor, leaving the note tucked in a pocket of the doctor's lab coat.

Squatting on his haunches, Thomas lightly slapped Andrew on the face. The recumbent giant stared up at him with eerily unfocused eyes.

Using his limited mental powers, Thomas broadcast to Andrew: *You know who I am. I am one who gives you orders.*

Andrew's malleable face tightened slightly as he nodded. *Here then are your orders. Go to the large city.* He sent the image of Andrew traveling on one of the trucks. *Find these people.* One by one, Thomas flashed the images of the five Lessers who could possibly upset Robert's plan— Harry Sturdley, John Cameron, Peg Faber, Emsisdin, and Matavi, along with suggestions of where they could be found.

His eyes bored into Andrew's vacant blue orbs. *Find each of them*, he ordered, *and kill them.*

A shaky sigh came from Andrew's slack lips. "Yessssss," he said. "Killlllll."

Shuddering slightly, Thomas led Andrew to the front gate, where the trucks were expected. He shouldn't mind leaving Andrew behind, any more than abandoning Gideon to his fate. The would-be rebel was now a walking dead man, to be destroyed by the fires that would consume the Lessers.

Although, Thomas had to admit, he'd have enjoyed a personal opportunity to settle scores with some of those on the death list.

Peg Faber wished she could wear her armor to operate the ancient manual typewriter she was using. The blasted thing's alleged touch control apparently ran from "very stiff" to "use a hammer." The armor might have made the job clumsier, but the exoskeletal muscle would make a welcome backup for her aching hands.

"Finished," she muttered, flexing her fingers. The phone rang, and Peg had yet another wish for armor between herself and a potential bomb. Picking up the handset, she held it well away from her ear, saying, "Harry Sturdley's office" in a loud voice.

"Peg Faber?" An equally loud voice, attenuated by distance from the phone and a lousy connection, whispered from the phone.

"Yes," Peg shouted.

"This is Quentin Farley. I'm calling from West Virginia."

She nearly dropped the phone. "Can you tell me something about—" Peg abruptly realized she was shouting very personal business at a phone. "What can you tell me?" she amended.

"It took a long enough time, with computers out and all this—" Farley's voice disappeared in a rush of static—

"civil disturbance. But I've personally gone out and checked, not only here, but in the sixteen nearest states. The, ah, gentleman in the picture you gave me is not listed as a missing person by any state authority. Wherever he disappeared from, it's nowhere near here."

"I love it when a good plan comes together," Senator Benjamin Fussock said aloud, but mainly to himself as he surveyed the Senate Chamber. The Vice president was in place, his noted confreres were taking their seats, and in a moment, he would enjoy the culmination of weeks' worth of cajolery, log-rolling, and plain old-fashioned blackmail.

His bill was never in doubt, because he knew he didn't need to recruit the votes with the special interests that would line up behind him. Big oil. Detroit. Wall Street. Aerospace. The banks. Any manufacturer who could afford a lobbyist inside the Beltway. Anyone who built, sold, or used anything electronic was getting killed by Mother Nature's novel interpretations of her supposedly immutable laws.

Fussock had chaired the panel that had listened to the big-domes explain what was going on. Few of the scientists had agreed, and none had a viable fix.

The best line of action for the near future was to adopt a more old-fashioned mode of existence. It made for a good political philosophy. Al Demagogua had been ecstatic at the idea of trumpeting the sturdy values of Early America. Of course, there were a few problems. America had a lot more inhabitants than it had in the early days. Amenities would have to be rationed.

The American Craft and Antique Regulation Act would set up the necessary system. For the public good, low-tech items created by modern craftsmen or saved from bygone days would be placed under national control for fair sharing. That sharing-out would be run by responsible figures from the corporate world. Figures who would owe Benjamin Fussock big-time.

Resistance from the craftspeople and antique-mongers had been negligible. *They* had no lobbyists worthy of the name. A couple of shrewdies sucking on other big-business teats had tried to horn in with bills of their own, but they had been either subsumed or beaten down. That left the few windbags who wanted to talk about public good.

I tell the public what's good for them. And with the way things are going in the city right now, we'll have to tell them with bayonets. He considered the army outposts ringing Capitol Hill. They couldn't trust their tanks to drive around, but thank goodness gunpowder seemed fairly low down on the electromagnetic scale.

Ah—they were calling the bill now. Fussock glanced around the room, keeping his face bland and confident. They had a majority and more. His contacts in the House were already crafting a similar bill. And if that idiot in the White House tried to horn in—well, Fussock thought, we can afford to give him a few low-tech goodies.

Time to vote. He stabbed the "aye" button on his desk with a brisk finger—and, quite literally, got the shock of his life.

Benjamin Fussock and more than half the Senate were simultaneously joined in a high-voltage electrical circuit. Most of the Distinguished Members were flung back a moment later, gasping and pale, when the nine-dimensional reality bubble which had fostered that particular electromagnetic anomaly dissolved.

But for nine of the older Senators, the more debauched, the ones like Fussock who were severely out of shape, the Crafts bill was the last they ever voted on.

Chapter Thirty-Six

Robert paced the lawns of the suburban Virginia estate he used as a base of operations for his Washington visits. He was not an indecisive person by nature—he couldn't be and rise as high as he had in Masterly society.

How far did Thomas and his people have to be from New York to be safe from a nuclear strike? What of his people, scattered across this domain, making their way to the Idaho haven? Barely a double handful were actually safe in the stronghold.

And if he waited too long, the Lessers' technology might become useless. He had to activate the warmaking machinery while it would still work.

Robert pulled out his portable phone and began dialing those leaders he'd psychically bound. He'd just have to hope that his people would reach some sanctuary before the fire fell.

For that matter, *he'd* have to get out of this city before its doom arrived.

Harry Sturdley sat in his office at the Fantasy Factory, his window the only one lit in the whole building. And that, he had to admit, was because Myra had provided him with candles and a hurricane lamp. The lamp came from the fireplace mantel at home, a handsome antique they'd bought many years ago.

The dim glow of the candles provided the only bright spot in Hairy's life, both literally and figuratively. The court case against Dynasty Comics had ground to a halt due to technical difficulties and legal sand in the gears. As for the business end of things, he scowled as he tried to read the reports in front of him. Some pages were laser-printed, right out of the computers. Some were typed, developed from paper files. Most of the recent ones were handwritten and represented educated guesses.

A new blow had landed this afternoon. The printing plant they depended on to produce Fantasy Factory books for the eastern half of the country had gone up. Bad enough that the printer had begun pushing his press time back to produce broadsides for press-starved newspapers, but now there were no presses at all—the damned things had blown up in the middle of the run on the first *Stalwart* issue.

"If we can survive this," Sturdley muttered, "it will turn out to be a valuable collector's edition."

The news of the plant's explosive demise had arrived on half a fax—the phone lines had gone out some-where—and verifying the story had taken most of his day. All he had in the way of consolation was the report that Marty Burke's first issue of *Deviants* had been printed, but there was no way to ship it.

Sturdley's real reason for staying late was that he was trying to come to a decision. Should he keep dragging the staff into the ever-scarier place that was New York? Should he close down the offices and let the people on the West Coast try to run things regionally? They were located in a suburban office park, after all. And *they* still had a printer. They didn't seem to be getting much shipped, but that was endemic. Nobody was shipping broccoli, either.

Could he furlough the staff on half salary? The bank's computers were down, and he didn't even know the extent of the company's liquid assets.

If Burke were still around, I'd hand him these headaches with my compliments, Harry thought.

No, he wouldn't. Lord knows what sort of a mess Burke would make. No, he had to keep plugging, keep trying. Screw the idea of shutting down. They'd find a new printer somewhere, maybe Bob Gunnar could scare up some trucks . . .

That just left finding paper to print on—and figuring out how to sell comics in an economy where a quart of not-too-fresh milk could go for six bucks on the gray market.

Sturdley's stomach rumbled, and he realized he'd had nothing to eat since breakfast. Had Myra gotten any food in? He'd mentioned to Peg the idea of suiting up and flying out to the boondocks to buy direct from farmers. Throughout all the unpredictability in the machinery of life, the steady improvement in their Argonian technology had been a welcome plus.

Sturdley turned to the closet behind him, digging a large, complicated key out of his pocket. The electric keypad he'd installed had burned out a week ago.

He unlocked the door, sliding it open to see if Peg's armor was there. An instant later, it was as if he were trapped in the recurring nightmare that had been killing sleep since he came back to Earth.

The office windows exploded inward, and arms longer than his body came groping in, trying to seize him. Sturdley cowered back for a second, and a huge hand plucked at his coat to drag him outside.

His coat! Harry's hand darted to the inside pocket and came out with the pen-sized blast projector he'd brought home from Argon.

He kept the beam short and tight, slashing at the fingers that pulled at him. They blistered as Sturdley's beam penetrated the psychokinetic force-fields.

Those hands fumbled back, as if in animal reaction to the heat. When they returned, they were balled into fists, seeking something to punch.

Sturdley slashed and burned again, but as he drove off one fist, the other would launch a blow. He retreated to the office door, getting out of reach. His giant assailant broke out the rest of the glass in the windows, trying to lean in and get at him.

It was an awkward fit, one arm stretched to the shoulder, the head hunched down, trying to squash in and extend at the same time.

Harry now recognized his attacker. It was Andrew, a giant he'd once thought of as having the looks and personality to get his own book someday. Both were gone now. Andrew's face was pale, slack, and dirty. His eyes were like a vacuum, glaring at Sturdley with no apparent thought but to crush him. Luckily, Andrew wasn't going about the job very intelligently. He stayed jammed in the window, fumbling and groping, as if he had no other idea of how to get at Harry.

Andrew could have pinned Sturdley with the desk, or hurled half a dozen pieces of furniture. But he kept up that stupid pawing. It would almost be funny, Harry thought . . . if it weren't so horrible. The sour smell of unwashed giant flesh struck him along with gusts of foul-smelling breath.

Stupid or not, Andrew was blocking the path to Sturdley's only safe egress from the building—the suit of

Argonian armor. Harry couldn't see any way out other than flying.

Harry withdrew further, into the hallway. An appalling, strangled growl came from Andrew, combined with an awful noise that Sturdley finally identified as the grinding of giant teeth.

The windowframe broke, and masonry began to crumble as Andrew forced himself further in. Sturdley waited until the giant was wedged in tight, his extended arm almost reaching the office door. Then Harry barreled in, using the blaster like a sword to scorch the questing fingers out of the way, charging straight at that staring face.

Now Sturdley launched a mental attack. There was no resistance. None at all, because there wasn't really a mind to direct opposition. All Harry's questing spears of psionic force discovered were the lowest life-maintaining processes in the lizard-brain, a self-awareness roughly comparable to an infant's, and a few simple, violent commands impressed in the cerebral cortex. This wasn't Andrew. It was a giant, mindless flesh robot sent out to kill people, with Harry Sturdley at the top of the list. The rest of the brain seemed—dormant.

Andrew was trying to crook his arm back to get at Harry. He was also trying to get his other hand in the other window. Sturdley reached out with tendrils of psionic force and sealed off the murderous programming. Andrew slumped, almost vegetative. If he hadn't been wedged in so tight, he'd have spilled right out the window.

Sturdley used his circuit-tracing abilities to try and see how much of the brain pathways were working. It was a frightening glimpse at a savage mental chop-job. Harry blundered into a less-dormant section of brain, where the tiny pseudopersonality had stored some fuzzy memories.

Flames danced in an almost impressionistic vision of a campfire. Giant figures sat around, sometimes in the light, often in shadow. They were talking, though there was no emotional content from the caretaker mind. But every word was recorded, and Sturdley blanched in horror as he perceived the giants discussing Robert's doomsday plan, and their expected move to safety in the mountains of Idaho.

Harry pulled out of the Andrew-zombie's brain and sent out an urgent psionic call for John and Peg. No response came from John. For all Sturdley could tell, he was asleep, dead, or in the Rift. Peg's mind, a little fuzzy as if she'd been dozing, responded almost instantly.

Get in your armor— Sturdley peered in the closet. Yes, his suit stood ready. *And burn gizmo getting down to the office. You'll find one of the giants—Andrew—or what's left of him.*

Dead? she asked.

Alive, but a vegetable, Sturdley responded. *Somebody— Robert, I think, gouged out most of the guy's personality and turned him into a mindless assassin. I'd be careful waking him up—you're on his hit list.*

Where is he?

Hard to miss. He's dangling out my office window. I guess we should be glad there are so many riots underway. The police haven't come to check out this little frolic.

Peg didn't respond, but Sturdley knew what she was expecting. *I want you to check his memories. Dig deep. I want anything he might have heard or imagined about Robert's plans. When you've got it, contact me on my suit radio. I'm flying to Washington, and I'll need every scrap you can find when I get there.*

A combination of dread and concentrated interest escaped Peg's shields. *You've managed to get a line on what Robert's up to?*

More like a taste, Sturdley responded grimly. *And the flavor of the day seems to be the end of the world.*

The missile silos were dug deep into the Nevada bedrock. So was the control room, only not as far down. For Lieutenant (j.g.) Ernest Manville, the air-conditioned silence contrasted most favorably with the noise, heat, and dust of the miles-long jeep ride from the airbase. Ernie always found the first hour underground to be the best. After that, he got into the Zen of desk duty, leaving the last hour to dread the return to the surface.

He was well into Zen state, sitting in companionable silence with Major Dalking, when the alarms started whooping.

"Damn! Nobody told me about a test," Manville complained, snapping to alert over his console. He was a little annoyed, considering himself well-plugged into the base grapevine.

"It's *supposed* to be a surprise," Dalking responded. The Major was a laconic, by-the-book type, known among the junior officers as "Dorking," although Manville found him a decent enough sort for a guy straight out of Washington.

They went through the standard procedures, removing their separate keys to activate the launch controls, receiving new coordinates to input for the navigation systems.

"Jeeze, this simulation must have us taking on the whole world," Manville said. "Look at these target centers."

Dalking said nothing, his fingers moving even faster than the lieutenant's as he input on his keyboard. Target coordinates went in, were rechecked, and the countdown began.

Manville began to sweat. "They're taking this to the wire."

The countdown droned on. Manville began typing.

"What are you doing?" Dalking suddenly demanded.

"I'm asking for confirmation. Something's wrong here. We should have stopped."

"Make sure *your* ID is on that. I'm not taking the blame for that sort of pussy stunt."

Manville stopped, then started typing again. "*You* checked the authorizations. Are you sure they were all right?"

Dalking's hand slammed down on his console. "Soldier—shut up and soldier."

"B-but those coordinates. Those are capitals of some of our allies." Manville turned a sweat-streaked face toward his superior. "We can't be launching a first strike!"

"We've suffered two strikes already," Dalking said grimly. "They blew up the Stock Exchange and attacked our lawmakers on the floor of the Senate. Looks like we don't know who's responsible, so we've decided to smear 'em all."

Manville fumbled for his sidearm. "You can't—"

Dalking was already drawing his gun. "This is mutiny."

The younger man was a hair faster. Manville's gun blasted, smearing the major's brains across the main display. The lieutenant clawed the dead man out of his way, reaching for the abort button, but he was too late.

The whole control room shook to the power of ten ICBMs launching.

Manville's face was streaked with tears as well as sweat. He reversed his service pistol and placed it in his mouth . . .

Sturdley pushed his Argonian systems to the limit flying to Washington, using so much gizmo that the armor began to shudder alarmingly. Framistat warnings blinked inside his helmet display until he had to throttle back.

He had feared there might be some sort of broadcast power fluctuation so far from the Hoozits, but his gauges read constant as he passed the outskirts of the capital. Whatever was going wrong with Earth technology just made Argonian products work to greater and greater tolerances.

Half an hour after leaving his office, Harry streaked down Pennsylvania Avenue, aiming for the White House. Peg was on the air with him, having passed along the few tidbits of information she'd been able to rescue from the ruins of Andrew's mind.

"Apparently it has something to do with *binding*— that's what they call taking over someone's mind," she said. "What happened to Andrew—that was sort of an extreme example."

"So Robert's been brainwashing people down here. The prez will be really upset to hear that," Sturdley said. "They were shown palling around on several—"

"Oh, my god!" Peg breathed.

Harry didn't want to think about it. "Here I go," he said. "Let's hope they don't think I'm trying to pull a kamikaze act."

Unfortunately, that's exactly what the Secret Service thought. Machine-gun fire opened up from several spots on the White House grounds, tracers arcing their way into the sky. Harry didn't mind the bullets. But he did get a little annoyed at the SAMs they launched.

He dodged one missile, aiming a tridigirector upward to explode it harmlessly in midair. The other he didn't have to worry about. The damned thing blew up at roof level, causing a few hundred thousand dollars worth of structural alterations to the home of the presidents.

Throughout this whole episode, Sturdley tried to establish radio contact with the defenders on the ground. The only answer to his desperate appeals was an increase in small-arms fire.

He detected somebody about to fire a Stinger, and in disgust blasted the thing while it was still on the ground.

"Obviously," Sturdley said, "I'm having trouble with the lower-level functionaries. I'll have to jump over their heads and talk to the big guy myself."

He extended immaterial probes into the building, searching for the President. No one in the Lincoln Room. The TV room no longer had a roof, thanks to that SAM. Bathrooms unoccupied. So was the Oval Office.

Finally, in a secure underground bunker, he detected signs of life—a very frightened junior agent, and with him was the President.

Harry took a peek through the agent's eyes. Depending on the party, the Chief Executive had a sly, shifty mug, or a very expressive face. But the face Sturdley saw now seemed pensive, with a faraway look in the eyes that reminded Sturdley of the emptiness he'd seen in Andrew.

A red telephone sat on the desk in front of the President, its clamor cutting through the tiny bunker. The President never answered the Hot Line, however. He continued to stare, seemingly unaware of it.

Chapter Thirty-Seven

To put it mildly, John Cameron had not had an easy day. After nearly twenty-four hours in armor and on patrol, he'd bumped into Matavi, been caught in a psychic trap, and nearly become the unwilling father of a new race. His response after being rescued had been to thank Peg rather inanely for saving him. Then he'd flown home and collapsed.

John was in a deep, dreamless sleep when a brusque hand seized him by the shoulder and tipped him out of his cot. He hit the floor hard and scrambled up, hands and mind ready for a fight, especially when he saw an armored figure looming over him.

But when his first probes brushed a mental shield, he recognized Peg. "What's the big idea?" he demanded in a hoarse whisper.

"The war with the giants has gone from cold to hot." Her voice was almost too calm as she spoke through her suit's speakers. "Robert sent someone to kill Harry."

John shrugged. "He sent people to kill me, too."

"But this time he sent a giant. Harry laid him out, and wants me to sort through his mind. Whatever he found on a once-over-lightly has him going to Washington." She reached down and pulled John upright. "I thought you'd want a look inside this head, too."

John rose, running his fingers through his hair and rubbing his face. There was a dent in his right cheek that almost matched the scar on his left. Only the dent, put there by a crease in his bedsheets, would go away. He went to the closet where the one-piece undersuit for his armor hung. John wasn't playing the modesty game. Whatever Peg was seeing, she had seen and enjoyed before.

His nose wrinkled as he pulled the undersuit on. It was getting a bit gamy, but there was no time to put it in the wash. Peg was tapping her fingers impatiently against her armored thigh.

John methodically donned his armor the quickest possible way, then turned to the window Peg had used as an entrance. Once it had been solidly shut with generations of dried paint. But when he'd made his home his crime fighting base, John had sprung for fresh glass and an entirely new frame—a frame that opened and closed soundlessly. But when he headed for the opening, Peg raised a hand. "We've got to get there fast," she said. "Let's go by Rift."

"That's not the best—" he began, but he could feel her determination. Sighing, he reached out, took her armored gauntlet in his, and began the vertiginous transition into the Rift.

John had always wondered what it would feel like to be in the tornado scene from *The Wizard of Oz*. Their appearance in the Rift was like living it. Currents in the one-time void tried to tug John and Peg apart with cyclonic force. They whirled helplessly for a moment until he pulled them into an eddy where they merely shook a bit. All around them, flotsam of alien realities swirled resistlessly, constructs built according to dimensional laws that did not apply on the world they knew. The alienness was palpable. Even the outward boundaries of these bubbles were governed by a geometry that human intellects couldn't grasp. Eyes used to dealing in three dimensions merely found it painful to behold.

"What the hell—" Peg began.

"Pretty much," John grunted in agreement. He'd gotten his bearings now, and found a current that would take them in the direction they wanted. It was still a rough ride, especially when John had to drop them out of the Rift before they were flung into a vastly deformed island universe.

They exited the Rift four blocks from the Fantasy Factory and a half-mile up in the air. John immediately activated his gizmoidal drive to hold them in place until Peg boosted her suit, too. "Sorry about that," he said, "but I didn't know what going through that bubble would do to us."

"Close enough," Peg said, starting in the direction of the office building. It appeared the authorities had made some sort of response to the reports of an unconscious giant. Several police cars and an EMS ambulance were parked down in the street. A handful of cops and technicians who barely came to Andrew's knee clustered around the giant, looking palpably baffled.

"They're not going to move him anytime soon," she said in relief.

"Not until he either wakes up or they get a couple of cranes in place," John agreed. He stared at the odd, contorted position Andrew had gotten himself into. One foot rested on the ground, the other had kicked in a groundfloor window and was resting in the sill for leverage. Andrew's right hand was in one of the windows of Harry's corner office. The giant's left arm, his shoulder, and most of his head were poked into the other window, frozen in the act of reaching into a constrained space.

They landed atop the building next door, scanning the giant's mind—what there was of it—from a distance while the city workers commenced a desultory search of the Fantasy Factory offices. As if in confirmation that the giant would be there a long time, some homeless people began setting up camp at Andrew's feet, using his dangling leg as a windbreak.

John was sickened as he saw the amount of damage that had been done to Andrew's mind. The personality was completely snuffed out, but the record of what had happened, step by step, was still recorded in dormant brain cells.

Peg, he knew, had hit on the scheme of using mind control when she had been stranded on the world of the giants, essentially binding a man who'd attacked her and turning him into her servant. But the method she had utilized was far different from the hack-and-slash method Robert had used. She sounded close to throwing up as she said, "We're supposed to look for memories of Robert—anything about his plans."

They dug for a while long-distance, but when the police left Harry's office, the armor-clad pair unobtrusively flew over to the roof of the Fantasy Factory's offices and entered the building for some closer work. Peg led the way down the darkened hall, stepping past her desk and into the open doorway of Harry's office. Using the infrared filters on their helmet visors, they could see Andrew clearly enough. He seemed unconscious and jammed in place. The emergency crews had done some first aid—John noticed bandages and some sort of ointment spread on burnt flesh.

Peg headed straight for the giant, detaching a gauntlet and opening her helmet. "Ugh!" she muttered as

Andrew's stertorous breathing wafted toward her. Averting her face, she nonetheless went straight to Andrew and got a hand on his cheek.

John, come in and help me, she sent.

John carefully kept his consciousness separate from hers as they sifted through memories. Most of the recollections of the Andrew-personality offered only hints—Robert's assurance that something would be done about the Lessers on this world, the fact that his visits to Washington would further his plans. The childlike memories of the caretaker-construct, indefinite and uncolored by emotion, gave the real story. They found the discussion by the fireside, and another combination pep rally and threat where Robert went into some detail on his plans while offering Andrew as an example of what would happen to those who didn't follow orders.

Peg finally stumbled back, her face pale. "Lord help us all," she whispered. Grabbing John's arm, she steered him away from the giant and down the hall to his own office— rather, he corrected himself, the office he'd used when he still worked for Harry Sturdley.

Putting her helmet back on, Peg got on the radio to relay the information they'd gotten. They heard Harry reach the White House. Before Peg could warn that the President might be bound as well, Harry came under fire.

"Looks like the Prez is out of it," Harry finally reported. "I'll have to go in and see if there's anything I can do. If there is, I'll let you know."

The radio connection cut off.

Peg tore her helmet off and confronted John. "Get out of that damned thing," she demanded. "I want to see your face."

He undid the connectors for his helmet and removed it. Peg looked at him long and hard. "Maybe I'm not the one who should ask," she said. "But because of what we once had—*can't you stop it?*" She almost seemed to be pleading with him.

"Stop what?" he said. "Robert's plan? We don't even know enough about it—"

"Not that," she said. "Or maybe I should say, not *just* that."

John stared at her. "I know you've been blaming me for a lot of stuff since we got home, but this I have nothing to do with."

"Are you *sure?*" Peg pressed. "The Fantasy Factory, our lives, the whole world—they've all gone topsy-turvy. What's the connection?"

"Me—or rather, the Rift," John amended.

"We've gone on a hell of a ride and accepted a lot of things at face value. At least I did, until I saw the leaders of the Deviants on Argon. You remember them?" Peg prompted.

"Skeletone, Megalomanik, Emsisdin, and Matavi," John said. "It looked like a Fantasy Factory rogues' gallery."

"Like something made up," Peg pressed. "Images in someone's mind come to life." Her face was tight, and her gray eyes were bigger than ever. "How could that happen, though? Whose brain would it come from? I'd like to think that any villains *I'd* think of would be a bit more . . . classical."

A brief smile tugged at her lips, then she grew serious again. "Harry might think in terms of supervillains, but he wasn't on Argon anymore."

John began to follow her drift. "That leaves me. You think I *created* those guys?" His face looked very young for a second. "No, it's more than that. You believe *everything* is my fault. Mike, all the people who died on Argon and in this mess here on Earth, your kidnapping, your folks thinking you were dead—" His voice cut off as bile rose in the back of his throat.

She seized his hands. "I don't *know*, and it's been driving me crazy! What if you don't know, either? Obviously, you've got—powers. And you told me right at the beginning that you're not sure how you do a lot of the things you do. Maybe using your powers causes shifts in reality—a side effect. It's not a conscious decision, but things in your head leak out—"

She fumbled for a concept, trying to explain, then shrugged. "You ever see the movie *Forbidden Planet?*"

"Sure. Anne Francis, and Leslie Nielson before he started playing comedy. It was supposed to be based on Shakespeare, wasn't it?"

"Right, but I was thinking more about Walter Pidgeon. He hooked himself up to an alien machine that could do anything he wished—"

"But his subconscious used that power to kill people," John finished. "You think that's what I'm doing?"

Peg looked at him, fear and pleading in her eyes. "I think that power brings responsibility—and danger."

He shook his head. "I can't believe this is happening to me."

"I can't believe what's happening to all of us," Peg said. "That giant sonofabitch is trying to kill everyone!"

"But it's not because of me," John protested, but his voice sounded weak even to himself. "I don't want this to happen. I sure as hell didn't *want* these weird powers. 1 don't even know where they come from."

He was all but begging her for assurance, and from the look on Peg's face, she couldn't give him any.

"It seems there's a lot you don't know about yourself," she said. "You told me your first memory is standing naked on a road in West Virginia a couple of years ago. So I put Quentin Farley to work checking for missing persons in the states nearby for that time period."

"And?" he asked, his voice tight.

"He couldn't find a match," she replied. "It's as though you came into existence right then and there—or invented yourself."

"Peg, I swear to you—"

"Words are cheap." She rubbed her eyes and her fingers came away wet. But her voice was brusque, even cold, as she said, "We need actions now."

Sturdley's voice came out of the speakers in her helmet. "I'm with the President and snapped him out of whatever spell he was under. But it's too late. Missiles have already been launched."

John and Peg looked at each other in shocked silence.

"You there?" Harry's voice inquired.

"John and I are both here," Peg replied, her voice sounding numb.

John suddenly stirred, reaching for his helmet. "Stay with the President and get as much information as possible on what got launched and what the targets are."

"Where are you going?" Harry asked.

"Very high up in the atmosphere," John said. He glanced at Peg. "We're going to try and take some action."

* * *

A moment later, the pair of armored figures linked hands and vanished from the office. Marty Burke felt a sort of sucking at his stomach and mind, as if he were being pulled off an endless cliff. The feeling subsided, but he still walked as if he were on the thinnest of ice as he stepped from behind the partition and glanced around his old office.

He'd taken his new secretary, Wendy Wentworth, along with him to Deviant Comics. But ample as Wendy's charms might be, an organized mind was not part of the package. She'd left a bunch of idea and sketch files in Burke's old office, and now that he'd finished the first *Deviants* title, Marty had decided to try and retrieve them.

As the former head of the Fantasy Factory, he'd not only gotten a key to the office and the executive john, but keys for the groundfloor entrance, fire keys to run the elevators, the whole schmear. He'd also been prudent enough to make copies before he'd turned the keys back to Harry Sturdley.

He'd just planned on an evening of gentlemanly burglary, but that had changed when he found the giant half-hanging out of Sturdley's window. After waiting for the cops to finish their search, he'd sneaked in, gotten his files, and was about to poke around in Sturdley's office when the Stalwarts arrived.

Burke dropped into his old desk chair and took a deep breath. The world was indeed going topsy-turvy. John Cameron and Peg Faber were the armored Stalwarts. Maybe Sturdley, too. They must have spent at least some of the time after their disappearance on the planet that Emsisdin and Matavi came from. John even seemed to know them.

And John Cameron, goofy gofer, had incredible powers and abilities—Burke shook his head. No. He didn't want to reduce this to comic book cliches. Whatever forces Cameron controlled, Peg believed he'd caused the chaos now overtaking the world just by existing.

And then they had flown off to try and stop World War III.

Marty Burke heartily wished them good luck, and not merely because he was doubtless sitting at ground zero for a significant proportion of the world's nuclear arsenal. He wanted to be able to survive and make a comic book out of tonight's activities . . . Burke began to chuckle . . . even if no one would believe it was reality-based.

Ham Belcher's piggy little eyes tightened with glee as he saw a passenger get off the bus. His partner in crime, Birdie Jockum, was already rising from the bench outside the old Toad and Stool, the local pub for the village of Weald on Wold in Merrie England.

Birdie was short and skinny, barely coming up to Ham's shoulder, with blond hair and fine-drawn, almost elfin features—a great help when he and Ham went to nearby cities for a bit of ponce-bashing. He could lure the poofters down a nice, quiet alley while Ham did the heavy work.

Ham was built for heavy work, big and porky, with coarse black hair in thick bristles on his head, arms, even in his nose. His features looked as if they'd been chiseled by an extremely inexpert sculptor on very porous stone.

They waited until the bus had pulled away, then Birdie approached the target. "A stranger in Weald on Wold," he said with a smile. "This is a red-letter day."

"Not many visitors?" the dark-skinned visitor asked in a flat accent. Ham felt a little disappointed. He had expected to hear heavily accented sing-song coming from the stranger's mouth.

"Nor many places to stay," Birdie picked up quickly.

The traveler adjusted the rucksack on his back. "I thought the local inn—" He glanced over at the Toad and Stool.

Ham's disappointment grew. If he got in there, and the regulars spoke up . . .

"Oh, not at all," Birdie said in a deprecating voice. "It's a bit on the dirty side, I'm afraid. And I wonder how often they change the sheets. I could show you a bed-and-breakfast place," he offered. "Small, but clean. For comparison's sake."

With a guileless smile, he led the stranger off.

For a small town, Weald on Wold had its share of back alleys. The perplexed traveler and his cheerful guide had reached a dead end in a particularly squalid one when Ham appeared to block the exit. Now the fun could begin. *"Bloody Paki,"* he growled.

"What?" The stranger glanced from Ham to Birdie, looking for some support.

"'E said 'bloody Paki,' you dumb brown bugger," Birdie amplified. "We want none o' your kind in Weald on Wold."

"Go back to Injah, or wherever the hell you come from."

"India?" the traveler stupidly repeated. "I'm from from New Jersey, on a walking tour—"

"We've enough Yanks already, thank you very much," Birdie jeered. "They come down from the R.A.F. base every weekend to throw their almighty dollars around and try their arms with our girls. And they're *white.*"

"That's no real Yank. Look at 'is kinky hair. He's some sort of nigger or yid." Ham set a hand in the stranger's chest and shoved. Birdie deftly yanked the rucksack free.

"Hey!" The protest ended as Ham caught the Yank, or Yid, or whatever across the mouth with a backhanded blow. The stranger flew back against a rough brick wall and stood there, blood leaking from a split lip. His face was pale under his heavy tan.

Birdie quickly inventoried the contents of the pack. "Pullover, change of clothes, knickers—" He dropped the items one by one into a mucky puddle. "A Yank passport."

"I still say he's a brown bastard," Ham insisted.

"Travelers checks." Birdie disgustedly let them flutter down into the mire. "Ah, and some real money."

He extracted the lot, perhaps fifty pounds, from the traveler's wallet and slipped it into his own pocket. "Think of it," Birdie said, "as your voluntary contribution to the fiscal well-being of Weald on Wold."

Ham grinned, imagining how many pints that contribution would buy at the Toad and Stool.

Birdie dropped the rucksack. "That will do," he said briskly. "On your bike."

The stranger squatted to retrieve his sodden belongings. They always did. "What?"

"Move your bleedin' arse out of town," Ham translated, adding a kick for emphasis.

The traveler tumbled into the filthy puddle. He stared up, his face mucky and scared.

"Hop it!" Birdie yelled as the Yank grabbed what he could and stuffed it in the bag.

They left the worse for wear traveler at the edge of town, on the main road. "Thumb yourself a ride," Birdie said. "If we see you in town again, our local constable here—" he reached up to pat Ham's shoulder—"will do you for vagrancy."

It was an outrageous lie, but their victims rarely put it to the test. The stranger silently put out his thumb. Ham heard a lorry pull to a stop as he and Birdie walked away.

The boys were the stars of the Toad and Stool, buying drinks for the NCOs from the R.A.F. base and relating how they'd gotten the better of the Wandering Yank.

"I still say he was some sort of Paki," Ham insisted, thrusting out his glass for a refill. "Those brown bastards—"

He was interrupted by a rumbling in the distance. An R.A.F. warrant officer ran to the pub's door. "Those are the missile silos!" he gasped.

The patrons crowded to the door, watching the ICBMs rise from beyond a copse of trees. They couldn't see the natural anomaly, a pocket universe barely larger than an adult pig, which happened to intersect with the nose of one missile. The warhead entered a new reality, where nuclear fission was a much easier proposition.

Birdie, Ham, and the others never saw any changes in natural law. They did, however, see a searingly white light as the fissionable core of the warhead suddenly detonated. Then onlookers, pub, village, and considerable countryside around disappeared in nuclear fire.

The heavy truck labored up an incline. Sitting in the passenger's seat—which would have been the driver's seat in his home country—Marv Leiber was blinded by a distant flash in the rearview mirror. Blinking his eyes, the recent victim of a rural mugging finally focused on a growing mushroom cloud rising from the road far, far behind.

"What the hell was that?" he asked as the rumble of the air shock reached them.

Clad in Earth-style clothing and carrying his armor in a gym duffel, Emsisdin frowned as he unlocked the door and walked into the apartment he and Matavi maintained for their civilian identities. The air was filled with savory smells, much *too* savory. His suspicions were justified when he entered the kitchen to find his partner opening bags of takeout food.

"You know, it wouldn't hurt if you'd *cook* every now and again," the male Deviant said.

"It could hurt *you* if you start that tired argument," Matavi snarled.

Emsisdin hurriedly retreated. His partner's temper had become ever-shorter of late. Perhaps something on this planet disagreed with her.

Matavi pursued him. "Food preparation isn't automated here the way it is back home," she continued. "And if you think I'm going to put on a pretty apron and cook for you, you've been watching too many commercials on the 2D."

"Television," he corrected, then wished he hadn't.

"Yes. You *like* the television here. You've got everything you want on this world. Wealth, a position as a hero—even a little blond slut to spread her legs for you."

Emsisdin's head went down in an almost ducking motion. Trust the bitch to read his mind. *"You* didn't seem to want—"

"Did it ever strike you to enquire what I *do* want?" Matavi raged. "What *I* need, and whether those needs are being met? Whether you could help—"

Abruptly, her tirade ceased and she collapsed over the table.

"Seven hells and devils," Emsisdin cried, leaping forward to clutch her arm. "Matavi, what's happened to you? Is it some Earth-illness? Are you all right?"

"Dead," Matavi said in a choked voice. Her face was white as chalk, and unbidden tears flowed from her eyes. Hundreds. . .thousands. . .dead. Far away, but I feel—"

Her hand slipped into his. "I feel their pain."

The panel truck had once been painted white, but that was many years ago. Its color now was a shabby, scabby gray. There were dents on the side and a hole had been torn in the metal at the front, where the boxy panel overlooked the driver's cab.

That hole had been punched mere minutes before by a giant hand wielding the truck's tire iron. The driver had sat in docile silence behind the wheel while Robert had prepared a peephole for himself. Then the giant had climbed inside and given the bound trucker the order to proceed.

The truck jounced uncomfortably as the driver maintained top speed heading out of Washington. Robert's posture, half-crouched as he peered through the hole, didn't add to his sense of ease or well-being.

They had already crossed the Beltway when a psychic scream impacted the giant's mental shields. Normally, even his enhanced senses wouldn't have had the power to detect death. But these were the death-screams of thousands of people, dying in totally unexpected agony, in terrible violence.

Robert frowned. His research had indicated that it would take the better part of an hour for the missiles of death to reach their destinations. Something must have gone wrong, somewhere.

It didn't matter. The cleansing of this world had just begun a little earlier than he'd planned.

Afterword

It's strange how we live in a world of opposites.

We have big and small, hot and cold, up and down, strong and weak, light and dark. . .the list is endless.

Yet, there are two opposites which are extremely difficult to reduce to absolutes, even though at first blush they seem to be totally dissimilar. I'm referring to good and evil, or, to put it into Fantasy Factory terms, heroes and villains.

From the outset, one of the unique things about Marvel Comics has been the fact that it dealt with a number of villains who occasionally possessed redeeming virtues, as well as heroes who were not without their own flaws. For example, one of Marvel's mightiest heroes is Iron Man, the alter ego of multimillionaire inventor/industrialist/bon vivant, Anthony Stark. One of our most successful Iron Man series dealt with the time he succumbed to alcoholism, an affliction which almost destroyed him. Of course, being the hero he was, he managed to overcome his alcoholism and rehabilitate himself.

Similarly, we've had stories in which it was revealed that the despotic Dr. Doom, one of Marvel's all-time greatest villains, despite his relentless quest for world domination, was truly a villain with his own code of honor and integrity. He might attempt to destroy a

Art: Dave Gibbons

M-16, also known as Emsisdin

civilization, but once he had given his word, no power on Earth would make him renege on a promise.

Yes, the more you study human nature, the more you realize that neither heroism nor villainy is a total absolute.

Another thing that has always fascinated me is the origin of legends. In every part of the planet, in every culture, the legends of mankind have so much in common. There is always the hero, the one who is nobler, braver, more virtuous than any foe. And, in juxtaposition, you will inevitably find the villain, whether man, beast or demon, with but one motive—to inflict pain and suffering upon hapless victims. This combination of good and evil, eternally in conflict, has stirred mankind's imagination and haunted its dreams since the dawn of creation and will undoubtedly continue to do so till the end of time.

Perhaps that's why the underlying theme of Riftworld so appeals to me. Just like the comicbook world itself, which furnishes the springboard for our series' action, Riftworld is a mysterious melange of heroes and villains, ever in flux, yet always constant in the sense that the battle never ends.

Another element of Riftworld that I find intriguing is the careful attention paid to character development. Just as you and I grow and evolve with each passing day and each new experience, so do those who inhabit our ever-changing world of fiction. Perhaps the greatest changes of all are in store for John Cameron, whose past is still steeped in mystery and whose destiny seems to involve far more than his own personal fate.

If I don't stop now, I'm liable to spoil some of the startling surprises in store for you in our following volume.

So, till we meet again, on the brink of Riftworld . . . Excelsior!

Stan Lee

www.ingramcontent.com/pod-product-compliance
Lightning Source LLC
Chambersburg PA
CBHW070540030726
47505CB00001B/103